oh no, not again....

"Oh, no, not again…"

Margo put on a burst of speed and propelled herself straight through a black rent in the air before she could halt her forward momentum. Margo had a brief, tunnel-vision view of a broad, silver river in flood stage, long low banks that sloped gently up to what appeared to be a vast flat plain, and a walled city. A two-part fortified bridge with a tower spanned the river. Standing at the crest of a low, open hill, the city clearly commanded a strategic position overlooking the river. Twin spires of a white stone cathedral were visible above the city walls. *Between* Margo and the walls…

It looked like a *battle*.

Then she was through the gate, right into the thick of it. Men in medieval-looking armor hacked at one another with swords. Horsemen on heavy chargers rode down men on foot. Volleys of arrows fell like black rain, pinioning anything unfortunate enough to be under them. A man right in front of her screamed and clutched at a steel crossbow shaft that appeared from nowhere and embedded itself in his chest armor. He went down with a terrible cry and was trampled by a screaming warhorse. Blood and mud and the smell of dying men and wounded horses spattered

Her gaze focused abruptly on a man who had stumbled to a halt right in front of her. Margo's heart slammed into her throat. And found an older, faintly familiar man staring at her, wild-eyed. He swung a spiked maul at least four feet long straight over his head, ready to crush her skull. Margo screamed and ran. She dodged unevenly ahead of her. She risked a glance over her shoulder. The madman with the maul was close behind.

She could just see the Commons as the gate shivered inward and outward again, a quivering hole in the light. *Don't close—oh, God, don't close yet—*

**The Time Scout series
(with Robert Asprin)**
Time Scout
Wagers of Sin

Baen Books by Linda Evans
Sleipnir
Far Edge of Darkness

TIME SCOUT

ROBERT ASPRIN
LINDA EVANS

TIME SCOUT

Copyright © 1995 by Bill Fawcett & Associates

A Baen Books Original

Baen Publishing Enterprises
P.O. Box 1403
Riverdale NY 10471

ISBN 0-671-87698-8

Cover art by Gary Ruddell

First printing, December 1995
Second printing, February 1999

Distributed by Simon & Schuster
1230 Avenue of the Americas
New York, NY 10020

Reset by Windhaven Press, Auburn, NH
Printed in the United States of America

CHAPTER ONE

It wasn't difficult to tell visitors from 'eighty-sixers. Visitors were the ones with the round mouths and rounder eyes and steadily decreasing bankrolls. Like refugees from Grandma's attic, they were decked out in whatever the Outfitters had decreed the current "look of the century." Invariable struggles with unfamiliar bits of clothing, awkward baggage arrangements, and foreign money marked them even faster than an uptilted head on a New York City sidewalk.

'Eighty-sixers, by contrast, stood out by virtue of omission. They neither gawked nor engaged in that most offensive of tourist behaviors, the "I-know-it-all-and-will-share-it-with-you" bravado that masks someone who wouldn't know a drachma from a sesterce, even if his life depended on it.

Which, in TT-86, it might.

Nope, the 'eighty-sixers were the ones who hauled luggage, snagged stray children back from the brink of disaster, and calmed flaring tempers in three different languages in as many minutes, all without loosening a fold of those impossible-to-wrap Roman togas or bumping into a single person with those equally impossible-to-manage Victorian bustles.

'Eighty-sixers were right at home in La-La Land.

Frankly, Malcolm Moore couldn't imagine living anywhere else.

Which was why he was currently threading his way

1

through the Commons of Shangri-la Station, decked out in his most threadbare woolen tunic (the one with the artistic wine and dung stains), his dirtiest cheap sandals, and his very finest bronze collar (the one that read MALCOLUM SERVUS _____).

The blank spot waited for the name of any person offering him a job. Adding the customer's name would take only seconds with his battery-powered engraver, and he had a grinder in his room to smooth out the name again for the next trip. The metal was currently as shiny as his hopes and as empty as his belly.

Occasionally, Malcolm felt the pun inherent in his name had become a harbinger of plain bad luck.

"Well, my luck's gotta change sometime," he muttered, girding metaphorical loins for battle.

His destination, of course, was Gate Six. Tourists were already beginning to converge on its waiting area, milling about in animated groups and smiling clusters. Hangers-on thronged the vast Commons just to watch the show. A departure at Gate Six was an Event, worth watching even for those not making the trip. Tables at little cafes and bars, especially those in the "Roman City" section of the terminal, were filling up fast.

In "Urbs Romae" hot-dog stands took the form of ancient sausage-and-wine-vendor shops visible on the streets of ancient Rome, complete with vats of hot oil in which the hot dogs sizzled. Countersunk amphorae in the countertops brimmed with higher quality wine than anything down time. Better cafes were designed like temples, private courtyards, even colonnaded gardens complete with fountains and flowerbeds. The clink of glassware and the rich scents of coffee, warm pastries, and expensive liquor caressed Malcolm's nostrils like a lover's fingertips. His belly rumbled. God, he was hungry. . . .

He nodded to a few friends already seated at cafe tables. They waved and were kind enough not to offer him a seat, since he was clearly dressed for business. As he approached the Down Time's narrow, dim storefront, half-hidden under the crossbeams of a support for a second-story catwalk (cleverly disguised as "marble" columns and balcony), he spotted Marcus and waved. His young friend was busy setting out shot glasses at one of the window-seat tables the bar boasted. A three-foot porthole affair, it gave the impression of peeping out through the side of an ancient sailing ship.

"Bona fortuna," the bartender mouthed through the glass; then he touched his temple and winked. Malcolm grinned. Marcus—who possessed no last name—had once expressed a private opinion that anyone who wanted to visit the genuine Urbs Romae was slightly off in the head.

"Go back?" he'd said the one time Malcolm had suggested they combine their respective talents as partners in the freelance guide business. Startlement in his young eyes had given way almost immediately to a glint akin to fear. "You do me honor, friend. But no. Shangri-la is more fun." The strain around his smile prompted Malcolm to change the subject with a mental note never to raise it again.

Urbs Romae was Malcolm's favorite part of Shangri-la Station, probably because ancient Rome was his specialty. Beyond the entrance to the Down Time Bar & Grill, the Commons stretched away like the inside of a shopping mall designed by Escher. Two hundred yards across and nearly three times that length, the Commons was a multi-level monstrosity of girders, broad catwalks, ramps, balconies, and cantilevered platforms disguised as an astonishing number of items. Many of them led absolutely nowhere.

Pleasant fountains and pools splashed under the perpetual glow of the Commons' lights. The occasional flash of color against blue-tiled fountains betrayed the

presence of exotic fish kept to graze the algae. Urbs
Romae's floor was a colorful patchwork of mosaics in
the ancient style, most of them put together by the
enterprising merchants whose shops bordered them.
Signs shrouded the walls at random intervals, while
staircases stretched upward past storefronts and hotel
windows to unpredictable levels along the walls.

Some ramps and catwalks were still under construction
or at least seemed to be. A number ended in blank
stretches of concrete wall, while others reached islands
that floated four and five stories above the main floor,
supported by open strutwork like scaffolding around a
cathedral under reconstruction. A few ramps and
stairways stretched from scattered spots to end in thin
air, leaving one to wonder whether they led up to
something invisible or down from a hole out of nothing.

Malcolm grinned. First impressions of Shangri-la
left most visitors convinced the time terminal's
nickname, La-La Land, came from the lunatic walks
to nowhere.

Large signs bordered several blank stretches, where
balconies and catwalks had been screened off with chain-
link fencing that made no pretense of blending in with
the rest of Urbs Romae. The signs, in multiple languages,
warned of the dangers of unexplored gates. The fencing
wasn't so much to keep things from wandering *in* as to
keep other things from wandering *out*. The signs, of
course, were a legal precaution. Most tourists weren't
stupid enough to wander through an open portal without
a guide. But there had been casualties at other stations
and lawsuits had occasionally been filed by bereaved
families. Residents of TT-86 were grateful for their own
station manager's precautions.

Nobody wanted the time terminal shut down for
slipshod management.

Nobody.

Today's batch of tourists and guides looked like

refugees from *Spartacus*. Most of the men tugged uncomfortably at dress-like tunics and expended considerable effort avoiding one another's eyes. Knobby knees and hairy legs were very much in evidence. Malcolm chuckled. *Ah, Gate Six* . . . Malcolm wore his own threadbare tunic with the ease of long practice. He barely registered the difference between his business costumes and what he normally wore, although he did note that his sandal strap needed repairing again.

Women in elegant *stolas* chatted animatedly in groups, comparing jewelry, embroidered borders, and elegant coiffeurs. Others wandered into the gate's waiting area, where they relaxed in comfortable chairs, sipped from paper cups, and watched the show. Those, Malcolm knew, were rich enough they'd been down time before. First-time tourists were too excited to sit down. Malcolm pushed past the periphery of the growing crowd in search of likely employers.

"Morning, Malcolm."

He turned to find Skeeter Jackson, clad elegantly in a Greek-style chiton. He held back a groan and forced a smile. "Morning, Skeeter." After the brief handclasp, he counted his fingernails.

Skeeter nodded to Malcolm's tunic. "I see you're trying the slave-guide routine." Brown eyes sparkled. "Great stains. I'll have to get your recipe sometime." Skeeter's wide smile, which was, as far as anyone had ever been able to tell, the only genuine thing about him, was infectious.

"Sure," Malcolm laughed. "One quart liquefied mare's dung, two quarts sour Roman wine, and three pints Tiberian mud. Spread carefully with an artist's brush, let dry for two weeks, then launder in cold water. Works wonders on raw wool."

Skeeter's eyes had widened. "Gad. You're serious." His own garments, as always, were fastidiously neat and apparently new. Where he'd obtained them, Malcolm didn't want to know. "Well, good luck," Skeeter offered. "I have an appointment to keep." He winked. "See you around."

The slim young man grinned like an imp counting damned souls and slipped off into the growing crowd. Malcolm surreptitiously checked his belt pouch to be sure the battery-powered engraver and business cards were still there.

"Well," he told himself, "at least he never seems to roll one of us 'eighty-sixers." He glanced at one of several dozen chronometers which depended from the distant ceiling and checked the countdown on Gate Six.

Time to get to work.

The crowd was growing denser. The noise volume increased exponentially. Hired baggage handlers worked to balance awkward loads comprised of odd-sized parcels and sacks and leather satchels, while Time Tours guides double-checked their customer lists and gave last-minute instructions. Ticket takers at the entrance to Gate Six's main ramp waved through a couple of company executives on their way to check the upper platform. Already Malcolm estimated the crowd at some seventy-five people.

"Too big for a tour group," he muttered. Time Tours, Inc. was getting greedy. The noise of tourist voices and baggage handlers grunting at their work bounced off girders high overhead and reverberated, creating a roar of confused echoes. At least with a group this size, he ought to be able to find something. He plastered a hopeful smile on his face, fished into the leather pouch at his waist for business cards, and got busy.

"Hello," he introduced himself to the first prospect, extending a hand to a tall, robust man whose tan and fair hair said "California tycoon." "Please allow me to introduce myself. Malcolm Moore, freelance guide."

The man shook his hand warily, then glanced at the business card he'd proffered. It read:

Malcolm Moore, Time Guide
Rome AD 47 ⚇ London 1888 ⚇ Denver 1885
Other Destinations Available upon Request
Experience Adventure without the Hassle of a Tour Schedule!
Private Side Tours and In-Depth Guide Services for
Individuals, Families, Students, Business Groups
Best Rates in Shangri-la
Contact: TT-86 Room 503, #111-1814

The tycoon scanned his card and glanced back up. "You're a freelancer?" The tone was more dubious than ever.

"My specialty is ancient Rome," Malcolm said with a warm, sincere smile. "I hold a Ph.D. in Classics and Anthropology and have nearly seven years experience as a guide. The formal tour," he nodded toward uniformed Time Tours employees taking tickets and answering questions, "includes the Circus Maximus chariot races and gladiatorial combats, but Time Tours is bypassing the extraordinary experience of the . . ."

"Thank you," the man handed back the card, "but I'm not interested."

Malcolm forced the smile to remain. "Of course. Some other time, perhaps."

He moved on to the next potential customer. "Please allow me to introduce myself . . ."

Begging never got any easier.

Given the chill of this crowd, Time Tours had been poisoning their customers against freelancers. Skeeter Jackson, drat the boy, seemed to be doing fine, whatever he was up to in that far corner. His smile glowed brighter than the overhead lights.

By the time the countdown clock read T-minus-ten minutes, Malcolm had begun to consider offering his services as a baggage handler just to pick up enough cash for a few meals, but a man had his pride. Malcolm was a guide and a damned good one. If he lost what was left of his reputation as a professional, his life here would be over. He scanned the crowd from one edge, counting heads and costumes, and decided glumly that he had, in fact, talked to everyone.

Well . . . damn.

A desperate attempt to hold onto the shreds of his dignity sent Malcolm in retreat. He retired from the immediate vicinity of Gate Six, accompanied by a return of nagging worries about how he might pay for his room and the next few meals. Overriding that, Malcolm suffered a keen disappointment that had very little to do with money or the loss of his old, full-time job. Malcolm Moore had no idea how guides for the big outfits like Time Tours felt; but for him, stepping through a portal into another century was a thrill better than eating regularly, almost better than sex.

It was that thrill which kept him at TT-86, working every departure, no matter the destination, for the chance to try it again.

Malcolm headed for the shadows of a vine-draped portico, close enough to Gate Six to watch the fun, but far enough away to avoid attracting attention from friends who would want to sympathize. Montgomery Wilkes, looking very out of place in his dark, up-time uniform, strode through the crowd with the singular intensity of a charging rhino. Even tourists scuttled out of his way. Malcolm frowned. What was Wilkes doing out of his inner sanctum? La-La Land's head ATF agent never attended a Gate opening. He glanced again at the nearest overhead chronometer board and found the answer.

Ah . . .

Primary, too, was due to cycle. He'd forgotten in the hustle of trying to line up a job that a new batch of tourists would be arriving today from up time. Malcolm rubbed the tip of his nose and smiled. A double-gate day . . . Maybe there was hope, after all. Even without a job, it ought to be fun.

Down at Gate Six, last-minute purchases were in full swing. Strolling vendors worked the crowd efficiently, burdened down with everything from ropes of "safe" sausages to extra leather satchels for souvenirs, the latest "must-have" survival junk, and local coinage for those stupid enough to leave money exchanges to the last minute.

Malcolm wondered if he should consider a career as a vendor? They always seemed to do well and it would be steady work. Connie, maybe, would give him a job. He shook his head absently as he watched everything from last-minute mugs of coffee to tawdry bits of jewelry exchange hands. Nah, he'd get bored too quickly trying to hold down a mundane job, even here. Setting up his own shop was out of the question. Besides the question of higher rent for business space and all that hideous government paperwork to cope with, where would he get the capital to buy inventory? Investors weren't interested in ex-guides, they wanted shrewd business acumen and plenty of sales management experience.

Of course, he could always go back to time scouting.

Malcolm glanced involuntarily toward the nearest barricades. The area had been fenced off because the gate hadn't yet been explored or was inherently unstable. Malcolm had risked down-time explorations into unknown gates as a freelance time scout only twice. A stray shiver crawled up his spine. Kit Carson, the first—and best—of all the time scouts, was famous all over the world. And damned lucky to be alive. Malcolm wasn't exactly a coward, but time scouting was not Malcolm's idea of a sane career. He was more than happy to settle for rubbing shoulders with giants and sharing war-stories with the real heroes of TT-86 over beer and pretzels.

A strident klaxon sounded, echoing five stories above the terminal floor. Conversation cut off mid-sentence. As abruptly as it had sounded, the klaxon died away, replaced by an amplified voice. Long-time residents leaned forward in chairs, absently twirling half-empty glasses or drawing designs in the condensate on table tops with idle fingertips. The throng in the waiting area paused expectantly.

"Your attention, please. Gate Six is due to open in three minutes. Returning parties will have gate priority. All departures, please remain in the holding area until guides are notified that the gate is clear."

The message repeated in three other languages.

Malcolm wished his tunic had pockets so he could thrust his hands into them. Instead he crossed his arms and waited. Another ear-splitting klaxon sounded.

"Your attention, please. Gate One is due to open in ten minutes. All departures, be advised that if you have not cleared Station Medical, you will not be permitted to pass Primary. Please have your baggage ready for customs . . ."

Malcolm stopped listening. He'd memorized the up-time departure litany years ago. Besides, departures down-time were always more entertaining than watching a bunch of government agents search luggage. The real fun at Primary wouldn't begin until the new arrivals started coming through. Malcolm's gaze found the countdown for Gate Six. Any second now . . .

A hum of sub-harmonics rumbled through the time terminal as Gate Six, the biggest of TT-86's active gates, came to life. Outside the range of audible sound, yet detectable through the vibration of bones at the base of one's skull, the sound that wasn't a sound intensified. Across the Commons, tourists pressed behind their ears with the heels of hands in an attempt to relieve the unpleasant sensation. Malcolm traced his gaze up a pair of broad ramps—one of which descended toward the waiting area from a wide catwalk, the other of which would handle departures—and waited eagerly.

Up at the edge of the catwalk an utterly blank section

of wall began to shimmer. Like a heat haze over a stretch of noonday highway, the air rippled. Colors dopplered through the spectrum in odd, distorted patterns. Gasps rose from the waiting area, distinctly audible in the hush. Then a black spot appeared in the dead center of the blank wall.

Tourists gaped and pointed. For most, it was only the second time in their lives they'd seen a temporal gate up-close and personal—their first, of course, being Primary on the down-time trip to Shangri-la. Conversation, which had begun to pick up again in the wake of the first shimmer, died off sharply. Baggage handlers finished tying off their loads. Last-minute transactions led to more money changing hands. More than one guide gulped down the last scalding coffee they'd taste in two weeks.

The spot on the wall dilated, spreading outward like a growth of bread mold viewed on high-speed film. In the center of the darkness, as though viewed through the wrong end of a telescope, Malcolm made out the shape of dim shelves and tiny amphorae stacked neatly in rows at the back of a long, deep room. Then light flared like a twinkling star as someone on the other side lit a lamp.

Tourists on the floor exclaimed, then laughed in nervous delight as a man dressed as a Roman slave, but moving with the purpose and authority of a Time Tours organizer, stepped through. He rushed at them like a hurled baseball, growing in apparent height from a few inches to full size in the blink of an eyelash, then calmly stepped through onto the metal grating. He landed barking orders.

Tourists, some looking dazed and ill, others talking animatedly, all of them visibly tired, spilled through the open gate onto the catwalk and down the ramp. Most clutched souvenirs. Some clutched each other. Guides had to remind most of them to slide credit-card-sized

Timecards through the encoder at the bottom of the ramp. Malcolm grinned again. The ritual never varied. The ones who remembered to "clock out" of Porta Romae were experienced temporal travelers. The ones clutching each other had discovered a deep-seated, unexpected fear of temporal travel, either because it was too dirty and violent for their taste or because they'd spent the trip terrified of making a mistake the guides couldn't fix.

The ones that looked dazed and ill either hadn't enjoyed the gladiatorial games as much as they'd thought or were still attempting to overcome the effects of too much boozing and not enough attention to proper diet and rest. Malcolm's clients never returned up time looking like they needed the nearest hospital bed. Of course, people with the sense to hire a private guide, even for a package deal like Time Tours offered, rarely had the poor judgement to get hung over after a two-week-long binge on lead-laced Roman wine.

Not for the first time, Malcolm permitted himself a moment's bitter resentment of Time Tours and their whole slick, money-milling operation. If not for their shady, underhanded tricks . . .

"Penny for 'em," someone said at Malcolm's elbow.

He started and glanced around to find Ann Vinh Mulhaney gazing up at him. He relaxed with a smile. She must have come straight from the weapons range when the klaxon sounded. She hadn't bothered to unholster the pistols at her belt or loosen her hair from its confining elastic tie. At five feet, five inches, Ann was a little shorter than Malcolm, but evenly matched with Sven Bailey, who strolled up behind her. He, too, was dressed for the weapons range.

They must've just released a new class, probably the one scheduled for London. Sven, who outmassed dainty little Ann by at least two to one despite their matched heights, nodded politely toward Malcolm, then watched the departing tourists with a despairing shake of his head.

"What a miserable bunch they were," he commented to no one in particular. "Stupid, too, if you're still here." He glanced briefly toward Malcolm.

He shrugged, acknowledging the well-meant compliment, and answered Ann's question. "I'm just watching the fun, same as everyone. How are you two?"

Sven, TT-86's recognized master of bladed weapons, grunted once and didn't deign to answer. Ann laughed. She was one of the few residents who felt comfortable laughing *at* Sven Bailey. She tossed her ponytail and rested slim hands on her hips. "He lost his last bet. Five shots out of six, loser picks up the tab at Down Time."

Malcolm smiled. "Sven, haven't you learned yet not to shoot against her?"

Sven Bailey regarded his fingernails studiously. "Yep." Then he glanced up with a sardonic twist of the lips. "Trouble is, the students keep trying to lose *their* money. What's a guy to do?"

Malcolm grinned. "The way I hear it, you two split the take."

Sven only looked hurt. Ann laughed aloud. "What a horrid rumor." She winked. "Care to join us? We're heading over to the Down Time to cool out and grab a bite to eat."

Malcolm was well beyond the stage of flushing with embarrassment every time he had to turn down an invitation from lack of funds. "Thanks, but no. I think I'll see the departure through, then head up toward Primary and try to line up some prospects from the new arrivals. And I've got to fix this blasted sandal again. It keeps coming loose at the sole."

Sven nodded, accepting his face-saving excuses without comment. Ann started to protest, then glanced at Sven. She sighed. "If you change your mind, I'll spot you for a drink. Or better yet Sven can pick up the tab from my winnings." She winked at Malcolm. Sven just crossed his arms and snorted, reminding Malcolm of a burly bulldog humoring an upstart chickadee. "By the way," she smiled, "Kevin and I were thinking about inviting some people over for dinner tomorrow night. If you're free at, oh, say about sixish, stop by. The kids love it when you visit."

"Sure," he said, without really meaning it. "Thanks."

Fortunately, they moved off before noticing the dull flush that crept up Malcolm's neck into his cheeks. If Ann Vinh Mulhaney had pre-planned a dinner party for tomorrow night, he'd eat his sandal, broken strap and all. Her gesture warmed him, though, even as he rubbed the back of his neck and muttered, "I've got to get a full-time job with *someone.*" But not with Time Tours.

Never with Time Tours.

He'd starve first.

Tourists over at Gate Six had started to climb the ramp, each one in turn presenting his or her Timecard to have the departure logged properly. Excited women could be heard clear across the Commons, shrieking and giggling as they plucked up the nerve to step through the open portal. That ritual never varied, either. Scuttlebutt had it, Time Tours had sound-proofed the exits on the other side of *all* their gates, rather than hush the tourists. He had to chuckle. He couldn't really blame them. Stepping through that first time was an unnerving experience.

Inevitably—this time about three quarters of the way through the departure—someone fumbled a load of poorly tied baggage. Parcels scattered across the catwalk, creating a major hitch in the traffic flow. Three separate guides, glancing wildly at the overhead chronometer, converged on the mess and snatched up baggage willy nilly. A fourth guide all but shoved the remaining tourists through the open gate. The edges of the gate had begun to shrink slowly back toward the center.

Malcolm shook his head. With years of experience behind them, Time Tours really ought to manage better than that. He grunted aloud. *That's what comes of exploiting stranded down-timers to haul baggage.* Somebody really should do something about the poor souls who wandered in through open gates and found themselves lost in an alien world. His old outfit had never used them as grunt labor.

Of course, his old outfit had quietly gone bankrupt, too.

The guides who'd snatched up the spilled parcels lunged through and vanished. Moments later, Gate Six winked closed for another two weeks. Malcolm sighed and turned his attention to Primary. He checked the chronometer and swore under his breath. He just had time, if he hustled. He left Urbs Romae behind and half jogged through Frontier Town, with its saloons and strolling "cowboys," then picked up speed through Victoria Station's "cobbled" streets, lined with shops whose windows boasted graceful Victorian gowns and masculine deerstalkers. The klaxon sounded, an ear-splitting noise that caused Malcolm to swear under his breath.

"Your attention, please. Gate One is due to open in two minutes. All departures, be advised that if you have not cleared Station Medical, you will not be permitted to pass Primary. Please have your baggage ready for customs . . ."

Malcolm cut across one edge of Edo Castletown, with its extraordinary gardens, sixteenth-century Japanese architecture, and swaggering tourists dressed as samurai warriors. He jogged past the Neo Edo Hotel, skirting a group of kimono-clad women who had paused to admire the mural inside the lobby. The desk clerk grinned and waved as he shot past.

Primary, less than a hundred feet beyond the farthest edge of Castletown, consisted of an imposing set of barriers, armed guards, ramps, fences, metal detectors, and X-ray equipment, plus dual medical stations, all clustered at the bottom of a broad ramp that led fifteen feet into thin air then simply stopped. Malcolm had once wondered why the station hadn't simply been constructed so that the floor was dead-level even with Gate One, or Primary, as everyone in residence called it.

Upon subsequent interaction with officials from the Bureau of Access Time Functions, Malcolm had decided ATF must have insisted on the arrangement for its unsettling psychological impact. Montgomery Wilkes, inspecting everything like a prowling leopard, stood out simply by the sweating hush which followed his rounds.

Malcolm found a good vantage point and leaned his shoulder against the station wall, extremely glad he didn't work for the ATF agent. He glanced at the nearest chronometer and sighed. *Whew . . .* Seconds to spare. The line of returning tourists and businessmen had already formed, snaking past Malcolm's position through a series of roped-off switchbacks. Customs agents were rubbing metaphorical hands in anticipation.

Malcolm's skull bones warned him moments before the main gate into Shangri-la dilated open. Then up-timers streamed through the open portal into the terminal, while departures cleared customs in the usual inefficient dribble. New arrivals stopped at the medical station set up on the inbound side of the gate to have their medical records checked, logged, and mass-scanned into TT-86's medical database. The usual clusters of wide-eyed tourists, grey-suited business types, liveried tour guides, and uniformed government officials— including TT-86's up-time postman with the usual load of letters, laser disks, and parcels—edged clear of Medical and entered the controlled chaos of La-La Land.

"Okay," Malcolm muttered, "let's see what Father Christmas brought us this time." Once a time-guide, always a time-guide. The occupation was addictive.

He double-checked the big chronometer board. The next departure was set for three days hence, London. Denver followed that by twelve hours and Edo a day after that. One of the quarterly departures to twelfth-century Mongolia would be leaving in six days. He shook his head. Mongolia was out of the question. None of that incoming group looked hardy enough for three months in deadly country inhabited by even deadlier people.

Gate Five didn't get much traffic, even when it *was* open.

He eyed the inbound crowd. London, Denver, or ancient Tokyo . . . Most of the tourists to Edo were Japanese businessmen. They tended to stick with Japanese tour guides. The only time Malcolm had been to sixteenth-century Edo had been on a scheduled tour for his old company and he'd been in *heavy* disguise. The Tokugawa shoguns had developed a nasty habit of executing any *gaijin* unfortunate enough even to be shipwrecked on Japanese shores. After that first visit, Malcolm had firmly decided he'd acquired a good knowledge of sixteenth-century Japanese, Portuguese, and Dutch for nothing.

London or Denver, then . . . He'd have three days, minimum, to work on a client. His gaze rested on a likely-looking prospect, a middle-aged woman who had paused to gape in open confusion while the three small children clustered at her side shoved fists into their mouths and clutched luggage covered with Cowboys and Indians. The smallest boy wore a plastic ten-gallon hat and a toy six-gun rig. Mom glanced from side to side, up and down, stared at the chronometer, and appeared ready to burst into tears.

"Bingo." Tourist in need of help.

He hadn't taken more than three steps, however, when a redheaded gamine clad in a black leather miniskirt, black stretch-lace body suit, and black thigh-high leather boots, hauling a compact suitcase that looked like it weighed as much as she did, bore down on him with the apparent homing instinct of a striking hawk: "Hi! I'm looking for Kit Carson—any idea where I might find him?"

"Uh . . ." Malcolm said intelligently as every drop of blood in his brain transmuted instantaneously to the nether regions of his anatomy. Not only did Malcolm have no idea where the retired time scout might be lurking this time of day . . .

God . . . It ought to be illegal to look like that!

Clearly, it'd been far too long since Malcolm had—

He gave himself an irritable mental kick. Just where *might* she find Kit? He probably wasn't at his hotel, not this late in the morning; but it was a little early for drinking. Of course, he enjoyed watching departures as much as any other 'eighty-sixer.

The delightful little minx who'd accosted him was tapping one leather-clad foot in an excess of energy. With her short auburn hair, freckles, and clear green eyes, she gave the impression of an Irish alleycat, intent on her own business and impatient with anything that got in her way. She was the darned cutest thing Malcolm had seen come through Primary in months. He kept his gaze on her face with studied care.

"Try the Down Time Bar and Grill. If anyone knows, the regulars there might. Or you could . . ."

He trailed off. She was already gone, like a bullet from the barrel of a smoking gun. That damned leather miniskirt did evil things to Malcolm's breath control.

"Well." He rested hands on hips. "If that doesn't . . ." He couldn't imagine why a girl that age—and in a tearing hurry, besides—would be looking for Kit Carson of all people. "Huh." He tried to put her out of his mind and turned to find his bewildered tourist with the cute kids. He needed a job worse than he needed a mystery.

"Oh, bloody hell . . ." Skeeter Jackson, the louse, had already collared the scared family and was hard at work playing with the youngest kid. Mom was beaming. God help them.

He considered warning her, then glanced down at his artistically filthy tunic and swore again. Compared with Skeeter Jackson's groomed appearance, he didn't stand a chance. Maybe he could get her aside later and explain the difference between reliable guides and the Skeeter Jacksons of this world. Malcolm sighed. The way his luck had been running lately, she'd slap him for maligning that "nice young man."

He decided maybe it wouldn't hurt to take up Ann's offer, after all. Malcolm strolled down the Commons on a reverse course through Castletown, Victoria Station, and Frontier Town. He entered Urbs Romae just as the klaxon for closure of Primary sounded, warning everyone that TT-86 was about to be sealed in again for another couple of days, at least. Up ahead, the pert little up-timer looking for Kit sailed straight past the Down Time without spotting it. He grinned and decided to see how long it took her to holler for help.

Just what *did* she want with Kit Carson?

Whatever it was, Malcolm had a feeling the next few days were going to prove most entertaining.

Margo thumped down the long, cluttered concourse, berating herself as she went. "Honestly," she fumed, "the first person you ask is a guy in a Roman tunic and slave collar? He's probably some poor down-timer who wandered through an unstable gate, like the articles warned about. Stupid, greenhorn idiot . . ."

Margo did not enjoy looking like a fool.

"No wonder he took so long answering. Probably had to translate everything I said first. At least he spoke *some*

English. And I've got the right station, that's something to celebrate," she added under her breath, glancing in restrained awe at the sprawling complex which stretched away in a maze of catwalks, shops, waiting areas, and cross-corridors that led only God knew where. The care she'd taken to research a time terminal's layout didn't begin to convey the reality of the place. It was enormous, bewildering. And none of the information she'd found described the private sections of a terminal, visible in tantalizing glimpses off the Commons. She found herself wanting to explore . . .

"First," she told herself sternly, "I find Kit Carson. Everything else is secondary. That Roman guy said he might be at some bar, so all I have to do now is find him. I can talk anybody into anything. All I have to do is find him. . . ."

Unfortunately, she didn't find the "Down Time" on the main concourse or any of the balconies connected to it. Margo set down her heavy suitcase, panting slightly, and scowled at an empty set of chairs clustered around a closed gate.

"*What* Down Time Bar and Grill?"

Grimly, Margo picked up her case again, regretting the decision to stuff everything into one piece of luggage. She looked for a terminal directory, something like she'd always found at ordinary shopping malls, but saw nothing remotely resembling one. She didn't want to betray complete ignorance by *asking* someone. Margo was desperate to give the impression that she was worldly, well-travelled, able to take care of herself.

But the Down Time Bar & Grill was apparently close kin to the Flying Dutchman, because it didn't appear to exist. Maybe it *was* down time? *Don't be ridiculous. Nobody'd put a bar on the other side of a time gate.* Finally she started hunting down the maze of cross-linked, interconnecting corridors that formed the private portion of TT-86. Stairways led to corridors on other levels, some of them brightly lit, others dim and deserted. Within minutes, she was hopelessly lost and fuming.

She set the case down again and rubbed her aching palm. Margo glared at a receding stretch of corridor broken occasionally by more corridors and locked doors. "Don't these people believe in posting a directory somewhere?"

"May I help you?"

The voice was polite, male, and almost directly behind her.

She spun around.

The guy in the tunic. Oh, shit. . . . Ever since New York she'd been so careful—and this was a down-timer, God knew what he'd try to pull—

"Are you following me?" she demanded, furious that her voice came out breathy and scared instead of calm and assured.

He scratched the back of his neck under the thick bronze collar. "Well, I couldn't help but notice you passed the Down Time, then took a really wrong turn off the Commons. It's easy to get lost, back here."

Margo's heart pounded so hard her chest hurt. She backed away a step. "I ought to warn you," she said in a tone meant to be forbidding, "I know martial arts."

"As a matter of fact, so do I."

Oh, God . . .

He grinned disarmingly, reminding Margo quite suddenly of her high school history teacher. "Most temporal guides do, you know."

Temporal guide?

He held out a business card neatly clasped between two fingers. "Malcolm Moore, freelance time guide."

Margo felt her face flame. "I . . . uh . . ." Clearly he knew exactly what she'd been thinking—and seemed to find it amusing. She took the card hesitantly and risked glancing at it. The card seemed genuine enough. "Uh, hi. I'm Margo."

If he was offended that she'd withheld her last name, he didn't show it. He said only, "Nice to meet you, Margo," and shook her hand formally. "If you like, I'll take you back to the Down Time."

She hesitated.

He grinned. "No charge. I only charge for tours on the *other* side of time gates."

"Oh. Okay." Then, grudgingly, because she was embarrassed she hadn't said it sooner, "Thanks."

"Don't mention it."

He had a nice smile. Maybe she could trust him, just a little. *Should'a worn something else, though.* His glance slid across her with inevitable—she almost might have said involuntary—interest. Most guys looked at her that way, thinking she was at least the eighteen she tried to appear rather than the almost-seventeen she was. Yes, she should have worn something else. But the boots were too bulky to pack in her case and she'd wanted to use every possible advantage she possessed when she finally came face to face with Kit Carson. . . . *Well, you made this bed. Lie in it.* Margo picked up her case and followed him back toward a corridor she was certain led in the wrong direction, only to emerge in a cross-corridor she recognized as the one she'd taken off the Commons. Margo sighed and relegated herself to having to overcome yet another handicap on her quest: a reputation for stupidity. Maybe Mr. Moore wouldn't say anything about having to lead her out by the hand; but she wouldn't bet on it. And she certainly didn't have enough money to bribe him.

They regained the Commons in silence, for which she was grateful. As they approached an enormous area caged to prevent tourist access, Margo frowned. She'd noticed it before, but only peripherally. Inside the cage was an irregular-shaped hole in the concrete.

"What's that?" she asked hesitantly, afraid she knew the answer already. *Unstable gate . . .*

Malcolm Moore glanced around. "What's what? Oh, the unstable gate."

"I know about those."

"Yes. Well, the floor collapsed when this one opened under it. A coffee stand fell through."

She edged closer for a better look and paled. The sight was unnerving. Air at the bottom seemed to ripple oddly. Every few seconds, she heard the splash of water. The bones behind her ears buzzed uncomfortably. "Fell through into where?"

"We think it's the Bermuda Triangle." His voice was flat, completely deadpan.

"The *Bermuda Triangle?* Don't jerk me around!"

"Hey," he held out both hands, "who declared war? Honest, we think it's the Bermuda Triangle. Katie and Jack Sherman almost drowned when the gate opened up the first time. Their coffee shop went straight to the bottom. I was on the rescue team that went through for them. Not only is it an unstable gate, the darned thing leads to a whole nexus of other gates popping open and closed. Picking the right one back to La-La Land was murder. Took us five wrong tries. We almost didn't get back."

"Oh." *Great. Unstable nexus gates, yet.* "I know about unstable nexus gates," Margo muttered, wondering why none of her research had turned up that little tidbit. Maybe the government didn't want to scare people? "I've been on time terminals before."

He appeared to accept the lie. She'd sooner have died than admit she'd sold almost everything she owned—and very nearly a good bit more—to raise the price of a down-time ticket onto TT-86. Margo eyed the hole in the floor with a slight chill of misgiving. Well, adventure was what she was here for, wasn't it?

"So where's this bar?" she demanded, turning her back on the watery chasm. "I have business with Mr. Carson."

Malcolm Moore eyed her for one heartbeat longer than he should have—did he suspect anything? ATF had accepted her faked ID without a second glance—then he shrugged and jerked his head. "It's down this way, in Urbs Romae. The Roman City," he translated, assuming she wouldn't know the meaning of "urbs."

Margo muttered, "I know where the word urban comes from." It was very nearly the only Latin she knew, but she knew *that*.

The corners of his eyes crinkled nicely when he smiled. Margo decided Malcolm Moore didn't remind her of any of the men she'd known, after all. "Come on. I'll show you where it is. It's a little tricky to spot."

She followed, hauling a suitcase that weighed more by the moment. When she had trouble keeping up, he glanced around and slowed his pace slightly to match hers.

"Are you by any chance planning to visit London? Or Denver?"

"Why?"

He grimaced expressively. "Just hoping. I'm looking for a client for one of the upcoming tours. We freelancers have to hustle for a job."

"Oh. No, I wasn't planning a tour. Sorry."

"Don't mention it." His eyes, however, remained bright with unspoken curiosity. Just how often did Kit Carson get visitors? If the world's most famous time scout turned out to be a cranky recluse . . . Given the difficulty she'd had ferreting out recent information on him, he probably was. Well, coping with her father ought to have been training enough to deal with any ill-tempered male ego. That training had gotten her out of New York alive, hadn't it?

Malcolm Moore led her at least half-way down the Commons, through areas that reminded Margo of history-book pictures. She knew where the various gates led, having researched TT-86 as thoroughly as possible before taking the plunge. This portion of the terminal led to ancient Athens, while the section over there was designed like a city in the High Andes. They passed shops that fascinated with glimpses of exotic interiors. One restaurant was shaped like a South American pyramid; its doorway was a replica of the Sun Gate at Teotihuacan.

Beyond that, Margo spotted intricate knotted patterns and interwoven mythical beasts carved around shop doorways. One restaurant had been built into a dragon-prowed ship, with signs painted to look like Viking runes. The scents wafting out of the restaurants made her empty belly rumble in complaint.

Should've eaten lunch before I came down time. I bet the prices here are sky-high. At least in New York, she'd been able to buy cheap hot dogs from street vendors. They passed into an area of mosaic floors and Roman-style shop fronts, then her guide ducked under a span of fake columns and steel supports and indicated a dim doorway. The clink of glasses and the unmistakable scent of beer wafted out from the interior. There was no shop sign visible anywhere. No wonder she'd missed it. *Must be a hangout for residents only, if they don't advertise.*

"Voilà," Malcolm Moore said with a courtly flourish and a smile. "The Down Time Bar and Grill."

"Thanks." She flashed him a quick smile of gratitude, then headed for the dim-lit entrance, leaving him to follow or wander off on his own, whichever he preferred. Her attention was already focused on what she was going to say to the legendary Kenneth "Kit" Carson, the man on whom her entire future—and more—depended. Mouth dry, palms wet, Margo gripped her suitcase in one hand and her courage in the other, then charged across the threshold.

". . . so anyway," Ann laughed above the sharp crack of billiard balls from the back room, "he learned a valuable lesson about concentrating on the front-sight post. Marcus, hello, yes, I'll have another."

Across the table, Sven groaned theatrically. Rachel Eisenstein's musical laughter provided a comical counterpoint to Sven Bailey's gloom.

"Oh, hush up and finish your beer," Ann told him. "I won fair and square."

"I know. That's what's so damn depressing."

Ann winked at Marcus while Rachel sipped from her wineglass and continued to laugh silently. Sven took another pull from his beer mug and sighed. The young bartender grinned and went in search of refills.

Granville Baxter wandered in, having to duck under the doorway, and paused to allow his eyes to adjust to the dim interior. His grey business suit was still crisp and neat, but the man who wore it had a wilted look that said, "I need a drink. Now." Rachel waved and indicated an empty chair. Baxter's maternal Masai heritage coupled with a few paternal ancestors who'd been NBA stars gave him a height advantage over every single 'eighty-sixer in La-La Land. Granville Baxter, however, had no earthly interest in sports, other than occasionally sponsoring special Time Tours package deals for rich franchises.

Time Tours considered Baxter a marketing genius.

"Mind if I join you?" he asked, ever polite even at the Down Time.

Sven gestured to one of several empty chairs. "Park 'em."

The Time Tours executive sank back with a sigh, fished in a pocket for a handkerchief, and blotted his dark brow.

"Double-gate day," he said, providing all the explanation any 'eighty-sixer needed.

Ann waved at Marcus and nodded toward Baxter. The bartender nodded back and drew a stein of Bax's favorite brew.

"How'd it go?" Sven asked, with a long pull at his own beer.

Bax—who had occasionally said dire things about his parents' decision to name him "Granville"—grimaced. "Baggage troubles again. Other than that, pretty smooth. Oh, we had the typical three or four who decide they want to switch tours after they get to the terminal and we had one woman who threw up all over a whole family on the other side, but nothing too rough. Forgot her scopolamine patch. I'll tell you, though, if my new baggage manager doesn't get his act together by the London departure, he's going to go begging a job somewhere else. —Oh, Marcus, bless you."

Half the beer vanished in one long gulp.

Ann sympathized. One transfer, one promotion, and one family crisis had led to four new baggage managers for Time Tours at TT-86 in the past six months. Bax's own job might be on the line if baggage handlers screwed up again. Rich tourists tolerated very little in the way of mistakes from hired underlings. Even geniuses were expendable if the right tourist pitched a loud-enough fit.

Marcus set out the rest of the drinks.

"So," Bax asked, "any problems at Medical with the new arrivals?"

Rachel had just begun to reply when a startling young woman clad entirely in black leather and lace, with short, auburn hair and a suitcase gripped like a set of nunchucks, charged through the doorway on a direct course for their table.

"Hello," she said, from halfway across the room, "I'm looking for Kit Carson. I was told he might be here."

Ann and Rachel exchanged glances. Even Bax lifted one brow. "No," he said in a friendly fashion. "I'm afraid he isn't, unless he's in back playing billiards."

The young woman swung around, clearly ready to

interrupt the game in progress. Every male eye in the room followed the swing of her short skirt.

"No, he isn't back there," Ann said, forestalling her. "That's Skeeter and Goldie, trying to outscam one another."

The crack of billiard balls underscored the statement. The red-haired girl all but scowled. "Any idea how I can find him? It's important."

"Well," Bax scratched the back of his head, "you could pull up a chair and wet your throat until he gets here." He looked hopeful. "He'll be here, probably sooner than later. Kit always stops by, especially on gate days."

Whoever she was, this girl didn't look in the mood to hang around and wait. Marcus, in his delightfully accented English, volunteered, "He has the hotel. He is there?"

Her eyes brightened. "Hotel? Which hotel?"

Sven set his mug on the table with a faint click of glass on wood. "The Neo Edo. It's right on the Commons, down by the big fish pond, with an entrance that looks like—".

She was gone before he could finish.

"Well," he said into the astonished silence.

Before anyone else could speak, Malcolm Moore stepped into the bar. He was still dressed for business and wore a wicked grin. "I see by the open mouths you've all met Margo. Anybody find out why she's looking for Kit?"

"Margo? You *know* her?" Bax demanded. "Who is she?"

Malcolm dragged over an empty chair. Ann highsigned Marcus for another beer. "No," he admitted with a chagrined air, "I don't know her. She came barrelling through Primary and collared me right off, asking about Kit, then promptly got lost back in Residential looking for the Down Time. I was hoping maybe she'd told you guys why she wants to find Kit. Prickly little cactus blossom, isn't she?"

Sven laughed at the look on Granville Baxter's face. "Bax, she'd put you in an early grave. Stick to Time Tours if you want to die young."

Bax shot him a look of utter disgust and studied his beer.

"Well," Malcolm nodded thanks when Marcus brought him a chilled mug, "I get the feeling things are going to be lively for a while." He saluted the group with his beer and grinned.

"You," Sven Bailey muttered, "just said a freakin' mouthful. The sixty-four thousand dollar question is, do we warn Kit?"

Ann and Rachel exchanged glances, Bax choked on his beer, and across the bar even Marcus started to laugh. Malcolm chuckled. "Poor Kit. Well, let's put it to a vote, shall we? All in favor?"

Solemnly, but with eyes twinkling, Kit's friends cast their votes with upraised hands. Malcolm plucked a few threads from the ravelling hem of his tunic. "Short thread does the honors."

Malcolm, of course, came up short. As always. He sighed, took the inevitable ribbing with a long drag at his beer, and headed for the phone.

CHAPTER TWO

Government paperwork was only one of many things about running a time-terminal hotel which Kit Carson hated. A laundry list of his favorite complaints, carefully filed away in one corner of his mind where they wouldn't distract, included laundry bills, the price of food brought in past customs, the cost of replacing towels, ashtrays, and plumbing fixtures carted off by the guests, a work force likely to vanish at a moment's notice, crushing boredom interspersed with ulcer-generating crises, and—near the top of the list—*tourists*.

Paperwork, however, was the thing he despised most. He'd almost rather have returned to academia.

The Neo Edo's executive office, larger than some modern, up-time homes, was one of the features of his current career that made it tolerable. His office boasted a video wall with panoramic real-time views of the Commons and equally panoramic taped views of multiple down-time vistas. A wet bar stocked with illegal bottles of liquid ambrosia (which both Kit and his predecessor, the builder of Neo Edo, had brought back up time) was available any time the job grew too hairy.

Priceless paintings and art treasures rescued from palaces destroyed by the Onin Wars in fifteenth-century Kyoto graced Kit's office, which also boasted pristine *tatami* rice mats on the floor and the clean, uncluttered look of sliding paper-screen walls and delicately carved woodwork.

The office's best feature, however, was a recessed light well which cast realistic-looking "daylight" over a miniature Japanese dry-landscape garden. The serene arrangement of raked white sand, upright stones, and elegantly clipped topiary which filled an entire corner of the office rested the eyes and soothed the soul.

It was Kit's salvation on paperwork days. He would periodically sit back in his chair, nurse a good bourbon, and contemplate the symbolic "islands" the rock formations represented, floating in their withered "sea" of sand. It gave Kit intense pleasure to symbolically consign the drafters of the requisite government forms to a long life marooned on one of those miniature desert islands, without hope of rescue.

Talk about the perfect Zen hell. . . .

The phone call interrupted him halfway through a form designed to require an entire battery of expensive lawyers to decipher. Kit grinned despite the fact that the call had come through on the "Panic Button." He tucked the receiver between shoulder and ear, allowed his gaze to stray to the corner garden, and said, "Yeah, Jimmy?"

Jimmy Okuda, at the front desk, was the only person with direct access to that particular intercom line. A call on the Panic Button usually meant another jump in Kit's blood pressure; today, the distraction was more than welcome.

"Call from Malcolm Moore, Kit."

"Malcolm?" What was Jimmy doing, buzzing him on the Panic Button for a call from Malcolm Moore? "Uh . . . put him through."

An outside line flashed as Jimmy transferred the call. What on earth could Malcolm Moore want? Kit had offered him a job more than once, only to be refused politely but firmly. Kit pressed the button. "Malcolm? Hello, what can I do for you?"

"Kit, sorry to interrupt whatever you're doing, but you're going to have a visitor in about five minutes."

"Oh?" Malcolm's tone invited all sorts of speculation. From the background noise, Malcolm was calling from the Down Time. That could mean *anything* might be on its way. Just as Kit had started reviewing lethal potentialities from his down-time adventures—and wondering where he'd left the soft body armor he'd used in his scouting days—Malcolm said, "An up-timer's looking for you."

"*Up*-timer?"

Malcolm chuckled thinly. "Some day, Kit, I will get you to tell me about that deal in Bangkok. Yeah, an up-timer. Real impatient, too. We took a vote and decided you deserved a warning before this one collared you." Malcolm was laughing at some inside joke to which Kit was clearly not privy.

"Uh-huh. Thanks, I think."

"Don't mention it. What're friends for? Relieve our curiosity, would you? Sven says he'll buy, if you'll tell."

Kit raised a brow. If Sven Bailey was that curious, something decidedly odd was up. "I'll let you know. Thanks for the warning."

Malcolm hung up. Kit shoved back his chair. Whoever was on his way, meeting the guy face to face, cold, was not Kit's idea of good strategy. He paused at the doorway to slip on his shoes, thought about his attire and hastily exchanged his comfortable kimono for a business jacket and slacks, then headed down to Neo Edo's main desk. "Jimmy, Malcolm says an up-time visitor is headed this way. Tell 'em I'm out, would you? I want to be scarce for a few minutes. Lay a false trail or something."

Jimmy, also a retired time scout, winked and nodded. "Sure thing, Kit."

Time scouts could never be too careful.

Particularly world-famous ones.

Kit damned all reporters everywhere and made tracks

through a gathering crowd. The Neo Edo's lobby was a modern re-interpretation of the receiving hall of the shoguns at Edo Castle, as it had appeared before Ieyasu Tokugawa's famous shogunate headquarters had burned to the ground in the Long-Sleeves Fire of 1657. The lobby's showpiece was the mural-sized reproduction of Miyamoto Musashi's famous, lost painting of sunrise over Edo Castle, commissioned from the master warrior-poet-painter by none other than Japan's third Shogun, Iemitsu Tokugawa. The painting drew the eye even from the Commons, which meant tourists who wandered in to admire the artwork often stayed to become customers.

Homako Tani had been a shrewd hotelier.

La-La Land scuttlebutt had it that the Neo Edo's builder had liberated the original during the 1657 conflagration which had destroyed Edo Castle; but Kit had never found any trace of it, not even in Homako's private safe. Of course, scuttlebutt also had it that Homako Tani had been murdered by the irascible Musashi, himself, during a down-time visit to feudal Japan, for some minor insult the *ronin* samurai hadn't been willing to overlook. Other rumors had him last seen stepping through an unstable gate into T'ang Dynasty China; and others that he'd gone into permanent retirement in Tibet as the Dalai Lama.

The point was, nobody knew what had become of Homako, not even the named partners in the law firm of Chase, Carstedt, and Syvertsen, who had delivered the impressive envelope deeding him ownership of the Neo Edo for "payment of debts." The only debt Homako Tani had ever owed Kit Carson was having his backside hauled out of that incendiary fiasco in Silver Plume, Colorado. So far as Kit knew, Homako never had gone back to the Old West. The stink of burnt saloons, banks, and cathouses had lingered in Kit's lungs for weeks afterward. He still mourned that sweet little four-inch "Wesson Favorite" he'd lost during the confusion. Only a thousand of the S&W Model .44 cal. DA revolvers were ever made, and his had gone up in smoke.

Kit sighed. Whatever the true fate of Homako Tani, the "inheritance" had come just as Kit was being forced into retirement. He'd needed a job, more to justify hanging around La-La Land than anything, since he didn't really need money. The Neo Edo had seemed a gift from the gods. After three years of managing the hotel, Kit had begun to suspect Homako Tani had simply come to hate government paperwork and tourists so desperately he'd bailed out before his sanity snapped.

Kit shouldered his way politely past incoming arrivals from Primary, nodding and smiling to customers whose loud voices grated on his nerves, and headed past the pebble-lined fish pond just outside his lobby. He glanced both ways down the Commons, but saw nothing out of the ordinary. Just the usual batch of new tourists gawking and lugging heavy suitcases while trying to decide which hotel they could best afford.

Kit wandered over toward a free-standing souvenir-and-information stall with a nonchalance born of long practice and pretended to study the trinkets. The stall's owner, Nyoko Aoki, raised a brow, but she said nothing, tending her genuine customers with studied diligence. Nyoko's stand provided a perfect view of the Neo Edo's main lobby. The hotel's graceful facade towered three stories above the Commons floor, rising to a peak two stories below the ceiling. The name was painted tastefully in gilt English script and Japanese characters. The tourists provided perfect cover as they busily bought up station maps, guide books, and T-shirts or wandered into the hotel lobby to admire Musashi's mural.

Kit didn't have to wait long, although the visitor's appearance startled him considerably. The minute Kit spotted her, he knew that *this* was the up-timer Malcolm had called about. She was young, redheaded, and apparently operated on full throttle as her natural mode.

Unlike any normal tourist, she was not gawking, window-shopping, or looking for a station guidebook. The way she was dressed—and the way she moved inside all that black lace and leather—got attention from ninety percent of the men on the Commons and not a few of the women.

Kit found it suddenly difficult to control his breathing properly. *Good God, she's easy on the eyes*. Hard on the pulse, though. . . . A man could get himself into serious trouble with that girl, just by smiling at her. She charged into the Neo Edo like a runaway bullet train and cornered poor Jimmy behind the desk. His eyes had bugged. Kit couldn't quite hear what was being said over the tourist babble, but he could see her impatient frown and Jimmy's shrug and uplifted hands. He could also read Jimmy's lips: "Try the Time Tripper."

Good. Wild-goose-chase time. She shot out of the Neo Edo's lobby at full tilt. Who in God's name was this kid? He'd expected . . . Well, Kit wasn't sure who, or what, he'd actually expected. But it wasn't a redheaded speed demon with an Irish wildcat manner and motives as inscrutable as a mandarin's. Malcolm, drat the man, hadn't given him even a hint. Of course, with Sven offering to buy drinks in exchange for information, maybe no one else really knew, either.

Kit followed her thoughtfully. He was certain he'd never run across her down time. *Her*, he'd have remembered. Vividly. He was equally certain he'd never met her up time, either. Hell, he hadn't *been* up time in years, probably not since that sexy little kitten had been wrapped in diapers. If that girl was past eighteen, it wasn't by more than a few days.

So who was she and why was she looking for him?

Probably a journalist, he thought gloomily, trying to make a name for herself. She had that supercharged "I'm going to get this story if it kills you" look of someone out for a first Pulitzer.

God . . .

Her skin was delightfully flushed, either from carrying that suitcase—which looked heavy—or from sheer pique. Kit grinned. Good. If she were sufficiently off-balance when they finally met, so much the better for him.

Kit bought a tourist map for camouflage and followed her at a respectable distance. She certainly didn't dawdle. Whoever she was, she headed straight for the Time Tripper, a modestly priced hostelry catering to families on tight budgets. Middle-aged fathers, respectable in their Hawaiian shirts and jeans, ogled her from over their wives' heads and ignored whining kids.

She cornered the hapless desk clerk, who shrugged, looked thoroughly irritated, and gestured vaguely toward the next hotel. When she stooped to retrieve her suitcase, Kit's viscera reacted mindlessly. The man standing next to him groaned, "Oh, *yes*, there is a God. . . ." Kit grinned. The guy pulled himself out of a trance when the woman next to him hit him on the shoulder.

"Hey! Quit drooling!"

Another man said, "Five minutes with her would probably kill a horse."

"Yeah," his companion moaned, "but what a way to go. . . ."

They were undoubtedly right on all counts. That girl spelled T-R-O-U-B-L-E—and her trouble had his name all over it. He sighed. When the redheaded whirlwind headed for the Tempus Fugit, Kit decided to let her continue the hunt alone. If Jimmy had laid his groundwork properly, she'd spend the next several minutes going from hotel to hotel. That would give Kit time to dig up what he could on her. He watched her eye-catching retreat toward the Fugit, then hastily backtracked toward the Down Time.

Margo rapidly received the impression that people were jerking her around, apparently for the fun of it.

None of the desk clerks had seen Kit Carson, despite what that grinning idiot at the Neo Edo had told her. If Kit Carson had "stepped out for a meeting with the other hotel managers, sorry, I'm not sure which hotel," Margo would eat her luggage, suitcase and all.

"This is ridiculous!" she fumed, heading for yet another hotel. "He's got to be here somewhere!"

The desk clerk at the Hotel Acropolis looked at her like she'd taken leave of her senses. "Meeting? What meeting? I *am* the manager." The middle-aged woman patted the back of Margo's hand. "Honey, Jimmy probably called Kit, wherever he was, and warned him you were coming. Kit doesn't much care for unannounced visitors. If I were you, I'd settle into a room someplace, call for an appointment, and meet him at his office."

Margo thanked her for the advice and left in a hurry, more determined than ever to track him down. If she simply called for an appointment, he'd find some excuse or other to delay meeting her, probably permanently. Margo might be a nobody, but she wasn't going to remain one and she wasn't going to let a little thing like impossible-to-get appointments stand in her way. Working as she was against a ticking clock—with a six-month countdown not even God could delay—she simply didn't have time for failure.

"If I were Kit Carson," she muttered half-aloud, "and I were trying to find out who was looking for me, where would I go?"

Someplace where he could talk to the people who'd already talked to her.

"Right. Back to the Down Time."

She transferred the hateful suitcase to her other hand, eyed the vast stretch of Commons she had to re-cross, and groaned aloud.

"Consider it training in physical endurance," she told herself. The scent of food wafting out into the Commons from various restaurants was nearly more than Margo could bear. She was sorely tempted to stop for a good hot meal, but didn't want the trail to grow any colder than it already had.

You'll see, she told a host of nay-sayers, beginning with that pig of a high-school guidance counsellor, moving on to Billy-the-rat-Pandropolous and ending—inevitably—with her father. Hateful, hurtful words rang in her ears, retaining the power to injure long after the bruises had healed. *Just you watch. You'll see.* Margo's eyes burned. She blinked back the tears. Small towns were terrible places to grow up with world-sized dreams—especially when those dreams were the only things you had left to hold onto. She was scared to death of Kit Carson already—had clung to this dream so long she was afraid to have it shattered, too. But the clock was ticking and Margo wasn't a quitter. No, by God, she wasn't. Just standing here was proof of that. Margo narrowed her eyes. *All right, Kit Carson. Ready or not, here I come.*

She closed in on the Down Time Bar & Grill.

Kit ducked under the girders and stepped across the Down Time's threshold.

"Hey!" Malcolm called from a crowded, jovial table. "Did you meet her?"

"Not exactly," Kit said drily. "I'll get with you in a minute."

Malcolm only grinned at the threat in his voice. Sven Bailey chuckled and popped a handful of peanuts into his mouth, washing them down with a sweating beer. Ann Mulhaney and, oh God, Rachel Eisenstein, leaned expectantly on their elbows, grinning in his direction. Rachel's eyes twinkled. Kit knew one helluva ribbing was coming, for sure—Rachel was the one person in La-La Land whose wit he could never top. Granville Baxter grinned and lifted his beer in a silent salute.

Kit stepped behind the bar and borrowed the phone.

A voice at the other end said, "Time Tripper, may I help you?"

"Yeah, Orva, this is Kit. What can you tell me about the girl who's been asking for me?"

Kit was tempted to hold the receiver away from his ear as Orva vented considerable irritation. She was just starting to say, "I have no idea why . . ." when the subject of their conversation stalked through the Down Time's door and dropped her suitcase with a bang. Kit held back a groan and tried to blend in with the wall. Sven grinned like the evil gnome he was. Rachel hid her eyes and shook with silent laughter. The redheaded wonder of the hour glared at Malcolm, who shrugged and nodded toward Kit.

Thanks, buddy, Kit thought sourly. *I owe you.*

Malcolm was grinning expectantly.

"Uh, gotta go," Kit muttered.

The line clicked dead. The outrageous little redhead cornered Kit behind the bar. "Mr. Carson? Kit Carson?"

She was standing directly in the center of the only narrow egress from this end of the bar, arms akimbo, hands on her hips, eyes flashing with barely suppressed irritation. Kit didn't think he'd ever seen a sight quite like her. She stood glaring up at him like an enraged scarlet parakeet.

Kit hung up the phone and said cautiously, "And you are . . . ?"

"Margo."

Uh-huh. He surveyed her silently, waiting for the rest. When she didn't offer it, he prompted, "Margo . . ."

She still didn't offer a last name. Instead, she said, "I have a business proposition for you, Mr. Carson."

Oh, God, here it comes. The story of your life, major news feature, blockbuster motion picture . . .

In that getup, she *looked* like a Hollywood wannabe. Who knew, maybe she did have studio connections. For all he knew, she was Somebody's kid, looking for a thrill.

"Lady," he said, with as patient a sigh as he could manage, "I never discuss business on my feet and I never, ever discuss business with someone who has backed me into a corner."

Her eyes widened. She had the decency to color an unbecoming shade of pink. Margo No-Name backed off sufficiently for Kit to edge out from behind the bar. Once he'd escaped, he leaned against the comfortably worn wooden bumper. "Now, if you want to talk business, kid, I suggest you buy me a drink."

From the way her mouth dropped open, one would've thought he'd suggested they get naked and mud-wrestle. He revised his estimate from Hollywood to Smallville. She closed her mouth and said primly, "Of course."

She moved one hand surreptitiously toward a small belt pouch, giving away her insecurity and lack of funds in one greenhorn motion. Kit sighed. Journalism student, he revised his mental estimation, and not overly bright at that.

He said, "Marcus, how about my usual—no, make it a bourbon—and whatever the kid wants. She's buying."

Marcus, who by this time was accustomed to the oddities of up-timers, only nodded. "House bourbon? Or the Special?" He glanced from Kit to the kid then back, smiling far back in his dark eyes. Marcus had seen it all, even *before* his arrival in La-La Land. The "Special" was a particular bottle Kit had brought back on one of his last trips. The Down Time kept it in a private cabinet for special occasions. Two matching bottles sat in Kit's private liquor cabinet. Getting through an interview with a journalism student called for more fortitude than a lone bottle of Kirin (his usual) could provide, but this was not a celebration.

"House will be fine."

Marcus nodded. Kit reluctantly led his mystery pursuer to a table. He chose a spot as far toward the back of the Down Time as he could get, in the dimmest corner of the dark room, far enough from his friends to prevent casual eavesdropping and dark enough to make it hard to read his face. If he had to endure this, by God, she was going to *work* for the story. The darker the corner, the better.

Wordlessly, Margo picked up her suitcase and followed.

CHAPTER THREE

Nothing was working out as she had planned.
Nothing.

Margo cursed her bad timing, bad temper, and bad luck and followed the retired time scout into the dingiest corner of what had to be the darkest, most miserable bar in Shangri-la Station. The atmosphere matched her mood: gloomy as a wet cat and just about as friendly. Even the carved wooden masks which dominated the bar's primitive decor seemed to be scowling at her.

As for Kit Carson, internationally famous time scout . . .

She glared at his retreating back. He looked nothing like the famous photos *Time* magazine had done a decade previously, or the even older photos from his days as one of Georgetown's brightest young faculty members. For one thing, he'd been smiling in those pictures. For another, he'd aged; or maybe "weathered" was a better term for it. Clearly, time-scouting was hard on the health.

Moreover, he wasn't in "uniform." She wasn't sure what she'd expected him to be wearing, but that drab suit and wilted tie was a considerable letdown. The *Time* pictorial, the one which had fired her childhood imagination and had given her the courage to get through the last few years, had shown the pioneer of all time scouts in full regalia, armed to the teeth and ready for the Roman arena. The man whose current scowl boded ill things for Margo's future, the man who had "pushed" the famous Roman Gate—the one right here in Shangri-la Station which Time Tours ran so profitably—was a real disappointment in the heroing department.

If legend were accurate, he had nearly died pushing that gate. Margo didn't put much stock in the legend, now. Kenneth "Kit" Carson didn't look a thing like a man who'd survived gladiatorial combat. Long, thin, and wiry, he wore that rumpled business suit the way a convict might wear his uniform and sported a bristly mustache as thin and scraggly as the rest of him. His hair—too long and combed back from a high, craggy forehead—was going grey. He slouched when he walked, looking several inches shorter than the six-foot-two she knew him to be. He darted his gaze around the dim room like a man searching for enemies, rather than someone looking for a private table in a perfectly ordinary bar.

He didn't look like a retired hero *or* a retired history professor. He looked like a thoroughly irritated, dangerous old man, past sixty at least. Margo, at sixteen and forty-some weeks, swallowed hard and told herself, *Get a grip. Remember the speech you rehearsed.* Unfortunately, not only had the body of her speech fled, so had the carefully prepared intro, leaving her floundering for words as she set down her case and scooted into the booth her life's hero had chosen. He'd already taken a seat at the very back. The booth reeked of beer and cheap smoke.

The bartender, a good-looking young man with a great smile, arrived with a tumblerful of bourbon and an expectant air. He slid the bourbon unerringly across the dimly lit table toward Kit Carson, then turned to her.

"Uh . . ." She tried to think what she ought to order. *Make a good impression . . .* Margo vacillated between her favorite—a raspberry daiquiri—and something that might rescue the shreds of her reputation with this man. She hadn't seen prices listed anywhere and tried to estimate how much this interview was going to cost. *Oh, hell* . . . Margo threw caution to the winds, figuring decisiveness was better than looking like a dithering idiot. "Bourbon. Same as Mr. Carson's."

The waiter, a dim shape at best in this hell-hole of a corner, bowed in a curiously ancient fashion and disappeared. Kit Carson only grunted, an enigmatic sound that might have been admiration or thinly veiled disgust. At least he hadn't asked if she were old enough to drink. The bourbon arrived. She knocked back half of it in one gulp, then sat blinking involuntary tears and blessing the darkness.

Gah . . . Where had they distilled this stuff?

"So . . ." She sensed more than saw movement across the table. "You said you had a business proposition?" The voice emanating from the dark was about as warm as a Minneapolis January. "I might remind you, young lady, I'm taking time out of a busy schedule at the Neo Edo. *I* already have a business to run."

This wasn't going well at all.

I'm not going to give up! Not that easily! Margo cleared her throat, thought about taking another sip of her drink, then thought better. No sense strangling again and cementing her doom. Her hands were trembling against the nearly invisible bourbon glass. She cleared her throat again, afraid her voice would come out a scared squeak. "I've been looking for you, Mr. Carson, because everyone agrees you're the very best time scout in the business."

"I'm retired," he said drily.

She wished she could see his face and decided he'd chosen this spot deliberately to put her off balance. Cranky old . . .

"Yes, I know. I understand that. But . . ." *Oh, God, I sound like an idiot.* She blurted it out before she could lose her nerve. "I want to become a time scout. I've come to you for training."

A choked sound in the darkness hinted that she'd caught him mid-sip. He gave out a strangled wheeze, coughed once, then set his drink down with a sharp click. A match flared, revealing a thin, strong hand and a stubby candle in a glass holder. Carson lit the candle, fanned out the match, then just stared at her. His eyes in the golden candle glow were frankly disbelieving.

"You what?"

The question came out flat as a Minnesota wheat-field. He hadn't moved and didn't blink.

"I want to be a time scout." She held his gaze steadily.

"Uh-huh." He held her gaze until *she* blinked. His eyes narrowed to slits, while his lips thinned to the merest white line under the bristly mustache. *Oh, God, don't think about your father, you aren't facing him so just hang onto your nerve....*

Abruptly he downed the rest of the bourbon in one gulp and bellowed, "Marcus! Bring me the whole damned bottle!"

Marcus arrived hastily. "You are all right, Kit?"

Kit, no less. The bartender was on first-name basis with the most famous time scout in the world and she was left feeling like a little girl begging her father for a candy bar.

Kit flashed the young man that world-famous smile and said, "Yeah, I'm fine. Just leave the bottle, would you? And get a glass of white wine for the lady. I think she damn near choked on that bourbon."

Margo felt her cheeks grow hot. "I like bourbon."

"Uh-huh." It was remarkable, how much meaning Kit Carson could work into that two-syllable catch-phrase.

"Well, I do! Look, I'm serious—"

He held up a hand. "No. Not until I've had another drink."

Margo narrowed her eyes. He wasn't an alcoholic, was he? She'd had enough of dealing with *that* for several lifetimes.

The bartender returned with the requested bottle and a surprisingly elegant glass of wine. Kit poured for himself and sipped judiciously, then leaned back against worn leather upholstery. Margo ignored the wine. She hadn't ordered it and would neither drink it nor pay for it.

"Now," Carson said. His face had closed into an unreadable mask. "You're serious about time scouting, are you? Who jilted you, little girl?"

"*Huh?* What do you mean, who jilted me?" Her bewildered question opened the door to as scathing an insult as Margo had ever received.

"Well, clearly you're bent on suicide."

Margo opened her mouth several times, aghast that nothing suitable would come out in the way of a retort.

Kit Carson grinned—nastily. "Honey, whoever he was—or she was—they weren't worth it. My advice is get over the broken heart, go back home, and get a safe little job as a finance banker or a construction worker or something. Forget time scouting."

Margo knocked back the bourbon angrily. *How dare he . . .*

She sucked air and coughed. *Damn, damn, damn . . .*

"I wasn't jilted by anybody," she gritted. "And I'm not suicidal."

"Uh-huh. Then you're crazy. Or just plain stupid."

Margo bit down on her temper. "Why? I *know* it's a dangerous profession. Wanting to scout doesn't make me a loon or a fool. Lots of people do it and I'm not the first woman to take on a dangerous job."

Carson poured a refill for himself. "You're not drinking your wine."

"No," she grated. "I'm not." She held out the empty bourbon glass. He held her gaze for a moment, then splashed liquid fire and waited until she'd choked it down.

"Okay," Carson said, in the manner of a history teacher warming to a lecture, "for the moment, let's rule out stupid. After all, you did have the sense to look for an experienced teacher."

Margo was sure she was being subtly put down, but couldn't nail down why. Something in the glint of those cynical eyes . . .

"So . . . that leaves us with crazy, which is a word that clearly sets your pearly white teeth on edge."

"Well, wouldn't you be insulted?"

That world-famous grin came and went, like an evil jack-o'-lantern in the dim candle glow. "In your situation? No. But clearly you are, so an explanation is in order. You want to know why you are crazy? Fine. Because you've got about as much chance of time scouting as Marcus, there, has of becoming an astronaut. Kid, you're flogging a dead horse."

She turned involuntarily and found the gorgeous young Marcus near the front of the bar. Smiling and waiting on new customers, he looked like a perfectly ordinary college-age guy in jeans and a T-shirt. Margo glared at the retired time scout. "That's a pretty big insult, don't you think? It's clear he's a friend of yours." Then she twigged to the name, the not-quite-Italian accent, the curious bow he'd given Kit. Marcus was still a popular modern name, but it had been a popular name in ancient Rome, too. "Oh. Down timer?"

Carson nodded. "Roman Gate. Some asshole tourist decided it would be fun to buy a slave and brought him through to La-La Land, then dumped him and vanished up time before the ATF could arrest him. Not only does Marcus have no legal standing whatever, he literally could never overcome the handicap he's carrying in terms of education, ingrained superstitions, what have you. He's an ancient Roman slave. And if you don't know what that means, not only here," he tapped his temple, "but also here," he tapped his heart, "then you have no business even trying to become a time scout."

"I'm not an uneducated slave dumped up time to cope with alien technology," Margo countered. "It's a helluva lot easier to understand ancient superstitions than it is to comprehend physics and math. And I got brilliant grades in dramatics, even had a chance to work off-Broadway." The half-truth sounded convincing enough; at least her voice had held steady. "I came here, instead. Frankly, I don't see how your argument holds water."

Carson sighed. "Look. First of all, there is no way I'm going to shepherd some greenhorn scout, regardless of who they are or how brilliant at dramatics they think they are, through the toughest training you've ever imagined, any more than I'm going to try to hammer some sense into that empty little head of yours."

She bristled silently.

"Second, you're a woman."

Congratulations, she fumed silently. *An MCP, on top of everything else. You and my father should start a club.* "I know all the arguments—"

"Do you?" Brown eyes narrowed into an intricate ladder of lines and gullies put there by too much sun and too many years of hard living. "Then you should've had the sense not to waste my time. Women can't be time scouts."

Margo's temper flared. "You're supposed to be the best there is! Why don't you stop quoting all the doom-sayers and find a way! From what I've gathered, you had to retire but didn't much like it. Think what a challenge it'd be, training the first woman time scout in the business."

His eyes glinted briefly. *Interest? Or acknowledgement of spunk? Impossible to tell. . . .* He knocked back his bourbon and gave her a long, clear-eyed stare. Margo, determined to match him, knocked back her own. This was getting easier. Either that or her throat was numb. The edges of Carson's face had begun to waver a bit, though. Bad sign. *Definitely should've had lunch.*

Carson, evidently sober as a stone, tipped more bourbon into his tumbler. Gamely she held out her glass. Very gently, he closed his hand around it and pushed it to the table.

"Point one: you're drunk and don't have the sense to quit. I will not ride herd on a greenhorn trying to prove a point to the whole world." Margo flushed. "Point two: the role of women down time, just about anywhere or anywhen you might land, is . . . less than what we'd consider socially respected. And women's mobility in many societies was severely limited. Then there's the problem of fashion."

Margo had thought all this through and had a counter-argument ready, but Carson wasn't slowing down long enough to voice it. She sat and listened helplessly while the man whose accomplishments had given her the courage to keep going nailed down the coffin lid on her dreams.

"Women's fashions change radically from locale to locale, often from year to year. What happens if you go scouting through an unknown gate and show up a couple of centuries off in clothing style? Or maybe a whole continent off? Any idea how ridiculous you'd look in 200 B.C. China, wearing an eighteenth-century British ball gown? You'd stick out like the proverbial sore thumb. Maybe—*probably*, even—you'd end up dead. Quite a few societies weren't real tolerant of witches."

"But—"

"At best, you'd end up in prison for life. Or even more fun, in some asshole's private harem. Just how fond of rape are you, Margo?"

She felt like he'd punched her. Painful memory

threatened to break her control. Margo was shaking
down to her fingertips and Carson, damn him, wasn't
done yet. In fact, the look in his eyes was one of growing
satisfaction as he noticed the tremor in her hand.

He leaned forward, closing in on the kill. "Point
three: I will not train a nice kid and turn her over to
the likes of some of the brutes I've encountered. Even
the nicest down-time men often had a nasty habit of
beating their favorite women for cardinal sins like
talking too much. Whatever your reasons, Margo, forget
'em. Go home."

The interview was clearly over.

Kit Carson didn't quite condescend to pat her head
on the way out. He left her sitting in the candle-lit
booth, fighting tears of rage—and worse, of crushing
disappointment. Margo downed a big glass of bourbon
and vowed, *One day, you're gonna eat those words.
Cold and raw, you'll eat 'em.* She couldn't bear to glance
in the direction of his friends. Margo flinched inwardly
at the spate of laughter from a crowded table across
the room. She closed her hand around the bourbon
bottle, gripping until her fingers ached. She was not
a quitter. She intended to become the world's first
woman time scout. She didn't care what it took.

The bill, when Marcus the displaced slave presented
it, represented a third of everything Margo possessed
in the world. The bill would've been higher, but the
glass of white wine didn't appear on it. She was being
charged only for the bottle of bourbon. Margo groaned
inwardly and dug into her belt pouch for money. How
she was going to pay for a room now . . .

"Well," she told herself, "time to put Plan B into
operation."

Find a job and settle in for a long, hard battle to
find someone willing to train her. If Kit Carson wouldn't
do it, maybe someone else would. Malcolm Moore,
maybe. Freelance time guide wasn't what she had in

mind, but it was a start. If, of course, he could be convinced to help train his own competition . . .

Margo poured another shot of bourbon. As long as she was paying for it . . .

Clearly, this would be a long, long day.

CHAPTER FOUR

The klaxon marking the re-opening of Primary
sounded just as Kit settled down for breakfast in Frontier
Town's Bronco Billy Café. He smiled to himself, wishing
a mental *bon voyage* to the redheaded Margo of No
Last Name. The computerized register of incoming
tourists had shown only "Margo Smith" who held a
transfer ID stamp from New York. In New York City
anyone could get any sort of credentials, could have
any fake name tacked onto one's mandatory medical
records, which had to match a person's retinal scans
and fingerprints to get past ATF Security.

After the orbital blowup which had created the time
strings that made temporal travel possible, so many
records had been damaged and destroyed, New York's
underworld had cleaned up issuing new identities.
Scuttlebutt had it that new ID's were cheaper than down-
time tickets to a temporal station.

If Smith were Margo's real last name, Kit would eat
his shoes.

He hadn't seen her since her arrival—thank God—
although he'd heard from several people she was asking
everywhere for a teacher. So far as he knew, everyone
had turned her down flat. Now she'd be departing for
home where she belonged. It was with a sense of
profound relief that Kit banished all thought of Margo
"Smith." He smiled at the waitress, clad primly in a
high-collared dress with a striped, floor-length skirt.

"Morning, Kit," she dimpled. "The usual?"

"Good morning, Bertie. Yes, please, with a side of hash browns."

Bertie poured coffee and produced a copy of this morning's *Shangri-la Gazette*. Kit was halfway through the "Scout Reports" section—which comprised at least a third of the small newspaper—when the klaxon announcing the closure of Primary sounded. Kit grinned. "Bye, Margo. Have a nice, safe life." He settled deeper into his chair, sipped coffee, and continued reading the latest reports from young time scouts who were busy continuing his work into all manner of unlikely places and times.

"Well, what do you know about that?" Some lucky scout over at TT-73 had pushed a gate into the middle of the Russian palace built by Catherine the Great and had inadvertently caught her *in flagrante delicto* with one of those infamous Russian boars. . . .

Kit chuckled, then raised a brow at the purported offers generated in a bidding war between up-time porno outfits. The clever scout had brought back a videotape. Another scout, over at TT-13, had returned from a hair-raising trip into the European Wurm glaciation with an anthropologist's ransom in documentation on Cro-Magnon lifestyles.

Sometimes, Kit really missed his old life.

Bertie returned with his breakfast and a smile. She glanced at the open newspaper. "I see you found the story on Catherine's palace."

Kit chuckled. "Yep. Lucky mutt."

Bertie rolled her eyes. "Personally, I think it's disgusting what the porno outfits are offering him. And who'd want to sleep with a giant hog? Now, the scout who took the video is another matter." She winked. "Any lonely time scout needs a room for the night. . . ."

Kit grinned, knowing Bertie's offer was only a tease, at least where he was concerned. Kit had a far-flung reputation as the world's straightest-laced time scout. It made most of the women on TT-86 treat him like a favorite uncle or a third grandfather. That had its advantages, but sometimes . . .

He sighed and pushed away thoughts of Sarah. *Ancient history, Kit.* But he still couldn't help wondering sometimes if he might have found a way to make it work. *Yeah. Right. You weren't good enough for her, Georgia Boy.* Despite the years, their last fight still had the power to hurt him. And when he'd gone looking for her, what her father and uncle had said . . .

Kit gave a deliberate mental shrug. She'd made her choices and he'd made his. He'd been through every conceivable argument over the years, trying to figure a way it might have gone differently, and he'd never found one. So Kit picked up his fork, carefully not allowing himself to wonder what had become of Sarah— or if she ever thought about him when she read the newspapers or watched the idiotic docudramas. . . .

Really, Kit told himself sourly, *after all this time, there is no point crying about it.* He smoothed the paper, turned to a fresh page, and dug into the heaping plate of Denver-style steak and eggs, with a bird's-nest side of golden-brown hashed potatoes drenched with melted cheese and liberally mixed with fried onions and green-pepper chunks. *Ahh . . .* Bronco Billy's knew how to make breakfast.

Kit was halfway through the steak, cooked rare just the way he liked it, when a shadow fell across his table. He glanced up—and nearly choked on a bite of half-swallowed beef.

Margo.

She was dressed conservatively enough in jeans and a semi-see-through sweater, but wore a look of determined sweetness that didn't fit the tilt of her chin. "Hello, Mr. Carson. May I join you?"

Kit coughed, still half-choked on the bite in his throat. He grabbed the coffee cup and gulped, scalding the roof of his mouth and his tongue. Kit burned the back of his throat, too; but the steaming liquid dislodged the bite of steak. He wheezed, swallowing while he blinked involuntary tears. He finally sat back and glared at her. This was the second time she'd nearly strangled him, catching him off-guard like that. *Christ, I'm losing my touch if a half-grown kid can damn near kill me twice in two days.*

"Still here, I see," he growled, still sounding half strangled. "I was hoping you'd gone home."

Margo's smile was chilly. "I told you, Mr. Carson. I have no intention of going home. I'm going to be a time scout and I don't care what it takes."

He thought about Catherine the Great and her Russian boar and wondered what this green kid would've done in that situation. Gone all schoolgirl incensed, or burst in protesting cruelty to animals?

"Uh-huh. Just how much money have you got, kid?"

Her face flushed unbecomingly. "Enough. And I've applied for a job."

"Doing what?" Kit blurted. "Serving drinks in that damned leather miniskirt of yours?"

Margo's eyes narrowed. "Listen, Mr. Carson, I will stay on this terminal, no matter how long it takes or who I have to find to teach me. But I'm going to be a time scout. I was hoping I could persuade you to change your mind. I'm not stupid and I have some pretty good ideas about overcoming the handicap of my gender. But I'm not going to stand here and be insulted like some truant schoolkid, because I am *not* a child."

You damn near are, Kit groused to himself, impressed with her tenacity and appalled that she was so determined to die. Kit sat back in his chair and ran one hand through his greying hair. "Look, Margo, I admire your determination. Really, I do."

The look in her eyes, sudden and unexpected, disturbed Kit. *Good God, is she going to cry?* Kit cleared his throat.

"But I won't be a party to your death, which is likely to be messy and very painful. Did you bother to read any of the scouting reports in this?" He held up the *Gazette*. "Or the obituaries section?"

Time-scouts' obituaries took up a whole page of the *Shangri-la Gazette*. The details were often gruesome.

She shrugged. "People die all the time."

"Yes, they do. So do time scouts. Let me tell you *how* time scouts die, kid. Sam One-Eagle over at TT-37 was killed by the Inquisition. They burned him alive, Margo, after taking all the skin off his back with whips and breaking all his major bones on the rack. His partner crawled back through with burns over most of his body from trying to rescue him. David lived for a month. The nurses said he spent most of it screaming."

Margo had blanched. But her chin came up. "So what? I could get run over by a bus, too, and plane crash victims get toasted just as thoroughly."

Kit tossed his hands heavenward. "Good God, Margo. The Inquisition is nothing to be flippant about. You haven't seen one of their torture rooms. I have. And I have the scars to prove it. Would you like to see them?"

Slim jaw muscles tightened. She didn't say a word.

"And do you have any idea, kid, what gave me away? What got me arrested by those bastards?"

She shook her head.

"A mispronounced word, Margo. That was all. A mispronounced word. And I speak fluent medieval Spanish."

She swallowed; but she had a comeback. "You lived through it."

Kit sighed and pushed his plate away. He wasn't hungry any longer. "Fine. You want to get killed, feel free. Just don't ask me to help you do it. Now scram, before I lose my temper."

Margo didn't say another word. She just stalked out

of Bronco Billy's and vanished into the bustle of Frontier Town. Kit muttered under his breath and glared at the passing crowds. Just what was it about this kid that needled him so thoroughly? She was every damned bit as stubborn as Sarah and made him very nearly as crazy.

Maybe it was genetic. He never had been able to resist petite women with heart-shaped faces and freckles.

"Huh. Women."

He shook out his newspaper irritably and folded it over to a new section.

"Mr. Carson?"

"What?" he snapped, glaring up at a middle-aged man he'd never laid eyes on. *Good God, can't a man eat his breakfast in peace?*

"I'm sorry to interrupt . . ." The man's voice trailed off. "Er, I, that is— Excuse me. I'll come back later."

He was already in the process of stepping away from the table. Kit focused on the slim portfolio he carried, the carefully pressed suit, the expensive shoes . . .

"Don't run away," Kit said with a lingering growl in his voice. "Sorry I snapped at you. I just finished a very unpleasant conversation, is all. Please, sit down."

And if you're a reporter, mister, you'll end up wearing what's left of my breakfast. . . .

"My name is Fisk, Harry Fisk." He offered a business card, which gave Kit no real clues other than his office was in Miami. "I represent the management of TT-27, located in the Caribbean Basin. We're looking for a consultant . . ."

Kit heard him out. The job sounded intriguing. A lucrative, full-time consultantship, unlimited trips to a time he was pretty sure he'd never visited, as primary consultant to the Time Tours agent looking to develop a new gate destination, paid apartments at TT-27's finest luxury hotel . . .

It was a magnificent chance to escape Neo Edo's

paperwork and the endless stream of raucous, thieving tourists. Kit scratched his chin and thought about it. Leaving TT-86 meant leaving friends. And he did owe it to Jimmy and the other retired time scouts in his employment to look after them. He wouldn't sell out to just anyone.

"No," he decided, "I don't think so, Mr. Fisk. I have a hotel to run."

"We would be more than happy to install a full-time manager for the duration of your consultantship, Mr. Carson. Time Tours wants the best for this project."

Huh. Now there was a fat offer. Paradise for as long as he wanted to live in it and he kept his steady income, too. And somebody *else* did the paperwork. The image of Margo, her face pinched and white as she stood over his table staring him down, flashed through his mind.

Dammit, kid, stay out of my head.

Kit toyed with his cold eggs, scooting them back and forth on the plate with the tines of his fork. He'd been waiting for something like this for a long time.

"No," he found himself saying. "I appreciate the offer, really; but not just now."

Mr. Fisk's face fell—ludicrously. "I really wish you would reconsider, Mr. Carson."

Kit shrugged. "Ask me again in a week or so. We time scouts are a changeable lot."

Fisk tightened his lips imperceptibly. "Yes, so I've discovered. Well, you have my card, but my employers are most anxious to press ahead with this project and there are other retired time scouts on my list."

Kit nodded. "I expect there are. And I'm sure most of them need the job more than I do." He held out his hand. Fisk shook it, betraying grudging respect in his eyes.

"If you reconsider your position in the next two days, please let me know."

He had until Primary cycled to change his mind.

Kit didn't foresee that happening.

Mr. Fisk left him with his cold eggs.

"Huh. It was probably a scam, anyway," Kit muttered. "Too good to be true equals dubious in my book. Besides, who wants to live in the Bermuda Triangle?" He could do that by jumping down La-La Land's unstable gate. He shoved Fisk's business card into his pocket and tackled his cold breakfast, telling himself his decision had nothing to do with keeping track of that stupid little imp, Margo.

Sure it doesn't, Kit. And toadie frogs got wings.

He muttered into his scraggly mustache and finished his morning paper, determined not to think about Margo or her suicide mission. Why was it, Kit mourned silently, that all the *real* trouble in his life inevitably came skipping in on the coattails of some irresistibly pretty girl?

If word of this got around . . .

Well, he'd just take his lumps and deal with the snickers. What Kit Carson did, or didn't do, was his own damned business. *Yeah. Mine and the rest of La-La Land's.* He signalled Bertie for a fresh cup of coffee and promptly fell to worrying about where Margo was going to find someone reputable enough to trust with her life. Maybe he could talk to Sergei or Leon or . . .

No, he told himself, *if you won't teach her yourself, do* not *try and line up somebody else for the job.* Frankly, he couldn't think of a single time scout who'd be willing to try it, anyway.

Vastly relieved by that observation, Kit put Margo firmly out of mind.

Why, Margo wailed silently, *does he have to be so beastly?* She'd found a quiet spot under a vine-covered portico in Urbs Romae where she could sit with knees tucked under chin and indulge in a good, long cry.

Mom warned me . . . .

That only brought fresh misery and a new flood of angry tears. She wiped her cheek with the back of one fist and sniffed hugely. "I won't give up. Damn him, I won't. There just has to be someone else on this miserable station who'll teach me."

So far, she had struck out with everyone she'd approached, even the freelance guides like Malcolm Moore. At least most of them had been nicer about it than Kit Carson. Even a brusque "Get lost, brat" was kinder than gruesome images of people being tortured to death.

"I'll bet he doesn't have any lousy scars," she sniffed. "And Sam One-Eagle probably isn't any more real than these stupid fake columns. He doesn't want me to be a scout, is all, so he's trying to scare me."

The thought of returning to Minnesota and the jeers . . .

Never mind her father. . . .

Margo shivered and hugged her knees more tightly. "Hell will freeze over first."

"Hell will freeze over before what?"

Margo jumped nearly out of her skin. The voice had spoken almost in her ear. She swung around and found a face peering at her through the vines. A male face. A *gorgeous* male face. Margo's personal-defense radar surged onto full-power alert. She'd had all she wanted of gorgeous men. But his winning smile was the friendliest thing she'd seen in two and a half days and after that miserable, gawdawful interview with Kit Carson . . .

"Hey, what's wrong?" He'd noticed the tears. Whoever he was, he ducked under the vines and dug for a handkerchief. "Here, use mine."

Margo eyed him suspiciously, then accepted the hanky. "Thanks." She dried her face and blew her nose, then wadded up the handkerchief and offered it back.

"No, keep it. You look like you need it more than I

do." He sat down cross-legged on the floor. "You're still a little drippy," he added with an attempt at a laugh.

Margo grimaced and blotted her cheeks. "Sorry. I'm not normally so weepy. But it's been a bad week."

"What's wrong? You look half starved."

Margo sniffed. She was. "Well . . . it's been a couple of days since I ate."

"A couple of *days?* Good grief, what happened? Some con artist steal all your money?"

Margo laughed, surprising herself. "No. I didn't have much to steal in the first place. And what there was, I've used up. All I have left is my suitcase and a hotel bill I can't pay tonight."

He tipped his head to one side. "Are you the girl everyone's talking about? The one who wants to become a time scout?"

"Oh, God . . ." *Insult on top of injury.*

"Hey, no, don't cry again. Honest, it's okay. I've been looking for you."

Margo blinked and stared at him. "Why?"

"I'm a scout. I've been looking for a partner."

"Honest?" Her voice came out all watery and breathy. It couldn't be true—but oh, Lord, how she wanted it to be . . .

He grinned. "Honest. My name's Jackson. Skeeter Jackson. I just got back from a quick run up time and heard you were looking for a teacher. I've been thinking I needed a partner for a while—that's why I was up time, actually—then I come back and what do I find? The challenge of a lifetime, right in my own back yard!" He grinned and held out a hand.

Margo couldn't believe it. A week of her precious six months gone and all she'd had to show for it was a collection of insults, and now . . . maybe there was a God, after all. She'd be careful—Billy Pandropolous, who was enough heartbreak for any lifetime, had taught her nothing, if not that. But Skeeter Jackson didn't appear to be hustling her. At least, not yet. She shook his hand. "Mr. Jackson, if you're for real—well, you'll be a lifesaver. I mean it. And I promise, I will work as hard as I have to. I'll make you proud." She ventured a tentative smile, appealing directly to what men seemed to value most. "I'll even try to make you rich."

Skeeter Jackson's eyes were warm, friendly. "I'm sure you will. Come on, let me buy you some breakfast."

He gave her a hand up. Margo dried her cheeks again and gave him a brave smile. "Thanks. I'll pay you back. . . ."

He laughed and gallantly offered his arm. "Don't mention it. I'll take it out of your wages."

Margo found herself grinning as she took Mr. Jackson's arm. Maybe, finally, her luck had changed for the better. Just wait until Kit Carson heard about this! He'd choke on his eggs again. And after the way he'd treated her, he deserved it! Dreaming of thrills, adventure, and plates of heaped bacon and pancakes, Margo accompanied her new teacher out into the bright, busy Commons of Shangri-la Station.

CHAPTER FIVE

The Down Time's pool room was a snoop's paradise. Thanks to the acoustics, it was possible to hear snatches of several conversations at once. Kit had always wondered if the place had been purpose-built. He lined up a shot, called it, and put the two ball neatly in a side pocket. Out in the bar proper, somebody was laughing about an invasion of grasshoppers at TT-37.

"Came right through a random gate into Commons. Tourists screaming, Station Pest Control tearing hair and swearing. Must've killed a million of 'em, minimum. Took days to sweep 'em all up."

In another corner, Robert Li's unmistakable bass voice rumbled, ". . . so when Wilkes said that, Bull told him all ATF courtesy passes were canceled, effective immediately. . . ."

Kit grinned. Another wrinkle in the continuing saga. The station manager's battle to keep ATF's nose where it belonged—out of everybody else's business—had spawned an entertainment form unique to La-La Land. Known as "Bull Watching," it involved avid betting on the outcome of any random encounter between Bull Morgan and Montgomery Wilkes.

Kit called and sank another ball, then lined up his next shot. Over in the corner, Goldie Morran frowned, looking every inch the disapproving dowager one might see on the Paris Opera House's grand marble staircase opening night, dressed to the nines and staring down that long, thin nose of hers like a Russian aristocrat. Even the hair—a particularly precise shade of purple Kit still associated with seventh-grade English teachers and aging duchesses—contributed to the overall impression.

Goldie eyed the line of Kit's cue stick and sniffed. "I knew I would regret this game. You're too lucky."

Kit chuckled. "Luck, dear Goldie, is what we make it." The next ball he called rattled musically into the far corner pocket. "As you, of all people, should know."

She only smiled, a thin hawkish smile that spoke volumes to those who knew her well. Kit suppressed the urge to look for the knife about to plunge into his back. He lined up his next shot and was just about set when Robert Li's voice interrupted from the doorway.

"Ah, Kit, there you are."

La-La Land's antiquarian, a long-time friend, *knew* that interrupting a game for anything less than catastrophic emergency was considered a hanging offense. Particularly when the opponent was Goldie Morran. Playing Goldie took concentration if you wanted to leave the room still wearing the shirt you'd come in with. Kit had momentary visions of Tokugawa samurai pouring through the Nippon Gate into the Neo Edo's main lobby, demanding room service.

"What is it?" he asked warily.

Robert lounged against the door frame and idly inspected his fingernails. "Seen the Wunderkind lately?"

The Wunderkind could refer to only one person: Margo.

Oh, great. Now what's she done?

In her four days at La-La Land, she had managed to set more tongues wagging than Byron and his sister had in four months of Sundays.

"Uh, no." He lined up his shot again. "Don't much care if I ever do, either."

He began the shot.

"Well, she's been hanging around with Skeeter Jackson. Says he's going to teach her to time scout."

The shot went wild. Kit's cue actually raked the felt table, leaving an ugly mar in its smooth surface. He swore and glared at his so-called friend, then at Goldie. She widened her eyes and shrugged innocence, reminding Kit unpleasantly of Lucrezia Borgia that night he'd accidentally surprised her in the infamous walled garden. . . .

"Huh."

Kit surrendered the table with as much grace as he could muster and said goodbye to the game. Robert Li, whose maternal Scandinavian heritage—fair skin and rosy cheeks—was overshadowed by a Hong Kong Chinese grandfather's legacy, only grinned. A completely scrutable scoundrel, he settled his shoulder more comfortably against the doorframe to watch. During the next two minutes, Goldie ran the table, hardly pausing for breath between shots. She spun the final shot off Kit's scratch, giving the ball just enough English off that long mar in the felt to sink it with a rattle like doom.

"Tough luck," she smiled, holding out one thin-boned hand.

Kit dug into his pocket and came up with the cash, paying her off wordlessly. Robert, still standing in the doorway, grinned sheepishly as she passed him on the way out.

"Sorry, Kit."

"Oh, don't mention it. I just love ruining a perfectly good pool table and losing a week's profits."

"Well, gosh, Kit, I just thought you'd laugh. How was I to know you'd take the news so personally? Don't tell me the famous Kit Carson has fallen for that redheaded imp?"

Wisely, Robert made himself scarce. But the antiquarian chuckled all the way out to Commons. Kit muttered impolite words under his breath. *With such friends* . . . He unscrewed the sections of his cue stick and slipped them into their leather case, then settled up the damages with Samir Adin, the night manager.

"You what?" Samir asked in gaping disbelief.

"I scratched. Here, this ought to cover the cost of refelting it."

"You scratched. Unbelievable. Did I miss the earthquake or something?"

Kit scowled. "Very funny. Frankly, I'd say it hit at least 7.5 on the Richter. Had Goldie's name all over it. Give me a Kirin, would you?"

Samir chuckled and dug for a cold bottle. "I keep telling you, Kit. If you want to beat Goldie Morran, play her when she's unconscious."

Kit downed the Kirin in five long swallows and felt better immediately. "Well, a man can dream, can't he? Hillary had Everest, Peary had the Pole, and I cling to the dream of beating Goldie Morran at pool."

Samir, a deeply sympathetic soul, broke into song, giving him a stirring rendition of "To Dream the Impossible Dream."

"Oh, you're no help," Kit grinned. "Why do I come in here, anyway?"

Samir chuckled. "That one's easy. All time scouts are gluttons for punishment. It's in the job description."

Kit laughed. "You've got me there. I *wrote* the damned thing."

Samir thumped him on the back by way of condolences and sent him on his way. Kit shoved hands into pockets, cue case tucked under one arm. *Well, that story ought to be a nine-day wonder. It'll be all over La-La Land by bedtime.* He strolled glumly through Urbs Romae, going nowhere in particular, then sniffed appreciatively at the scents wafting from the Epicurean Delight. *Dinner sounds good, after that beer. Hmm . . .*

He wondered what Arley Eisenstein had written on

the Special Board for tonight. Arley's restaurant was *the* place to eat in La-La Land. Other restaurants boasted more posh in their decor, but Arley had discovered the secret of enticing the world's best chefs to take turns in his kitchen. Down-time agents on his payroll obtained recipes in exchange for a slice of the Epicurean Delight's profits. Some of what they brought back, of course, made haggis sound appetizing. But he came up with enough "lost" winners to make a tidy profit.

Chefs who wanted access to Arley's culinary secrets paid through supervising Arley's kitchen for a stipulated number of days per year. Since most tourists couldn't identify ingredients in what they ate, never mind figure out procedure . . . From the rumors, the arrangement was wildly profitable in up-time restaurants.

It certainly was for Arley. Unless you were a resident, you booked reservations two months in advance. Eighty-sixers, on the other hand, sampled the Delight whenever they liked. Arley made it a policy always to hold back at least three tables for station residents. Any given night, all three would be full.

Kit's mouth was already watering.

He cut around a column to head for the restaurant and very nearly ran down Connie Logan. She emitted a tiny screech and teetered. Kit grabbed her arm and steadied her.

"Sorry," they said simultaneously.

Kit blinked. She was about a foot too tall.

"Good God."

Connie was clad in a silk kimono held together by sewing pins and basting threads. Peeping out from under the pinned hem were "shoes" that resembled beach thongs, except they were made of wood and the soles were at least eleven inches thick.

Connie blinked, owl-like, from behind her glasses. "Hi, Kit. What do you think?" She held out both arms to display the half-finished work to its best prickly advantage.

"Let me guess," Kit said drolly. "Your customer wants to join the semi-annual grand procession of harlots through Yoshiwara?"

Connie rolled her eyes. "No. He wants to give his favorite down-time mistress a present. I'm trying it out, to be sure it *can* be worn. Now I understand why those old woodcuts show guys walking on either side of those poor girls, balancing them. These shoes are murder."

Kit grinned and offered his hand. "Shall we dance?"

Connie stuck out her tongue, but accepted the offer with alacrity. "Just help me over to that bench and I'll get rid of these lousy clogs. I was afraid to kick them off. Didn't want to lurch off balance and break an ankle."

Kit glanced around and guided her toward the targeted seat. Even in La-La Land, Connie was attracting stares. The shoes thunked with every step.

"So who is this customer?"

Connie shuddered. "Don't ask. He's about seventy-five and covered with tattoos."

Yakuza. Japanese mob . . .

Sixteenth-century Edo's Yoshiwara district had become a popular spot for Japanese businessmen's tours. Japan's recovery from the tsunamis, volcanic eruptions, and economic disasters left behind in the aftermath of *The Accident*, as that fateful orbital blowup had come to be called, had astonished most of the world. For the survivors, it was back to business as usual and most of the businesses were rich and getting richer. Japanese corporate tours were mostly organized by Yakuza gangs—which had *really* cleaned up in the re-construction, since they apparently controlled the lion's share of the Japanese construction industry.

Kit wondered how Time Tours guides enjoyed rubbing shoulders with Japanese gangsters. He knew Granville Baxter hated them, but business, as they say . . . Grant didn't make corporate decisions. He just dealt with the field problems and gritted his teeth while making the home office a ton of money.

Kit eased Connie down to the bench. "There," he smiled. "All safe and sound."

She winced and wriggled to avoid pins, then sighed. "Thanks a million. Computer design may be my forte, but it just doesn't take the place of field testing. Sometimes," she grimaced at her feet, "it's a little rough on body and soul."

Kit stooped and eased off her shoes, earning a deep sigh. Connie's feet, clad in tabi socks, were visibly swollen even through the cotton. He rubbed gently. She collapsed bonelessly against the backrest.

"Oh, God . . . I love you, Kit Carson."

Kit chuckled. "That's what all the ladies say. Had dinner yet?"

She peeled one eyelid. "No, but I don't have time. Still have a special order for the London run to finish designing and after that I have a new batch of sketches from Rome and some samples that you just wouldn't believe, how gorgeous they are. . . ."

Kit grinned. "I'll take a rain check, then. Don't forget to order pizza or something."

"Scout's honor." Connie melted another few inches down the bench while Kit finished her feet, then sighed and stood up. She wriggled cotton-clad toes against the concrete. "Blessings on your soul, Kit. I may be able to limp back, now."

"Mind if I ask a stupid question?"

"Shoot."

"How come you tortured yourself into walking halfway down the Commons in those things?"

Connie grinned. "I paced it out beforehand, to the exact distance of the harlots' processions through Yoshiwara. If I can go the distance in those infernal shoes, anyone can."

Connie Logan wasn't exactly sickly, but she was fragile. Kit scratched the side of his jaw. "Well, I guess you have a point. Still seems a helluva way to design costumes."

Connie laughed. "This, from the man who pioneered masochism into a new art form. Just why *did* you become a time scout?"

"I cannot tell a lie." He leaned closer and whispered, "Because it's fun."

"There you have it. *I* get to play dress-up, every day." She stooped for the hideous shoes, then gave him a quick hug full of pins. "Thanks, hon. Gotta go. Oh . . . I saw that kid the other day, with Skeeter Jackson."

Kit groaned.

Connie's brows twitched down. "Good grief, Kit, she really got to you, didn't she? You ought to say something to her. She worships you, and Skeeter's going to get her killed. You wouldn't believe what he had her wearing."

"Great. Since when did I get promoted to greenhorn-daddy?"

Connie flashed him a grin. "You don't fool me, Kenneth Carson. You care. It's why we like you. Gotta run."

Kit was still grumbling under his breath long after Connie had vanished back toward her outfitters' shop. "Sometimes," he groused, "this Mr. Nice-Guy rep is more trouble than it's worth." He sighed. "Well, hell." He really couldn't countenance allowing Skeeter Jackson to pass himself off as an instructor of time scouts.

Normally residents didn't interfere in other residents' business dealings. But there was a difference between fleecing obnoxious tourists out of a few dollars and perpetrating negligent homicide. Skeeter, never having been a scout—having rarely even been down time— probably didn't realize just how deadly his current scam was. Kit swore under his breath. He probably wouldn't earn any thanks, but he had to try.

Kit dropped by the Neo Edo just long enough to put away his cue case and be sure Jimmy had the business well in hand, then started asking around for Skeeter. Typically, nobody recalled seeing him. Kit knew some of his favorite haunts, but the rascal wasn't in any of them. Skeeter generally avoided Castletown, since even he didn't care to risk fleecing the wrong person and end up someplace really nasty, minus several fingers. Kit checked all of Skeeter's favorite watering holes in Frontier Town, then hit the pubs in Victoria Station. Nothing. Skeeter Jackson was making himself mighty scarce.

"Well, he's got to be someplace."

With no gates currently open, Shangri-la Station was closed up tight. The only exits were hermetically sealed airlocks leading—if the main chronometers and Kit's own equipment were correct—into the heart of the Tibetan Himalayas, circa late April of 1910. The only reason those airlocks would ever be opened would be to escape a catastrophic station fire. And since halon systems had been built into every cranny of La-La Land . . .

Skeeter hadn't left the station, not unless he'd fallen through an unstable gate somewhere.

"We should be so lucky," Kit muttered. "Well, genius, now what?" He planted hands on hips and surveyed the breadth of Victoria Station, which wound from one side of Commons to the other in a maze of pseudo-cobbled streets, wrought-iron "street lamps," park-like waiting areas, picturesque shop fronts, and the inevitable cobwebbing of catwalks and ramps which led up to the Britannia Gate near the ceiling.

A tourist in a garish bar-girl costume left the Prince Albert Pub and fumbled in a small purse that would have been more appropriate for an American frontier matron. Slim white shoulders rose above a shocking neckline. Kit couldn't see her face. A drooping bunch of black feathers from a hat that should have been paired with a tea gown hid her features. The hemline of her dress was cut rakishly high enough to reveal shoes that were completely out of period.

"Huh. She went to a lousy outfitter."

The tourist closed her purse, then turned on an emphatic stilt heel. Kit groaned. *It figured.*

Margo . . .

"Well, Connie did warn me." He squared metaphorical shoulders and moved to intercept her, stepping out from behind a "street lamp" into her path. "Hi."

Margo glanced up, badly startled, and teetered on high heels. Kit let her regain her balance.

"Oh. It's you." Belatedly, she said, "Hi." Then her chin came up. "I found a teacher."

"Yes, I know. That's why I want to talk to you."

Margo's eyes widened. "You do?" Almost instantly, suspicion flared. "Why?"

Kit sighed. "Look, can we just declare a truce for about fifteen minutes?"

She eyed him narrowly, then shrugged. "Sure." She tossed her head slightly to bounce feathers out of her eyes.

Kit started to say, "That hat's on backwards," then bit his tongue. He didn't want to antagonize her. He wanted to save her life. So he suggested, "Let's go over to the library. It's quiet. We shouldn't be interrupted."

Margo eyed him curiously. "Why are you taking the trouble? I thought you hated me."

"Hated you? I don't hate anybody, Margo. Time scouts can't afford the luxury of hate."

Or love . . .

Margo's eyes had gone curiously wide and vulnerable. "Oh. Well, I'm glad."

Kit recalled what Connie had said—"she worships

you"—and sighed. He wasn't cut out to be anybody's personal hero.

"Come on, Margo. The sooner I get this said, the sooner you can tell me where to jump off, then we can both call it quits." He eyed her unhappily. "And contrary to what you clearly believe, I don't enjoy hurting people's feelings."

For once, she didn't come back with a sharp remark. She just followed him wordlessly toward the library.

Margo knew time terminals had libraries. Tourists, guides, and time scouts all used them, to one degree or another. Her original legwork had revealed that time terminal libraries were among the most sophisticated research facilities in the world. But Skeeter Jackson hadn't suggested they go there and she hadn't given it much thought. Margo had never been fond of books. She preferred direct, dramatic action and firsthand experience. Poring through dusty, musty pages nobody had cracked open in fifty years only made her crazy. Besides, all those experts disagreed anyway, and a time scout's job was to go places and find out what the truth was.

Still . . .

La-La Land's library overawed.

Margo repressed a delicate shudder and didn't even try to calculate the number of books contained in this . . . the word "room" seemed inadequate. And computer terminals, too, with recognizable CD-ROM and video drives, all voice-activated. Judging from the snippets of soft-voiced commands she heard from a dozen busy users, they were programmed for multiple-language recognition. The computers drew Margo's attention more thoroughly than any of the books.

Mr. Carson—she had trouble thinking of him as "Kit"—spoke briefly with a slim, dark-skinned man in his mid-thirties, then steered her toward the back.

Several private cubicles had been built into the back wall, complete with computer and sound-board hookups.

"What are these for?"

"Language labs," Carson said quietly. "I take it you haven't been here yet?"

Margo detected no particular edge to his voice, but the question irritated her. "No. Skeeter has me busy doing important things." *Like earning a living to pay for the equipment I'm going to need.*

"Uh-huh. This one's empty." He pushed open a door and held it for her.

Margo fluffed inside and took the only chair. Her nemesis closed the door with a quiet click of the latch.

"Now. About this teacher of yours . . ."

"I suppose you're going to tell me how he's charging more than I can afford and what a fool I am and how I'll starve before I get my first big contract with Time Tours or some other outfit. Well guess again. He's not charging me anything but an advance on expenses and most of what I need I'm earning with the job he helped me find. *He* wants a partner."

Kit Carson just looked at her. He leaned against the door, crossed his ankles comfortably, and looked at her like she was the most recalcitrant, lame-brained child he'd ever encountered. It made her mad.

"Don't smirk at me, you egotistical—!"

"Margo," he formed a classic "T" shape with his hands, "time out, remember? No insults, no temper tantrums. And I'm not smirking."

"Huh. Could'a fooled me." But she subsided. He was trying to be nice for a change; the least she could do was listen. "Okay, go on."

"Skeeter Jackson has told you he's a time scout, looking for a partner. True or false?"

"True." She bit one fingernail, then folded her arms and tried not to fidget. "What of it?"

"He's not a time scout. Never has been, never will be. Frankly, he's neither crazy nor stupid and he knows his limits."

Oh, no . . .

"Are you calling Mr. Jackson a liar?" she asked quietly.

His smile held a certain strained quality. "Yes. And before you say anything, I'd like to point out that liar's not the worst thing he's been called. Backstabbing cheat comes a little closer."

"How *dare* you—"

"*Shut up and listen!*"

The indolent pose had vanished. Margo shut up. She'd never heard such cold authority in *anyone's* voice. He wasn't angry—just relentless. And Margo was scared. After Billy Pandropolous . . .

"Skeeter Jackson is a *con artist*. A two-bit operator who makes his living fleecing tourists. If there's a scam on the books, he's used it. Currency exchange scams, luggage theft, pickpocketing, black-marketeering, you name it."

Margo didn't want to hear any more. Every word he clipped off reduced her closer to the status of gullible fool—again.

"Skeeter doesn't touch 'eighty-sixers, which is the only reason Station Security tolerates him. He's probably wanted in half the sovereign nations in the world on various charges. Nothing violent, nothing dangerous . . . until now."

"What do you mean?" Even Margo realized how petulant she sounded.

"If I thought all you'd lose was the shirt off your pretty back, I'd let you have all the rope you want to hang yourself. But if you keep 'studying' with Skeeter Jackson, then walk through an unexplored gate thinking you're a time scout, you won't come back."

"Well, you didn't leave me much choice, did you? I *did* come to you first, if you'll recall."

He nodded. "Yep. And I gave you a fair assessment of your chances. I just thought you deserved to know how deadly this little game of yours is. Walking in with eyes wide open is a little different from being conned. Like I said before, I don't want your death on my conscience."

"Thanks for caring!" Margo snapped. "I can do without your advice, if that's all you've got to say!"

He sighed and didn't offer to move.

"Well? Are you leaving or what?"

"Just what is he teaching you?"

Margo crossed her arms again. "None of your business. If you won't teach me, why should I bother answering questions you'll just charge me money to answer?"

His eyes narrowed. "Don't be insulting. Who picked out that ensemble you're wearing?"

She just glared at him. Clearly, she'd made some mistakes—and vowed she'd die a torturous death before she admitted it.

"Okay," he muttered, "the kid gloves come off. Let's say Skeeter sends you through the 'safest' tourist gate there is, just for practice. If you walk through the Britannia Gate wearing that getup, the first thing that's going to happen is some well-bred lady on the other side will either scream or faint. Whores don't generally stroll through Battersea Park."

Margo paled, then flushed bright red. "I'm not a whore! And I'm not wearing this dress in London, you'll notice! I'm wearing it for a bunch of drunken tourists in Victoria Station! Besides, what's wrong with it? Skeeter showed me photos—"

"Margo, you look like a two-bit trollop in that thing. Skeeter likes skin and he doesn't have the faintest idea what decently bred Victorian women wore. If he had a photo, it was of a Denver saloon trollop. Denver cathouses are among the few down-time attractions Skeeter Jackson *has* visited."

Margo wanted to hide. At least she'd had the sense to tell Skeeter no the couple of times he'd suggested . . .

"Margo, you've just illustrated my point for me: you don't know what you're doing and neither does Skeeter. If you'd tried walking through the Britannia Gate in that dress, here's what would've happened: After some poor, shocked matron had a fit of vapors, her outraged gentleman companion would have called for a constable. You'd either have ended up in the Old Bailey for peddling your wares in the wrong part of town or landed in an asylum. Street walkers who went mad from syphilis weren't handled particularly gently."

Margo didn't want to hear any more. Rose-colored balloons of hope broke with every word, but Kit Carson showed no inclination to stop. "Let's even suppose you didn't get nailed by the law. That by some miracle you actually found the slums where that getup might look more appropriate. Do you even know what they were called? Never mind where they were? If you stumbled into them by sheer chance, you'd still be in trouble. Because some whore would carve you up for encroaching on her territory or some tough would decide to make you his meal ticket—after trying out the wares for himself first. Unless, of course, you were *really* lucky and the Ripper decided you were a likely looking target."

Margo went cold all over. *Jack the Ripper?* She couldn't help glancing at her dress, any more than she could hide an involuntary shudder. Carson, to give him his due, didn't crack a smile. He just nailed home the point like a vampire hunter pounding in the stake.

"The Ripper liked his victims helpless. Most psychopaths do. Step through the Britannia Gate without training or a guide, and you'll end up looking more helpless than any other walker on the street. Believe me, it won't be long before Red Jack starts having a bloody good time gutting you like a market fish—"

"STOP!" Margo had covered her ears.

He stopped.

Margo was breathing as hard as she did after a sparring session in the *dojo*. Kit Carson, curse him, might have been sipping tea at a garden social for all the emotion he betrayed. *I won't give up! I can't!* Margo literally had nowhere else to go. And she was running out of time. Her six months were nearly one sixth gone already.

"I can take care of myself," she said stubbornly. "Skeeter's all I've got left. Any teacher's better than none and you won't help me."

He straightened up from the door. "That's right, kid. I won't. And if I let you stick with Skeeter, he'll get you killed. Not even he realizes what he's setting you up for. Believe me, when I catch up to that young fool, I'll roast his ears good."

"*What?*" She came to her feet, shaking to her pinched toes as panic set in. She was out of money, out of hope, out of everything. If Kit forced Skeeter to kick her out . . . "You *can't!* If you bully him off the job . . . You just *can't!*"

Blue eyes glinted like hard sapphires. "Oh, yes I can."

"Dammit—!"

"Don't you have any brains in that decorative little head of yours?" He took a step forward, evidently intent on opening her skull to look.

She held her ground. "I will not give up! And you don't have any right to interfere! It's my life, not yours. I'll risk it as I please, Mr. Hot-Shot Retiree!"

He flushed. "Look, you stubborn little—"

"Stubborn?" Margo laughed shrilly. Then, before she could quite believe she'd said it, Margo heard herself say, "Well, if I'm stubborn, I come by it honestly! With you for a grandfather, what else could you . . ."

Kit Carson halted mid-stride. His face collapsed into a tangle of weathered lines, aging him ten years in an instant. Despite the tan, he had blanched the color of dirty snow.

A knot of panic condensed in Margo's belly, the germ of a glacier. *Shit . . . oh, shit, me and my big mouth . . .*

For at least ten thudding heartbeats, he just stood there, looking like a stray word might knock him to the ground. Piercing blue eyes had lost their focus. Margo groped uncertainly for the chair and shoved it aside, anxious to put room between herself and the forceful man who would be coming out of shock any second.

Empty blue eyes focused slowly on her face. His brows came together. He studied her for another thudding stretch of heartbeats. Margo didn't know what to say or do to fix this. When he drew a halting sip of air, she braced for the worst, but he didn't say anything. He seemed incapable of speech. After a moment, he shut his eyes. Then, without a single word spoken, he turned and opened the door. He left her standing behind the chair, feeling like she wanted to die and get the hurting over with, rather than face what she'd just done.

Kit didn't hear or see much of anything. He navigated the library on autopilot and found Brian Hendrickson behind the main reference desk. He located the desk by bumping into it.

"Good afternoon, Kit. What can I— Dear God, what's wrong?"

The librarian's face swam into focus. Kit gripped the edge of the reference desk until his knuckles hurt. "Am I awake?"

"Are you *what?*"

"Am I awake?"

Brian blinked. "Uh—yes?"

Kit swore. His belly did another drop into oblivion. He wished for the tiniest of moments he could follow it. "I was afraid of that." He left Hendrickson gaping after him and literally ran into Margo halfway back to

the cubicle. She staggered, blinking tears, then made
to cut around him.

"Oh, no you don't!" He sidestepped quickly, blocking
her path. "Back where you came from!" He pointed
imperiously.

Her face was blotched and red. *"Leave me alone!"*

She tried to bolt. He cut her off neatly and resisted
the urge to seize her wrists. The last thing he wanted
her to do was scream. But when she shoved him hard
enough to stagger him off balance, he reacted before
his brain could catch up—which wasn't very difficult
in his current state of mind. Kit snatched her off balance,
swearing under his breath, and forcibly pulled her toward
the back of the library.

Predictably, she resisted.

Kit swung her around hard enough to jounce her
teeth together. "Do you really want me to turn you over
Grandpa's knee, *little girl?*"

Margo worked her mouth like a drowning fish. "You—
you wouldn't—" She halted mid-protest. "You would."

For a moment, they stalemated in the center of La-La
Land's library. Then she wrenched free of his grip, with
an against-the-thumb movement that spoke of some
martial arts training, but she didn't try to leave. She
stood glaring at him, chest heaving against the plunging
neckline of her dress in a fashion that made him want
to throw a flour sack over her torso. Then she broke
and fled toward the language lab. Kit drew a deep, shaky
breath.

Dear God . . .

He needed time to absorb this, time to figure out
when and how . . .

Sarah, why didn't you ever tell me?

The hurt in his chest made his whole soul ache.

Kit lifted a shaking hand to his eyes. *Gotta think.
Sarah and I broke up in . . . If she was pregnant then,
and had a child before . . . Sarah's child would've had*

to be about seventeen when Margo was . . . "Dear God. She could be."

Teenage pregnancies had very nearly become the rule, rather than the exception, during the years Margo's mother would have been a teenager. Margo had reminded Kit all along of someone. Now he knew. She didn't look much like Sarah, but that temper, not to mention the pride . . . even the determination to get what she wanted and everything be damned that stood in her way. Margo was Sarah van Wyyck all over again.

He didn't know whether to laugh or cry or swear aloud.

Meanwhile, his *granddaughter* had to be faced.

"Christ, and she's still set on being a time scout."

His viscera did another swan dive into a bottomless chasm. *I can't let her do this.* . . . Hard on the heels of that thought came another. *And just how do you propose to stop her?*

The whole library wavered in his vision for a moment as he superimposed Margo's face over some of the sights that still gave him nightmares. *She doesn't understand . . . thinks it's high adventure and she'll live forever . . . and I can't even insist on partnering her, can't even go along and watch her back.* . . .

If Kit stepped through another unknown gate, odds were extremely high the attempt would kill him.

"What am I going to do? She wants this . . ." And was it any wonder? What must the kid have grown up thinking and dreaming every time she heard about her famous granddaddy?

"Dammit, Kit, pull it together. . . ."

Walking back into the language lab was possibly the hardest thing Kit had ever done.

Margo had pulled the chair into the far corner; but she wasn't sitting in it. She'd taken up a stance *behind* it, gripping the back as though he were a savage lion in need of taming. He recalled some of the ugly things

he'd said to her and swallowed. *Damn* . . . Kit closed
the door softly and faced her. Tear streaks ran down
her face in jagged paths. But her chin was still up, still
defiant, despite visible fear in her eyes.

"I'm not an ogre," Kit muttered. "You can put down
the chair."

Very slowly, Margo let go her death grip. The front
legs settled with a quiet thump. She swallowed a couple
of times. "I didn't mean—I mean, I didn't plan to—"

"It's said," Kit interrupted brusquely. "And yes, you
do come by it honestly."

For some reason, that brought a fresh flood of tears.
Kit felt as though he'd just hit her and couldn't for the
life of him figure out how to repair the damage. The
sense of helplessness which paralyzed him reminded
Kit unpleasantly of the times Sarah had dissolved into
tears.

"I—Skeeter, he—and you—" Margo's voice control
was gone.

Kit finally thought to hunt for a handkerchief and
found a rumpled one in a back pocket. "Here."

She all but snatched it out of his hand, then turned
her back and struggled visibly to regain the shreds of
her dignity. Kit waited quietly, aware that a woman's
pride was a far more serious matter than a man's—
and men had been known to do murder when theirs
was injured. She hiccoughed a few times and blotted
her face, then blew her nose.

"Sorry," she muttered. "I ruined Skeeter's hanky, too."

Kit winced. He decided he did *not* want to know how
Skeeter Jackson had comforted his granddaughter. If
he'd hurt her . . . *I'll toss him through the next unstable
gate that opens.* She finally faced him, a watery-eyed
waif in a bedraggled strumpet's gown. *No wonder she
paid somebody to change the name on her ID card to
"Smith." Didn't want anyone to know who she really
was, desperate to do this on her own merits* . . .

Kit knew only too well how that felt. He cleared his throat, more to gain time than anything. "You're dead set on this time-scouting business."

She swallowed. Her eyes, red and angry as bee stings, still brimmed with unshed tears. "I've wanted it all my life."

Once again he cleared his throat. "Things as they are, I can't say I blame you. . . ." Then he eyed her critically, studying her for the first time as a potential scout. He shook his head over the visible cleavage. "Best thing to do would be disguise you as a boy, but you're not really built for it."

Her eyes widened. "You mean—" Then, hastily, "It's not real. I mean, they're *real*, but I'm wearing stays. A corset. Skeeter bought them for me at an outfitter's. They really make me look . . . well, more voluptuous." Kit, thoroughly familiar with the bio-mechanical effect of a woman's corset stays, flushed. *I'm talking to my granddaughter about the size of her breasts.* . . .

Margo was still talking as fast as possible. "I could wear baggy shirts, you know, to hide things, and my hips aren't really that wide, it's just I have a narrow waist. . . ."

Kit shook his head. The kid really did want this. *God help us both.* . . .

Her face fell. He realized she must have misinterpreted that head shake. Kit sighed. "All right, Margo. I'll do it. But under conditions—"

"*Really?*" Her voice squealed into the soprano register. Her bedraggled face lit up like Christmas.

"*Under conditions!*" Kit repeated sharply. She gulped and heard him out. "First, I decide when—or if—you're ready. Second, you agree to do everything I tell you, exactly as I tell you. Understand? And you *don't* do anything I don't specifically tell you to do. If, after we're into training, I decide you don't have what it takes, you agree to switch to something else. Time guiding, maybe.

There's a world of difference between the two professions. Guiding's fun. Sometimes dangerous, but mostly not. Scouting's deadly. If you thought convincing me to train you was hard, you don't even know the meaning yet. By the time I've put you through training, you will. Any time you want to quit, holler."

"I won't quit."

Kit managed a wan smile. "I expected you'd say that. But I mean it. Remember the bourbon. Knowing when to quit can be just as important as fighting for what you want."

A flush of pink crept into her cheeks. She rubbed her nose with the back of one hand and sniffed hugely. "Okay."

"Any questions?"

She shook her head.

"Okay." He had about a million of his own—but now wasn't the right time to broach them. He took a deep breath and struggled against the cold in the pit of his belly. "Let's get started."

CHAPTER SIX

A rattle of glassware punctuated the low buzz of voices like frogsong through the hum of mosquitoes. Familiar and comforting, the sounds rose in a welcoming chorus from the Down Time's open doorway. Kit ushered Margo in first, aware that speculative glances were levied in their direction. Several glances lingered, some on Margo, some on the scouting equipment he conspicuously carried in the trademark leather satchel he'd been the first to construct. Dirt-stained and battered, it nevertheless remained sturdy and functional. At one time, Kit wouldn't have felt fully dressed without it.

Behind the bar, a young woman with a long-boned face the British royals would've been proud to claim wiped up a spill and nodded. "Evenin', luv."

"Hello, Molly. Any seats left?"

In answer, she jerked her head toward a small table at the side of the room, missing all but two of its chairs. The Down Time was jam-packed, of course. *Too much to ask for a quiet night, tonight of all nights.* Kit recognized nearly everyone. Laughter punctuated a dozen conversations. "Thanks, Molly. How about a couple of ice waters?"

Molly's long, clear-eyed gaze followed Margo as she made her way toward the indicated table, but the barmaid withheld comment, as she generally did. She filled a couple of glasses with ice cubes and water and handed them over. "Anythin' else?"

Kit shook his head. "No, not just now. Maybe later."

"Luv . . ."

Kit paused mid-step, causing the ice cubes to clink faintly. The chill of condensate sank into his hands, echoing the coldness which still gripped the rest of him. "Yeah?"

Molly's brow had furrowed the tiniest bit, betraying intense worry. "Keep 'em open, Kit. She's a sharper, she is."

Kit glanced over to the table. Margo had taken up residence in the outer chair, which would leave Kit with his back against the wall. Margo's cheeks were visibly flushed despite the low-light conditions which prevailed this time of night in the Down Time. She was all but quivering with excitement.

"I suspect she's had reason," Kit said quietly. "I'm just trying to keep her alive."

Molly nodded. " 'at's awright, but keep 'em open, luv. Tike care she don't steal yer bees an' 'oney while yer's back's turned."

Her concern that he might lose money to Margo surprised Kit—and touched him. "I'll do that."

She nodded briskly and turned to cater to another customer's needs. Kit eased his way between tables, greeting friends as he went and parrying curious questions with a smile and offhand jokes. Margo watched the ritual with wide eyes. He finally set the water glasses down and took the other chair. Margo sipped—then shot him a startled glance.

"*Water?* I'm not a baby!"

"You're drinking what I am. Pay attention."

Kit didn't think he'd ever seen a more skillful disgruntled female flounce—stationary, no less, in a straight-backed bar chair—but she didn't argue. "I'm listening."

Given the rapt attention on her face, she *was*, too. "All right, Margo. Phase One: Equipment Lecture."

Kit rummaged in the satchel for his personal log and ATLS. Margo would need her own set. Kit made a quick note on his mental to-do list, then set both items out for inspection. "These two pieces of hardware are your lifeline."

Margo peered at them without offering to touch. "What are they? I read that scouts used microcomputers and some gizmo to determine absolute time and Skee— I mean," she flushed, "I was saving money from my job to buy whatever I'd need. Is that what these are?"

"Yes." Kit picked up the personal log. A compact unit, smaller than an average letter-sized sheet of paper, it weighed more than it looked. "This is a time scout's personal log." He opened the case, pressed a latch, and lifted the tiny screen, revealing a keypad and the mesh grid of a microphone. "The casing is waterproof, shockproof, just about everything we can protect it from, except maybe immersion in strong acid or molten metal— or molten rock. It can be used in either voice or key mode. Scanners and digitizing micro-cameras can be attached. The personal log operates on a solar-powered system backed up with batteries that last about twenty-four hours between charges. It writes automatically to a micro-layer space-grown crystal matrix for storage, so there's no chance of losing data even if you do experience catastrophic power failure. They're expensive, but you don't set foot through a gate without one."

"So, they're like a trip diary, for recording notes and stuff?"

Kit shook his head. "Much more important and much more detailed. This," he tapped his log, "is quite literally what keeps me from killing myself."

A tiny vertical line appeared between Margo's brows. The uncertainty in her eyes mirrored a chain of thought that was almost comical.

"No," Kit smiled, "I'm not suicidal. Although a large percentage of the population would argue any time scout is. How much reading have you done? Do you know what Shadowing is?"

Margo hesitated, clearly caught between answers.

"Don't be embarrassed to say no."

"Well, no. I mean, I know there's something weird about the gates and time scouts have to retire early because you can't ever be in the same time twice, but I never read the word 'shadowing' or heard it used."

As though to underscore her admission, a shadow falling across the table interrupted them. Kit glanced up—and held back a groan. Malcolm Moore had pulled up a chair. "Mind if I join you? This looks interesting." He glanced from the scouting equipment to Kit to Margo and back to Kit, then grinned expectantly.

Kit considered telling him to buzz off, then thought better. Malcolm's assistance might actually be useful. He'd scouted a couple of times and had given it up for guiding.

"Sure. Park it."

Malcolm turned the chair around and sat down. "Hello, Margo. You look, um . . ."

"Ridiculous," Kit said drily.

Margo flushed. "I didn't have time to change." She snatched the hat into her lap and ruffled her short hair. Kit winced at the movement of cleavage—and at Malcolm's interested attention.

"Malcolm," he said under his breath, "as you are a friend, don't do that again."

Malcolm's brows soared. "Good Lord, Kit, what's eating you? Can't a man even pay a lady the compliment of noticing?"

"No."

Margo just put her hands over her face.

"She's, uh . . ." *Oh, hell.* . . . "She's my grandkid."

Malcolm rocked back on his chair and stared. "Margo's your *granddaughter?*"

Conversation cut short throughout the bar. Kit felt the flush start in his neck and work its way up into his hairline. Margo risked a peek, then groaned and hid her face again.

"Well, I'll be . . . suckered." Malcolm Moore was grinning like the proverbial village idiot. "Miss Margo, you can't imagine what a wonderful surprise this is."

The buzz of conversation picked up again, livelier than ever.

"I, uh," Margo floundered for words. She shot a stricken glance at Kit, then settled for a faint, "Thanks."

Kit glowered at Malcolm. "What I'm trying to do, here, is keep her alive. She wants to scout."

Malcolm's grin widened, which Kit would've bet was physically impossible. "Really? What was it you said the other day—"

"Never mind what I said the other day. I'm training her. Maybe. If—" he turned a severe glare on Margo "—she listens and learns."

"I'm listening! So show me, already!"

"Good." Kit drew a breath and downed half his water in one gulp, wishing it were something stronger. "Malcolm, here, has scouted a couple of times."

Malcolm nodded. "Exactly twice. Then I switched to guiding."

Margo rested her chin on her hands. "Why?"

Malcolm chuckled. "Because I wanted to live to see thirty."

"Why does everyone keep saying scouting's so dangerous?"

Malcolm glanced over. Kit just shrugged, leaving Malcolm on his own—and Kit was sure any answer the guide provided would be more than effective.

"Well," Malcolm said quietly, "because it is. My first time out, I beat the witchfinders to the gate by about four minutes. One of them actually got through on sheer momentum and had to be tossed back through just as the gate was closing. If the gate hadn't opened up, I'd have . . . Well, never mind. The second time, I missed

Shadowing myself by about half an hour. Promised myself I'd never set foot through an unknown gate again."

Then he chuckled and rubbed the back of his neck. "Well, I did risk it just once more, when we rescued the folks who fell through that unstable gate in the floor, but I didn't stop to think, then, I just jumped. I was lucky. Someone, thank God, had their log and ATLS with them, so at least I have a record of which gates we stumbled through trying to get home again."

"Okay, so it's dangerous. What's this Shadowing stuff all about, exactly?"

Kit tapped the personal log absently with one fingernail. "It means you can't cross your own shadow. Not and survive. If you step through a gate into, say, Rome on A.D. 100, March twenty-fourth, 2:00 P.M. sun time, you log into this machine exactly when and where you are. How you determine when and where you are, I'll explain in a minute. The point is, you note down exactly when you arrived, where you arrived, how long you stayed, and when you left. You keep track of when and where you've been. Okay, let's say somebody else pushes a gate into Meso-America, A.D. 100, March twenty-third. If you step through that gate, and stay past March twenty-fourth 2:00 P.M. *Italian* time, one of you disappears. The current you. The Roman you is alive in the past, but the real-time you just died. You cannot cross your own shadow. Paradox doesn't happen, because you vanish completely, forever."

Margo shrugged. "Sounds easy enough to avoid. You just don't try to watch Julius Caesar murdered twice."

Malcolm said, "You couldn't do that, anyway. The two ends of the time strings that form gates are connected. They move at the same pace. If a week goes by here, a week goes by there. Once you miss an opportunity to see something, it's gone forever, unless another time string opens up to the same point in time.

Of course, if you tried to go back, you'd cross your shadow and end up not seeing it—or anything else—ever again."

"The point is," Kit nodded, "the more down-time trips you make, the greater the odds that when you step through a gate into some unknown time, you'll already exist somewhere and somewhen else. Eventually the odds catch up and you die."

Margo chewed her lower lip in a thoughtful fashion. "So . . . you take this gamble every time you walk through an open gate, because you never know when—to what time—it leads? Why bother to keep records at all, if you could just vanish anyway? Seems like a lot of fuss, when you could blip out before you knew what hit you, no matter what you put in this thing. I mean, you don't know when you're going, so what does it matter that you know when you've been?"

Kit told himself that Margo was very young. "A couple of reasons. First, it's your job, as scout, to keep meticulous records. Scholars and tour companies will want to review any data you bring back. Second, if you don't keep records, you could accidentally kill yourself just trying to take a vacation or by trying to visit another station, or even the wrong gate in the same station."

"*Huh?*" She levelled an incredulous stare in Kit's direction. Clearly, she hadn't done enough research. Margo damned small-town libraries, high schools controlled by school boards opposed to things like "Evil-lution" and a father who'd drunk every penny she might have saved toward a computer to hook into the big information nets.

Malcolm nodded. "He's right. Even guides have to be careful about that. Every station is built at least as far back as 1910, to get around the problem of people stepping into a time after they were born. That's why up-time lobbies have warning signs. Surely you saw the one on the other side of our Primary? 'IF YOU

WERE BORN ON OR BEFORE APRIL 28, 1910, DO NOT STEP THROUGH THIS GATE. YOU WILL DIE IF YOU ATTEMPT TO ENTER THE TIME TERMINAL.' The date on that sign changes every day, to match Shangri-la's relative temporal location. They had to beef up security about ten years ago when a few desperate senior citizens committed suicide by stepping through, rather than face starvation or terminal cancer."

"Well, I understand that danger," Margo sniffed, "and I remember seeing TV shows about those poor old people who killed themselves. But what's this stuff about dying if you visit some other terminal or the wrong gate on the same terminal?"

"We're not just trying to scare you off," Kit said quietly. "The temporal position of any station, in its relation to absolute time, is different from any other station's temporal position. Terminals 17 and 56 are absolutely deadly to *anyone* on Shangri-la. If I tried to visit TT-56, I'd accidentally emerge into last week, when I was very much present at Shangri-la Station, which is currently . . ."

He checked the chronometer built into his personal log. "Which is currently April 28, 1910, 22:01:17, local— i.e. Tibetan—time zone. Time guides have to be careful, too."

Malcolm nodded. "It's why we guides tend to specialize in tours through just a handful of gates leading out of one terminal. I could go to one of the other terminals and look for a scouting job, but I'd have to do careful homework first to be sure which terminals and which tours were safe for me. The Denver and London gates here in La-La Land can be just as deadly. The Denver gate is currently opening into 1885, the London gate into 1888. If I try to take a tourist to Denver during the same week I'd already taken someone else to London three years previously . . ." He shrugged. "I'd accidentally kill myself. So we keep damned good records of where and when we've been. That little credit card you were issued when you bought your Primary Gate ticket? The one they encoded for you before you came down time? When tourists use the gates, their Timecards are encoded in both directions—going down time and coming back—so they have a record of when they've been. If the computer catches an overlap, it sounds an alarm."

Margo's eyes were beginning to take on a glazed look.

"Careful as the precautions are," Kit added grimly, "there are still accidents, even with the tourists. Time scouts have to be paranoid about it. For instance, I could only visit TT-17 if I went up time and stayed for at least a year. TT-17's always twelve months and six hours behind this one, same geographical zone, about a thousand miles north of here. If I went through TT-17's Primary without letting it "catch up" and pass by my last exit from TT-86, I'd never live to see the other side."

Malcolm said, "There have even been organized-crime murders committed that way, particularly *yakuza* killings. They select a victim, get them to take out a huge insurance policy naming a gang member as beneficiary, treat them to an Edo Castletown tour out of Shangri-la on a false ID, then some other gang member takes them to Terminal 56 on their *own* ID, so they shadow themselves in front of witnesses. Instant profit."

Margo shivered. "Okay. I think I get it."

"Now that you've been here, you'll have the same problem. The longer you stay, the greater the chance of overlap. The more gates you step through, the more complicated the whole mess becomes. That's why the log is essential."

Margo rested her elbows on the table. "Okay, point taken. We have to be careful. But I still say you can get run over by a bus, not paying attention. What's the other thing for?"

Kit sat back in his chair. Was she being flippant to hide fear? Or was she just that silly? Or that stubborn? He wondered how often she'd gotten what she wanted just by smiling that enchanting smile or by coming back with a wisecrack that set people to chuckling. Just what sort of life had Margo known before hunting him up? Given her prickly defenses and that over-sharp tongue, Kit wasn't too sure he wanted an answer.

"It's an ATLS. Absolute Time Locator System. That 'gizmo' you mentioned reading about. It works on a combination of geo-magnetic sensors and star-charting systems. The ATLS places you more or less exactly in time and geographic location, relative to absolute Greenwich time."

"More or less?" Margo echoed. "Isn't it precise?"

"Scouts always fudge by at least twenty-four hours in both directions when using the ATLS, just to be sure. Most of us build an even larger safety margin in, because as good as the ATLS is, it isn't absolutely precise. It can't be. Our lives are riding on how closely we cut it. Without it—and the personal log—we couldn't function at all. Even time touring would be impossible, because the tour companies need scouts to push new tour routes. The ATLS's casing gives it the same kind of protection your personal log has."

Margo was frowning at the ATLS. "If it's so dangerous to step through, why not just put the ATLS on a long pole and shove that through, then let it do its thing? That way nobody'd ever have to risk going 'poof'."

Kit shook his head. "It isn't that simple. For one, you have only a fifty-fifty chance of a gate opening at night. If it opens during the day, you can't take a star-fix, so the long pole idea would be useless. Or it might be a cloudy night—no stars. We *could* roboticize the whole thing, I suppose, and send it through to take the proper magnetic and star-fix readings, but it would cost a ton of money for each robot and there are thousands of unexplored gates with new ones opening all the time. Anything could still go wrong and recovering the robot might prove impossible. Frankly, human scouts are cheaper, more reliable, and have the advantage of being able to gather detailed social data no robot could. That's important particularly when scholarly research or potential time touring is involved.

"We," he tapped his breast bone, "are expendable. We're independent businessmen, on nobody's payroll. No insurance company in the world will touch us, not even Lloyd's of London. That's another downside to scouting. No health coverage, no life insurance, no disability policies. You sign on for this job, you take your chances. There is a guild, if you care to pay the dues, but the treasury's almost always empty. Time scouts tend to suffer catastrophic illnesses and injuries with depressing frequency. I hope," he added grimly, "that you have a high pain threshold and don't faint at the sight of blood—yours or anyone else's."

Margo didn't answer. But her chin came up a stubborn notch, despite sudden pallor beneath already fair skin.

Kit sat back. "Huh. I'll give you credit for guts, girl. All right, let me show you how these operate."

He and Malcolm took her step by step through the operation of both machines, although they couldn't shoot a star-fix from inside La-La Land. The personal log she caught onto fairly quickly. The ATLS' geo-magnetic sensors gave her trouble.

"No, you're plotting that reading backwards, Margo. You've just put yourself half a continent off target, which means you've just calculated the time zone completely wrong, as well. Run it again."

"I hate math!" Margo snapped. "How was I supposed to know I'd need all this crap?"

Malcolm visibly suppressed a wince. Very gently, Kit

took the ATLS from her. "All right. We'll begin by having you hone up on basic skills. I'll schedule study times for you in the library. And not just for remedial math. You'll need language skills, historical studies, costuming and customs, sociological structures . . ."

Margo was looking at him in wide-eyed horror.

"Let me guess," Kit said drolly. "You thought time scouting was a way to avoid college?"

She didn't answer, but he could read it in her eyes.

"Kid, if you want to be a time scout, the first thing you have to become is a *scholar*. Scouts are a rough and ready bunch—we have to be—but most of us started life as historians or classics professors or philosophers or anthropologists. We're the best-educated bunch of roughnecks this side of eternity."

Malcolm laughed. "I have a Ph.D. in Roman antiquities."

Margo sat back and crossed her arms. "This is maddening. If I'd wanted a Ph.D., I've have gone to school. All I want to do is explore neat places!"

Kit started to say something that would have been entirely too heartfelt, but Malcolm beat him to the punch.

"Fame and fortune and adventure?" he asked in a voice dry as fine wine.

She flushed.

Kit felt like cheering. "That's fine," he told her. "But you have to pay the dues. And we have an agreement, Margo. You do what I tell you, when I tell you, or you don't set that first pretty pink toe across the threshold of a gate."

She pouted at the ATLS. Then sighed. "All right. I'll go to the library. Isn't there anything to this job besides studying?"

"Sure." Kit sat back. "Plenty, in fact. How much martial arts training have you had?"

She shrugged. "High school stuff. I have a belt."

"What kind, which discipline?"

"Brown belt, Tai Kwan Do."

Kit grunted. All flying kicks and damn near no full-contact sparring, not compared to what she'd need. Tai Kwan Do spent too much time "pulling" its punches short to give a student a taste of what it was like to hit—or be hit. He saw the chance for an object lesson that might just sink home.

"All right. Let's go."

"Go? Go where?"

Kit returned the log and ATLS to their leather satchel. "To the gym. I want to test how much you know."

"You . . . now?"

Kit grinned. "Yep. What's the matter, Margo? Afraid an old man will whip you?"

Slim jaw muscles took on a marble hardness. She came to her feet and planted hands on hips. "No. I'm not afraid of anybody or anything. Where's the damned gym?"

"Watch your language," he said mildly. "The gym is in the basement, next to the weapons ranges."

Her eyes widened. "Weapons ranges?" Her expression hovered somewhere between excitement and dismay. "You mean, like guns and stuff?"

Kit exchanged glances with Malcolm, who rolled his eyes. Kit forcibly held back a sigh. "Yes, Margo. I mean exactly like guns and stuff. If it can be shot, slashed with, or jabbed into someone, you're going to learn how to use it."

"Oh."

Clearly, this was another aspect of time scouting his granddaughter had not considered. She looked like she'd rather have picked up a live cobra than picked up a weapon. Good. Maybe this would convince her to quit. Given the set of her jaw, Kit rather doubted that, but it made for a pleasant fantasy. He had a sinking feeling *nothing* he did or said would dissuade her.

Margo said primly, "If we're going to spar, I'll need to visit the lady's room first."

Malcolm shot to his feet and hovered at the back of her chair, but didn't quite offer to take her hand to assist her. Kit glowered. Margo gave Malcolm a sweet smile that left Kit's glower even darker. Malcolm had the good grace to look sheepish as Margo made her way through the crowded bar. Very nearly every eye in the place followed her progress. Kit shook his head. The dress had to go. Preferably into the trash. Or maybe over Skeeter Jackson's head.

"How about you, Malcolm? You coming to the gym, too?"

The freelance guide chuckled. "Just try and get rid of me. I wouldn't miss this for a full-time job."

"You," Kit muttered, "are a pain in the neck."

"Hey, don't blame me," Malcolm laughed. "You're the one who agreed to teach her."

"Yeah, I did. I figure it's either teach her or bury her."

Malcolm's laughter vanished. "Yeah. I know. You need help, you let me know."

Kit gave him a pained smile. "I'll do that. I figure I owe you."

Malcolm groaned. "How come I have a bad feeling about this?"

"Because," Kit punched his shoulder, "your luck stinks."

The younger man chuckled. "Well, I won't argue that. All right, here she comes. Smile, Grandpa."

Kit muttered, "You'd better salute when you say that, mister." Malcolm just laughed. Kit said forlornly, "I will never live this down. Never." He pasted on what he hoped passed for a smile. "Okay, Margo, let's go."

Phase One underway.

And a lifetime's worth of worrying yet to come.

CHAPTER SEVEN

News travels fast in a small town.

And despite its enormous size for a complex under one roof, TT-86 was, in fact, a very small town, as isolated in some ways as a medieval village. There was no live television, no live radio, no satellite hookups to talk to relatives left behind. Electronic recreation was available, of course, for a price. Most private quarters had televisions and laser-disk players and nearly every resident owned some kind of computer.

But in order to satisfy the craving for live entertainment, 'eighty-sixers resorted to a time-honored form of recreation first invented by bored cave-dwellers who found themselves stuck in cramped quarters with nowhere to go. 'Eighty-sixers gossiped. About everything. Tourists, other stations, down-time mishaps and adventures, each other . . .

Someone had once laughingly suggested that station management install "backyard fences" in the residential sections. The jokester had immediately initiated a six-month wrangle over where, what color, who would pay for them, wood vs. chain-link, and installation vs. maintenance logistics, until Bull Morgan had finally put his authoritative foot down in the middle of the ruckus and quashed it with a succinct "No fences!"

Long-time 'eighty-sixers still occasionally grumbled over it.

Kit had no more than opened the gym door than someone called out, "Hey, Grandpa! How's the arthritis?"

Kit shot back a time-honored response and told Margo, "That way. You'll find clean gym shorts and T-shirts at the window. Tell 'em to put it on my bill."

"Okay."

At least nobody wolf-whistled at Margo's stilt-heeled progress toward the women's shower room. Kit changed and emerged to find Malcolm leaning easily against one wall. Margo had not yet put in an appearance.

"Aren't you going to spar with us?" Kit asked with a wolfish grin.

Malcolm feigned surprise. "Me? End up wrestling around on the floor with your grandkid? Kit, stupid I ain't."

"You're twenty years younger than I am, dammit. Dress out. If you're short of pocket cash, I'll pay for the rental. Hell, I'll pay for the sparring session. If we knock her flat enough, maybe she'll give up."

"Well, okay. It's your party. But I wouldn't count on it. She does remind me a little of you."

Kit tossed his towel at Malcolm's head. The younger man grinned, caught it, and tossed it right back, then headed for the shower room. Margo emerged decently clad in shorts, a loose T-shirt, and rented cotton-soled shoes. She moved well, but that might just have been youth and an unfortunate tendency toward exhibitionism. Clearly, she was perfectly well aware that every male eye in the room was on her.

Huh. It's not bad enough she's my granddaughter, but she has to be sexy as a minx, too. And legally old enough to make her own decisions if the age on her ID were accurate. She *looked* eighteen, anyway. He'd tackle her about her exact age later. Kit tried to adjust himself to the uncomfortable new mindset as she crossed the last couple of yards and came to a halt. She balanced lightly on the balls of her feet. "Well, are you ready?"

Kit shook his head. "Malcolm's joining us. I want to watch you two spar first. Then you and I will pair off."

She didn't look happy about that.

Malcolm finally arrived. "Okay, boss. Shoot."

"Let's see what the two of you can do, shall we?"

Malcolm nodded and gave Margo a formal bow. She returned it in classic sportsmanlike fashion—and Malcolm charged. Half-a-second later, Margo grunted sharply. Her back connected with the mat. Kit shook his head and tsk-tsked.

"Margo, didn't your instructor ever teach you to keep your eyes on your opponent?"

She glared up at him from an extremely indelicate position with Malcolm between her knees. He'd pinned her wrists to the floor. "How was I supposed to know he'd cheat?"

Malcolm grinned. "This isn't a *dojo*, Miss Margo."

"And it sure as hell ain't a high school match," Kit added drily. "We're here to see how you can fight. If you want to discuss customs and courtesies in the competitive arena, go talk to an etiquette master."

Malcolm rose easily. Margo scrambled to her feet, mastering a huffy glare on the way up. "All right," she muttered. "Let's see you try that again. This time, I'll be watching."

Malcolm moved in fast and grappled her, using classic Greco-Roman grappling styles. The unexpected move completely flummoxed Margo. She staggered backward, trying to extricate herself from wrestling holds she didn't have the strength or technique to break.

"Hey! What is this?" She tried stamping on Malcolm's instep. He picked her up, leading to chuckles from across the gym. Interested spectators had halted all pretense of continuing any workouts.

Kit suppressed a grin, wisely deciding that laughing at her would be a mistake. Wordlessly, he separated them. Margo stood glaring and huffing for breath. Malcolm offered a polite bow which she ignored icily.

"All right," Kit said, stepping off the mat once more, "let's see what else you can do."

She turned that alley-cat glare on him—and Malcolm came in fast. But this time he didn't catch her off guard. Margo snapped out a beautifully executed snap kick, lifting her knee and extending her leg so fast it was difficult to follow the motion. Her foot brushed Malcolm's cheek. That kick would've scored wonderfully on the sporting circuit. If she'd kicked him in the nose or forehead, she might even have rendered him unconscious.

Unfortunately for Margo, neither Malcolm's nose nor his forehead were in the right spot. He kept coming. Margo's heel sailed straight over his shoulder. Before she could snap back from the unexpected move, she found herself on the floor, in exactly the same position as before with Malcolm between her knees.

"It's not fair!" she wailed. "That would've knocked him out!"

Kit nodded. "Yep, if you'd actually kicked hell out of him, it probably would've. But you didn't."

"Look, I don't want to break your friend's face!"

Malcolm chuckled. "I appreciate your concern, Miss Margo." He let her up, and she rubbed her wrists, then eased a strained muscle in her thigh.

Kit said, "Take five."

He went back to the equipment room and found sparring helmets, gloves, and padded shoes, then returned to find Margo glowering silently at Malcolm. "Okay, this should be pretty much like what you used in karate competitions."

She eyed the equipment dubiously.

Oh, great. "Let me guess? You never did any full-contact competitions?"

"Well, no," she admitted. "We always pulled the

punches short and made sure the kicks didn't connect. Our high school didn't have money for this kind of stuff."

Kit thought dark thoughts at any school administration that would allow kids to risk injury in a "sport" that was designed to cripple and kill, then showed her how the padded helmet worked. Similar to the leather helmets boxers wore, it was made of soft plastic, with a big pad across the forehead and down the sides of the face, straps under the jaw, and a pad that extended around the sides of the head a bit. Malcolm strapped on his own helmet, then slipped into shoes and gloves while Margo struggled with hers.

When she was ready, she said uncertainly, "I still don't want to cripple him or anything."

Kit nodded. "Just make him go *oof* and I'll be happy."

"Okay."

Once again, Malcolm charged in, giving her almost no time to react. Margo executed a side check kick and hit him right across the pelvis. He said "oof!" and stopped abruptly. As he folded over, Margo hit him just above his right ear with her left fist. Another sharp "oof!" accompanied the punch. Margo struck with her right fist across the back of the skull on his way down. A third ludicrous "oof!" tore loose. When his face hit the mat, a final, muffled *"oof . . . ."* prompted grins all across the gym.

Margo said sweetly, "You mean, like those four?"

Kit just looked at her. "Aren't you going to finish him off?"

From near Margo's feet, Malcolm muttered into the mat, "Oh, God, don't encourage her."

Kit chuckled and nudged him with an unsympathetic toe. "C'mon, Malcolm, get up and do it again. This doesn't prove she's any good, it just proves you've gotten overconfident."

Margo huffed and crossed her arms.

Malcolm scraped himself off the mat and stood up,

moving a little awkwardly. Kit grinned. "What's the matter, Malcolm? A little slow on the rebound?"

"You," Malcolm muttered, "are a pain."

"Every chance I get."

Malcolm charged without warning. Margo threw up another check kick, but Malcolm stopped short, leaving the kick whistling through empty air. By the time she'd finished executing it, she was turned away from him. Malcolm rushed in gleefully. Kit winced and braced himself for Margo's wail of protest. Her back was toward him as Malcolm rushed forward—

Then she astonished them both.

Margo stepped *toward* Malcolm. When he hit her, Margo brought her elbow straight back with the forearm parallel to floor, fist clenched, palm up. She leaned into it and hit him in the solar plexus. He snapped forward with an ugly sound that caused Kit to grimace in sympathy. Margo dropped as he did, then grabbed him around the neck with both arms and jerked him forward. Poor Malcolm landed dead on his backside with Margo balanced lightly on her feet behind him. She grabbed his hair in her gloved fist and punched him in the base of the skull with her right hand, pulling the punch so that it just popped him.

While Malcolm's eyes and nose streamed wetness, Margo said even more sweetly, "You mean finish him off like that?"

Kit crossed his arms to hide his amusement. He didn't want Margo getting cocky. Poor Malcolm was blinking and struggling manfully to dry his face with his gloves. "Well, that's one," Kit drawled, "but in a real situation, you always need to kill or cripple at least twice."

"Twice?" Margo echoed. "Oh, so he doesn't surprise you when you think he's down."

When she made to finish Malcolm off again, Kit waved her back.

"No, Malcolm is clearly finished. This time."

The freelance guide glared at Kit as though to say, "Malcolm does not want to play any more. Malcolm is in pain and will pay you back for this, good buddy."

Kit shrugged as though to say, "Who knew?"

Malcolm had struggled to his feet. "You . . ." he wheezed at Kit, ". . . should be damned glad Bull doesn't allow litigation lawyers in La-La Land."

"So I should," Kit said mildly. "And so should you. Go one more time."

"Cripes, Kit, what're you trying to do? Give Rachel Eisenstein more business?"

Margo was literally preening.

Kit's grin was entirely unsympathetic. "The day Margo puts you in the hospital is the day I'll eat your shoes. C'mon, buddy. Brace up."

Margo gave him a mocking bow, carefully keeping her eyes on him. Malcolm groaned and settled himself. "All right," he muttered. "We'll just see."

Malcolm, forced into the role of attacker by the requirements of the sparring session, came in again— but this time, he surprised her. Malcolm came at her like a trained Tai Kwan Do fighter, throwing a beautiful front snap kick of his own. It knocked her back with an unladylike sound. Malcolm charged in flailing, punching with both fists, one-two, one-two. Margo staggered back, moving away, bringing her arms up as he tried to hit her. Then she threw up a hook kick, sweeping his arms down out of the way with her foot. Before he could recover, she punched him twice in the face, using the momentum of her forward motion. As he backed away from her, Margo threw her shoulder into his gut, knocking him backwards. Then she really surprised Kit—not to mention Malcolm. She grabbed the back of his leading knee and snatched it up past her own hip while continuing to push with her shoulder. Malcolm smacked the mat flat on his back and gave out an ugly "whoof!"

Margo landed between his knees in a parody of his early pins. She said, "Your turn!" and raked his face with one gloved hand, then popped him in the Adam's apple with the other.

"Gak!" Malcolm's eyes bulged and crossed, simultaneously.

Margo jumped up, grinning impishly, then actually curtsied to Kit. Laughter erupted across the gym, along with sporadic applause. Margo curtsied again to the audience, drawing greater applause. Malcolm rolled over onto his hands and knees, coughed, and wheezed in Kit's general direction, "Stuff it, Kit. Mamma always taught me never fight with girls. Mamma was usually right."

Kit managed to return Margo's triumphant grin with a bored expression. "Thought you were trained in Tai Kwan Do," he observed drily. "What was that little flip at the end of Malcolm's second fall?"

Margo's grin widened. "Well, my freshman year in high school, I took Judo until I found out they weren't going to let us roll around on the floor like that with boys."

"Don't be nasty, little girl," he said mildly.

Margo just laughed. "Next?" she challenged.

He privately conceded her the right to be pleased with herself, but cocky was dangerous. Time for a reality check. He stepped out onto the mat.

Malcolm wheezed, "Wait a sec. Lemme get out of the way."

All across the gym, spectators pressed a little closer. Someone gave Malcolm a cup of water, which he gulped down. He took the ribbing surprisingly well, grinning and unfastening the gloves, pulling off the helmet and rubbing at the base of his skull.

Margo watched him with a glow of satisfaction warming her all the way through. She'd scored big time and she knew it. She saw grudging respect in Malcolm's eyes and open interest in several faces as they appraised her. *Finally,* she thought, *finally, I do something right around here!* Maybe now Kenneth "Kit" Carson would start showing her a little respect!

Flying high, Margo playfully lunged straight toward him.

Afterward, she wasn't sure what he'd done, except that he turned and raised one hand while the other came down. She was never sure if she touched him or he touched her, but she was abruptly sitting on her butt clear off the edge of the mat on a cold, hard floor. The ache jolted all the way up her spine.

When Margo recovered from shock, all she could find to say was a wailing, "Ow!" Then she turned to glare at Kit. "You threw me off the mat!"

"No," he disagreed with a tiny smile, "*you* threw you off the mat."

HUH?

"Okay," he said kindly, "ready to do a little serious sparring now?"

That was more than Margo's bruised ego could bear. She charged in, launching another nice high front snap kick—only Kit's head wasn't there. It was down around her belt level and the left foot she was using for support was suddenly up a little higher than her left ankle used to be, and at least a foot forward, while her backside travelled rapidly straight toward the floor.

This time, Margo was the one who blinked involuntary tears. *Owww . . .* Malcolm was in her line of sight, grinning insufferably.

Kit Carson, damn him, said, "Well, don't just sit there, kid. Come on, I thought you wanted to fight."

She scrambled up and launched herself forward with a flurry of fists, as fast and furious as the punches Malcolm had thrown at her. Margo saw his open palms come up between her blows, but her fists never hit quite where she expected. Then, quite suddenly—due to a light pressure on her right wrist and elbow—she found it necessary to throw herself at top speed straight toward the floor. She landed hard, face-first. At least this time she'd landed *on* the mat. Margo saw red. She regained all fours while he just stood there, smiling down at her. She lunged straight for his crotch, determined to grab whatever she could.

He grasped her wrist. Lightly. With nothing but his thumb and center finger. Adding insult to injury, he even left his index finger lightly extended. Before she could recover, he backed up enough to straighten her arm, then turned slightly. Her elbow straightened painfully across the front of his knee. He continued his turn, in slow motion to emphasize the point. Margo gasped—then gasped again as that lazy turn forced her to attempt crawling around him in a circle, just to prevent her elbow from being popped out of joint. Howls of amusement erupted throughout the gym. *Oh, God, they're laughing at me. . . .*

While she continued crawling around in a state of growing panic and embarrassment, Kit told her, "That's enough for today, I think. Get showered and we'll talk about this."

He finally let her go. Margo stuffed a wail back inside before it could burst loose, but she couldn't stop the impulse to rub her wrist. All around men were chuckling and returning to their own workouts. She bit back a scathing comment, realizing even through a haze of humiliation that she had a lot to learn. *He set me up, dammit, he set me up. . . .*

Well, she'd asked for it, hadn't she?

That thought got Margo through a long, miserable shower. Hot water pounded against bruises and relaxed knots of muscle from her neck to her toes. When she emerged, wrapped in a towel, she found the locker room attendant and tried to reclaim her clothes. The woman smiled and handed her another set of clean workout clothes.

Margo groaned. "Oh, God, not another torture session?"

"No," the attendant smiled, "just something a little less, um, I think Kit said *scandalous* than your dress." She handed that over, too, along with the stilt heels, bedraggled hat, and corset. "Keep the gym shoes, too."

"Thanks," Margo muttered, earning a sympathetic laugh.

Margo considered putting her own clothes back on, Kit Carson be damned, but she was so muscle-sore, even the thought of cinching herself into that corset was unendurable. Besides, she'd had enough humiliation for one day. She didn't want any reminders of her own poor judgement where Skeeter Jackson was concerned. She hoped that rat made himself *scarce*. She never wanted to see him again, let alone talk to him. Margo wadded the dress, corset, and shoes into a ball and balanced the hat on top.

"Well," she sighed, "chalk one up to experience, Margo. It's going to be a longer day than you thought."

She lifted her chin, refusing to acknowledge utter defeat. She'd bested Malcolm Moore and convinced Kit to train her. That was worth a great deal. With those moderately cheering thoughts, Margo headed toward her next confrontation with the maddening man she'd chosen as teacher. *Surely*, she told herself by way of a pep talk, *it'll get better soon.* And if it didn't? Or if he decided she didn't have what it took?

Well, he could toss her out, but she wasn't by God going to quit!

While Margo showered and changed, Kit sent Malcolm off with enough pocket change for a good, solid meal, then phoned to transfer funds into Malcolm's account to cover the sparring session and damages sustained. He had further plans for the guide concerning his granddaughter's training, which meant he didn't want

Malcolm quitting for good before Margo's lessons had even begun. Malcolm didn't know it yet, but he was about to become substantially richer—and probably a little bit greyer. Kit shook his head. Who'd have guessed the kid would work him over so thoroughly?

He took advantage of Margo's tardiness in the shower to hunt up the next of Margo's instructors. The weapons ranges were nearly empty. Ann Vinh Mulhaney was seated cross-legged on the floor next to an empty shooting bench, cleaning several break-action revolvers.

"Hi, Kit," she smiled. "I hear Margo gave Malcolm a working over."

"News travels fast," he chuckled. "Poor Malcolm. He'll get over it, though. Especially when I offer him the chance to get even."

Ann laughed. "Poor Margo. Where is the Wunderkind, by the way?"

"Showering. I think she's in there sulking, actually. She, er, didn't do so well against Aikido."

"So I heard. What's up? Rumors are flying that you plan to teach her to scout, but I didn't put much stock in them."

Kit scratched the back of his head. "Well, actually . . . I want you to teach her to shoot."

"You want me to what?" Ann Vinh Mulhaney's eyes widened. TT-86's resident firearms instructor planted hands on slender hips, ignoring smears of carbon residue and solvent on her hands. "Don't tell me those rumors are *true?*"

Kit cleared his throat.

Ann stared at him in dawning horror. "Oh, God, you *are* teaching her, aren't you? Any particular reason? I mean other than you've clearly lost what brains you ever had?"

Kit flushed. "Dammit, Ann, she'll do this on her own if I don't. You know how stubborn I am. She's just as bad, and just turned eighteen, and convinced the world's hers for the plucking, and she doesn't give a hoot about the risks, she just wants to follow in my goddamned footsteps. . . ."

Ann's demeanor changed at once. "Oh, Kit. You poor thing." She rested a hand on his arm. He relaxed slowly, letting the anger and worry go muscle by muscle. When he could breathe without hurting his chest again, Ann said, "All right, Kit. I'll teach her. But if I pass judgement and it's bad . . ."

He met her eyes. "Maybe she'll listen to another woman."

"Maybe. I've got a lesson starting in a few minutes or I'd offer to take her on right now. Go talk to Sven and see what he has to say; then come back tomorrow morning and we can get started."

"Thanks, Ann." He squeezed her arm in heartfelt gratitude.

She smiled. "Don't thank me. This is going to cost, Kenneth Carson." But she winked to remove the sting.

Kit just groaned. "What do you want?"

"How about the honeymoon suite for a week?"

"A *week?* Do you have any idea what I could get for . . ." He trailed off. "Okay. A week."

"And my normal fees, plus fifty percent for private tutoring."

Grandkids were expensive. "Anything else? My signature in blood?"

Ann chuckled. "You think I'm expensive, wait until you tackle Sven."

"Great. Thanks. What does *he* want?"

"Out of the whole deal. I can hardly wait to see what you offer him that changes his mind."

Kit decided to kiss an entire quarter's worth of profits goodbye and went looking for Sven. Kit found him in the armory sharpening a *gladius*.

"Hi, Sven."

"Hi, yourself. The answer's no."

The scream of naked steel on the whetstone didn't encourage argument. Kit found a chair and plopped down. "Bull hockey."

Sven glanced up. "No way. She gets killed, you come hunting me, I have to break your neck. . . . Nope. No thanks."

"Would you rather have her go down time without lessons?"

"Huh. You'd rope her down, first."

"Yeah, but she'd have to go to the bathroom sometime and that's one determined kid. I mean it, Sven. I need you on this one. Ann can teach her anything she needs to know about projectile weapons, but she needs blades, too, and more martial arts than she's got. She needs lessons. Good lessons. *Your* lessons."

Sven put a finer edge on the *gladius*, then turned it and started working the other side. "You won't interfere?"

"Nope."

"Or get pissed off if she gets hurt?"

"Not a bit. The rougher it gets, the more likely she is to wake up and pick another career."

Sven snorted. "You're all heart, Grandpa. Well, the answer's still no. She's cute. She'll come to her senses."

Kit counted ten. Searched for some other argument. "I've got a Musashi sword-guard."

Sven halted mid-stroke, then swore and reshaped the ruined edge. "Bastard. Is it signed?"

Gotcha. "Yep."

Sven glared at him. "Where the hell did you get an original Musashi *tsuba?*"

"Found it in the Neo Edo's safe. There's some amazing stuff in that safe."

Sven laughed darkly. "I'll just bet there is." He set the *gladius* aside and leaned back. "If it was just the *tsuba,* Kit, I'd tell you to get the hell out of here." He held Kit's gaze. "You really want to teach the kid that bad?"

"Yes, I do," Kit said quietly. "If I thought there was

a way out of it . . . but I haven't found one yet. I want her to have a fighting chance."

Sven shook his head. "A woman scout. And a raw kid, at that. My friend, you're crazy." He gave Kit a lopsided smile. "But then, we always knew that. All right. I'll do it. And Kit—keep the Musashi. God knows, I owe you a couple of favors here and there. Just let me look at it now and again and we'll call it even."

Kit, who couldn't have taken the priceless Musashi sword-guard back up time in any case, decided he'd just found Sven's next birthday present. "Thanks, buddy."

"Sure. Any time you want to go off the deep end, you just let me know. When do you want her to start?"

"Any time you're ready."

Sven sighed. "Well, hell, I guess that's now. Have you eaten dinner?"

Kit shook his head. "No, and I suspect Margo's half starved. Why don't I call and see if the Delight has a table open?"

"Sounds good to me. I'll meet you upstairs as soon as I finish locking up down here."

The Epicurean Delight's decor reflected its location in Urbs Romae: mosaic floors, frescoed walls (some of them painted by a muralist who'd spent a year down time studying with ancient master artists), and tables interspersed with genuine Roman-style dinner couches for those with the desire to eat lying down. Live music was provided by an accomplished lyrist dressed in Greek slave's robes. The waiting staff, too, dressed as well-liveried slaves. The evening's clientele boasted six instantly recognizable millionaires, one anonymous Japanese billionaire and his current mistress, a member of Great Britain's House of Lords and *his* current mistress, and three world-famous actresses who chatted animatedly about the down-time research they planned to do in London for their next film.

All in all, it was another typical night at the Delight. Kit noted Margo's eyes widen when the head waiter seated them next to the actresses.

"That's—"

"Yep," Kit said, cutting her off. "Get used to it, Margo," he grinned. "TT-86 is a magnet for the jet set, miserable lot of deadbeats that they are. Just don't plan on joining their ranks and you'll live a happier life. Now, while we wait for Sven to join us . . ."

Margo's face took on a shuttered, wary look. "Yeah?"

"Relax, kid, I don't bite. Those three," he nodded toward the actresses, "are here doing role research. You said you wanted to be on stage, right?"

She nodded.

"Good." Kit leaned forward and interlaced his fingers comfortably. "I want you to think of scouting as role research for the most challenging stage play you've ever been cast as lead actress in."

Margo grinned. "That's dead easy."

"No, it isn't. If you flub your lines, there won't be any prompters backstage. You won't have a director to yell, 'CUT! Take it from page six. . . .' You'll be on your own. Your performance won't be judged by a critic, it'll be judged by survival. Your audience will be the down-time people you encounter. Fool them and maybe you'll get back in once piece. Now . . . about your performance in the gym."

Her eyes flashed. "I'll get better!"

"I'm sure you will. I want you to answer one question for me, but I want you to think about it before you answer."

"I'm listening."

Kit nodded. "I want you to tell me what the goals of a timescout are. Ah, hello, Arley, how are you?"

Arley Eisenstein greeted Margo warmly, welcoming her to TT-86, then recommended the House Special. "It's a new recipe, Egyptian, wonderful. You're my guinea pigs."

Kit smiled. "I'm game. Margo?"

With a combative look in her eye, Margo said, "Anything he's having, I'll have."

"Anything?" Arley said with an uptilted eyebrow.

"Anything."

Arley rubbed his palms together in gleeful anticipation. "Oh, good. This ought to be fun. I'll tell Jacque to get started. Is anyone else joining you?"

"Just Sven, far as I know, but I don't mind company if somebody wants a chair."

"Good, good. The more the merrier," Arley laughed. "Wine? Appetizers?"

Kit glanced at Margo, who was clearly tired but still on edge. "Is this Special of yours poultry, fish, pork, or beef? Or something else altogether?"

Arley winked. "Seafood. Mostly."

"All right, why don't we start with a half-carafe of Piesporter Michelsburg and some fresh fruit and bread and I'll let you choose the wine for the main course?"

Arley flashed a delighted smile. "Mead. Egyptian mead. I'll send Julie out with the appetizers," Arley promised. He smiled warmly again at Margo, then threaded his way through the Delight, pausing now and again to speak with other clients. Sven Bailey arrived.

"So this is the one, huh?" he said without preamble. His long, shuttered stare brought an uncomfortable flood of color to Margo's cheeks—and a glitter of irritation to her eyes.

"I'm the one what?" she asked coldly.

Sven just grunted and ignored her. He plopped into a chair. "You're sure about this?"

Kit shrugged. "Yep."

"Huh."

Margo glanced from Sven to Kit, then back. She clearly wanted to ask a question and just as clearly wasn't sure she wanted to risk the answer yet. Kit took pity on her.

"Margo, this is Sven Bailey, acknowledged far and wide as the most dangerous man on TT-86."

Margo's eyes widened. Sven just snorted. "Damned right I am. Last man who tried to prove otherwise ended up dead." He guffawed, leaving Margo to stare uneasily anywhere but at him. Kit didn't bother to explain that the gentleman in question had been a mad tourist who'd insisted on using the Biddle style of formal knife-fighting, despite Sven's solemn warnings that it would get him killed (which it had, in some filthy little Soho alley, where he'd found out that "knife fencing" and street fighting were not the same animal, after all).

Sven high-signed Julie, who beamed in their direction while balancing a wine carafe and glasses on a silver tray. "Hi, guys," she said brightly, setting down glasses and a perfectly chilled carafe of Piesporter, along with tumblers of icewater. "What'll your poison be, Sven?"

He sniffed at the wine. "Not that. How about a Sam Adams?"

"Any thoughts on dinner? We have a wonderful seafood special tonight, a new dish from ancient Egypt . . ."

"Hell, no. Let Arley experiment on somebody else. You still doing that beef thing you had in here last week?"

Julie dimpled. "We sure are. Rare?"

"Make it moo."

Margo looked like she was about to lose her appetite—or worse.

Kit grinned. "What's wrong, kid? No stomach for blood?"

Margo compressed her lips. "I'm fine."

Sven eyed her. "You sure act squeamish for a kid about to try time scouting."

She fidgeted in her chair, but refrained from comment.

"Speaking of time scouting," Kit said, rubbing the

side of his nose, "any thoughts about the answer to that question I posed?"

Margo glanced at Sven. She looked suddenly very young and uncertain. Then her chin came up. "Well . . . A time scout's job is to find out where a gate leads."

Kit shook his head. "I didn't ask what a scout's job was, I asked what a scout's goals are. That's a little different proposition."

For a second, she looked so tired and hungry and miserable and confused, Kit thought she might cry. He prompted, "Just tell me what pops into your head. What's a scout's primary goal?"

"To make money."

Sven let loose an astonishing guffaw that startled diners in a circle three tables deep, then pounded Margo's back with friendly affection. She nearly came adrift from her chair, but managed a sheepish smile. Kit grinned. "Money, eh? Well, yes, if you're lucky. If the gate you push doesn't lead to the Russian steppes in the middle of the last ice age. A few scientists might want a peek, but there's not much commercial potential in a mile-high glacier. What else?"

"To stay alive," she said, with a tiny toss of her short hair.

"Absolutely," Kit agreed.

"You're gettin' there, girl. What else?" Sven asked, taking the burden of grilling her off Kit's hands.

She chewed her lower lip thoughtfully. "Learn stuff about where you are, of course. Do you take a camera?"

Kit thought about Catherine the Great and her Russian boar and winked at Sven. He'd clearly read the same article, judging by the sudden twinkle in his eyes. "Sometimes. Usually not. Cameras aren't essential equipment."

"What else ought to be my goal, then?"

Kit nodded. "Good. You're asking questions." He leaned forward. "Point number one: the kind of karate you've learned in high school might be great for a soldier attacking someone else, but soldiering—fighting battles—isn't the primary goal of a scout."

"Hell, no," Sven muttered. "You want a battle, go live in Serbia or anywhere from Istanbul down to Cairo. Last I heard, Israel was threatening to pop a nuke or two if the Moslem states didn't stop recruiting *jihad* fighters from down time and I can't say as I blame either side. Gad, what a mess."

Even Margo had the sense to shiver. What the time strings had done to the incendiary Middle East didn't bear thinking about. A coalition of Moslem and Jewish women had come together to try and stop the fighting, but so far neither side was listening to the voice of sanity. The whole region had been declared off limits after TT-66 had been bombed into oblivion. Kit, like most 'eighty-sixers, had lost good friends during the death of the station.

Kit cleared his throat and defused the sudden chill by pouring wine for Margo and himself. "All right, then," Kit said, "a scout's goal isn't to engage in battle. It's to go someplace, to learn whatever he can, *then get away clean*, doing the least amount of damage to the local environment—including the denizens of that environment."

"Especially the denizens," Sven said, by way of emphasis. "Anything else is borrowing trouble. Big trouble. If you piss off somebody who can't be killed and you end up in a life-or-death situation with them, you'll be the one kissing your backside goodbye."

"Wait a second," Margo said with a frown. "What do you mean, somebody who can't be killed? Anybody can be killed."

"Not exactly," Kit said quietly. "If someone's death would alter history, then that person can't be killed. At least, not by an up-timer. Paradox will not happen. History won't change. People have tried. It never works.

Never. Let's say you try to assassinate somebody famous, like George Washington. Your gun will jam or misfire, or you'll trip at the last second so the knife doesn't hit a vital spot. *Something* will happen to prevent you from changing anything critical. The tricky part here is, it can happen when you least expect it."

"Like if you get into a fatal fight with somebody who seems unimportant," Sven said quietly. "If their death would affect history, then they won't die. That doesn't mean *you* won't."

For once, Margo looked worried instead of flippant. She glanced at Sven, then back to Kit. "Okay." It came out surprisingly subdued. "What else?"

"Another point to remember is that we're the outsiders, down time. Even if somebody is unimportant enough that their death wouldn't matter to history, we don't have a moral right to go barging in with a macho attitude that we'll just smash anything that puts us in danger, without taking precautions to avoid problems in the first place."

"The best way to win a fight," Sven put in, "is to avoid fighting in the first place. The real kicker, of course, is learning how to avoid the fight."

Margo chewed one thumbnail. "And if you can't? I mean, what if some psychopathic kook jumps you?"

His cruel comments about Jack the Ripper had clearly made an impression. Kit refilled her wineglass. "That's always possible, of course, and sometimes there may be nothing for it but to break a neck or shatter a kneecap, but most of the time your goal is to be invisible. If you can't be, then your goal is to keep someone from breaking *your* neck or shattering *your* kneecap. And, of course, to get the hell back to the terminal in one piece. When it comes to scouts, heroes are just people who confuse cowardice with common sense."

Sven gestured lazily with one thick hand. "Anybody knows that, Kit does. A real running expert on smash and skedaddle. And the only man on the station I can't throw five out of five times, sparring."

Kit chuckled thinly, drawing little circles in the condensate on the tabletop. "Only before I retired, buddy. I wouldn't go near you, right now."

"Only proves you should," Sven came back with a grin. "Keep you on your toes. Keep you young."

"Don't rub it in too deep," Kit laughed. "You're not that far behind me. Let's see, how old will you be come June?"

"Old enough," Sven said with a mock glower that fooled no one.

Margo was staring, oogle-eyed, from one to the other. Then quite suddenly she relaxed, as though she'd finally decided Sven didn't plan to pick up his steak knife and do her in between the salad and the main course.

"Now, that's not to say," Kit said with a smile, drawing the discussion back to the topic at hand, "that there's anything inherently wrong with good karate. I've got a black in Sho Shin Ri and another in . . . Well, I have several and they're all useful now and again. But Aikido—which is what happened to you, by the way— is probably the perfect defensive art."

Margo did another beautifully executed stationary female flounce and glared at him—although less murderously than in the gym. "That was humiliating."

"So's dying," Sven said laconically.

Margo flushed. "Okay, so I have a lot to learn. That's why I came looking for a teacher. At least it'll be more interesting than *math*."

Sven grinned. "You don't know math, you'll kill yourself just as dead as a back-street punk with a dirk would. Now, if you really want to kill, Korean Hap Ki Do or Hwarangdo are interesting forms to get into. If you have six or eight years. Of course," Sven rubbed his hands together and grinned, "Kit will tell you the years spent studying Hap Ki Do's art of invisibility would be far more useful to a scout than its fighting style."

Kit ignored the gambit to reopen a favorite discussion. "Unfortunately," Kit told Margo, "you don't have years because you'll be spending most of your time studying, not sparring. So what we'll do is set you up with an Aikido instructor to give you a good grounding in basics and a few specific moves, things that maybe could get you out of tight spots."

Sven punched Margo good-naturedly in the shoulder, causing her to wince. "That's right. Stuff to let you use those damned attractive legs of yours to run like hell."

Margo scowled at Sven. "My legs are none of your business!"

"Oh, yes they are," he grinned, an evil, thickset imp who leaned back and cracked his knuckles while staring her down.

Margo turned a dismayed look on Kit. "He isn't . . ."

Kit nodded.

"Oh, no . . ." She sat back in stunned horror. "My *teacher?*"

"Yep," Sven said as his beer arrived with the bread and fruit plate. "Tomorrow morning, 7:00 A.M. Dress out and be prompt. Because if you're late, I am going to wipe up the mat with you." Then he laughed. "Hell, I'm going to wipe up the mat with you either way, but if you're late, I'll be irritated when I do it." He held up his glass in a toast. "Enjoy your dinner."

The look of stricken horror Margo tried to hide was comical.

Kit grinned and refilled her wine glass. "Drink up, kid. Tomorrow you go into training, which means no more alcohol." The stricken look deepened.

"None? Not even wine?"

"None," Kit and Sven said simultaneously.

"A muddle-headed scout—" Kit began.

"I know, I know," Margo groaned. "Doesn't live long."

Thus proving she can learn, if she hears it often enough. "After you finish up with Sven, Ann Vinh Mulhaney will be ready for you."

"What does *she* do?" Margo wailed.

"She shoots the pants off me," Sven chuckled.

Margo just covered her face. "I'm doomed."

Kit tousled her hair, earning a fierce glare. "You could always quit and go home."

"Never!" The alley-cat snarl prompted a grin of anticipation from Sven Bailey.

"Well, then," Kit smiled, "eat your dinner and pay attention. Uncle Sven and I are about to start your first lesson in survival theory."

She gave them both a dubious glance. "That being?"

Sven guffawed. "When the fight starts, be someplace else. And always remember, nobody watches your butt for you when it's You versus the Universe—and Margo, the universe just don't give a damn. Death's a high price to pay for stupidity or carelessness, but they'll get you eventually if you don't do your job. And that job," he took another sip of his Sam Adams and warmed to the subject, "ain't pushing gates to get rich and famous. Now. The underlying principle of Aikido is real simple. There's you," he dropped a couple of droplets of water into the bowl of his spoon, "and there's the universe." He dropped another couple of drops nearby, carefully balancing the spoon so they remained separated.

"The trick with Aikido is to become one with the universe," he allowed the droplets to run together, "so that nothing catches you by surprise. Master that and you can offer an enemy reconciliation instead of battle. The rest is just vigilance and practice."

Margo was staring dubiously at the water droplets. "You're kidding."

"Nope."

She sighed. "Okay. What do I have to do to snuggle

up to the universe? Chant 'om' a couple thousand times an hour?"

Sven and Kit exchanged glances. Sven's questioning look clearly said, "Are you *sure* about this?"

Kit's grimace said "Yeah, dammit, wish I could say otherwise."

"Well," Sven said almost tiredly, "no, you don't chant 'om.' There isn't a secret key, some trick that will do it. Either it happens or it doesn't. The way you begin in Aikido is to start by doing wrist exercises." He demonstrated as Julie made her way toward their table with a heaping tray on which their dinner plates had been cast in the starring role. Sven shook out his napkin. "Why don't you practice that while Miss Julie puts that plate of eels and steamed octopus in front of you?"

Margo swung around in her chair. "*What?*"

Julie dutifully conjured a dish of baby octopus— tentacles artistically arranged around the eels— swimming in a garlic sauce that brimmed with unidentifiable spices and grated vegetables.

"Oh, my God . . ."

Kit couldn't help it. He started laughing. Sven was already wiping tears.

"C'mon, Margo," Kit teased, "what happened to your brave challenge? I thought you'd try anything I was game to try."

"But . . . but . . ."

"Let me guess," Kit said drily, "they didn't serve octopus in whatever little town you grew up in?"

Margo was still transfixed by the sight in front of her. The eels, which had been gutted and de-boned, still had their heads, producing the indelible impression that the plateful of slippery food was staring back. She swallowed convulsively. "I, uh . . ." She picked up her fork with an air of grim determination. "All right. *How* does one eat them?"

"That's the spirit," Sven laughed. "The eels, you cut into pieces. The octopi, you eat whole."

She shut her eyes and swallowed again, then tried a bite. She widened her eyes. "Hey, that's good!"

Kit chuckled. "Of course it is. Arley Eisenstein wouldn't serve it, otherwise. *Bon appétit.*"

He dug in with gusto.

True to her word, Margo matched him bite for bite—and enjoyed every last morsel.

The best thing Margo could say about her first lesson with Sven Bailey was that she didn't have to pay for it. The worst thing was, Malcolm Moore showed up to watch. After the first five minutes, she seriously regretted the previous day's sparring session. He enjoyed her utter trouncing far too thoroughly to outlast the brief satisfaction it had given her to show him up. After the first seven minutes, she had more bruises than she'd given Malcolm—and Sven Bailey was just getting warmed up.

She gritted her teeth and stood it.

After fifteen minutes of hell, which proved beyond any doubt that Margo was in over her head, Sven Bailey stepped back and said, "Okay. What've you learned?"

Margo rubbed the freshest set of bruises and said, "That I have a lot to learn. I knew *that* last night."

"That's it? That's all you've figured out?" His tone relegated her to the realm of idiots, worms, and cockroaches.

Margo bit her tongue with difficulty.

Sven rested hands on hips and studied her. "I was under the impression you were here to *learn* something."

"So show me something to learn! All you've done so far is throw me around like a sack of flour!"

"Sit down."

"What?"

He jabbed an emphatic middle finger toward the mat. "Sit!"

She sat.

"Close your eyes."

She did so.

"Now, breathe."

Margo felt like an idiot, sitting in the middle of the gym with people staring at her while she did nothing but breathe.

"Forget Malcolm, forget the other people. Concentrate on your center. Breathe. Down to the bottom. Hold it. Hold it. . . . Exhale. Again."

Grudgingly, her body began to relax. Tension made itself known in burning muscles from neck to hips. She shifted slightly for a more comfortable position.

"What are you feeling?"

"My neck is tight. My shoulders, too. My back hurts."

"Good, that's where you're fighting yourself. That's what I'm talking about when I ask what you've learned. You're fighting yourself as hard as you were fighting me. Keep breathing."

For half an hour, all Sven Bailey let her do was breathe and listen to her body's multiple complaints. When he finally allowed her to stand up again she felt looser, but restless.

"Now," Sven said, circling her slowly, "let's practice wrist exercises. The strength in your wrists is pathetic. To study Aikido, that has to change. Like this . . ."

For another half hour, Margo exercised her wrists until her arms trembled and her wrist-bones ached.

"Very good. Now, let's practice standing."

"*Standing?*"

Sven crossed his arms. "Are you going to question everything I tell you or do you want to learn something?"

"Yes! I'd just like to learn it before I'm eighty!"

Sven's appraising stare was about as warm as last winter's icicles. "You can't even crawl yet and you want to run the marathon?"

Margo clamped her lips shut. If she antagonized her

teacher, Kit would yank her right out of training. Her mother's voice came back to her: *Margo, you're too impatient for your own good. Slow down. You'll get it all done.* Yes, she would—but would she get it done in *time?* She was still fighting a relentless deadline, but if she hoped to succeed, she *had* to do things their way. *If only you hadn't gotten sick, you bastard . . .* But he had. And like Sven Bailey's relentless personality, there was nothing she could do to change that. She could only adapt and incorporate the fact into her plans.

Margo drew several deep breaths. "Okay. All right. I'm sorry. Mom always told me I was in a tearing rush to do everything, even when I was learning to crawl. I'll do better. I promise." She tried a sweet smile and knew she'd succeeded when a little of the darkness left his scowl. "Okay, Mr. Bailey, how am I supposed to stand? Show me."

Sven put her in position, then began to talk— surprisingly enough, about something besides breathing and strengthening her wrists.

"The idea we have in mind is to give you a broad foundation in unarmed combat before we move to armed combat. No, Margo, sink down a little further, that's right, hold it. If you rely on the weapon alone, without backup layers of self-defense, you risk being caught helpless if you lose use of the weapon. Whether you're carrying a firearm, a knife, some kind of chemical, or a club, you need to have other layers of protection in your defenses. One layer is alertness. If you don't notice an attacker, he'll take you by surprise. And once that happens, you're in trouble. For the next twenty-four hours, I want you to practice a little game. Tomorrow, tell me how well you do. See how many times you notice someone before they're aware of you and how many times they notice you first. Keep a record and we'll talk more about alertness tomorrow."

For once, Margo could see the immediate usefulness

of the lesson. She vowed to score a hundred percent on this particular test. Nobody would catch her napping.

"All right, shift your stance like this. Good. Now . . . one reason to stay alert. Suppose you have a gun."

Margo nodded. "Okay."

Sven backed up at least twenty feet. "I've got a knife." He brandished a closed hand as though holding a knife in a fencing grip. "Lady, I'm gonna cut your throat. Draw from your holster and shoot me."

He rushed at her. Margo grabbed for her hip, pretending to go for a gun—

And landed hard on her back. Sven's hand slashed her throat.

She widened her eyes. "Hey! No fair!"

"There's no such thing as fair, girl." He let her up. "Get back into your stance. Remember, a man armed with a knife can cover twenty feet faster than you can draw a gun. Keep your distance from potential threats and stay alert."

Quite suddenly, the game wasn't so funny.

Margo reassumed her stance. "What else?"

"Forget everything you've ever seen in movies. I'm talking martial arts, knives, fistfights, or guns. Movies are crap. They'll get you killed. A knife fight is likelier to leave you dead than a gunfight—dead or crippled— if you don't know exactly what you're doing. Know how to use your weapon. Ann will teach you projectile weapons: firearms, archery, even blowguns. I'll teach you the rest. Getting tired? Good. Next, you fall."

And she did, too. Repeatedly. Sven taught her a better way to fall than her karate instructors had ever shown her. By the time Sven was satisfied that Margo had at least learned how to fall down, she was shaking with exhaustion and covered with sweat.

"Okay," Sven finally told her, "shower and change into fresh clothes. Ann's waiting for you on the range."

Margo held back a groan and scraped herself off the

mat. Malcolm Moore abandoned a *kata* of his own and intercepted her halfway across the gym.

"Please," Margo said, holding out both hands to ward him off, "don't rub it in."

"No hard feelings." He smiled, surprising her with the friendliness in his eyes, and held out one hand. She shook it warily. "Really, Margo," he said with a self-conscious laugh, "you pointed out how badly I need to practice. I've been lax lately. Thanks for reminding me to get back in shape."

"Oh. Well, you're welcome."

"Sven gave you a hard time." It wasn't a question.

His friendly smile prompted a heartfelt response. "All he let me do was breathe, stand in one place, and fall down!"

Malcolm grinned. "I can think of worse things he might have made you do."

Much to her surprise, Margo found herself laughing. "Well, yeah, I guess that's true." She nodded toward the shower. "I, uh, have to get cleaned up. I'm supposed to learn how to shoot."

Her lack of enthusiasm must have communicated itself to Malcolm Moore, because he chuckled. "I'll make a wager with you. An hour from now, you'll be singing a different tune. In fact, I'll bet you enjoy it so much by the end of the week, you'll be sneaking in to practice when you're supposed to be studying math."

Margo rose to the challenge with glee. "That's a bet! What'll you wager?"

Malcolm grinned again. "Me? Hell, Margo, I'm broke."

She laughed. "Me, too."

"Okay, how about something besides money?"

"Like what?" She was abruptly wary.

Malcolm blinked, clearly taken aback for a moment by her tone. Margo gave herself a mental kick. Malcolm wasn't Billy Pandropolous or even Skeeter Jackson. Kit

Carson wouldn't trust him if he were, for one thing, and he wasn't like any guy Margo had ever met, for another.

"Well," he said slowly, "about the only thing I have to offer is guide services. I could take you down time to London—if Kit agreed to pay for the tickets," he added hastily.

Margo's pulse started to pound. *Down time to London? Oh, please . . .* But what to wager in return? And would Kit Carson say yes even if she won the bet?

"All right, one down-time trip with all the trimmings against . . ." She swallowed and risked it. "What do you want?"

Malcolm eyed her thoughtfully. Margo braced herself for the worst. But Malcolm Moore didn't say "An hour in my bedroom" or anything even remotely close to that. "How about your life story?"

"Huh?"

"Well . . . " That nice smile of his made her feel warm and funny inside. "How else do people get to be friends, if they don't know anything about one another?"

But . . .

Her life story? She turned away. "There's not much to tell." To her horror, her voice wobbled.

He touched her arm gently. "Margo, I'm sorry. I didn't mean to pry. I just thought it might be nice to get to know you."

She wrapped both arms around herself and wondered about that. Was she a person worth getting to know? Her father had certainly never thought so. Billy Pandropolous had—for reasons of his own, involving sex and cold, hard cash and a booming market for pretty young things fresh from Minnesota. But Malcolm wasn't like that. Was he? Billy had seemed nice at first, too. Or maybe Malcolm was just looking for a chink in the armor, to get even? It was silly of her, perhaps, but she didn't think so.

But tell Malcolm about her father's drunken rages? Or finding her mother and a stranger she'd never seen beaten to death on the kitchen and living room floors? Or running for New York the second she turned sixteen to try and earn the cash to find her grandfather, only to land in Billy Pandropolous' loving hands?

She blinked back tears. Well, she could always lie.

"Okay," she said reluctantly. "I guess it wouldn't be much of a bet if I didn't have an incentive to win?"

He smiled. "True enough. Do we have a deal?"

She shook his hand. "Deal. And now I really do have to go. I don't want to keep a teacher waiting."

"Mind if I watch? Or would I make you nervous?"

Margo thought about it and decided she really didn't mind. "No, I think maybe I'd feel a little less nervous if I had a friendly face around."

"Scared of guns?" he asked sympathetically.

"Well, wouldn't you be?"

Malcolm chuckled. "You've been watching the evening news too much. Get showered. I'll tell Ann it's my fault you're late."

"Thanks."

"Don't mention it."

Irrationally, Margo felt better as she headed for the showers. Maybe—just maybe—she'd found her first real friend.

Hearing protectors and range glasses were mandatory on TT-86's firing line. The range was indoors, of necessity. One lane was a hundred yards long, designed for high-power rifles as well as rimfire rifles, shotguns, and pistols, but most of the lanes were ten yards long, about the right distance for most personal defense training. La-La Land's weapons trainers dreamed of a three-hundred-yard lane, but the cost for that much space was just too high. There were no clay pigeons to shoot at, no cute little metal animals or numbered bull's-eyes. All targets were either blank sheets of paper, human silhouettes, or plain, circular steel plates. Other time terminals which boasted safari tours included animal-shaped targets marked with kill zones.

Ann Vinh Mulhaney's targets were marked with kill zones, too: centered around the human torso and braincase.

Margo looked a little green already. Malcolm, lounging comfortably on a bench nearby, felt sorry for her.

"Get used to it," Ann told her. "Time scouting is not a picnic."

"So everybody keeps telling me," Margo said with a shaky little laugh that didn't fool anyone.

"Did anyone talk about the dangers of tangling with people who can't be killed down time?"

Margo nodded. "Last night, yes."

"Good. People who are critical to history can often be . . . dissuaded . . . even if they can't be killed. Self-defense is a dangerous proposition at best, but self-defense down time is really tricky, because you never know if what you try will actually work. So it's good to have a variety of options—fast legs, the ability to ride horses or drive a harnessed team, a good grounding in martial arts. Remember, the first lesson of self-defense is—"

"Avoid the situation in the first place," Margo sighed. "That's what Sven said."

"Then you'd better remember it. All right. A gun is only one layer of your defense. But if you're going down time, it's useful to know how to use one. You won't carry one with you, because you'll never know whether or not a firearm will be an anachronism there. But once you get where you're going, you may need to pick one up in a hurry, if they exist. Firearms have changed a lot since their invention in the 1300's. So we're going to start with something simple and fairly modern, something easy to shoot, just to get you used to marksmanship principles. Once I'm convinced you can hit what you're shooting at, I'll start teaching you historical firearms all the way back to the early pole guns. You're going to have homework, too."

Margo groaned and looked to Malcolm for support.

He grinned and shrugged. "Can't learn without studying. Remember, I already have my Ph.D. and I spend my spare time studying everything I can get my hands on."

Margo managed a smile that looked a little strained. "All right. *What* will I be studying?"

"Principles of safety. Types of mechanical actions. Types of ammunition. How to load and unload. How various specific firearms function and differ from one another."

"Yuck."

"You could always find another career," Ann said sweetly.

"So show me!"

To Margo's horror, her "shooting lesson" began with a three-hour NRA course on basic safety. Granted, her teacher covered several basic types of modern guns, too, but she was required to pay attention while Ann Mulhaney just stood there and talked, showed her photographs and models, and repeated "Keep the muzzle pointed in a safe direction; keep your finger off the trigger until you're ready to shoot; and keep the action open and the gun unloaded until it's ready for use" so many times Margo thought she'd go mad.

"All right, what's the first safety principle?"

"Keep the damned thing pointed in a safe direction!"

"That being?"

"Away from what I don't want to shoot. My foot. The neighbor's window. Not up, if there's a second floor to the building I'm in, or down if I'm upstairs somewhere." Margo crossed her arms. "When do I get to shoot?"

"Later. Let me see you de-cock that single-action revolver again."

Margo fumbled the job three times before she got it right. She grinned in proud relief when she finally managed it correctly.

"Remember, a lot of these older-style guns and some of the modern ones have no mechanical hammer blocks, Margo. Screw this up with a loaded single-action that *doesn't* have a way to block the hammer from striking the firing pin, and you'll have an accidental discharge. If it's pointed at your stomach—" Ann forcibly moved the muzzle away from Margo's middle "—you'll end up gutshot."

Margo's sense of accomplishment dissolved. She felt like crying. First Kit had roughed her up, then Sven had *hurt* her, and now Ann Mulhaney was making her look like a dangerous fool. "I'm sorry! I'm tired and hungry. . . ."

Ann said shortly, "Get used to it, Margo. You won't have the luxury of choosing the time and place for a gunfight to save your life."

She wanted to scream. Instead she tried to reason with her tormentor. "Yes, but I could choose the time and place for the lessons! How am I supposed to learn this stuff when I'm beat on my feet? Don't you people ever *eat?*"

Her tummy rumbled in echo. Malcolm Moore must've heard it, too, because he chuckled.

Ann sighed and smiled ruefully, then retrieved the Colt Army single-action pistol. "All right, Margo, point taken. Eight o'clock tomorrow morning and don't be late this time. I have other lessons tomorrow besides yours."

Margo wanted to collapse right where she was. "I'll be here."

Where she'd find food, Margo had no idea. She didn't have enough money even for a hotdog.

"Well," Malcolm said on their way out of the gym, "what do you think?"

"You haven't won your bet yet," Margo said sourly.

He laughed easily. "I have until the end of the week, remember? That gives me a couple of days. How about lunch?"

"I'm broke. I mean really, truly broke. I think I have ten cents to my name."

"Where are you staying?"

"On a couch in Kit's living room."

The chagrin in her voice caused Malcolm to chuckle. "How come you never call him 'Grandpa' or 'Grandfather'?" He watched curiously for her reaction. She looked uncomfortable. It took her a moment to answer.

"Well . . . he's not exactly the kind of person it's easy to call that."

Malcolm drew his own conclusions. "He scares you."

She glanced up swiftly. The little-girl vulnerability in her eyes shocked Malcolm nearly speechless. Then the moment passed and the flippant "who cares" look was back. "Nothing scares me."

Malcolm stopped several feet short of the elevator, causing Margo to stop short as well.

"What?" she wailed. "What'd I do now?"

"Margo," he said gently, "if nothing scares you, then I may not have very long to get to know you. And that's sad. Sadder than you can know."

A tiny vertical line appeared between manicured brows the color of bright new flames. She studied him with frank curiosity, head tip-tilted to one side like a canary faced with an unknown beast beyond its wire cage. It occurred to Malcolm that she was very, very young and trying desperately to hide it. Hard on the heels of that thought was another: *She's been roughed up by life already. Dammit, she's too young to look like that. What the hell happened to this kid before she found Kit?* The interest he felt turned suddenly protective.

Margo sighed, which prevented him from saying

anything he might have later regretted. "You're odd, Malcolm," she said slowly.

"Am I?"

"Yes. You . . . ." She didn't finish.

I don't hit on you like the other boys? Is that it?

Or maybe, considering the wary tension in her body, it wasn't just boys her own age who'd . . .

Malcolm forced his thoughts into less private realms of speculation. "How about some lunch? I have sandwich fixings in my fridge. We could meet somewhere for a picnic on the Commons. Unless you have another lesson?"

Margo relaxed fractionally. "Not that I know of," she said a trifle ruefully. "A picnic on the Commons sounds nice. I . . . " She broke off abruptly.

"What?"

She mumbled something that sounded like "Never mind" and avoided his gaze.

Malcolm touched her shoulder very gently. "Hey. It's me, remember? The guy you wiped up the mat with?"

Almost as though disobeying a stern command to stay downturned, a corner of her lips quirked upward. She sniffed once. "Huh. I gotta beat up a guy before he'll ask me out?"

Malcolm laughed. "No, but it ought to give you a little peace of mind, knowing you can."

She gave him an odd look, then both corners of her lips twitched upwards.

"That's better," he smiled. "Why don't you find a nice spot somewhere in Castletown, maybe by one of the garden pools. We'll have a quiet lunch."

Her smile brightened. "All right. You know, that sounds wonderful. Thanks, Malcolm."

"My pleasure."

He held the elevator door with a courtly flourish that brought sparkling laughter to her eyes. *That* brought a sense of dismay to Malcolm's determination to remain an utter gentleman. He could fall for this kid—hard—without much trouble at all. Margo got off at the Commons level with a cheery smile and headed toward Castletown. Malcolm watched her go, then punched the button for his floor. Whatever that little girl was hiding inside, it was hurting her. He'd started out the week feeling sorry for Kit. Now he felt sorry for them both.

"Well," he told himself philosophically as the elevator rose with an efficient whir, "looks like another job for Mr. Fix-It." He just hoped Kit's granddaughter didn't get them all into a jam they couldn't untangle. Given what he'd seen so far, she could wreak havoc just by breathing.

She could also break Kit's heart without even trying.

The insight left him with a chill chasing itself down his back. Malcolm made himself a promise, then and there: *I'll do whatever I can—whatever Margo and Kit will let me—to keep that from happening.*

Where that promise might lead him, Malcolm didn't even want to consider.

CHAPTER EIGHT

Kit was looking for ways to avoid finishing a stack of bills when he spotted Margo on one of the real-time screens on his office video wall. She was sitting beside a pebbled fishpond in Edo Castletown, staring into the water and looking so vulnerable and alone, Kit felt his heart thump.

He shoved back his chair and headed downstairs, pausing only long enough to slip on shoes. He didn't even change out of the vintage kimono he habitually wore while working. Kit wasn't sure what he'd say to her, but maybe the excuse of just getting to know her better would suffice. She was trailing one fingertip in the clear water when he arrived.

"Hi."

She glanced up. Her eyes widened slightly. "Good Lord. You're wearing a kimono?"

Kit grinned. "I'm running away from paperwork. I, uh, usually try and wear the most comfortable thing I own when I have to tackle stacks of bills or government forms. Mind if I join you?"

"Oh. Sure."

"Such enthusiasm," he tut-tutted, settling down beside her.

She tucked knees under chin and stared at the colorful fish. "I'm tired," she admitted, "and hungry. Malcolm thought it might be nice to eat a couple of sandwiches on the Commons. So I picked a spot."

"Malcolm?"

She grimaced. "He watched my lessons today."
Ahh . . .

They fell silent for a few moments, just watching the fish make lazy circles above artistically arranged slate-blue pebbles. Finally Margo glanced up sidewise. "You don't like paperwork much?"

Kit rubbed his nose. "No. Tops a whole list of things I loathe."

She smiled. "I guess everybody's got their own list, huh?"

"What's on yours?"

She rested chin on knees again. "Oh, stuff."

"Like for instance?"

"I dunno. Snow, for one. Minnesota winters suck. Snow gets old real fast. Especially when you're too old to make snow angels in it. All that's left is cussing because the roads are closed and you're late to wherever it is you need to be."

Kit smiled. "You sound eighteen going on forty-two." She stuck out her tongue, prompting a chuckle. "I was twenty, you know, before I saw more than a quarter inch all at one time."

"You're from Georgia. Doesn't snow much."

"Just what do you know about me? I mean, besides what's in all the tabloids?"

Margo grinned. "They're awful, aren't they? I think my favorite was the one where you were abducted by mad scientists from way, way up time and they altered your sex and you got pregnant and then they changed your sex back and sent you home after you had the baby."

"Oh, good God, you're kidding?"

Her eyes twinkled. "Nope. They even had a picture, you were out to here." She indicated a very pregnant stomach. "I love what they can do with computer graphics programs, don't you? The little old ladies that buy those things in the grocery stores actually believed it."

Kit just groaned. "I knew there was a reason I didn't go up time much these days."

Margo chuckled.

Kit decided the time was right, but he hesitated anyway, reluctant to destroy their fragile rapport. "Margo . . . ."

She looked up again. "Yeah?"

"Would you tell me about my . . . I don't even know if I have a son or a daughter."

The sparkle vanished from Margo's green eyes. She swallowed and turned her face away. "Daughter. You had a daughter."

"*Had?*"

Margo wouldn't look at him. "Mom died. A few years ago."

The ache of losing something he'd never had a chance to cherish left Kit struggling against sudden tightness in his chest. He blinked rapidly several times, fighting a salty sting behind his eyelids. *How* had Kit's only child died? His daughter . . . She couldn't have been very old, if she'd died several years ago. An auto accident? Catastrophic illness?

"What was her name?" Kit whispered, trying to keep his voice steady. "What did she look like?"

Margo didn't answer for a moment. Then, in a low voice, "Mom's name was Kitty."

Quicksilver pain flashed through him. Sarah had actually named their child *Kitty*—

"She had hazel eyes. Kind of sandy-colored hair. When I was a little girl she laughed a lot. Look, I know . . . I know you want to hear about this and I want to tell you, but—" She blinked rapidly. Kit realized quite abruptly his grandchild, too, was on the verge of tears.

"Margo?"

She turned away again. "I was the one who found her. Can we talk about something else? Please?"

How old had Margo been when her mother died?

Kit wanted to ask a thousand questions, but Margo wasn't ready to answer them.

"What about your grandmother?" Kit tried, remembering with cutting clarity the last time he'd seen Sarah.

Margo sniffed. "I've never seen her. Mom ran away with Dad when she was seventeen. I'm not sure Grandma van Wyyck even knew where Mom was or that we existed. I . . . I had a picture. But everything I had was stolen. In New York. I even had to buy new shoes."

Kit, too, mourned that photograph's loss. "What was the picture like? How did she look? Did she seem happy?"

Margo seemed to come back from someplace even farther away than Kit had been. She studied him for a long moment. "You're still in love with her. Aren't you?"

Kit managed a pained smile. "Does it show?"

"Well, you're crying."

"Am I?" He swiped at his cheeks. "Damn . . ."

Margo dug in a pocket and held out his hanky. She'd laundered it somewhere. "Here."

Kit managed a shaky laugh. "Thanks, imp. You've rescued my reputation as an unflappable time scout."

She started to say something, then stopped.

"What? Whatever it is, say it. Or ask it."

Margo frowned. "It's nothing much. Just . . . Everything I ever heard or read . . . Mom used to say you grew up a dirt-poor Georgia boy, had to scrap and fight for everything you had. I used to think about that, sometimes. It made me proud, knowing you'd made it, but . . . I always thought . . ."

"You thought I ran out on Sarah van Wyyck? Because she stood in the way of my plans?"

She flushed, but her silence answered the question.

"I loved your grandmother very much, Margo. But

sometimes even when people love one another, they have different dreams, different goals. Your grandmother's life and mine . . . it didn't work. Probably never would have worked. But I still loved her, even when she left me."

Margo's eyes widened. "*She* left *you?*"

Kit cleared his throat. "At the risk of sounding like my granddaughter, mind if we talk about something else?"

Margo blinked. Then she said, "I guess we all have stuff it hurts too much to talk about, huh?"

"Yeah. I guess we do."

She gave him a funny little smile. "Did you ever go back to Georgia?"

"No. I didn't really see much point. You plan on going back someday? To Minnesota?"

Her face hardened. "Yeah. I do. But not for very long."

"Unfinished business?"

She sniffed. "Something like that." She shook herself slightly. "Anyway, that's about it for my life's history. I had a twin brother, but he was killed in the big quakes caused by *The Accident*. That's when my folks left California and moved to Minnesota. I don't really remember it. I was just a baby." She shrugged. "I grew up, left home, came here. The rest isn't worth telling."

Kit thought it would have been, but didn't want to press the issue. He'd already learned more than he'd dared hope. A daughter, a grandson—both lost to him— and a granddaughter who didn't like snow and thought tabloids were stupid and was the kind of person who'd go back and settle old scores. Or maybe debts. Just what sort of unfinished business did she have and with whom? She was hardly old enough to have made the kind of enemies Kit had occasionally made.

An affair of the heart, maybe, despite her protestations that she hadn't been jilted. A man didn't have to jilt a girl to make her want to come back and settle affairs. Sometimes all he had to do was fail to notice. Or fail to act. Or maybe it was simply that she needed to repay someone who'd helped her buy that ticket to New York. Or . . .

Maybe someday she'd trust him enough to tell the rest.

Kit spotted Malcolm heading their way from Residential, an honest-to-goodness picnic basket slung over one arm, and decided to let his granddaughter have her picnic without Grandpa hanging around. "Well, here comes your lunch date. I guess I'd better tackle that paperwork. Just do the fish a favor and don't flip Malcolm into the pond between the sandwiches and the desserts?"

The sparkle came back to Margo's eyes. "Okay. Although after what Sven did to me, I don't think I could flip a soda straw into the fish pond."

Kit rumpled her hair affectionately. "Good. Proves you're doing it right. See you at dinner, imp."

Her smile brightened his whole mood. "Okay."

Kit returned Malcolm's wave, then headed back up to his office. Very deliberately, Kit switched the camera view on one particular video screen, leaving his grandkid her privacy. Besides, with Malcolm Moore as chaperon he didn't really have anything to worry about. Kit chuckled, recalling the full-blown panic in Skeeter Jackson's eyes when he'd cornered *that* worthy and made matters crystal clear, then settled down to the bills in a better frame of mind than he'd enjoyed in days.

Two days into Margo's weapons training, Kit started getting bad news. First came the altercation on Commons when a drunken tourist accosted her. She flipped him straight into a fishpond, almost as though deliberately recalling his advice not to toss Malcolm into one. Bull Morgan had not been amused when the drunken idiot turned out to be a billionaire who threatened to sue. Fortunately, Margo'd had plenty of witnesses for Kit to counter-threaten with sexual assault charges. The billionaire had slunk away down time on his tour, muttering into his expensively manicured beard.

Kit told Margo, "Next time, try not to dislocate shoulders or drown importunate perverts. Nothing excuses his behavior, but there's such a thing as overreaction."

She had sulked for hours. He supposed he couldn't blame her. Frankly, if he'd been there, the jerk might've suffered more than a wrenched shoulder and a publicly humiliating dunking into a goldfish pond. But as a scout in training, she had to learn self-control and alternative methods of extricating herself from sticky situations.

Then he checked in with Ann and Sven.

"She has the attention span of a two-year-old," Ann Vinh Mulhaney complained. "Either she doesn't want to learn or she's afraid of the guns."

"She wants to learn, all right," Kit said grimly. "But she wouldn't admit to fear of a live cobra in her shower stall if she thought I'd halt her training over it."

Ann frowned. "That's not good."

"I know."

Kit ran a hand through his hair. After their heart-to-heart by the fishpond, Kit knew it would be doubly—triply—difficult if he had to tell Margo her dreams weren't going to come true. His heart was still in his throat just thinking about letting her scout. He didn't know what he'd do if he lost her, too. But he wanted as much as any other grandfather on the planet to make his grandchild happy. If he had to tell her two days into training that it was hopeless . . .

"Is there any hope?"

The tiny firearms instructor hesitated. "Well . . . maybe. Her hand is very steady and she has a good eye. When she's actually shooting, she scores well. But she won't apply herself to the *learning*. Has she been doing her homework?"

Kit frowned. "Homework? Not unless she's doing it in the library. She drags in like a half-dead cat, gulps supper, then collapses for the night. I didn't think it was possible to wear out an eighteen-year-old."

Ann didn't smile. "She needs to study. She keeps forgetting basics, like working the pump on the pump shotgun. Then she gets angry with herself when it won't function like a semiautomatic. The double-action revolver isn't a problem, but the self-loading pistols . . ." Ann just shuddered. "I haven't even tried historical firearms yet. I don't dare."

"Great. I'll start working her on basic firearms mechanical actions while she eats."

"Good. She needs it."

The story was much the same from Sven. The stocky martial arts instructor saw him coming from across the weapons range, clearly considered ducking out the nearest exit, then visibly braced himself.

"That bad?" Kit asked without preamble.

"Kit," Sven growled, "you got a big problem in that kid."

"You don't need to tell me that. All I get these days is trouble. Let me guess. She won't apply herself to the learning."

"Oh, no," Sven shook his shaggy head. "She's nuts to absorb the stuff, fast as I can teach her. And she's good, for a novice. Problem is, her attitude stinks."

"What about her attitude?" Kit asked tiredly. "In a thousand words or less."

Sven's evil grin came and went. "Rough, is it? *Teenagers.* If they weren't so cute, we'd drown 'em."

"The cuter they are, the bigger the occasional desire to hold their heads underwater. So what *is* Margo's problem?"

"No patience, no *feel* for Aikido. She just wants to make the moves like an automaton and hurry on to something else. Kit, that kid is in one damned big hurry to do *something* and I'm not sure it'll be healthy once she does it."

Great. Sven was waxing philosophical about his only grandkid, who was in a tearing *hurry* to die. He wondered if her impatience were part of her general personality, part of that mysterious unfinished business she'd mentioned, or just eagerness to get past the lessons and into something she could consider an adventure?

"Maybe she just wants to get down time," Kit sighed. "In her place, I would. Here she is on TT-86 watching the tourists go places she can't and all I let her do is read books and take lumps from you and Ann."

Sven pursed his lips, looking faintly like a thoughtful bulldog. "Could be, I guess. She's young, wants an adventure. Maybe you should give it to her. Settle her down."

"Give her an adventure?" Kit echoed. "You mean send her down time? Before she's ready?"

Sven shrugged. "Sure. Why not? I'm not talking about a scouting trip. Send her on a tour. Britannia Gate's due to open soon. Outfit her for a tourist jaunt and send the kid to London for a few days. Might take the itch out of her trousers, give her a taste of what it is she's letting herself in for."

"I can't go with her," Kit pointed out unhappily.

Sven's sympathetic glance didn't help much. "Stinks," he agreed. "So send Malcolm. He owes her a guided tour, anyway."

Kit sharpened his gaze. "He what?"

Sven widened his eyes innocently, then chuckled. "Well, now, so Grandpa *doesn't* know all. I'm disappointed—and surprised you hadn't heard. They made a bet. Malcolm thought she'd end up liking the shooting, she said she wouldn't. They bet on it."

"What in God's name did they bet? Margo's broke. I know. I won't give her an allowance until she's earned one."

Kit trusted Malcolm as far as any man would with a granddaughter who looked and behaved the way Margo did; but he couldn't imagine what she might have wagered—and given the effect she had on men, he knew the male libido well enough to imagine the worst, even from Malcolm.

Sven patted his shoulder. "Not to worry. Scuttlebutt has it she bet her life story against a guided tour."

"Her life story? Huh." The rest of Margo's life story was something *Kit* would have paid a ransom to hear. "Too bad Malcolm lost."

Sven grinned. "You said it. There'll be other bets. I'll start her on bladed weapons next, but I'd like her to settle down before then. Think about the Britannia Gate. Might do her some good."

"Yeah," Kit said glumly, thinking about that billionaire and the fish pond. "But will it do the rest of us any good?"

Sven just laughed at him. "Your grey's showing, Grandpa. How about a sparring session?"

Kit considered it, then shook his head. "No, I think I'll take your advice. Which means I'd better hunt up Malcolm before he accepts a job to Mongolia or someplace equally improbable. Thanks, Sven."

"Don't mention it."

Kit found the freelance guide working the newcomers who planned to do the London trip. He waited until a curvaceous young thing had turned him down, then approached while Malcolm was looking bluer than a well-aged round of Roquefort cheese.

"Any luck?"

Malcolm grimaced. "Nope. Time Tours is getting nasty about sharing business with freelancers."

Kit made a mental note to "lean" a little on Granville Baxter. There was enough money to be made for everyone. Malcolm's freelance business didn't hurt Time Tours' profits in the slightest. "Tell you what. I'd like to hire you."

Malcolm just stared. "*You?* For Pete's sake, why?"

Kit laughed. "Let's wet our throats someplace and talk business."

"Well, sure," Malcolm agreed readily. "Anytime you want to pick up the tab, Kit, you just holler."

The Prince Albert Pub was the handiest place to sit down and cool their thirst. The interior was a good bit cleaner than most genuine Victorian-era pubs, the prices were moderate for La-La Land, and the place was virtually empty in the post-lunch-hour vacuum. They found a table near the front windows and sat down.

"Have you eaten yet?" Kit asked, glancing at the menu. "I worked through lunch." Then he grinned sheepishly. "You're a good excuse. I'm playing hooky from paperwork day."

"Oh, ho," Malcolm chuckled, picking up his own menu. "Better not let Big Brother find out."

Kit grimaced. "Paperwork sucks," he said eloquently, half quoting Margo. "Hmm . . . I haven't had kippers in years."

"Never could abide them."

"A Victorian time guide *and* a born Brit and you can't abide kippers? What's the world coming to?"

"A better sense of what's edible, hopefully."

Kit laughed. "Then for God's sake, don't order lunch in medieval Edo."

Malcolm shuddered. "Once was enough to convince me, thank you. I'll stick to steak and kidneys, any day of the week."

"Beats some of what I've eaten," Kit agreed. He set his menu down and flagged a waitress. They ordered lunch and started emptying glasses of dark ale.

"So, what's on your mind?" Malcolm asked.

"Margo. What else?"

The younger man just grinned. "Anything in particular or everything in general? Or both?"

"Both, actually," Kit admitted, "but her lack of progress in her studies, particularly."

Malcolm's smile vanished. "She isn't stupid, Kit. What's the problem?"

"Sven thinks she's too hyped on going down time to concentrate."

The time guide sat back and fiddled with his ale glass, leaving a series of wet rings on the wooden tabletop. "He could be right," Malcolm said slowly. "That probably isn't all of it, but he could have something, there. Going down time is all she talks about."

"How much time are you spending with her?"

Malcolm flushed. "Not enough to warrant that tone, Kit. But I worry about her. I figure if she's with me, she's not falling prey to someone like Skeeter. And you know we get sharks through here every time Primary opens."

Kit knew. He relaxed. "Yeah, don't we just? Any feel for how she's coming with her lessons? Ann and Sven are underwhelmed."

Malcolm shook his head. "No, we don't talk much about her studies, not the bookwork part of them. Mostly she asks questions about my experiences down time or what I know about *yours*. She's . . ." He hesitated.

"She's what?"

"I don't know. Guarded, I guess. She doesn't let the thorns down long, if you catch my drift."

"Tell me about it. She sleeps on my couch, eats my food, showers in my bathroom, and about the only thing I can get her to relax and talk about is how much fun it is living in La-La Land. Do you have any idea how many obscure television celebrities that girl knows by sight?"

Malcolm chuckled. "Really? Well, she did want to be an actress. But then, what little girl didn't at some point in life? As I recall, my sisters went through the 'I'll die if I'm not an actress' phase shortly after the

'I'll die if I don't have a horse' phase and the 'I'll die if I'm not an Olympic figure skater' phase."

Kit grinned. "I didn't have any sisters. Sounds like I missed out on all the fun. But seriously, Margo and I have had only one real heart-to-heart since she's been here and what I found out then . . ." He shook his head. "She's so full of hurt, she doesn't want to talk about any of the million or so silly little details I'd give the Neo Edo to know."

Malcolm sighed. "I figured as much. What are—" He paused, visible startlement passing over his mobile features, then pressed a hand to the back of his ear. "There's no gate due to cycle—is there?"

Kit felt it too: that subharmonic sensation which heralded a gate opening nearby. Whatever it was, it was out of phase—and from the feel of it, this was one *big* gate.

"New gate!"

"Right!"

They scrambled for the door and all but collided with the Prince Albert's owner. "Where is it?" Peg Ames demanded breathlessly. She was holding her head. "Mother Bear, that's going to be a big gate. That *hurts*."

It did, too, much worse than the Porta Romae—which was La-La Land's biggest active gate. 'Eighty-sixers converged on the Commons at a dead run from storefronts, even from residential corridors. Several carried scanners designed to search for the unstable fields that heralded a gate's arrival in the temporal-spatial continuum. Tourists looked bewildered. They huddled in groups, holding their ears. A klaxon's strident *SKRONNK!* echoed off girders and concrete walls in a mad rhythm. Someone had sounded the special alert siren activated only during station emergencies. Last time that siren had sounded, the semi-permanent unstable gate under the Shermans' coffee shop had endangered the lives of more than a dozen rescue workers.

Station Security converged from various points around the Commons. Several men and women in innocuous grey uniforms arrived in their wake, carrying everything from capture nets to tranquilizer rifles and riot shotguns. Discreet black lettering across grey uniform pockets read *Pest Control*. Their stalwart corps had risen considerably in status ever since an outbreak of Black Death on TT-13—and that wooly rhinoceros fiasco on TT-51—had been traced to station managers' refusals to pay for adequate pest control services. *Nobody* argued now with anything a Pest Control officer requisitioned.

Bull Morgan, a stocky man who wore his suit like a casino pit boss wore a scowl, shouldered his way through the crowd, a fireplug on legs. Worry had creased his brow above a nose broken in one too many fist fights. Mike Benson, head of La-La Land's security, followed in the Station Manager's wake, blue eyes narrowed as he scanned the air for the first telltale sign of the new gate's location. He spoke urgently into a walkie-talkie.

Bull high-signed someone with a scanner. "Has anybody—?"

"Oh, shit!"

A dozen scanners were pointed straight upward.

Then the ceiling opened up. A chronometer board vanished into blackness. The air dopplered through the whole visible spectrum in a chaotic display. Kit clamped hands over his ears in reflex action, even though the gesture did nothing to damp out the sound that wasn't a sound. Everyone—tourists and 'eighty-sixers alike—backed away from the area, leaving wrought-iron benches empty near the center of Victoria Station. The gate widened, ragged and pulsating unsteadily near the edges. It shrank visibly, then expanded with a rush like an oncoming freight train, only to collapse back toward its center again just as fast.

It didn't take a sophisticated scanner to determine this gate's condition. It was *visible* to the naked eye.

"Unstable!" Malcolm shouted.

Kit just nodded and hoped to hell nothing fell through it from a height of five stories. Even the floor pulsed angrily in the backlash of subharmonics. The gate widened savagely once more. Blackness swallowed more and more of the ceiling, crept outward and engulfed the upper level of the nearest wall, taking catwalks with it. *Biggest damned gate I've ever seen.* . . .

Ragged light flared: lightning bolts against a backdrop of black storm clouds, seen in miniature through the gate's distortion. For a split second, Kit glimpsed what looked for all the world like a rain-lashed seacoast. Then driving rain spilled into TT-86. Tourists broke and ran for cover under the nearest storefronts. Kit narrowed his eyes against the sudden deluge. Another wild gust of rain burst through, soaking them to the skin. He lifted a hand to protect his eyes—

Something enormous crashed through.

"LOOK OUT!"

Whatever it was, it let out a scream like a frightened schoolgirl then plunged five stories toward the floor. Kit threw himself backward as it dropped straight toward them. A long, sinuous body impacted messily less than three feet away.

A gout of blood and entrails spattered Malcolm. "Aw, bloody *damn!*"

Another drenching gust of rain blasted through the gate, washing spattered onlookers clean. A trail of gore and broken bone stretched twenty feet across cracked cobblestones and smashed benches. Before Kit could cast more than a cursory glance at it, another dark shape dove through. This one was winged.

"Holy—"

A defiant scream like bending metal echoed through the Commons. A smaller winged shape darted through the black madness, then another and another, until a whole seething flock of wildly gyrating winged things darted frantically amongst the girders. Lightning sizzled through and struck a catwalk near the fourth floor. Blue fire danced across steel gridwork. Thunder smashed through the station, shattering upper-level windows. Glass tinkled in sharp slivers on the cobbles.

Then the gate collapsed.

It vanished, almost in the blink of a stunned eyelash. A final drizzle of rain drifted down in a bewildered sort of mist to settle into forlorn puddles. Silence—profound and complete—reigned for a full heartbeat. Then someone pointed and someone else screamed. An enormous shape with leathery wings skimmed low above the crowd. Kit dove instinctively for the floor.

My God . . .

Its wingspan was nearly the size of a Learjet's. It snapped a long, sharp beak with a clacking sound like striking two-by-fours and passed less than a foot above the nearest "streetlamp."

This time, 'eighty-sixers broke and ran. A silver underbelly caught the lights as it winged around toward the ceiling. Dark markings in black and grey mottled its back and wings. An enormous, broad vertical crest was patterned like a moth's wings, with huge eyespots and scarlet streaks. It snapped at a tourist on the third floor and narrowly missed her head. The woman screamed and hugged the catwalk. Pest Control tracked it with shotguns.

"DON'T SHOOT IT!" Bull yelled. "TAKE IT ALIVE!"

Half a dozen Pest Control officers swore, but dropped shotguns in favor of big capture nets. Kit scrambled up and grabbed the edge of the nearest net. Malcolm latched onto another section and lifted it in readiness for the beast's next pass.

"What is that thing?" a nearby Time Tours employee gasped.

The enormous animal soared toward the ceiling on thirty-foot wings, scraping a catwalk with one wingtip.

Sue Fritchey said calmly, "Looks like a *Pteranodon sternbergi* to me. Damned near as big as a Quetzalecoatlus—and that's the biggest pterodactyl we know about. That gate opened right into the Upper Cretaceous. Here it comes! Ready . . . wait . . . wait . . ."

Kit hung onto his nerve and faced down a lethally sharp beak as the giant pterosaur swooped directly toward them. The head and neck alone were longer than Sven Bailey was tall. Kit's lizard-brain, that portion of the human cranium that controls fight-or-flight reactions, was screaming "RUN!" at the top of its lungs.

Kit ignored it.

Sue was still cautioning them, "Wait . . . almost . . . almost . . . NOW!"

A dozen men heaved the big net. It tangled in leathery wings. Another net hit it, settling over the sharp beak and soaring crest. The huge pterodactyl came down hard in a mass of screaming, struggling beak, wings, and claws. Someone fired tranquilizers into it, three shots in rapid succession. Bull Morgan darted over to help hold the nets. A powerful wing lifted Kit off the ground then flung him back toward the shattered cobbles, but he hung onto the rope. Malcolm came loose and vanished from Kit's immediate awareness. Kit thought he heard a cry of pain and an explosive curse, but he was abruptly confronted by a baleful scarlet eye and a snapping, upcurved beak that severed half-inch hemp fibers like spaghetti strings.

One of the Pest Control officers darted in with a coil of rope and risked hands in order to rope the sharp beak shut. A twist of the pterosaur's neck lifted him off the floor and sent him flying, but the ropes around its beak held. The tiny crimson eye rolled murderously; then, slowly, that wicked little eye began to close. By the time the tranquilizers had taken effect, Kit was bruised and battered, but La-La Land had quite a zoological prize.

"Good work," Bull said, panting slightly. "What're those?"

He pointed toward the ceiling.

Sue Fritchey was studying the smaller winged figures—perched now amongst the rafters—through her field glasses. "Those over there are *Ichthyornis*, looks like. Little primitive birds, beak full of teeth, about the size of a seagull. Fish eaters. They'd be about the right time period and ecosystem to come through with a *sternbergi*. Must be twenty of 'em up there. And over there," she swung the glasses around, "we've got about fifteen little pterosaurs the size of crows. Hell, I have *no* idea what those are. Those, either." She'd swung the glasses around toward a pair sitting by themselves near the rafters. "They look like predators of some sort, but I'm not sure. *Could* be fish eaters, but the beaks look wrong. Far as I know, there's nothing in the fossil record anything like what I'm seeing."

"Are there enough of any of those things for a breeding colony?" Bull asked sharply.

"Maybe. Those two by themselves, probably not. Those pterosaurs, though, and the *Ichthyornis* flock . . . Close to critical failure of the gene pool, of course, but we've rescued species from that close to the brink. Depends on the number of breeding—or gravid—females up there. It's hard to sex birds without plumage differences to go by and I'm not seeing any. And I have no idea how to sex pterosaurs."

Nobody cracked the obvious jokes.

"Any danger to the tourists?" Bull asked, glancing unhappily at the damage and the white-faced tourists still cowering in storefronts.

"Dunno. Probably not, unless the animals feel threatened. I doubt they would unless somebody went after 'em. Birds, anyway, aren't as violently reactive as, say, killer bees, although the pterosaurs may be. Not as likely, but we just don't know."

"Then we don't disturb them until we get additional expert advice," Bull decided. "Next time Primary cycles, send for whoever you need. Those things eat fish? Okay, stock all the fish ponds in the station and keep 'em stocked. Watch the little buggers and let me know if they put anybody in danger. Well, more danger than being spattered with dinosaur droppings."

The Pest Control crews chuckled. Sue Fritchey said, "They're not dinosaurs, they're pterosaurs and proto-birds. But don't worry, we'll handle it."

Bull nodded, then glanced at Malcolm and Kit. "Thanks for the help, boys."

"Glad to pitch in," Kit smiled. "It's not every day even I get to wrestle a giant pterodactyl to the ground."

Bull chuckled. "Point taken. You all right, Malcolm?"

Kit looked around. The young guide was nursing his wrist. "Yeah, just bloody bruised."

Bull peered closely at the wrist, which was visibly swelling. "Have Rachel look at it and don't argue. My tab. I'll call her."

Malcolm sighed. "Thanks, Bull. Me and my lousy luck."

Kit grinned. "Don't think you get out of this job so easily."

Malcolm gave him a sour glance. "*What* job? You haven't even told me what it is, yet."

Kit formed a sling from Malcolm's shirt and suspended his wrist at chest height. "What I had in mind was nursemaiding Margo through the Britannia Gate."

Malcolm stared, then eased the sling into a more comfortable position. His eyes had already begun to glow. "Are you serious?"

"Dead serious. Speaking of dead, what the devil was that thing?" He jabbed a thumb at the creature which had fallen through the ceiling. Judging from the remains, it had been all teeth, tail, and claws. Several tourists had crowded closer already.

Sue Fritchey waded in. "Sickle-claw killer of some kind, about the size of Utahraptor, but a different species from the look of it. We didn't know they'd survived that late into the Cretaceous. Just be real glad it's dead."

Malcolm shivered absently. "Am I *ever*. Say, that thing is warm!" He leaned over for a better look.

Sure enough, heat was rising from the dead sickle-claw.

"Yep," Sue said, moving back after a cursory glance. "Get back, please."

"But, it's *warm!* Surely *you* can appreciate what this means for the scientific debate over ornithischian endothermy!"

Sue glared at him. "Yes, I do! I also appreciate that it's a cooling corpse. Its parasites are going to start leaving in droves—and I don't want *anyone* finding a tick the size of their own pinkie or a pinworm the size of a ballpoint pen! Jimmy, scour and disinfect this whole area!"

Malcolm moved hastily away. Tourists abandoned attempts to see the dead 'raptor and crowded around the netted pterodactyl instead. Pest Control was bringing up a forklift hoist and a large wooden pallet to transport it.

"C'mon, hero," Kit said, taking Malcolm's elbow. "Let's clean you up and look at that wrist." He steered Malcolm through the crowd and hustled him off to Rachel Eisenstein's infirmary. She fussed over the wrist, told him he'd sprained it heroically and warned him, "Don't tackle anything more strenuous than dinner for a couple of days, okay?" She suspended his injured wrist in a real sling. His shirt, retired from sling duty, had begun to dry, revealing tears and gore stains. The rest of him, however, was squeaky clean: Rachel had given him a *bath* in disinfectant and new clothes.

"Yes, ma'am." He saluted her with his unbandaged hand.

"Good," Rachel smiled. "Now, scoot. I have work to do. Some of the tourists were hurt during the ruckus and others are having hysterics. Unstable gates," she grimaced, "are not conducive to integrated psyches. Wish I'd been there to see it. Just my luck I was stuck on call and couldn't leave."

Kit sympathized, then they left Rachel to the demands of her profession. Once in the corridor, Kit said, "You never did answer. Are you game for the Britannia Gate?"

Malcolm chuckled thinly. "You should know without having to ask. Where shall I take her? A night at the opera? Or maybe a stay in the East End to discourage girlish romantic fantasies?"

"I leave that to your discretion and wisdom. I would suggest we collect my granddaughter, though, and head over to Connie Logan's. Kid'll need a good down-time kit."

Malcolm nodded. "Are we playing tourist for this trip or am I getting her ready for her role as disguised boy?"

Kit considered. "Again, use your discretion, but I'm inclined to think a little of both."

"So am I. I'll, uh, meet you at Connie's," he said. "In, say, fifteen or twenty? These pants Rachel gave me, uh, pinch."

"Make it the Prince Albert and we'll finish lunch before we collar her."

Malcolm grinned. "Whatever you say, boss! You may shower me with free food and money all you like."

Kit just snorted. "I'd tell you to go soak your head, but you already did. See you at the Albert."

Connie Logan's establishment was—in keeping with La-La Land's reputation—one of the true first-class Outfitters in the business. Connie was young for it, barely twenty-six, but she'd started with an advantage. A

theatrical aunt who'd owned a small touring company
had raised her in the business of historical costuming,
then died and left her with an inventory, a room full of
cloth waiting to be turned into historically accurate
clothing, considerable skill as a seamstress and designer,
and enough money to attract venture capital.

Connie Logan was sharp, creative, and a delight to
'eighty-sixers. They often laid wagers on what she'd be
seen wearing next. The sign over her doorway was short
but effective: CLOTHES AND STUFF. A few tourists were
stupid enough to prefer shops with fancier names, but
not many. On their way across the Commons, Margo
admitted that she hadn't been inside yet.

"I hate to shop when I'm too broke to buy anything,"
she admitted. "It's depressing."

"What about that barmaid's dress?"

Her cheeks colored. "Skeeter gave me money for that.
He told me to buy it in Costumes Forever because the
prices were better. I, uh, haven't been shopping since."

"Well, you're in for a treat, then." Kit smiled, but he
wondered privately if this scheme would help or only
exacerbate matters. When he steered her through Clothes
and Stuff's doorway, Margo spent a full minute in the
center of the main aisle just staring. Then she gave a
low sound of utter ecstasy, turned in a complete circle
to gape at shelves, display racks, and glass cases, then
ended with a wide-eyed, "Shopper's freaking *paradise!*"

She thereupon bolted for the nearest dress racks.

Malcolm took one look at Kit's face and convulsed
with silent laughter.

"Oh, shut up," Kit groused. "Some help you are."

"Kit, you have to admit, there's a pretty darned funny
side to this. She's eighteen. She's female. She's just been
given an expense account in heaven."

"Oh, great. Make me feel better."

Malcolm's long face creased in a wide grin. "I suspect
the Neo Edo can support it."

"Huh. *Your* taxes aren't due next time Primary cycles."

Malcolm's eyes twinkled. "Oh, yes they are. I just don't have enough income for it to matter."

Kit thumped his shoulder. "Just wait. I'll take care of that little problem."

"Thanks," Malcolm drawled. "I'll go from owing zip to owing a third of whatever you pay me."

"Well, I could just pay you two thirds of what we agreed on. . . ."

"Fat chance. A man's got his pride, after all. Hey, look, Connie has a new line ready for the London season."

He wandered off to do his own window shopping. Intrigued as always by the content's of Clothes and Stuff, Kit cruised the aisles as well, just to get a feel for what they'd need. Neat racks displayed costumes appropriate to La-La Land's resident gates. Costumes were situated in carefully arranged groupings, neatly labelled as to geographic location, exact time period, and appropriate occupation or social occasion. Items could be either rented (for those on a budget) or purchased (for those with essentially sky's-the-limit funds).

Shelving units and glass cases held every manner of accessory, including an astonishing variety of footgear, belts, undergarments, gloves, fans, hosiery, hats, coats and cloaks, appropriate equivalents of the modern handbag, jewelry, timepieces, even items designed to conceal weapons: shoulder holsters for guns and knives, belt holsters and sheaths, ankle rigs, even garter-belt sheaths and holsters. One entire case was devoted to wigs and false hairpieces in every conceivable shade, most attached to hairpins or combs to be added as necessary to elegant coiffures. Every one of them was styled after authentic period hairpieces.

Another section of the shop included appropriately designed luggage, lighting equipment from candle lanterns to oil lamps, sanitary and survival gear, tools, weapons, even historically appropriate eyeglasses. One employee on Connie's payroll did nothing but grind prescription glasses and long-wear contact lenses to order for those who needed them.

If it had existed down time and people had used it, or if it was necessary to survival and it could be disguised, Clothes and Stuff stocked it or was prepared to manufacture it.

Connie herself, in direct contrast to her shop, was anything but neat and organized. She emerged from the back where she kept her office and design studio, noticed Kit, and waved. Kit chuckled. Beneath a hand-basted kimono that gaped open because she hadn't tied on an *obi* to hold it closed, she was clad in bits and pieces of Victorian undergarments. She wore hobnailed Roman "boots" on her feet and an ancient Meso-American feathered headdress appropriate for a jaguar priest over long, glossy black hair. Her eyes, a startling Irish blue, sparkled as she came across the shop, clomping every step of the way in her ancient footgear.

"Hi, Kit! What brings you in?"

He met her beside a glass case containing lace-and-lawn caps, feathered and plain fans, plus silk, leather, and cloth gloves while Margo emitted the most outlandish sounds he'd ever heard a female make off a mattress.

"What do you think?" he smiled, nodding toward the enraptured figure pawing through a rack of ball gowns. "Margo, of course. I'm sending her down the Britannia Gate with Malcolm. Sort of a trial run just to get her feet wet, give her a taste for time travel."

"Good idea. Hang on a sec, would you? These feathers itch."

She lifted off the headdress. The glossy black hair came with it. She shook out her own hair, then vanished into the back. When she returned, the kimono had gone as well, replaced by a set of cowboy-style leather chaps, worn over woolen drawers and a boned corset. Occasionally Kit had known her to change clothing five times during the course of a twenty-minute conversation as she tried out various new creations. Across the room, Margo noticed. She stared for a full thirty seconds, round-eyed, then returned to her window shopping with another silly squeal as her attention rested on something else utterly wonderful.

"Very becoming," Kit drawled.

Connie laughed. "They're hideous and the corset is cutting me in half, but I had to be sure the busks and side steels were bent to the right shape before I had William stitch the cover closed."

"And the chaps?"

"The customer said they chafed him. I'm testing them out to see what the problem is."

"Uh-huh."

Kit, like most 'eighty-sixers, had eventually realized that when she was working, Connie Logan was completely unconcerned about her appearance. And since she worked most of the hours she was awake— "What do you mean, do something fun for a change? I *love* designing clothes!"—Connie Logan was at first glance the most eccentric loon in a time station crammed full of them.

Kit thought she was the most charming nut he'd ever known.

Even he deferred to her encyclopedic knowledge.

"London, is it?" Connie asked, peering toward Margo, who had discovered the Roman *stolas* with their richly embroidered hems. "What's the program? Simple tour? Teaching experience? Test-run scouting trip?"

"All the above. I leave the outfitting choices to you and Malcolm."

"But not to Margo?" Connie smiled.

He rolled his eyes. "Let's see what she picks on her own and judge from that."

"Fair enough. Rent or buy?"

"Rent what's rescuable when they get back. I'll buy what's ruined."

"Okay." Her glance travelled beyond Kit's shoulder to a group of tourists selecting accessories for the dresses they carried. "Oh, damn . . ." She bolted past Kit's shoulder. "No, no, no, not that fan, that's an evening fan for the opera, what you have there is a morning dress for strolling and paying calls. You'd stick out like an idiot, carrying that around London. Here, what you need is this, or this, or maybe this . . . And that pair of slippers is completely wrong, what you need are these side-button boots. Size six? Hmm . . . a little narrow, I think. Try this six-and-a-half."

The astonished tourists gaped at the figure Connie made, her girlish pudginess stuffed into a lawn shift, woolen combinations peeking out from under several layers of petticoats, the tightly laced corset which created unsightly bulges both above and below, topped off with the leather chaps—tied on *over* the petticoats. The Roman "boots" were icing on the cake.

"Uh . . . thank you . . ."

They accepted Connie's choices a bit reluctantly, but obediently sat down to try on the boots.

Connie came back shaking her head. "If they'd just read the signs . . . You have to watch 'em like hawks. Let's check on Margo. Oh, Lord, she's already in trouble. . . ."

And Connie was off again, before Kit could open his mouth to add a single comment.

"No, no, Margo, not that, you've got a charity schoolgirl's cap paired with a lady's tea gown. . . ."

"Malcolm," Kit waved to get the guide's attention, "get over here! Connie's on the warpath and we need some decisions!"

Malcolm, looking for all the world like a truant schoolboy caught in a candy store, hastened over. "Sorry. Just catching up on the newest down-time styles.

There've been changes in top hats since last season—
they're more tapered from crown to brim—and the new
dress lounge coats are magnificent, with that new rolled
collar. But did you see those hideous woolen jersey
Jaeger suits?" Malcolm shuddered. "They wore those
things in July and August, even while exercising. No
wonder people died of heatstroke."

"Malcolm, I didn't know you were a clothes horse,"
Kit teased.

The guide—currently dressed in faded jeans and a
cheap T-shirt—grinned. "Me? Never. But I'd better
update my wardrobe before I step through the Britannia
Gate or I'll look like an old fuddy-duddy."

"You *are* an old fuddy-duddy," Kit laughed, "and so
am I. Let's get this over with. Gad, but I hate shopping."

"Only when you're not stepping through the gate,"
Malcolm smiled.

"Too true. Now, about what she'll need—"

An animal scream lifted from Commons, high and
piercing, followed an instant later by a woman's shriek
of terror. Kit and Malcolm jerked around, then ran for
the door. Surely another new gate hadn't opened? The
warning klaxon hadn't sounded and Kit hadn't felt the
telltale buzz in his skull bones. Someone started cursing.
Then Kit rounded an ornamental garden plot and found
a woman in medieval regalia staring at the ceiling and
sobbing in rage.

"They killed her! Goddamn them, they killed her!"

The men with her, also dressed in medieval garb,
were struggling to soothe terrified, hooded falcons on
their arms. One bird had already sprained a wing trying
to escape its jesses.

"Who killed whom?" Malcolm blurted.

A few spots of blood on the concrete and a couple
of feathers gave Kit the clue. "I'd say those two bird-
things Sue couldn't identify made lunch of this lady's
falcon."

The lady in question affirmed Kit's guess in most unladylike language. Malcolm coughed and turned aside to hide a grin. Pest Control came running, Sue Fritchey in the lead.

"What happened?"

The woman whose valuable hunting falcon had just become a paleo-hawk's dinner told her—scathingly.

"Uh-oh. I was afraid of something like this. Where are they now? Ah . . . there. Okay. Jimmy, Bill, Alice, we need capture nets and tranks, stat. We let those things keep feeding, we won't have any pterosaurs or *Ichthyornises* to study. And maybe a tourist will get hurt."

That last had clearly been an afterthought. Kit hid a grin. The tourist who'd lost her falcon began demanding reimbursement. Someone called Bull Morgan to mediate.

"C'mon, Malcolm. Looks like the fun's over. We have a trip down time to plan."

Margo, not surprisingly, hadn't even heard the ruckus. She was still flitting from rack to rack, cooing and all but drooling on the clothes. Even Connie was laughing at her. Kit shook his head. An unlimited expense account in heaven . . .

"Well, let's see what our prodigy's chosen, shall we?"

"Don't I get an opinion?" Margo demanded. The three faces ranged against her grimaced simultaneously. If Margo hadn't been so flaming angry, it would've been comical. "Well, don't I? I'm going to be the one wearing these!"

She held out the ridiculous embroidered smock, the baggy pants with their hideous flap front that fell open if the buttons popped loose—never mind the rags she was supposed to tie around her knees to hold the pants off the ground—then kicked at the scuffed, wide-toed leather boots. The shapeless felt hat was so pitiful she couldn't even bring herself to look at it.

"This is only one of the outfits you'll be wearing," Malcolm Moore told her, sounding infuriatingly patient.

"But they're *ugly!*"

"You're not in training to be a fashion model," Kit said sternly.

Margo subsided, but not happily. "I know."

"Now, about the choices you made," he continued, "Connie has a few words."

"Starting with the ball gown," the outlandish outfitter said, hanging it back on its rack. "The first word is 'No.' Your job isn't to go down time and party it up. It's to learn scouting. If you want to revisit London later for a vacation, on your own time and money, fine. Until then, the party dresses stay here."

Margo sighed. "All right. I'm supposed to go down time and be miserable."

"Not at all!" Connie said, somewhat sharply. "You have a remarkably negative attitude, Margo, for someone who's been given the chance to go down time for free. Britannia Gate tours cost several thousand dollars each."

Margo felt her cheeks burn. She hadn't thought of it quite like that. "I'm sorry. It's just I got so excited when you said I could go and that we could pick out clothes. . . ." She turned an appeal for forgiveness on Kit. "I'm sorry, really I am. I was just so disappointed after I saw those," she pointed to the glittering silks, velvets, and satins, "then you said what I would get to wear was these."

The humble farm clothing—men's farm clothing—lacked only mud to make the hideousness complete.

"Apology accepted," Kit said quietly. "Once you learn your trade, Margo—and you have a great deal yet to learn—you can play dress-up as often as you like. But not while you're on the job. *Never* while you're on the job."

Margo felt like crying. She'd been rude and

ungrateful—her temper *always* got her into trouble—
and they were being desperately nice to her. It wasn't
a situation she was accustomed to. She felt lost as to
how she ought to respond.

Connie Logan said more kindly, "Here, let's see what
else we can find. Malcolm, what about having her pose
as a charity girl?"

"We'd need a chaperon for that," Malcolm said slowly,
"but I like the charity girl idea. Her hair's short and
that'll either have to be disguised or explained. Charity
girl is the perfect cover. As for a chaperon, I could hire
someone from an agency and rent a flat for the week
we'll be there."

"I don't understand," Margo said. "What's a charity
girl? Why would that make a good cover story for my
hair?"

"Poverty-stricken children—orphans, children with
destitute parents—were sometimes taken in by
charitable institutions," Malcolm explained. "There were
dozens of schools supported by patrons and patronesses.
Children wore uniforms and numbered badges to
identify them. Because sanitation was a problem and
head lice were common, even girls' hair was cut short."

"*Head lice?*" Margo grabbed the sides of her head,
instinctively trying to protect her scalp from an invasion
of vermin.

Kit cleared his throat. "Sanitation in Victorian London
was quite a bit better than many places you'll end up
as a scout. Head lice—and other nasties—can be
eliminated once you get back."

Margo just stared, overcome with an intense desire
to be ill. She hadn't thought about *lice*. The more she
studied for this job, the clearer it became there was a
great deal she hadn't thought about.

"Well, I'm not quitting," she said stubbornly,
straightening her spine. "Nobody ever died from being
dirty."

Malcolm exchanged glances with Kit, who said repressively, "Millions have done just that. The point is, you keep yourself as clean as you can and deal with medical problems when you return. If you return. Why do you think you're required to receive so many inoculations before coming to a time terminal? Up time, we don't even vaccinate for smallpox any longer. It's an extinct disease. Yet even in someplace as relatively sanitary as Denver of the 1890's you could still contract it. Not to mention lockjaw or blood poisoning from a simple cut or scrape. So you take your medicine, keep yourself clean, and hope you don't come back with anything Medical can't handle.

"Now, I think this charity girl idea's a good one, but that leaves us with another question, Malcolm. Namely, how to explain your association with her. You're known in London."

"Fairly well, in certain circles," Malcolm agreed.

"So people will know you wouldn't have a reason to associate with a charity girl of eighteen. And her accent's all wrong, anyway, to pose as a British orphan."

"The few people I know down time believe me to be an eccentric gentleman from British Honduras—which helps explain away the occasional wobble or two in *my* accent."

Margo blinked. He'd sounded astonishingly British during that sentence, which he hadn't before. In fact, given the small amount of stage training she'd had, she'd have bet everything she owned it had been genuine, not affected.

"How did you do that?"

"Do what?" He sounded American again, as American as Minnesota winters.

"Sound British? I thought you were American."

Malcolm grinned. "Good. I've studied hard to sound like that. Heading down time to Denver with an English accent isn't a good idea. Fortunately I have a quick ear and years of practice. But I was born in England." He cleared his throat and glanced away. "I survived The Flood, actually."

Margo said breathlessly, "*The* Flood? From *The Accident?*"

Malcolm rubbed the back of one ear. "Well, yes. I was just a kid. We lived in Brighton, you see, near the seaside. We ran a little tourist hostel during the summers. My family was lucky. We only lost my elder brother when the house caved in."

Margo didn't know what to say. The English coast had been wiped out by tidal waves. All the coastlines of the world had been hit hard. Several dozen cities had been reduced to rubble and the ensuing chaos, rampant epidemics, and starvation had reshaped world politics forever. Margo hadn't been old enough to remember it. She forgot, sometimes, that most of the people on this time terminal *did* remember the world before the time gates and the accident which had caused them.

She wondered quite suddenly if that was why her father had been the way he was. Had he blamed himself all those years ago for her brother's death, then found himself unable to cope with the changed world? She shivered, not wanting to sympathize with him, but something in Malcolm's voice had triggered memories of her father during his more sober moments. The look in her father's eyes during those moments echoed the desperate struggle not to remember she saw now in Malcolm's dark eyes.

"I'm sorry, Malcolm. I didn't know."

He managed a smile. "How could you? Don't dwell on it. I don't. Now, what were we saying? Oh yeah, my background. The people I know down time think I'm a gentleman from British Honduras, with no visible means of support and no daily job to distract me from gentlemanly pursuits. I just happen to have a lot of wealthy, scatterbrained friends who pay me visits from the other side of the water, particularly America." He grinned. "That way it's natural for my tourists to gawk at the sights. Londoners in the 1880's considered Americans boorish provincials just this side of savagery."

Margo sniffed. "How rude."

Connie laughed. "Honey, you don't know the half of it. Victorian Londoners took class consciousness to new extremes." She gestured to the Britannia section of her shop. "It's why I carry such a varied line of costumes for the Britannia Gate. Clothes said *everything* about your station in life. Wear the wrong thing and you become a laughingstock—"

"Or worse," Kit put in.

"—or you just blend into the background and become invisible."

Malcolm nodded. "Yes. But you have to be careful. The wrong clothing could get you hauled off to jail or Bedlam Hospital to be locked in with the other madwomen."

Margo shivered. "What about this charity girl stuff, then?"

"Well," Malcolm said, glancing at Kit, "given my reputation as something of an eccentric, it wouldn't be out of character for me to sponsor a young girl who'd been orphaned in a cholera epidemic, say, or by one of the tropical fevers that laid so many Europeans low in Honduras. You could be the child of some deceased friend or even a relative. A niece, maybe, brought back to England for schooling."

Kit was nodding. "I like it. All right, choose something appropriate. Connie, why don't you fit her out while Malcolm and I update his wardrobe? If he's going to keep up his reputation in London, I suspect he'll need a new item or two. And you'll need a couple of 'incognito' getups as well, I think, so your down-time friends don't recognize you when you two go slumming."

Connie beamed. "Help yourselves. Gosh, I love it when scouts and guides put their heads together and go shopping!"

Kit groaned. Malcolm laughed. "Don't worry, Kit. I'll try to be gentle with your budget."

"Pray do, sir," Kit drolled. "It isn't unlimited, you know."

They strolled off in the direction of the men's clothing. Margo watched them go. "They're . . ." She paused, suddenly embarrassed.

"They're what?" Connie asked curiously.

"Nothing," Margo mumbled. She'd been about to say, "They're really sweet, aren't they?" but had stopped herself just in time. She'd gotten where she was by being tough and uncaring. Now wasn't the time to let down her guard, not with her dreams almost within grasp. But she couldn't help thinking it. They *were* sweet. Even Kit, when he wasn't glowering at her for whatever she'd done wrong most recently. A flash of insight told Margo he glowered because he didn't really know how to talk to her.

That was all right. She didn't really know how to talk to him, either, not without a whole retinue of defenses in place. A smart mouth and a lifelong habit of sarcasm—skillfully combined with pouting frowns and winning smiles—weren't exactly the most useful skills if she wanted to learn more about this man as a human being, rather than a legend.

Get real, Margo. Remember the fish pond. Try to get better acquainted with him—with either of them—and you'll have to talk about yourself. The less said on that subject, the better. For everyone concerned.

Margo sighed unhappily, earning a long, curious look from Connie, then she shook herself free of the mood and said brightly, "Okay, about this charity-girl costume. Show me!"

CHAPTER NINE

Brian Hendrickson had come from a family whose older sons enlisted for life in the Royal Navy. Brian— a third son born in the islands—had become a historian rather than a sailor. But his military upbringing lingered in a meticulous personality and a tendency to run his library with martial efficiency. His accent, a delightfully odd one, was right at home in La-La Land.

Kit, taking advantage of Margo's mood after the shopping trip, escorted her from Clothes and Stuff directly to the reference desk in La-La Land's library. It was high time she started learning more than remedial math, firearms history, and martial arts.

"Brian, this is Margo, my granddaughter. Margo, Brian Hendrickson, TT-86's resident librarian."

He smiled pleasantly and kissed the air above her hand, Continental-style. "Most pleased to meet you, Miss Margo."

She blinked, clearly startled. Brian Hendrickson startled most newcomers to TT-86.

"Where are you *from?*" Margo blurted.

A dazzling smile came and went. "It is more a matter of where I am *not* from, actually. I was born in the British Virgins, spent the first three years of my life in Glasgow, then my father was posted to Hong Kong. Let's see . . . I've nearly forgotten the Falklands, haven't I? I took my university degrees from Cambridge."

"Oh." She looked a little round-eyed.

Kit grinned. "Which brings us to the reason we're here. She needs advanced lessons."

"Hmm, yes, I should think so, if rumors are true."

"They're true," Kit sighed. "Detailed histories, languages, the works."

The librarian tapped well-manicured fingertips against the desktop. "Yes. I should think Latin to start, followed by French—modern, middle, and old—to cover all bets. And Italian and Greek. And we'd better throw in the main Chinese dialects—"

"You're not serious?" Margo broke in, her voice echoing the panic in her eyes. "*Latin?* And . . . and Chinese and all those Frenches . . . and . . ."

Brian blinked. "Well, yes, I am serious. Goodness, Miss Margo, you can't expect to scout if you don't speak at least ten languages fluently."

"*Ten?*" She glanced wildly at Kit. "*TEN?*"

Kit only rubbed the side of his nose. "Well, that's a fairly limited beginning, but yes, ten might prove just barely adequate. I speak twenty fluently and can make myself understood in considerably more than that. I did warn you, Margo. Scouting is a scholarly business, above all else. When you're not down time exploring a gate, you're studying. Constantly."

"But—"

"I don't make up these rules just to upset you."

"I know, I know," she wailed, "I understand that, but . . ."

"He's right, Miss Margo," the librarian said quietly. "My steadiest customers are never the tourists. They're the guides and the scouts. Particularly the scouts. They spend hours here every day, learning and learning. In fact, if you'll examine the gentlemen at the computers over there or back in the language labs, you'll discover half the scouts who work out of TT-86 on a regular basis. Excuse me, please."

Kit glanced around. John Merylbone, a fairly new

scout despite his age—he was pushing fifty—had come up to the desk.

"Brian, sorry to interrupt, but I need help. I'm looking for information on early British scholars' costumes. I'd heard there was a good general reference by Cunnington and Lucas from 1978."

Brian stared at the scout for long, unblinking moments, giving the distinct impression that John's request was utterly beneath his notice. Margo whispered, "Isn't that a little rude?"

Kit smiled. "No, actually he's thinking. Watch."

Brian started talking. "Well, yes, that's a very good general reference, but it contains a good bit more than you'll need. Covers all manner of charity costumes, through several centuries, actually. I'd recommend Rymer's *Foedera*, vol. VII, or *Statutes of the Colleges of Oxford for the Royal Commission*—that's translated from the Latin, which is useful—or perhaps Gibson's *Statua Antiqua Universitatis Oxoniensis*. Loggan also did some excellent work in *Cantabrigia Illustrata* and *Oxonia Illustrata*."

The librarian was busy jotting down names and titles while he spoke.

"Good grief! He didn't even use the computer!"

Kit only smiled. "Don't look so horrified. Nobody's asking you to learn as much as Brian knows. *Nobody* knows as much as Brian Hendrickson. He has a photographic memory. Useful for a research librarian on a time terminal."

"Oh. I was beginning to worry."

"You do that," Kit laughed. "I like it better when you're worried. Proves you're thinking."

She put out a pink tongue. "You're mean and horrible. Why does everybody else like you?"

Kit scratched his head. "Search me. Guess it's my good looks and charm."

Margo actually laughed. When she relaxed, his

granddaughter was a remarkably pretty girl, with no
trace of that Irish alleycat glare. He sighed, feeling old
before he was ready for it.

"What's wrong?" Margo asked.

"Nothing," Kit said, forcing a smile. "Let's set up your
study schedule."

Brian returned from helping the other scout and they
got down to business. He assigned Margo a language
lab, where she was to spend four hours every other
day learning the first of the languages on her list. The
next four hours of her library days (after lunch, which
Kit agreed to have delivered to her from the Neo Edo
so she wouldn't need to leave the library) were to be
devoted to detailed historical studies.

"Let's start her with American history, since that's
what she's likeliest to absorb readily," Brian suggested.
"Then we'll put her on European history, working
backwards from the twentieth century. We'll tackle
Africa, Asia, South America, India, and the Middle
East a little later in the program, after she's settled
down into the study routine and is capable of
absorbing cultural detail significantly different from
her own."

Kit and Brian agreed she'd be better off leaving the
library during the evenings to eat dinner and do
homework, and to alternate library days with continued
weapons training. With any luck, the physical exercise
would leave her tired enough to sleep after homework
sessions.

By the time they were done setting up her schedule,
Margo was visibly horrified and trying hard not to show
it. She gave him a brave smile as they left the library.
"One thing's for sure, life'll never be the same around
you. Latin, Chinese, and French, oh my . . ."

"Better that than lions, tigers, *or* bears," Kit chuckled.
"Just remember, you can never truly understand a nation
or its people until you can speak its language."

"Right," she sighed, giving him another brave smile. "I just hope scouting is worth all this agony."

Kit resisted the urge to ruffle her short hair. "I doubt you'll be disappointed. Surprised, probably—almost undoubtedly. But disappointed? No, I don't think so. Time travel is *never* what people expect it to be. And that," he smiled, "is half the fun."

"Well, goodness, I hope so. My head already hurts and I haven't even started yet!"

Kit laughed. "That's because you're stretching your brain, possibly for the first time. Cheer up. By the time you're done, not only will you have the equivalent of several Ph.D.'s you didn't have to pay some university to earn, you'll have the ability to do field research most Ph.D.'s still can't afford to do. Education," he smiled, "is *never* a waste of time."

She gave him an odd look, but said nothing. Kit found himself fervently hoping London convinced Margo she needed every bit of the "brain work" he and Brian had outlined. Margo loose for a week in London, even with Malcolm Moore along to protect her . . . Kit was so apprehensive, before he went to bed that night he found himself standing in the living room doorway, just watching her sleep.

Young, vulnerable . . .

He turned away silently and went to bed.

But not to sleep.

Malcolm came for Margo early in the morning the day the Britannia Gate was due to open.

"Hi!" The world was wonderful this morning. Today was the day she would finally step through a gate into history.

"Sleep well?" Malcolm asked.

Margo laughed. "I was so excited I hardly closed my eyes all night."

"Thought as much," he chuckled. "Kit up yet?"

"In the shower."

"All packed?"

"Yes!"

"Good. We have one last appointment before we go."

Uh-oh. Margo regarded him suspiciously. "What is it?"

A pained smile came and went. "You're not going to like it, but I think it's vital."

"What?"

"We need to visit Paula Booker."

Margo wondered who the devil that was. "For?"

"Your hair."

Margo touched her short, flame-colored hair. "What's wrong with my hair?"

"Nothing—for here and now. Everything, for down time. That color stands out. We want to be inconspicuous. The less noticed you are, the better."

"What are you going to do about it? Dye it?" Margo asked sarcastically.

"Yep."

She stared. "Oh, no."

Malcolm sighed. "I knew this wouldn't be well received. That's why I wanted Kit's opinion."

"On what?" Kit asked, emerging from the bathroom. He was—uncharacteristically—clad only in a towel. His hair was still wet and he hadn't shaved yet. Margo stared, knowing it was rude, but she couldn't help it.

There *were* scars. Terrible ones.

"Margo's hair," Malcolm said. "I think Paula should dye it."

Margo managed to drag her gaze off Kit's whip-scarred torso and met his gaze. He ignored her stricken look and merely studied her critically. "Yes," he said slowly, "I didn't think it was too important yet, but you're probably right. She's awfully noticeable."

"Thanks for the compliment," Margo muttered. The last thing she wanted to be was "noticeable" if attracting attention earned her scars like Kit's, but the timing was *rotten.* She'd spent the last twenty-four hours trying hopelessly to memorize Latin declensions and conjugations and whatever else all those verb and noun forms were called. All those fickle, changeable word endings left her head spinning. She'd tried—really tried—and now as a reward they wanted to dye her best feature some hideous, drab color to match the clothes they'd picked for her to wear.

Margo wanted to cry or scream at something or wail about how monstrously unfair it was. Instead, she swallowed it raw. Time was ticking away and she was still very little closer to scouting than the day she'd stepped through Primary into La-La Land with a heart full of bright hopes and no notion how murderously difficult it was going to be.

You'll see, she promised. *When we get to London, you'll see. I'll prove to you both I can do this.*

"Okay," she said finally. "I guess I go down time looking like a mud hen. Sven keeps telling me, be invisible. I should've seen this coming, huh?" Then, in a bright tone that turned a bitter complaint into a cheery joke, she said, "Let's get this over with and get down time before I'm too old to enjoy it!"

Kit laughed and even Malcolm chuckled. Margo swept out of the apartment before she gave it all away by crying. Malcolm caught up and fell into step.

"You know, Margo," he said conversationally, "it might help to think of this as the biggest game of dress-up you ever played."

She glanced up, startled. "*Dress-up?* Oh, good grief, Malcolm, I haven't played dress-up since—" She broke off abruptly, recalling the beating her father had given her for liberating her mother's makeup. "Well, not in a long time," she temporized, covering the stumble she'd made with a bright smile. "It's just you caught me off guard and . . . well . . . nothing's like I expected it to be. Nothing."

"Very little in life usually is," Malcolm said, without a trace of a smile.

"I suppose so. But I don't have to like it."

Malcolm's glance was keen. "No one said you had to, Margo. Do you think I enjoy grovelling for a job every day of my life, living on rice and dried beans, and swallowing my pride when people are rude, callous, or downright cruel? But I do it and smile because that's the price of living *my* dream."

Margo chewed that over as they left Residential behind and emerged into the throng crowding Frontier Town. A kid sporting an oversized cowboy hat and an undersized leather gunbelt drew and fired his pretend six-shooter at a diving pterosaur. It splashed into a nearby fishpond.

"Got him!" the kid crowed.

Unperturbed, the pterosaur emerged with a wriggling goldfish nearly as large as it was. The kid's father laughed and called him over. He practically swaggered back.

Margo smiled. "I'd say *he's* living his dream, huh?" Then more seriously, "Not too many people ever get the chance to try that, do they? I think you're the first person I ever met who *was* doing it." Except, maybe, Billy Pandropolous, and his dream was more akin to nightmare for everyone who came close to him. "I envy you."

"You know," Malcolm said quietly, "you may be the first person ever to do *that*."

"Huh. You got lousy friends, then. They can't see what's right in front of 'em. Money's not everything." She flushed suddenly, realizing she'd just insulted Malcolm's friends—at least one of whom was Kit Carson.

"How right you are," Malcolm said with a smile. "I'm glad you're beginning to see that. Some people never figure it out. This way." He nodded toward Urbs Romae. "Better hustle or we'll be late."

Paula Booker's establishment was tucked away in one corner of the Commons. Margo was expecting a hair styling salon. What they entered looked more like the waiting room of an upscale medical clinic. Just as they entered, two men emerged from an inner sanctum. One assisted the other, who shuffled awkwardly as though his groin hurt. The first one said sympathetically, "You think that's bad, you should see what she did to mine."

"Yeah," the second man said through clenched teeth, "but a whole new foreskin? God, I hurt. . . ."

Margo stared until they had passed through the outer door and vanished down the Commons.

"What was *that* all about?"

"Zipper Jockeys." Astonishingly, Malcolm Moore wore the blackest scowl she'd ever seen.

"Zipper Jockeys?" she echoed.

"They're here for one of the sex tours. Bastards go down time and spend the whole trip brothel hopping. Paula takes revenge on 'em, though. Does corrective surgery they more than deserve, so their modern circumcisions won't arouse suspicion. Most places TT-86's gates lead to, circumcisions were practiced only by the Jewish. Anti-Semitism being the ugly thing it was in many down-time cultures . . ."

"Oh. That's lousy. The anti-Semitism, I mean."

"Yes. Bigotry is. But Zipper Jockeys deserve what they get. Paula ranks them down around the level of flatworms, which personally I think is too high on the evolutionary scale. She makes sure they hurt good and hard before they head out to rape women. If she could get away with it, she'd castrate them."

Margo glared after the departing men. "Someone should do something! Someone should stop it!"

"Yes," Malcolm said tightly. "Someone should. Time Tours won't. They make money off the trade. So does the government. A *lot* of money. Half the Zipper Jockeys that go down time have to be quarantined when they come back, until Medical can deal with the venereal diseases they pick up."

"That's disgusting!"

"Personally, I think they should be marooned down time to die from whatever they catch."

No compromise softened Malcolm Moore's voice. All at once, Margo realized how very much she liked this time guide. "Thanks, Malcolm."

He shot her a startled look. "For what?"

"Nothing. Just thanks. What about my hair?"

He shook himself visibly and gave her one last penetrating look, then stepped over to a reception window. "Malcolm Moore, for the 8:15 appointment."

"Have a seat, please."

They didn't have to wait long. The inner door opened to reveal the most astonishing individual Margo had ever laid eyes on. She knew her mouth had fallen open, but she couldn't help it.

"Hi, Paula," Malcolm said, rising to his feet.

"Hello, Malcolm."

Paula Booker was . . .

Cadaverous.

That was the only word to describe the cosmetologist's appearance. Tall—she topped out at six feet in flat, surgical-style shoes—and gaunt, Paula's face had hollows like a skull's. White hair wisped around a face the color of a bloodless corpse. But she wasn't old. If Paula Booker were a day over thirty-five, Margo would eat her own shoes.

With those pale eyes and that funereal expression, TT-86's cosmetologist looked very much like a female Lurch, from an unknown branch of the Addams Family Tree.

"How are you this morning?" Paula asked as Malcolm shook her hand.

Even Paula's *voice* was soft and creepy.

Margo realized how intensely she was staring when both Malcolm and Paula turned and stared back.

"I—uh—"

To Margo's astonishment, Paula started laughing. The sight was so disturbing, Margo actually had trouble getting to her feet. She tripped over her own shoe and stumbled.

"Malcolm," Paula Booker winked, "let's show this young lady my photographs, shall we?"

Margo followed uneasily as Paula Booker escorted them into a private office. One wall was covered—literally covered—with photos of one of the most beautiful women Margo had ever seen. Ash-blonde hair, sparkling blue eyes, fine bone structure above hollowed cheeks—

"My God! It's you!" Margo blurted.

Paula laughed again. "Aren't I a great walking advertisement?"

"You . . ." Margo stared from the photos to the apparition before her and back again. "You did *that* to yourself?"

Paula's grin was a terrifying vision. "Indeed I did. Every morning I put on the finishing touches with makeup."

"But you could've been a movie star! A world-famous model!"

"Oh, I was. A model, that is. It was dead boring." Paula's eyes twinkled. "This is much more fun. And I get to do such interesting plastic surgery, too. I have a medical degree just for that. Somebody Caucasian wants to go to Edo, I doctor them a little and presto, they're virtually indistinguishable from a native-born Japanese. I can alter skin tone, hair color, whatever's required."

Margo thought about the man limping out of Paula's clinic and grinned. "That's terrific!" She fluffed her own hair. "What can we do about this? Everyone says I have to dye it."

Paula studied Margo for several moments. "Yes, but we won't want to go too dark, unless you want her looking as funereal as I do?" She glanced at Malcolm. "Black hair with that skin tone will look terrible. Even dark brown is going to make her look anemic."

"Can't be helped. Use your judgement on how dark, but she can't go scouting looking like that."

"No," Paula agreed. "Definitely not. Red hair was associated with witches throughout most of the Middle Ages. Probably one reason red hair is relatively rare today—the gene pool was reduced through burning at the stake. All right, Margo, let's get started. Malcolm, you're welcome to sit in the waiting room. This will take a while."

How long could it take to dye one head of very short hair brown? Margo's answer came when Paula revealed her intention to dye every *bit* of Margo's hair: body-wide.

"You can't be serious!"

"Dead serious. And you'll need to touch up the roots every four weeks."

"But—but—" That seemed to have become virtually the only thing Margo was capable of saying, lately.

Three hours later, Margo emerged, forlorn as a wet cat. She took one look into the waiting room's mirror and burst into tears—again.

"Hey," Malcolm said, rising hastily to his feet, "you look great!"

"No, I don't!" Margo wailed. "I look . . . I look *awful!*"

The mirror revealed a pinched, pale face like an orphan someone had beaten and left for dead in some unspeakable sewer. She'd have died before revealing the ignominy of having hair dye applied elsewhere with a cotton swab.

"Hey, shh. Let's grab a bite of lunch somewhere then change into our costumes and pick up your luggage. We only have a couple of hours before the Britannia Gate opens."

Not even that prospect had the power to dispel the gloom that had settled over Margo. Just one other little consideration she hadn't foreseen in becoming a time scout. To get what she wanted, Margo had to give up being pretty.

That blow, after all the other battles she'd fought through nearly seventeen miserable years of being made to feel stupid, unwanted, unloved, and a burden to everyone who knew her was nearly more than Margo could bear. The solitary, single thing that kept her from breaking down into hysterical tears was the knowledge that such a childish display would destroy her chances of scouting forever.

Her chin quivered despite her best efforts to keep it still, but she held it high. She was *going* to do this. No matter what it took, no matter how many obstacles Kit Carson threw in her path. She was going to scout or die trying.

And nothing was going to stand in her way.

Nothing.

CHAPTER TEN

Victoria Station hadn't yet recovered from the damage of the unstable gate, but the worst debris had been hauled away and repairs had begun. Margo, palms sweating, clutched the handle of her frayed carpet bag. Malcolm smiled down at her, causing a sudden triphammer lurch under her breastbone. Malcolm Moore, dressed as a wealthy Victorian gentleman, was enough to set Margo's pulse racing.

He grinned suddenly. "You look nervous."

"I *am* nervous. This is real. It isn't a stage play, it's *real*. Do you get used to it?"

Malcolm's eyes took on a faraway look as his gaze focused on something Margo couldn't see. "No," he said softly. "You don't. At least, I don't. I could've found any number of teaching positions up time, particularly with my scouting and time guiding credentials in addition to my degrees. But I don't want to go back. Stepping through a gate . . ." He grinned again. "You'll see."

The air began to buzz. Margo pressed a hand to the bones of her skull. "Ow."

"Any moment, now."

Malcolm sounded even more excited than Margo felt, which was saying quite a lot. She checked her "uniform" again to be sure everything was in place. Under a heavy walking cloak, Margo's deep azure dress and starched white pinafore were immaculate. A pretty white cap and an enormous straw hat mercifully covered her hideous brown hair. Thick knitted stockings, ankle-length boots, and fingerless mittens completed the ensemble, topped off by a beautiful badge in which a crown and the letters R.M.I.G. enclosed a setsquare and compasses.

"This," Connie Logan had told her with a smile, "is a particularly prestigious school uniform."

"What does R.M.I.G. stand for?"

"Royal Masonic Institution for Girls."

Malcolm, it turned out, was a Freemason, both in real life and in his down-time persona.

"I've found it helps enormously," he'd told her. "If you're in trouble—and it's very easy to fall into trouble, even for an experienced guide—having a network of sworn brothers dedicated to a creed of helping those in need can literally be a lifesaver."

"Are all guides and scouts Masons?" Margo asked, wondering with a sinking sensation if this would be yet another barrier to be overcome.

"No, but quite a few are. Don't worry about it, Margo. Membership isn't required."

At the time, Margo had felt relieved, but now, reviewing the details of her costume again, she wondered if anyone down time would expect her to know secret rituals or anything. Maybe this uncertainty had been part of Kit's plan? To impress upon her how much she had to learn? Margo shifted the carpet bag to her other hand and stiffened her back—although slouching was all but impossible, anyway, what with the horrid undergarments that were already pinching and chafing.

Doubtless physical discomfort was just another part of Kit Carson's plan to discourage her. Well, it wasn't going to work.

The air began to shimmer up near the ceiling. Well-dressed men and women stirred excitedly. Then the gate began to cycle. Rather than opening out of the wall, darkness grew out of thin air right off the end of the high, gridwork platform, a ragged hole, a widening maw . . .

Margo gasped. Through it, she could make out the colors of twilight, the twinkle of a high, lonely star. Nearer at hand, a breeze stirred barren, low-hanging branches. She could see—but not hear—dead leaves which gusted into view. A warm, golden glow appeared, then a dark shape occluded the lantern light—

Titters of laughter ran through the crowd when a figure in a tall hat and opera cape stepped through, rushing at them like an oncoming train. The gentleman doffed his hat politely to the waiting crowd below. "Your patience, please, ladies and gentlemen."

Tourists had begun to emerge from the Britannia Gate. Women in smart dresses, men in evening suits, ragged servants hauling steamer trunks, carpet bags, and leather cases, young women dressed as housemaids, all poured through onto the platform and made their way down the ramp to the Commons floor. Many were smiling and chatting. Others looked grim. Still others staggered with assistance from Time Tours employees.

"Never fails," Malcolm murmured. "Always a few come back sick as dogs."

"I won't," Margo vowed.

"No," Malcolm agreed drily. "You won't. That's what I'm here for."

She suppressed a huff, wanting to point out that she didn't need a nursemaid, but even she realized she *did* need a reliable guide. And then, before she expected it, their turn came.

"Oh," Margo said excitedly, "here we go!"

Malcolm gallantly offered his arm. Margo laughed and accepted it, then laughed again when he insisted on carrying her carpet bag. Their "porter," a husky young man named John, took charge of their hefty steamer trunk. Margo slid her Timecard through the encoder, then hurried up the long ramp at Malcolm's side while

John waited with the other baggage handlers. Margo paused at the very threshold of nothingness, mortified that her hindbrain whispered, "If I step off, there's nothing there but a five-story drop to the floor."

She screwed shut both eyes and followed Malcolm off the edge of the platform. For an instant she thought she *was* falling.

"Open your eyes!" Malcolm said urgently.

She opened them—and gasped. The ground was rushing at her—

Malcolm steadied her through. "That's a girl," he said encouragingly.

Margo shuddered with sudden cold.

"Are you quite all right, my dear?"

Margo blinked. The smiling, relaxed Malcolm with the easy American voice had gone completely. In his place stood a distinguished British gentleman peering anxiously down at her.

"Uh—yeah."

Very gently, Malcolm drew her to one side, making room for other tourists. "Margo, the proper response to such a question is not 'Uh, yeah.' That's terribly anachronistic here."

Margo felt her cheeks burn. "All right," she said in a low voice. "What should I have said?"

"You should have said, 'Yes, sir, thank you kindly, it was just a passing dizziness. Might I have your arm for a moment more, please?' To which I would naturally respond by offering to escort you to some place of rest where I might fetch you a glass of water or stronger spirits if such might be required."

Margo was so fascinated by the archaic speech patterns and the wonderful sound of his voice, she almost forgot to pay attention to what he'd actually said. "All right. I mean, very well. I'll . . . I'll try, Malcolm, really I will."

"Ah-ah," he said with a smile. "Here, I am Mr. Moore. You are Miss Margo Smythe, my ward. Never fail to call me Mr. Moore. Anything else would be seen as unforgivably forward."

Behind them, the gate had begun to shrink. Porters rushed through with the last of the luggage, then the gate into La-La Land vanished into a tangle of brown vines and a high stone wall. For a terrible instant, Margo experienced complete panic. *We're cut off. . . .*

Then Malcolm high-signed John, who joined them and set the trunk down with a sigh. " 'at's good, Mister Moore, sir."

Malcolm grinned. "Good show, John. Your Cockney's coming along nicely."

"I been doin' a study on it, sir." John's eyes twinkled. Malcolm had introduced him as a graduate student who planned to stay down time for several months working on his doctoral dissertation on the London underclass. He and Kit had come to an agreement: John would "work" as a manservant for Malcolm and Margo during their week in London, doing whatever was required of him. In return, Kit would front him the money for the initial gate ticket. He'd provided for his own living expenses and gear.

"Where are we?" Margo asked quietly. She stamped her feet to keep them warm.

"In the private garden of a house near Battersea Park at Chelsea Reach."

"Chelsea Reach?"

"A stretch of the Thames. We're across the river from where we shall need to be for most of our stay."

Gas lights illuminated a garden where the tourists now milled excitedly. Time Tours guides dressed as liveried servants organized sixty-some people into a double line, gentlemen escorting ladies, while the porters struggled with heavy trunks. They carried luggage into a three-story, graceful house where gas lights burned warmly. The interior seemed warm and inviting compared with the damp, frigid garden.

"It's cold," Margo complained.

"Well, it *is* late February. We shall have a hard frost tonight or I'm no judge of weather."

She tucked her hands inside the cape. "Now what?"

"First, fetch out your ATLS and log, please." He glanced toward the darkening sky. "We'll need to take readings and start our trip chronometers running. Remember, Miss Smythe, it is essential that you start your trip chronometer running very quickly after passing a gate. And shoot an ATLS and star-fix as soon as possible. And as I suspect we'll have fog soon, do hurry with it. London generally does in the early evenings."

"But we already know exactly when we are," Margo pointed out.

"On a tour, yes. As a scout, you won't. You'll have to determine that as the opportunity arises. Just because your Timecard was logged in for the Britannia Gate, doesn't mean you may skip this ritual. Most gates you'll step through as a scout won't *have* an encoder available yet, for the simple reason that you'll be the first one stepping through it. And when you come through in broad daylight, you'll have to wait until nightfall to update your exact geo-temporal reading."

Margo dug out her equipment and took the ATLS reading. Malcolm checked her and made a small correction, then showed her how to take a star-fix. She mastered the knack after three tries and proudly entered the readings in her log.

"There! How did I do?"

"Your ATLS reading was off far enough you'd have placed yourself in the Irish Sea, but not too bad for a first attempt under field conditions. We'll take readings each night we're here, to give you the practice."

Malcolm finished entering data into his own log, made certain Margo had properly initiated the chronometer sequence, then put away their equipment.

"Now what?"

The tourists had lined up along a garden path and were filing slowly into the house.

"Time Tours will have made arrangements for cabriolet carriages to take us to various good hotels for the evening."

"I thought carriages were called hansoms."

Malcolm smiled. "Hansom cabs are very popular just now, but they're small, two-wheeled affairs. Hansoms cannot carry any significant amount of luggage. Hence the need for something a bit sturdier."

They joined the line and moved steadily toward the house. Margo wanted to rush forward and explore. She found it increasingly difficult to stand still.

"Patience," Malcolm laughed. "We've an entire week ahead of us."

"When will our cab be here?"

"Our hosts," Malcolm said, glancing a little coldly at the liveried Time Tours guides, "will serve refreshments while carriages are summoned. We'll be departing in small groups at least fifteen minutes apart, to help reduce the chance that anyone will notice the number of people coming and going from this house."

"How did Time Tours get hold of this place?"

Malcolm said quietly, "I'm told the spinster lady who owned it had a fit of the vapors the first time the Britannia Gate opened in her garden. When it happened several weeks in a row, she sold the place cheaply to a scout and retired permanently to Scotland. Time Tours bought it from the scout."

Margo hadn't considered what people *down* time must think when a gate opened right in front of them.

"Who was the scout?"

Malcolm shrugged. "Your grandfather."

Oh.

"I would suggest," Malcolm said as they moved across the threshold into a surprisingly chilly drawing room, "that we refrain from discussing up-time affairs for the week, as far as possible. You are here to learn, certainly, but discussing anything from up time is very dangerous within earshot of people who understand the language you're speaking. If you must ask a question, keep your voice down and try to ask it where others can't hear you. I'll pass along my advice under the same set of strictures."

Again, Margo was trying to get the rhythm of Malcolm's new speech patterns. "Very well, Mal—Mr. Moore."

He patted her hand. "Very good, Miss Smythe. And now, if you would be so kind as to permit me, I will introduce you to London."

He led her toward a warm coal fire and beckoned to a "servant" who brought steaming cups of tea.

"My dear, warm yourself while I see about our luggage and transportation."

He signalled to John, who carried their steamer trunk toward a long front hall where other porters waited. Margo sipped astringent tea, grateful for the warmth; the room's lingering chill surprised her. Other tourists were talking excitedly, admiring the furnishings, the rugs, the draperies, the view out the windows. Margo was a little envious of the women's dresses. One elegantly attired lady smiled and approached her.

"That's a charming costume," she said. "What is it?"

Feeling vastly superior, Margo said, "It's one of the most prestigious school uniforms in London, from the Royal Masonic Institution for Girls." She dredged up Connie Logan's lecture and added, "It was founded in Somers Town, London, by a chevalier in 1788."

"It's delightful. Could I see the whole costume?"

Margo dimpled and set down her teacup, then slipped off the cape and pirouetted.

"Oh, look!" exclaimed another tourist. "It's darling!"

"Where did you get it?"

"Connie Logan, Clothes and Stuff."

"I wish I'd thought to dress Louisa like that," one lady laughed. Her daughter, looking dowdy in a plain grey morning dress, was pouting under a stylish hat decorated rather hideously with dead birds.

"And look at that brooch. What an intriguing design. Is that the school's crest?"

"Yes. It's a badge. All the charity schools issued them to identify their pupils."

"Ladies," Malcolm smiled, bowing slightly, "if I might rescue my ward, our cabriolet is waiting. Here, let me help you on with that cape, my dear. The night is dreadfully chilly and John neglected to bring along our lap rug."

A flutter of excited laughter ran through the room.

"Who *is* that gentleman?"

"Oh, I wish our guide sounded like that!"

"Or looked like him . . ."

"I don't care what Time Tours says, the next time I come here, I'm going to hire him. I don't care *what* it costs!"

Malcolm smiled, murmured, "A moment, my dear," and handed around business cards with a polite bow and smile to each lady. He then offered Margo his arm. "A moment's attention to business works wonders, don't you agree?"

Margo laughed, waved goodbye to her brief acquaintances, then strolled out into the London night on Malcolm's capable arm.

By the time their cab had swayed through five dark streets, thick fog had left them blind. Swirling, foul yellow drifts blanketed the streets. Even the horse vanished from view. Only the soft clip-clop of its hooves assured Margo they weren't drifting along by magic.

"London stinks," Margo whispered. "Like a barnyard. And that fog smells awful."

"London is full of horses," Malcolm whispered back.

"Some hundred tons of manure fall on London streets every day."

"Every *day*?"

"Daily," Malcolm affirmed. "And the fogs have been known to kill hundreds in a single day. If you find it difficult to breathe, you must tell me at once and we'll take a train for the country until the worst of it clears."

"I can breathe," Margo whispered, "it just isn't pleasant. Are we going to a hotel?"

"Actually, no. We'll stay at a boarding house near Victoria Station for the night, then rent a flat on the morrow. That will give us privacy to come and go without undue notice. John, here, will be staying on at the flat once we've gone."

"Mr. Carson be terrible gen'rous, Mr. Moore," John said in the darkness.

Margo giggled. "You sound so funny."

"He sounds exactly as he should," Malcolm said sternly. "You do not. Charity schoolgirls are demure and silent, not giggling, brash things given to rude comments."

"Well, excuse me," Margo muttered.

"Certainly not. Study your part, young lady. That is an order."

Margo sighed. Another domineering male . . . She almost looked forward to trading the schoolgirl getup for the rough clothes of a country farmer or the even rougher getup of a costermonger. Masquerading as a boy, she wouldn't need to worry so much about observing all these confining social conventions. She began to catch a glimmer of what Kit had meant when he'd insisted women would have a rough go of it trying to scout.

The sound of water lapping against stone and a hollow change in the sound of the horse's hooves told Margo they were very near the river. The occasional complaining grumble of a steam whistle drifted on the evil yellow fog like the distant cries of dying hounds.

"Where are we? I can't see a thing."

"Crossing Lambeth Bridge."

A few rents in the murk revealed a distant, dark wall. "And that?"

"Millbank Penitentiary. New Bridewell's not far from here, either."

"New Bridewell?"

"A rather notorious prison, my dear. You do ask the most shocking questions."

Fog closed in again the moment they left the open bridge with its fitful breeze. Margo heard the heavy, muted rumbling of not-too-distant trains. A shrill whistle shivered through the foul, wet air, so close Margo jumped.

"Don't be alarmed, Miss Smythe. It is merely a train arriving at Victoria Station."

"Will we hear that all night?"

Malcolm's chuckle reached her. "Indeed."

Fiend. He'd done this on purpose, to leave her groggy and off balance tomorrow. He *knew* she was already running on virtually no sleep. *Well, when you start scouting, you may be short of sleep, too. Consider it part of the lesson.* At length, their driver halted. Malcolm left her shivering inside the cold carriage. He made arrangements with the lady who ran the boarding house, then offered his hand and assisted her from the cab.

"Oh, you poor dear, you must be tired," the plump lady smiled, ushering them up a long, dark staircase. A gaslight at the landing threw feeble light down the stairwell. Margo had to watch the hem of her dress to keep from tripping in the shadows. "Your guardian said how you'd come all the way from Honduras and then by train, poor thing, orphaned by them terrible fevers, and now he's enrolled you in the School, but can't bear to part company wi' you yet. Such a nice gentleman, your guardian, watch your step, dear, that's good, and here's your room. Mr. Moore's is directly along the hall, there, second on your right. I'll have hot water sent up. And here's your bag, dearie," she said, taking the carpet bag from John and setting it on a heavy piece of furniture that evidently was meant as a dry sink, judging from the basin and pitcher her hostess took from its lower recesses.

"I'll leave you now to rest and see you at breakfast, dearie. Pull the bell if you need anything."

And that—Margo gaped as the landlady left in a rustle of petticoats and firmly closed the door—was that.

And she died more than a hundred years ago. . . .

Margo shivered, momentarily overcome by the unreality of it. It wasn't at all like watching an old film or even like participating in a stage play. It was like stepping into someone else's life, complete with sounds and smells and the sensation that if she blinked it would all vanish like a soap bubble. But it didn't. She sank down slowly on the edge of a feather tick. Bed ropes creaked. The room smelled musty. Gaslight burned softly behind a frosted globe on the wall. Margo wondered how in the world to turn it off. She untied her hat and took it off then removed the cap and the heavy woolen cape. The once-white cap was grey from coal smoke. She shivered absently. The room was freezing and damp. No central heat.

"Now what?" she wondered aloud.

A soft tap on the door brought her to her feet. Margo clutched the cap in knotted fingers. *"Who is it?"* Her voice came out shaky and thin.

"It's Mr. Moore, Miss Smythe. Might I speak with you for a moment?"

Margo all but flew across the room. She snatched the door open.

He smiled widely at her expression, then nodded toward the gas light. "See that little chain on the side?"

Margo peered toward the light. "Yes."

"Pull it once to turn off the lamp. Don't blow out

the flame or your room will fill up with gas and we'll all die rather messily."

Oh. "Thank you. I—I was wondering about that."

"Very good. Any other questions before I retire for the evening?"

Margo had about a million of them, but the only thing that popped into her head was, "How do I get warm? It's freezing in here."

Malcolm glanced around the room. "No fireplace. No stove, either. The landlady is doubtless afraid of fires and rightly so. But there should be plenty of quilts in that linen press." He pointed to a heavy piece of furniture across the room. "Pile them on and snuggle in. Anything else?"

Margo didn't dare admit that she wanted—desperately— to say "I'm scared." So she shook her head and gave him a bright smile.

"Very good, then. I shall see you at breakfast." He bent and kissed her forehead. "Good night, my dear. Lock your door."

Then he stepped down the hall and entered his room. His door clicked softly shut. A key turned in the lock. Margo stood gazing down the dimly lit corridor for several moments while her brow tingled under the remembered feel of Malcolm Moore's lips.

Oh, don't be ridiculous! All you need is to pull some stupid schoolgirl stunt like falling for a poverty-stricken time guide. He's too old for you, anyway, and thinks you're silly into the bargain. Besides, you had enough heartache from Billy Pandropolous to swear off men for all time.

She closed her door and locked it, experiencing a swift prickle of tears behind her eyelids. She didn't want Malcolm Moore to think she was silly. She wanted to prove to him—and everyone else—that she could do this job. Do it and be good at it.

She lay awake far into the night, listening to the rumble

of carriages and wagons through London's filthy streets and wincing at the shriek of steam locomotives. And the whole time she lay there, Margo wondered miserably what that kiss would have felt like against her lips.

Workaday London enthralled.

Malcolm made arrangements for a small flat in western London, several streets east of Grosvenor Square, which was itself just east of the ultrafashionable Hyde Park in Mayfair. The West End was where—according to Malcolm—Britain's ten thousand or so members of "Society" (some fifteen hundred families) made their London homes. The houses were splendid, but their construction surprised Margo. Most of them were more like condos than individual houses. Immensely long stone and brick facades took up entire city blocks, subdivided into individual "houses" that each wealthy family owned.

"It's a law," Malcolm explained, "passed after the Great Fire of 1666. Not only fewer combustible materials, but this construction plan was adopted to help combat the spread of another disastrous fire."

"How bad was it?"

Malcolm said quietly, "Most of London burned. Only a tiny corner of the city was spared. One of its blessings, of course, was that the fire evidently destroyed the plague, since there haven't been any outbreaks since then. Cholera, on the other hand, remains a serious difficulty."

Margo gazed in rapt fascination at the long, mellow facades, the immaculately clean walks, the ladies being assisted by liveried footmen into carriages for their round of "morning calls." They were gorgeous in heavy silks, furs, and luxuriant feathered hats. Margo sighed, acutely conscious of her charity-school costume and short, dyed hair; but she didn't let that spoil the fun of watching the "quality" pass by.

"We're far enough from the heart of Mayfair," Malcolm told her once they had settled into the six-room flat, "to go unnoticed in our seedier disguises, but close enough to avoid the filth and crime of the East End and allow me to continue my persona as independent gentleman."

"Have you been here before?"

"Not this particular flat, no; but this general area, yes. I bring my tourists here rather than to a hotel, unless they insist otherwise. Living in a flat and buying vegetables and fish from the markets gives one rather a better feel for life here. Unpack your things, Miss Smythe, and we'll begin our work."

He had John hire a carriage and horses for the week while they unpacked. Malcolm arranged with the landlady for deliveries to be made from a reputable chandler to victual them with staples. Once the food arrived, he showed Margo how to prepare a British-style luncheon for a country outing.

"A country outing?" Margo asked excitedly. "Really?"

Malcolm smiled. "I doubt it's what you have in mind. Pack that set of tweeds for me, would you? That's a dear. And bring along that loose shirt, those trousers, and that pair of boots for yourself. Yes, those. As a scout, one of the most important things you'll need to know is how to handle horses. I'm going to teach you to ride."

The closest thing to a horse Margo had ever ridden was a carousel at the state fair. And only then because her neighbors had taken her with their kids, pitying a child whose father spent most of what he had on liquor—and, eventually, worse.

"I don't know anything about horses," she said dubiously.

"You will." Malcolm's cheerful smile removed the hint of threat.

The horses John hired—four altogether—came in

two distinct pairs. As John shook out the reins over the carriage horses, Malcolm explained.

"Those are cobs, sturdy draft horses used for pulling loads. This isn't the fanciest carriage available, although it's smart and very up-to-date in keeping with my persona here."

"What's it called?"

"It's a four-wheeled brougham, with a hard top," he rapped the ceiling with his knuckles, "which will make it easier for you to change your attire without being noticed. This is the family vehicle of the 1880's, very respectable."

"And the horses tied behind?" They were much sleeker than the stocky carriage horses.

"Hacks. General riding animals, not nearly as expensive or handsome as hunters, but much easier to manage and cheaper to rent for those who don't care to feed a horse year-round, pay for its stabling, a groomsman, a blacksmith . . ."

"Expensive, huh?"

"Very. That's why livery stables do such a brisk business hiring animals and carriages."

Margo thought about what Connie had said on the subject of class distinction and decided to risk a question. "What do the really rich people think about people who hire carriages and horses?"

Malcolm's mobile features lit up. "Very good, Miss Smythe! Generally, we're snubbed, of course. Anyone with pretensions to society keeps a carriage and horses of his own. I am absolved through the eccentricity of my comings and goings from Honduras. Providing I ever acquire the capital, I intend to take out a long-term lease on a small house where I might entertain guests. All my down-time acquaintances urge me to do so, in order to keep a permanent staff rather than relying on the vagaries of agency people."

Margo wondered how much that would cost, but

didn't quite dare ask. That seemed like an awfully personal question and she was still feeling very uncertain in the aftermath of that harmless kiss last night.

"Speaking of money, do you remember my lecture on currency?"

Oh, no . . .

"I, uh . . ." Margo tried frantically to recall what Malcolm had taught her during their visit to Goldie Morran, one of TT-86's money changers. "The basic unit's the pound. It's abbreviated with that little 'L' thing."

"And a pound is made up of . . ."

She cast back through the confusion of foreign terms. "Twenty shillings."

"Twenty-one shillings being called?"

Oh, God, it was some sort of bird . . . "A hen?"

Malcolm sat back and covered his eyes, stricken with helpless laughter. "The association," he wheezed, "is flawlessly logical, I'll have to credit you that much. A *guinea*, Margo. A guinea."

"A guinea," she repeated grimly. "Twenty-one shillings is a guinea."

"Now, what else do we call twenty shillings, other than a pound?"

Margo screwed shut her eyes and tried to remember. Not a king, there was a queen on the throne. "A sovereign."

"Or quid, in slang terms. What's it made of?"

"Gold. So's a half-sovereign!" she finished triumphantly.

"And half of that?"

Something else to do with royalty. But what, she couldn't remember. She lifted her hands helplessly.

"A crown. Five shillings is a crown, or a 'bull' in slang usage."

Margo took a deep breath. "A crown. A quarter sovereign is a crown. Then there's the half-crown, or two-and-a-half shillings." Her head hurt.

"Two shillings is . . ."

"I don't know," Margo wailed. "My head aches!"

Malcolm produced a card from his waistcoat pocket, hand-written with what was clearly a period inkpen. "Study this. If you forget and must refer to this, please explain that you're a recently orphaned American with a British benefactor and you just can't keep all this straight, then bat your eyelashes and look helpless and the shopkeepers will probably fall over themselves trying to assist you."

Margo couldn't help it. She burst out laughing at the ludicrous face Malcolm presented. He grinned and handed over the card. Margo settled herself to study the rest of the currency—florins, pence, groats, pennies, farthings, and all the rest—with a much improved frame of mind.

Horses, Margo learned, were tricky beasts.

Changing clothing in the cramped carriage was easy compared to managing an animal that weighed half a ton and scared her to death every time it blew quietly at the front of her shirt.

"All right," Malcolm said patiently when she succeeded in bridling the hack without losing a thumb or fingers, "do it again."

She shut her eyes, summoned up every erg of patience she possessed, and unbuckled the bridle. Then performed the whole terrifying procedure again. They'd been at this an hour and she still hadn't even *saddled* the horse, much less gotten on its back. The "riding" lesson had begun with a bewildering new set of terms to learn: withers, fetlocks, gaits, snaffles, cinches, leathers, headstalls . . .

Oh, God, why did I ever think time scouting would be easier than college?

But even she could see the practical necessity of learning to control *the* mode of transportation from prehistory right down to the invention of the mass-produced automobile.

Margo finally mastered haltering and bridling, moved on to saddling, then spent twenty minutes exercising her hack on a lunge line to learn the difference in its gaits and learned to judge what it took to control a horse from the ground. By the time she passed muster, she was exhausted. Her toes, fingertips, and nose were numb with cold.

"Shall we break for lunch," Malcolm suggested, "then try our first ride afterward?"

Oh, thank God.

"Cool out your horse by walking him up and down the lane for about five minutes while John spreads out a blanket. Then we'll water him and rest a bit ourselves."

At least Malcolm accompanied her on the walk. The horse's hooves clopped softly behind them. Margo had begun to feel less nervous asking questions. "Why do we have to cool him out? It's freezing out here!"

"Any time you work a horse, cool him out. Particularly in cold weather. An overheated horse can catch a fatal chill if he's not properly cooled down afterward. Horses are remarkably delicate creatures, prone to all sorts of illness and accident. Your life literally depends on the care you give your horse. Treat him with better care than you treat yourself. Your horse is fed and watered before you even think of resting or eating your own meal. Otherwise, you may not have a horse afterward."

It made sense. It also sounded remarkably similar to Ann Vinh Mulhaney's lecture on caring for one's firearms: "Keep them clean. Particularly if you're using a black-powder weapon. Clean it every time you use it. Black powder and early priming compounds are corrosive. Clean your gun thoroughly or it'll be useless—and that can happen *fast*. Don't ever bet your life on a dirty weapon."

"Mal— Mr. Moore," she amended hastily, "are you carrying a firearm?"

He glanced swiftly at her. "Whatever brought on that question?"

"You just sounded like Ms. Mulhaney, about keeping firearms clean or losing the use of them. So then I wondered."

"One generally doesn't ask a gentlemen, 'Sir, are you armed?' As it happens, I am. I never travel to London, never mind outside it, without a good revolver on my person."

"Isn't that illegal?"

His lips twitched faintly. "Not yet."

Oh.

"There are a few things about down-time cultures," Malcolm said with a sigh, "that are vastly preferable to up-time nonsense. Self-defense attitudes being one of them. Let's turn about, shall we? I believe he's cooling out nicely."

Margo turned the horse and they returned to the hired carriage, where she tied the reins and draped a warm blanket over his back. She then watered the animal from a pail John produced.

"Thank you, John," she smiled.

"Me pleasure, miss."

Margo grinned, but refrained from comment, since they were supposed to stay "in character" as much as possible to avoid slip-ups.

Lunch was simple but good: slices of beef and cheese on crusted rolls and red wine in sturdy mugs. John had built a warm fire and spread out a blanket for them. Margo relaxed, draping her heavy cape around her shoulders and leaning close to the fire to keep from catching a chill. Clouds raced past through a lacing of barren branches above their little fire. She couldn't identify the tall tree but sunlight filtering down through the spiderwork of twigs and branches was wonderful. "Nice."

Birdsong twittered through the silence. One of the horses blew quietly and let a hind leg go slack as it dozed. Tired as she was, it would have been incredibly easy just to close her eyes and fall asleep to the hush of birdsong and the profound silence behind it. Far, far away Margo heard voices, the words indistinguishable with distance. And beyond the voices, the faint hoot of a train.

Margo hadn't realized the world before automobiles and jet aircraft could be so quiet.

"Ready for that riding lesson?"

Margo opened her eyes and found Malcolm smiling down at her.

"Yes, Mr. Moore, I believe I am."

"Good." He offered her a hand up.

Margo scrambled to her feet, refreshed and ready to tackle anything. *Today*, she told herself, *I become a horsewoman*.

The horse—of course—had other ideas.

Margo learned the first critical lesson about horseback riding within five minutes. When you fall off, you get back on. Heart in her mouth, she tried again. This time, she rechecked the cinch first, as Malcolm had told her before lunch—and which she'd forgotten in the interim—then clambered back aboard.

This time, the saddle held. She started breathing again and relaxed her death grip on the mane. "Okay, I'm on. Now what?"

Malcolm was busy mounting his own horse. Margo discovered an intense envy of the ease with which he floated into the saddle and found a seat. "Follow me and copy what I do."

He set off by thumping heels sharply against the horse's belly. Margo tried it. Her hack moved off sedately with a placid "I have a novice on my back" air about him.

"It works!"

"Well, of course it works," Malcolm laughed. He reined in to let her pass. "Heels down, toes in."

"Ow! That hurts!"

"And don't forget to grip with your thighs. But leave your hands relaxed. You don't want to bruise his mouth with the bit."

What about my *bruises?*

Concentrating on heels, toes, thighs, and hands all at the same time while steering and not falling off was nerve-racking. For the first ten minutes, Margo sweat into her clothes and was thoroughly miserable. The horse didn't seem to mind, however.

"Keep right on," Malcolm said over his shoulder. "I'll follow you for a bit."

He reined around behind her. Margo's horse tried to follow. She hauled on the reins, overcorrected, and sent her horse straight toward a hedgerow. She straightened him out after wandering back and forth across the lane several times. Eventually she mastered the knack of keeping a fairly steady course.

"You're doing fine," Malcolm said from behind her. "Sit up a little straighter. That's good. Toes *in*. Heels *down*. Better. Elbows relaxed, wrists relaxed. Good. Gather up the reins slightly. If he bolts now, he'll have the bit in his teeth and there'll be no stopping him. Firm but relaxed."

"If he *bolts?*" Margo asked. "Why would he do that?"

"Horses just do. It's called shying. Anything can scare a horse. A leaf rustling the wrong way. A noise. An unexpected movement or color. Or a particular item. A parasol. A train. A lawnchair."

"Great. I'm stuck way up here on something likely to jump at a shadow?"

"Precisely. Tighten your thighs. Heels *down*."

Ow . . .

After half an hour, Malcolm let her trot. That was worse. The gait jolted her from top to bottom. Learning to *post* a trot put cramps in her thigh muscles. He brought her back down to a walk again to let her rest.

"I hate this!"

"That's because we haven't tried the canter yet," Malcolm smiled.

"And when we get to do that? Next week?"

Malcolm laughed. "Patience, Miss Smythe. Patience. You can't fly until you've learned to flap your wings properly. Now, the post again."

Margo held back a groan and kicked her horse into the posting trot that jolted everything that *could* be jolted. She missed her timing, rising on the wrong swing of the horse's withers, and discovered that was worse. She jolted along for a couple of paces before she got it right again. Eventually, Margo mastered it.

"All right," Malcolm said, drawing up beside her, "let's see if the nag will canter."

Malcolm clucked once and urged his horse forward with thighs, knees, and heels. He leaned forward—

And shot away in a thunder of hoofbeats. Belatedly Margo kicked her own horse to greater speed. One moment they were jolting through a horrendous trot. The next, Margo was flying.

"*Oh!*"

It was wonderful.

She found herself grinning like an idiot as her horse caught up with Malcolm's. "Hi!"

He glanced over and grinned. "Better?"

"Wow!"

"Thought you'd like that!"

"It's . . . it's terrific!" She felt alive all over, even down to her toes. The horse moved under her in a smoothly bunched rhythm, while hedgerows whipped past to a glorious, stinging wind in her face.

"Better pull up," Malcolm warned, "before we come to the crossroad."

Margo didn't want to pull up and go back. Greatly daring, she kicked her horse to greater speed. He burst into a gallop that tore the breath from her lungs and left her ecstatic. Eyes shining, she tore down the country lane and shot into the crossroad—

And nearly ran down a heavy coach and four sweating horses. Margo screamed. Her own horse shied, nearly tossing her out of the saddle. Then the nag plunged into a watery meadow at full gallop. Margo hauled on the reins. The horse didn't slow down. She pulled harder, still to no avail. Freezing spray from the wet meadow soaked her legs. Patches of ice shattered under her horse's flying hooves. Then Malcolm thundered up and leaned over. He seized the reins in an iron grip. Her horse tossed its head, trying to rear, then settled down to a trot. They finally halted.

Malcolm sat panting on his own horse, literally white with rage. "OUT OF THE SADDLE! Walk him back!"

Margo slid to the ground. Rubbery legs nearly dumped her headlong into muddy, half-frozen water. She wanted to cry. Instead she snatched the reins and led the horse back toward the crossroad. Malcolm sent his own mount back at a hard gallop, spattering her with mud from head to foot. That did it. She started crying, silently. She was furious and miserable and consumed with embarrassment. Malcolm had stopped far ahead, where he was talking with the driver of the coach. The carriage had careered off the road.

"Oh, no," she wailed. What if someone had been hurt? *I'm an idiot. . . .*

She couldn't bear even to look at the coach as she slunk past, leading the horse back down the lane. When Malcolm passed her, back in the saddle, he was moving at a slow walk, but he didn't even acknowledge her presence. When she finally regained the carriage, Malcolm was waiting.

"Fortunately," he said in a tone as icy as the water in her shoes, "no one was injured. Now get back on that horse and do as I tell you this time."

She scrubbed mud and tears with the back of one hand. "M-my feet are wet. And freezing."

Malcolm produced dry stockings. She changed, then wearily hauled herself back into the saddle. The rest of the afternoon passed in frigid silence, broken only by Malcolm's barked instructions. Margo learned to control her horse at the canter and the gallop. By twilight she was able to stay with him when Malcolm deliberately spooked the hack into rearing, shying, and bolting with her.

It was a hard-won accomplishment and she should have been proud of it. All she felt was miserable, bruised, and exhausted. Whatever wasn't numb from the cold ached mercilessly. John solicitously filled a basin for her to wash off the mud. He'd heated the water over the fire. Her fingers stung like fire when she dunked them into the hot water. She finally struggled back into the hateful undergarments, the charity gown and pinafore. Then she had to take another ATLS and star-fix reading and update her personal log. When Malcolm finally allowed her to climb into the carriage for the return to town, she hid her face in the side cushions and pretended to sleep.

Malcolm settled beside her while John loaded the luggage and lit the carriage lanterns, then they set out through the dark. As a first day down time, it had been a mixed success at best. They rattled along in utter silence for nearly half an hour. Then Malcolm said quietly, "Miss— Margo. Are you awake?"

She made some strangled sound that was meant to be a "Yes" and came out sounding more like a cat caught in a vacuum cleaner.

Malcolm hesitated in the dark, then settled an arm around her shoulders. She turned toward him and gave in, wetting his tweed coat thoroughly between hiccoughs. "Shh . . ."

With the release of tension—and the sure knowledge

that he'd forgiven her—crushing exhaustion overtook Margo. She fell asleep to the jolt of carriage wheels on the rutted lane, the warmth of Malcolm's arm around her, and the thump of his heartbeat under her ear. The last, whispery sensation to come to her in the darkness was the scent of his skin as he bent and softly kissed her hair.

Nothing in Margo's experience prepared her for the East End.

Not an abusive father, not the crime and violence of New York, not even the barrage of televised images of starving, ragged third worlders, brandished like meat cleavers by charities desperately trying to stave off global disaster.

"My God," Margo kept whispering. "My God . . ."

They set out very early in the morning. Malcolm thrust a pistol into a holster under his jacket and pocketed a tin wrapped with waxed cord, then asked John to drive them to Lower Thames Street, near the famous London Docks.

The Docks had been cut out of the earth in Wapping to form a deep, rectangular "harbor" filled with river water. The city surrounded it on all sides. Steamers and sailing ships were literally parked at the end of narrow, filthy streets.

They picked up an empty pushcart cart John had procured and began walking through the pre-dawn chill. Margo's old boots and woolen, uncreased trousers chafed. Her ragged shirt and threadbare pea jacket barely kept out the chill. Swing docks afforded occasional glimpses of the river as they passed the stinking, bow-windowed taverns of Wapping. Sailors accosted everything female with such gusto Margo huddled more deeply into her boy's garments, desperately grateful for the disguise.

Okay, so they were right. She didn't have to be happy

about it, but she could disguise herself. Fortunately, none of the sailors so much as glanced at her twice. Malcolm steered them toward the riverbank, where the stench of tidal mudflats was overwhelming. They watched young kids, mostly barefooted, picking through the freezing mud.

"Mudlarks," he explained quietly. "They scavenge bits of iron or coal, anything they can sell for a few pence. Most children are supposed to be in school, but the poorest often dodge it, as you see. There used to be much fiercer competition down there, before mandatory schooling laws were passed. On Saturdays, the riverbanks are alive with starving mudlarks."

One romantic illusion after another shattered into slivers on the cold road.

"What are those?" she asked, pointing to a boat mid-river with large nets out. "Fishermen?"

"No. Draggers. They look for dropped valuables, including bodies they can loot for money and other sellable items."

"*Corpses!*" Margo gasped. "My God, Malcolm—" She bit her tongue. "Sorry."

"Dressed as a boy, it's not such a grave error, but I'd still prefer you said Mr. Moore. People will take you for my apprentice. You've seen enough here. We have to get to Billingsgate before the worst of the crowds do."

"Billingsgate?"

"Billingsgate Market," Malcolm explained as they neared a maelstrom of carts, wagons, barrels, boats, and human beings. "Royal Charter gives Billingsgate a monopoly on fish."

The stench and noise were unbelievable. Margo wanted to cover her ears and hold her breath. They shoved in cheek-to-jowl with hundreds of other costermongers buying their day's wares to peddle. Liveried servants from fine houses, ordinary lower class wives, and buyers for restaurants as well as shippers who would take loads of fish inland for sale, all fought one another for the day's catch.

"Salmon for Belgravia," Malcolm shouted above the roar, "and herrings for Whitechapel!"

"What do we want?"

"Eels!"

Eels?

After that dinner at the Epicurean Delight, Billingsgate's eels came as another rude shock. Malcolm filled their cart with the most repugnant, slithery mess Margo had ever seen. Jellied eels went from huge enameled bowls into stoneware pots. From another vendor they procured hot "pie-and-mash" pies, plus a supply of hideous green stuff the screaming fishwife called "liquor." Malcolm bargained the prices lower in an earbending accent. The language the fishwives used put to shame anything Margo had heard on the streets of New York—when she understood it at all. Malcolm stacked the pies in their cart, layered them on boards and wrapped them in worn woolen cloth to keep them warm. Margo—under instructions to pay attention to details—tried to keep track of what she witnessed, but there was so much to take in she found it all running together in a screaming blur.

They finally escaped Billingsgate's scaly stench and set out. Malcolm did a surprisingly brisk business selling eels and pies as they entered the cramped streets of Wapping. Of Malcolm's colorful patter, however, Margo didn't understand one word in four.

"Give yer plates of meat a treat," he called out, "rest a bit, I've eels to eat!" Then, another block onward, "Yer trouble and strife givin' you worries? Tike 'ome 'ot eels, thankee and tip o' the titfer t' you, mate." Then, to a hollow-cheeked lad who eyed the cart longingly, "Wot, no bees 'n' 'oney? Rough days but I gots mouths ter feed meself." And finally, in a completely incomprehensible exchange with a sailor, "Aye, let's 'ope ain't no pleasure an' pain t'day. 'A penny, an' enjoy."

When they moved out of earshot, Margo could no longer contain burning curiosity. "What in the world are you *saying?*"

Malcolm grinned. "It's Cockney speech. Cockney's more than an accent, it's a way of speaking. Rhyming sales patter and no real attention to grammar."

"But what does it *mean?*"

He chuckled and eased the cart over to one side of the narrow street. "All right. I'll try to translate what I've been saying." He glanced upward, evidently casting back through his patter of the previous few minutes. "Plates of meat—those are your feet. Essentially I said, 'Give your feet a treat. Sit down and rest a while, have some delicious eels.' Then let's see, what did I say next?"

"Something about trouble and strife giving you worries. That made sense, at least."

"Did it?" His mobile mouth quirked upward at the corners. "Trouble and strife means 'your wife.' "

"Your *wife?*"

Malcolm laughed. "That phrase meant 'Is your wife giving you problems? Take home some hot eels.' Hinting of course, that a warm breakfast might soothe her ragged temper."

"What's a titfer?"

His eyes twinkled. "Tit for tat means hat. Cockney loves to abbreviate as much as any other language. A tip of the titfer—"

"Is a tip of the hat," Margo finished.

"Right. Bees and honey is money—and without it, you're sunk if you want breakfast from this cart."

"What about the pleasure and pain bit?"

Malcolm chuckled. "I told him I hoped it didn't rain."

Margo rolled her eyes. "Good grief. How is anyone supposed to learn all this? And what's that horrible stuff made of, anyway?" Margo asked, pointing to the green "liquor" in the cart.

"Parsley sauce."

"Parsley sauce? Oh. I couldn't imagine what it was." She'd had visions of some Cockney fishwife growing mold in vats and adding gelatin.

"Actually, it's quite good. Want to sample the wares?"

Margo was starving. "Uh, no. Thanks."

Malcolm cut up one of the pies anyway and spread parsley sauce on it. "You need to eat. The day's cold and it'll be long."

She shut her eyes and bit into it. Then glanced up, startled. "Hey, not bad!"

Malcolm grinned and wolfed his own down. "You look too healthy. Suck in your cheeks a little. Better . . ." He scooped up a handful of filth and smeared mud across one cheek. "Yes, that's it."

Margo tried to hold her breath. The mud stank.

He smeared his clothes artistically then washed his hands from a bottle in the bottom of the cart. "Next stop, Whitechapel. Watch your step—this is a rough area."

Whitechapel's main roads were surprisingly wide—and every last inch of roadway was jammed with wagons and ox-carts. Behind the main streets, however . . .

London's deadly slum was a sunless maze of narrow alleyways, winding, dangerous streets, and courtyards where nothing green found purchase in the filthy soil. Crowded conditions left some people living on ramshackle staircases. Mud and filth reeked underfoot. Everywhere Margo looked were ragged, filthy people: sleeping on stairs, in puddles of filth, in rooms whose doors sagged so far open she could see drunken men and women snoring in piles of decaying refuse. The stench was overwhelming. Here and there, men and women urinated openly in the streets.

Margo whispered, "Isn't this where Jack—"

He hushed her. "Not until later in the year. August."

Margo shivered and eyed ill-kempt women, wondering which of them might fall victim to the notorious serial murderer. It was an unsettling thought. Kit Carson's brutal assessment of her chances in this slum rang in her ears. *All right,* she grudged him, *you've got a point.*

Malcolm sold a few eels, mostly to sleepy women whose clothing still reeked of their previous night's customers. Everywhere the stench of human waste, cheap gin, and rot rose like a miasma from the ground.

"Are *all* the women in Whitechapel prostitutes?" Margo whispered.

Malcolm shook his head. "Not all." Then in a cautious whisper, "There are some eighty-thousand whores in London, most trying to stave off starvation." Margo understood that statement now in a way that would have been impossible two hours previously.

"Do they stay prostitutes?"

"Some yes, many no. Many take to the 'gay' life, as prostitution was known, only long enough to find a better-paying job. Northwest of here, up in Spitalfields for instance, a woman can get work in the garment district sweat shops. If she doesn't have too many mouths to feed, she might eke out a living without going back on the streets."

They glanced at a yawning fourteen-year-old who eyed Margo speculatively, appraising the "young man" for potential business even this early in the day. She switched her attention to Malcolm and smiled. "Tumble for a pie?"

Malcolm just shook his head, leaving the girl hurling curses at them.

Margo was fascinated and repulsed at the same time. She felt as though she'd stepped into a living play whose author had no real ending in mind. *Study your part, study the background.* That was what Kit and Malcolm had brought her here to learn.

"With so many women in the business," Margo asked slowly, trying hard to understand, "isn't competition fierce?"

"Ye-esss . . . in a manner of speaking. Officially, you understand, sex was considered extremely bad for one's health. Led to a breakdown of one's physical constitution and mental faculties. Privately, our straight-laced Victorian gentleman considered sex his natural right— and any woman born lower than his station was fair game. London had several million souls, recall, not to mention seafaring crews. Remind yourself to look up an eleven-volume personal memoir called *My Private Life* when we return to the station library. It's available on computer now. You'll find it . . . revealing of Victorian social attitudes."

"What happens to all these women? When they're too old or ill to work?"

"Some go to the Magdalen for help."

"Magdalen?"

"South of the Thames," Malcolm murmured as they trundled their cart along, "you will find four kinds of 'charity' institutions, if one can call them that. Bedlam— Bethlehem Hospital—is for mental patients. Old Bridewell was originally a school to train apprentices, but it turned into a brutal prison. Eventually a new school was attached to the prison grounds to house legitimate apprentices. Bridewell apprentices are notorious delinquents, the terror of the city. Then there are protected girls in the purple uniforms of the Lambeth Asylum for Female Orphans, and of course the grey of the Magdalen Hospital for seduced girls and prostitutes. A number of the girls rescued by Magdalen go mad anyway from incurable syphilis."

Margo shuddered. She'd grown up taking medical miracles for granted. How long did it take the "social disease" to deteriorate a person's brain into insanity?

While she tried to take it all in, they sold eels and

pies and moved steadily westward. Then, astonishing her with the abruptness of the transition, the dome of St. Paul's Cathedral loomed up over the dreary skyline. They found themselves abruptly in the heart of the bright, sunlit "City" where London's Lord Mayor ruled from Mansion House. Margo gaped at the wealthy carriages which jostled for space on the narrow streets.

"It's amazing," she said, staring back the way they'd come. "I can hardly believe the change."

"Yes. It is startling, isn't it?"

The respite didn't last long, though. Past Lincoln Inn Fields, they plunged once more into a realm of dark, sagging rooflines which overhung one another. The bright sunlight they'd left behind seemed centuries as well as miles away.

"How can they live and work so close to this misery and not *care?*"

Malcolm gave her a long, penetrating look. "They haven't wanted to see it. An effort is eventually made, particularly after Red Jack ensures that conditions in Whitechapel are widely reported upon. And the Salvation Army got its start here a few years ago, so there is some—" He broke off and swore under his breath. "Damn, I hadn't noticed we'd left Charing Cross Road. Heads up, now. We've wandered into St. Giles."

They'd entered a "traffic circle" marked "Seven Dials" but there was no traffic, pedestrian or otherwise. At the center of the circle stood a dilapidated clock tower with seven faces. Running outward from the tower like mangled spokes from a wheel were seven sunless alleyways and wretched, filthy courtyards. They vanished into a slum that made Whitechapel seem luxurious. A noxious vapor rose from the houses, hanging like fog over sagging rooftops. Broken gin bottles littered the filthy ground. Under layers of filth and dirty ice might have been paved streets.

"Malcolm . . ." She felt as though the blank windows—

many of them without glass—were staring at her like malicious eyes.

"These seven streets are the most dangerous place in all London. Watch our backs until we're well out of here."

From out of the gloom in the dank alleyways, rough men in tattered clothing watched through narrowed eyes. Margo kept a sharp lookout and wished they could break into a run. *You'll cope with this on your own as a scout. This is the career you asked Kit Carson to give you.*

At the moment, Margo would almost have traded this for another beating at her father's hands.

Almost.

Then she saw furtive movement in the shadows, the glint of steel—

The man who grabbed her from behind laid a straight razor at her throat. She froze, a scream dying in her throat. Two other toughs materialized in front of Malcolm. Margo realized with a shock, *They're younger than I am!*

The feel of sharp steel at her throat left her trembling. Margo's attacker tightened his arm around her waist. "Lookit, 'ee don' even shave yet." The boy's breath was foul. " 'ow bouts I teach 'im?"

The other boys grinned. Their straight razors glinted evilly. Malcolm had gone very still, trapped between them.

" 'and over the tike, mate, an' mibey we let 'im shave 'is own self?"

While Margo tried to sort out what, exactly, he'd demanded, Malcolm reached for the money pouch at his waist.

"Quick, now," the boldest said. He dropped his gaze from Margo to watch Malcolm pluck at his purse strings.

Margo moved instantly. She grabbed her assailant's wrist, twisting toward him as she shoved the wicked straight razor away from her throat—then grabbed a handful of his crotch and *crushed*.

The boy screamed. She continued the turn, dragging his arm up behind him, then kicked the back of his knee. He went down with a gurgling sound and writhed on the ground, holding himself.

She whirled—

Malcolm had gone absolutely *white*. "You little *idiot*—"

Before either of the other boys could strike, an enormous bull of a man stepped out from the alleyway and shoved them aside.

"You 'urt me boy," he said, staring at Margo. The bludgeon he held was as thick as Margo's thigh. His shoulders were twice the size of Malcolm's. He wore a thick woolen coat that covered him almost to the knees. Rough work pants and low, broken shoes completed the picture of the quintessential murderous lout. He grinned at Margo. "First I cracks your skull." He licked dirty lips. "Then me nephews cuts up wot's left."

Margo was suddenly conscious of other grimy faces in the shadows, watching with inhuman detachment. Malcolm swore and backed away from the trio, turning so they couldn't see him draw his revolver from concealment. The moose in the center hefted his cudgel—

He charged. So fast Margo didn't even have time to scream.

Malcolm fired three shots and dove to one side. One of the shots hit the man's right ankle. The would-be killer screamed, lurched, and sprawled into the filth. The teenagers ran clattering down an alley. Malcolm whipped around like a cat and grabbed Margo's wrist, dragging her in the opposite direction. They dashed the length of a filthy, stinking alleyway and emerged into St. Giles-in-the-Field. Malcolm dodged into a rank, overgrown churchyard and dragged her behind a crumbling gravestone, then pressed a hard hand over her mouth. They waited, hearts thudding, but Margo heard no immediate sound of pursuit.

"Reload this," Malcolm said brusquely, thrusting his pistol and the tin from his pocket into her hands. He crept out of the graveyard and eased his way to the edge of the churchyard, peering back the way they'd come.

Margo stared stupidly at the gun. The tin was heavy. It rattled. She had no idea how to reload this revolver. It wasn't anything like the revolvers Ann Mulhaney had taught her to shoot. She was still staring idiotically at it when Malcolm returned.

He took the pistol—then swore in language she hadn't known he could use. "You didn't reload!"

Tears prickled behind her eyes. "I—"

"First you pull a stupid stunt like fighting that street tough—"

"But he was robbing us!"

Malcolm's pallor turned to marble coldness. *"I was going to give him the goddamned money!* My God, it's just a few pence! You nearly got us both killed—and I had to risk shooting that lout—"

"You didn't even shoot to kill!"

If she'd used that tone with her father, he'd have blacked half her face. Malcolm didn't hit her. Instead, his voice went as icy as the filthy stone against which she huddled.

"We are not at liberty to shoot whomever we please. Getting out of a fatal jam without killing *anyone* is a time scout's job. If the Britannia Gate opened up right now and Kit stepped through, I'd tell him to send you packing back to whatever miserable little town you came from. Give me the goddamned bullets."

She handed over the tin. Her hand shook. Malcolm jerked the cord loose, opened the sliding lid, and dumped three rounds into her hand.

"You're going to reload this gun right now. Pull up on that T-shaped handle."

It blurred through hot tears, but she jerked up on it. The whole top of the revolver swung forward and down, revealing the back of the cylinder. Three empty cases and the two unfired rounds popped up slightly. Her fingers shook but she pulled out the spent cases and reloaded the empty chambers. Then she closed the gun up again.

"You were supposed to know how to do this. Skip your lessons again and . . ."

He left the threat hanging. He'd already destroyed any hope she'd ever entertained of becoming a scout. Her whole chest ached with the need to sob. But she held it all inside, except for the hot, miserable tears she could not quite contain.

Malcolm checked the alleyway again, leaving her to huddle against the wretched gravestone. She slid down into the weeds and fought the tightness in her throat. *I won't give up. I won't. It isn't fair!* She'd only done what Sven Bailey had taught her. Hadn't she? *Know when to quit,* Kit had told her. *I won't quit! Not when I've come so far!* Somehow, she'd find a way to get back into Malcolm's good graces. She *had* to. She'd sooner commit suicide than go back to Minnesota a failure.

During the endless walk up through Spitalfields, Margo listened with everything in her, ruthlessly shoving aside humiliation and terror for the more immediate need to *learn.* She picked up slang, names for items she'd never seen before, tidbits of news and gossip that led her to several startling conclusions about the state of the world in 1888.

"Malcolm?" Her voice quavered only a little.

"Yes?" *His* voice was still icy.

"This isn't an ordinary slum, is it? Spitalfields, I mean. It isn't like Whitechapel or St. Giles."

He glanced back. Some of the chill in his eyes thawed into surprise. "Why do you ask?"

She bit her lower lip, then nodded toward women who spoke in a language that wasn't English, toward men who dressed in dark coats, wore their beards long, and looked at the world through eyes which had seen too much hardship. "These people look and sound like refugees. Who are they?"

Malcolm actually halted. Absently he blew against his fingers to warm them while giving Margo an appraising stare.

"Well, I'll be suckered. . . ." he said softly.

She waited, wondering if she'd get a reprieve.

"Who do you think they are?" He'd given her a challenge.

She studied the older women, who wore shawls over their hair, watched the younger girls with shining black tresses and shy smiles, the old men with wide-brimmed black hats and hand-woven, fringed vests. The younger people looked hopeful, busy. The older ones seemed uncertain and afraid, suspicious of her and of Malcolm. The language sounded like German, sort of. Then the whole picture clicked.

Yiddish.

"They're Jewish refugees," she said slowly. "But from what? Hitler . . . has he even been born yet?"

"Hitler was not the first madman to order pogroms against the Jewish communities of Europe. Just the most sweepingly brutal. Stalin was almost as bad, of course. The bloody pogroms going on all across Europe started about eight years ago, in 1880. Jews are being murdered, driven out of their homes, out of their own countries."

"Then . . . what went on during World War II was a . . . a sort of continuation of this? Only much worse? I never realized that." Margo looked up and down the street, where kosher slaughterhouses and butcher shops fought for space with tailors' establishments and bakeshops. In that moment, echoing down empty places in her mind she hadn't even known existed, Margo saw connections, running forward into the future from this moment and backward from it. In an instant, her narrow Minnesota universe expanded with dizzying explosiveness into an infinitely larger place with more intricately bound pieces of the human puzzle to try and understand than she had ever thought possible.

She understood, in a flash, why Malcolm Moore was willing to endure gruelling poverty and the humiliation of a freelance guide's life, just to step through one more gate.

He wanted to *understand*.

Margo gazed down those infinite corridors in her mind, filled with endless blank gaps, and knew that she had to fill them in—or at least as many of them as she could before she died trying.

When she came up for air, Malcolm was staring at her in the oddest fashion, as though she'd just suffered a stroke and hadn't yet found the wit to fall down. The only thing she could think to say was, "They must have been . . . I can't even imagine what they must have thought when Hitler started bombing London."

Something far back in his eyes changed, in response to what must have been visible in her own. For a moment, Margo knew he understood exactly what was shining inside her. Sudden, unexpected tears filled his eyes. He turned aside and blew out his breath and cleared his throat. A steaming vapor cloud dissipated in the freezing February air.

"It's half my own fault," he mumbled, "if not more. You were already badly upset and I should have made certain you knew how to operate a top-break revolver before we even set foot through the gate. It's just there's so much to remember, sometimes even experienced guides forget little things like checking up on what your partner knows." A crook of his lips and an embarrassed flush surprised her. "And, well, I'm not really used to *having* a partner along."

Margo found it suddenly impossible to swallow properly. "I'm starting to understand, Malcolm. Really, I am. I'm studying every minute we're here. I'm trying to learn *how* to learn, not just *what* to learn."

Malcolm touched her chin. "That's a good beginning, Margo. We'll give it another go, shall we?"

Her eyes filled in turn. Scouting was about so much more than just adventure and money, that for the first time, Margo wasn't sure she had what it took. She dashed knuckles across her eyes and sniffed hugely. "Thanks, Malcolm. Ever so."

He tousled her short hair. "Well spoken, young Smythe. It's barely gone noon. You have a good stretch of London left to study." His grin took any possible sting out of the words.

Wordlessly, Margo set herself the task of trying to understand what she saw around her, rather than just staring at it like a sun-struck tourist.

Margo studied hard for the duration of their stay. She learned—slowly and painfully—but she learned, nonetheless. Malcolm grilled her endlessly in the evenings with help from John, who was amassing quite a wealth of notes for his own research. Margo recorded observations in her personal log each evening, while they were still fresh in her mind. Even she was surprised by the detail she could recall when she put out the effort.

Then Malcolm told her he'd been in touch with some friends who were in town for the Season. An invitation for dinner had been received and duly accepted. She panicked. "What should I do? What should I *say?*"

"As little as possible," Malcolm said drily.

She managed a smile. *Don't screw this up* was the message, loud and clear. Of course, a scout wouldn't have to worry about things like formal social evenings with the British peerage very often. . . . She dreaded returning to the book work she knew would be waiting for her on the time terminal. Learning by *doing* was so much more interesting. But she clearly needed some of that tedious cultural and historical reading. She held back a shudder. Margo had learned more about Victorian England in three days than she would have in three *years* cooped up in some stuffy classroom.

"Well," she said philosophically, "everyone keeps telling me charity girls are supposed to be demure and silent. I can always blush and stammer out something silly and let you rescue me."

"That's one solution. In this case, actually not a bad one, since socially you are not yet 'out.' Have you been reading the newspapers as I suggested?"

"They're weird."

"And the magazines?"

"No photographs. Just those dull black-and-white etchings."

"You're supposed to be reading the articles," he said, brows twitching down in exasperation.

"Well, I can't make sense of half of them."

"Ah," was all the comment he made.

"Yeah, yeah, I know. I have a lot to learn."

"Yes," he said, looking down that extremely British nose of his, "you do."

"Well, you don't have to rub it in."

"Mmm, yes, I think I do. We very nearly died in St. Giles and . . . Well, the less said about your first riding lesson, the better. An unprepared scout has a very short career."

If he was aware of the pun, he wasn't smiling.

Margo sighed. "Okay. I'm trying. Really, I am."

"I know. Now, about dinner. Let me explain cutlery. . . ."

Margo's last three days in London were as glorious as the first four had been miserable and terrifying. She mastered the knack of fluttering her eyelashes and deferring questions with naive requests of her own.

"Oh, but I'm so dull, you don't want to hear about an orphan. Please, tell me about riding to hounds. I don't understand anything about it and it seems so exciting. . . ."

In her school-girl mob cap and pinafore, she wasn't taken seriously by anyone. Even the ladies thought she was adorable.

"Mr. Moore, what an absolutely delightful child. Your ward is a charm."

"You really must bring her out in a year or two."

"Oh, no, not back to that dreadful tropical backwater, surely?"

And so the evening went, in a wonderful haze of wine, sparkling conversation, and more food than she could possibly eat, course after course of it, with delicate little desserts between. She floated to bed that night and dreamed of long formal gowns, bright laughter, and an endless round of parties and dinners with Malcolm at her side. . . .

The next day they went riding again, this time in Hyde Park, with Margo sidesaddle in a long riding habit and Malcolm in immaculate morning attire. Some of the women they'd seen last night at dinner smiled and greeted Malcolm, then smiled at her. Margo returned the greetings with what she hoped was a properly humble air, but inside she was bubbling.

Hyde Park was glorious in the early morning sunlight, so glorious she could almost forget the horror of disease, squalor, and violent death such a short distance east. Because she was not yet "out" socially, none of the gentlemen they had dined with noticed her, but that was all right. It meant Margo had been accepted as a temporal native. She'd passed a difficult test with flying colors, as difficult in its way as that lethal little confrontation in St. Giles.

They spent the afternoon window shopping beneath the glass roof of the Royal Arcade on Old Bond Street, which linked the fashionable Brown Hotel to Bond. John trailed along as chaperon. Margo gawked through the windows into Bretell's at #12 where Queen Victoria herself bestowed her considerable patronage. Margo left the Arcade utterly dazzled.

On their final day, Malcolm took her by train down to Brighton, where they wandered along chilly streets and Malcolm pointed out the myriad differences between the city of 1888 and the city where his family had been caught in the great Flood of 1998. They paused within sight of the waterfront. Malcolm gazed out at the leaden spray crashing against the shingle and went utterly silent. Margo found she couldn't bear the look in his eyes. She summoned her nerve and took his gloved hand in hers. He glanced down, eyes widening in surprise, then he swallowed hard.

"Thank you, Miss Smythe. I—"

He couldn't continue.

Margo found herself moving on instinct. She guided him down the street to a warm inn and selected a seat in the corner. When the innkeeper bustled over, she smiled and said, "Stout, please, for my guardian and might I have a cup of hot tea?"

"Surely, miss. Is there anything else I can get for the gennleman? He seems a mite poorly."

Malcolm was visibly pulling himself together. "Forgive me, innkeep," he rubbed the bridge of his nose with a gloved hand, "but I lost a dear brother not far from here. Drowned in the sea. I . . . hadn't been back to Brighton since, you see."

The innkeeper shook his head mournfully and hurried away to bring the dark beer and a steaming cup of tea. Margo sipped in silence while Malcolm regained his composure.

"I shouldn't have come back," he said quietly.

"Don't the tourists come here on holiday?"

"Not often in February," he smiled wanly. "If one of my guests desires a holiday at the seaside, I generally recommend the Isle of Wight or even Man. I've avoided Brighton. Particularly during February."

The orbital blowup, Margo knew, had occurred in February, catching Atlantic coastlines in the middle of the night. The loss of life had been devastating even in the relatively sheltered English Channel.

Malcolm sipped his dark stout again. "You did very well just now," he murmured. "I'm not accustomed to being rescued by someone I'm guiding. You kept me from considerable embarrassment out there. This," he lifted the glass in a tiny salute and gestured at the inn, "was just what I needed: the shock of staying in persona to wake me up and the stout to deaden the hurt. Thank you."

"I— It just seemed the right thing to do."

A faint smile creased wan cheeks. "You've a good instinct, then. That's important. More so than you might guess." He drained the last of the stout, then took out his pocket watch. "If we're to make that return train, we'd best be leaving."

When Malcolm squeezed her gloved hand, Margo felt as though she were flying.

By the time the scheduled re-opening of the Britannia Gate forced them to leave London, Margo knew she'd found what she wanted to do for the rest of her life. *I've done it, I've gone through a whole week down time, and I've come out just fine.* She had a lot to learn yet, of course—she'd endured humiliation and learned valuable lessons—but now that she'd done it, she knew this was exactly what she'd wanted all along.

You'll see, she promised an unshaven face in her memory, *you'll see, damn you. I'll do it. This was harder than anything you ever did to me, but I did it. And I'll do it again. Just you wait. I'll prove it to you.*

Margo had found where she belonged. All that remained now was to convince Kit Carson. And Malcolm Moore. Margo cast a last, longing glance at the gaslit windows of the Time Tours gatehouse, then stepped boldly through onto the grated platform in La-La Land. It felt like she'd come home at last.

CHAPTER ELEVEN

"There are," Sven Bailey told her patiently, "three basic grips in knife fighting." He demonstrated. "The hammer grip is the way most people pick up a knife, even kitchen carving and paring knives. It's a good, solid grip."

Margo practiced on the slim knife he handed her.

"Then comes the fencing grip." He shifted the knife in his hand as though he were holding an envelope out to someone else. His thumb rested on the top of the grip. "This is a deadly grip in the hands of a trained knife fighter, very difficult to defend against. Learn to use it."

Margo copied the hold on her own knife. It felt odd.

"Third," Sven shifted his blade again, "we have the icepick grip." He now held the knife upside down, so that the blade lay flat against the length of his forearm.

"That looks silly," Margo commented. It felt silly, too.

Sven lifted his forearm toward her. "Would you care to hit my arm with that sharp edge in the way?"

"Well, no."

"Right. It guards your arm somewhat. Moreover," he moved with lightning speed, "you can come across your body with a wicked slash and follow up with a powerful stab."

The knifepoint stopped half-an-inch from Margo's breastbone. She gulped. "Oh."

"Limited, but useful. You'll master all three grips and the moves useful or unique to them."

"All right. Where do we begin?"

"With the types of knife blades and what each is useful for." He retrieved the practice knife he'd loaned her, then rummaged in a case he'd brought out to the practice floor. Sven laid out half-a-dozen knives, all carefully sheathed.

"All right. There are two very basic blade shapes, with multiple variations. This," he drew a ten-inch, thick-bladed knife, "is a Bowie. The spine is thick for strength. This whole side has been cut away, so the knife isn't symmetrical. The curved upper edge is called a false edge. It's often sharpened, but not always. Sometimes these blades have 'saw teeth' added. Mostly saw teeth are a sales gimmick, based on bad twentieth-century movies. The teeth are too large to be any good sawing anything. Avoid them. They can get caught on ribs, then you're stuck with no knife."

"No saw teeth," Margo repeated.

"The Bowie is an excellent *survival* knife. It's strong enough to use for camp chores like cutting small branches for firewood if you don't have a hand axe. The blade's thick enough to use as a prybar without too much risk of snapping the tip off. Unfortunately, it has drawbacks as a fighting knife, such as sheer size, lack of a second sharp edge all the way back to the guard, not to mention its worst drawback: it's anachronistic as hell most places or times you'd end up in. But you'll learn to use one because we're being thorough."

"Okay."

"This," he unsheathed a beautiful, perfectly symmetrical blade some eight inches in length, "is a leaf-point or spear-point dagger. The shape is exactly the same as ancient spear points, even the Roman short sword, the *gladius*. Unlike the *gladius*, it's small enough and sharp enough along both edges to make a nearly perfect fighting knife. It'll slash the hell out of anything you cut with it. And it's thin enough and symmetrical enough to make a beautiful stabbing point, although the point isn't strong and it may snap off. A bodkin or stiletto," he drew out a thing like a knitting needle or an ice pick with slim grips, "is a perfect stabbing weapon, designed to stab through the links of chain-mail armor. Its use is limited, however, to stabbing."

He put away the blades he'd shown her so far.

"Now, something that's neither Bowie nor leaf-point is the world-famous Randall #1." He slipped a glittering ten-inch blade from a worn sheathe. "Some people will tell you it's a modified Bowie. Bo Randall, who invented it back before World War II, pointed out rightly that the shape of this second edge is nothing at all like a Bowie. It's straight, not curved. He didn't design it as a Bowie and he took great exception to having his knife classified as a Bowie. This is one of the best all-around fighting knives ever made. Again, the problem you have is the anachronistic shape for most of history."

Margo sighed. "Why am I learning to use knives I won't carry?"

"Because I'm thorough and careful. Don't argue."

"What are these others?"

"This is a skinning knife." It was a relatively flat, wide blade with a thin spine, and very delicate compared to the fighting knives. "It's specialized for skinning an animal. This," the next blade was curved, thick, and shaped nothing like any of the others, "is a hunting knife. Filleting knives," he held up yet another, "are similar to skinners and completely useless for our purpose. Now, this odd-shaped little jewel is a Ghurka knife."

It was a strange, zig-zag shape, with an ornate hilt.

"This," he drew a crescent-moon sword blade, "is called a scimitar. You'll learn to use them, but the chances of your running across them are fairly slim because of relatively limited geographical distribution. Now, this Tanto," he drew a blade shaped something like an Exact-O knife, "was designed to penetrate enamel-style armor in the Orient. It has the same tip shape as some Asian fishing knives. Again, limited usefulness as a fighting knife, but we'll work with it because you may run across one if you end up in the Western Pacific Rim. Japanese samurai swords and halberds had the same blade shape, just longer and heavier. Now, last but not least is this little jewel."

The final knife was a T-handled thing like a corkscrew, but the blade was shaped exactly like the spear-point dagger—except that the whole blade was only three inches long and the inch closest to the handle was little more than a dull-edged, narrow rectangular bar.

"What's that thing?" Margo laughed.

"A push dagger. Far too many instructors ignore them. That's stupid. The push dagger," he demonstrated the hold, with the T-handle clenched in the fist and the short blade extending beyond the knuckles, "is a very deadly weapon. It's next to impossible to dislodge it from your hand. You can slash," he demonstrated rapidly, "or stab with a simple punch, or," he opened his hand, seized her wrist, and without letting go of the knife, said, "you can grab an opponent without cutting them. The push dagger gives you some *nice* options."

Margo widened her eyes and stared at her wrist. "Good God."

Sven Bailey grinned wickedly and let her go. "Yeah. Isn't it great?"

Margo laughed. "I'm just thinking what a karate punch would be like with that thing in your fist."

"Exactly. You," he pointed with the tip of the push dagger, "will learn to use this very well. It's particularly suited to women who don't have much experience knife fighting—but then, that won't apply to you, will it?"

Margo chuckled ruefully. "Not by the time you're done with me."

"Right. Now, as to the tactics of knife fighting, forget *everything* you've ever seen in any movie. Stupid doesn't begin to cover it. Movie knife fighting—like movie gunfighting or fistfighting—will get you killed. Knife fights are dirty, dangerous affairs carried on by people who want to cut your guts open and spill them in the mud. Literally. Unless you're very careful and very good, you'll bleed to death within seconds of losing a knife fight. The idea," he smiled grimly, "is to avoid fighting in the first place. But if you can't, you make damn sure it's the bastard who attacks you who bleeds to death, not you. Knife fighting is, encounter for encounter, far deadlier than any gunfight. If a bad guy shoots you, chances are extremely good you'll live through it."

"What? Are you pulling my leg?" Margo demanded, thinking of a lifetime's worth of newspaper, magazine, and television news articles.

"Unless it's a sawed-off shotgun at close range, or the shot hits a vital organ, chances are you'll live given relatively decent medical care. But if you're cut up in a knife fight, shock and blood loss will kill you quick. And I mean *quick*. In seconds, if you're hit in the right places. One good slash," he traced a finger across her lower arm, "will sever muscles to the bone, cut arteries, veins, may even fracture bone itself. If you're hit across the femoral, the jugular, or the carotids, you're dead. Period. Same with abdominal or chest wounds, most times. You'll bleed out or die of shock before you can get help."

Margo swallowed. "Wonderful. What happens if some guy jumps me by surprise?"

Sven held her regard steadily. "Easy. You never *let* anyone jump you by surprise."

He wasn't kidding.

"Pay attention to your surroundings *constantly*. What's potentially hiding in the shadows of that bush? Behind that tree, around that corner, in that doorway? Is the man behind me just strolling along for a walk or following me? What about the guy lounging around

on the steps up ahead? *Pay attention.* Somebody takes
you by surprise, you've already lost. Remember that
exercise I had you practice before you went tripping
off to London. Notice everyone else before they notice
you."

Margo flashed back to the attack in St. Giles. If she
hadn't been watching so carefully . . . "All right, point
taken."

"Your homework on alertness is simple but effective.
You've tried it once, for a day. Now we get serious about
it. For the next week, keep track of everyone you
encounter. Strangers, people you know, people who
know you. As before, keep a count of how many times
they notice you before you notice them, and vice versa.
Every time someone sees you and reacts before you
do is a potentially lethal encounter you won't walk away
from."

"Isn't that a little paranoid?"

Sven shook his head. "This is standard training for
self-defense on urban streets, never mind military
situations. Your job as scout combines features of both.
Learn to notice everything around you. Alertness is half
the fight. Being prepared to act on an instant's notice
is the other half. No moments of doubt, hesitation, self-
questioning. Go for a crippling blow whenever you can,
but if it comes down to a lethal fight and you're not
prepared to kill the other bastard to stay alive . . . well,
then, you're in the wrong job, kid."

Margo chewed her lip. Would she be able to pull a
trigger? Or cut someone's throat? Martial arts was one
thing, with its focus on getting the hell out with minimal
damage; knifing or shooting someone was something
else. Clearly, she had some soul searching to do.

"Problems?" Sven asked quietly.

That question deserved an honest answer. "Maybe.
I don't know. I survived St. Giles, but it shook me up.
I need to do some heavy thinking tonight."

Sven nodded. "Good. That's critical. Unless you're prepared to use deadly force, and I mean prepared here," he tapped her head, "and here," he tapped her chest, "you *won't* use it when the flag drops on a lethal encounter. You'll be the one carried home. Think it out. Meanwhile, you might as well start learning technique."

Kit finished up at the Neo Edo's office and checked his watch. Time for Margo's next firearms lesson. After the hair-raising conversation he'd shared with Malcolm, Kit intended to watch every single one of Margo's shooting lessons. He slipped on a pair of shoes at the door and headed out to the Commons, then stopped at a little "open-air" stand for a quick lunch.

"Hi, Kit," Keiko smiled. "What'll it be?"

He pored over the selection of soups, sniffed the yakitori appreciatively, and glanced over at the large fish tank where customers could make their sushi choices—live fish being the best way to ensure freshness in a setting like a time terminal. The tank was five feet deep and eight feet long, filled with salt water and swimming sushi delicacies.

"That young yellowtail," Kit pointed to the fish he wanted, "looks good."

"Hai!"

Keiko turned to pick up the dip net—and shrieked.

A leather-winged shape zipped past, skimmed the top of the tank, then flapped off with Kit's lunch. Japanese didn't precisely have the same corrosive vocabulary available to English speakers, but Keiko had no shortage of colorful curses to heap on the heads of fish thieves and other assorted miscreants.

"They eat all my profits!" she stormed, shaking a fist at the pterodactyl. It had perched in the girders high overhead, busily gulping the profit in question.

"I, uh, think I'll try the yakitori," Kit hastily amended,

trying to suppress a grin. "Talk to Bull Morgan about the problem."

"I have," Keiko said sourly as he fixed Kit's lunch. "He says, let them eat my fish. He will pay me. This does not make my customers happy when they steal my fish and leave messes!"

There was no doubt about the messes. Paper parasols—particularly those with hideous monster faces painted on top—had become all the rage in La-La Land. Kit stole a glance over his shoulder at the pterodactyls and the primitive birds busy swooping and diving on La-La Land's ornamental fish ponds, sidewalk cafes, and open-air food stands and grinned. Half the people in sight carried open parasols.

Across the nearest pond a very elderly Japanese man missing a couple of fingertips (and probably tattooed over his entire body) cursed at one of the *Ichthyornises* when it dove after a goldfish he'd been admiring, not only swallowing it in two gulps but splashing his suit in the process of flapping away again. Its feathers were so waterlogged, the primitive, short-tailed bird made it only as far as the top of a nearby shrub, where it spread wings to dry in the manner of cormorants or anhingas. The singular difference was a beak filled with extremely sharp teeth. That tooth-filled beak—and an angry hiss—changed the elderly gentleman's mind when he advanced, evidently intent on wringing its neck. His subsequent retreat was calculated to look thoughtful and planned. Kit managed not to laugh. He'd never seen a yakuza thug back down from a bird. Kit felt like cheering.

"Thanks," he said when Keiko handed him a plate filled with rice and barbecued chicken chunks on little wooden skewers. "Mmm . . ."

He strolled over to a seat and hurried through his lunch while tourists snapped photos of the *Ichthyornis* drying its wings. Sue Fritchey was sweating it out until Primary cycled again, waiting for a message from colleagues up time about La-La Land's newest residents. The giant pterosaur was supposedly recovering just fine from its adventure and was eating all the fish they could toss into its enormous beak. They'd urgently need a resupply of fish by the time Primary cycled, what with a thirty-foot fish eater and two separate flocks of smaller ones to keep happy.

Bull had given standing orders that station personnel were to secure fish from any down-time gate that opened. What would happen if they couldn't get permission to ship the beasts to an up-time research facility? . . .

Kit had visions of shopkeepers like Keiko buying shotguns.

Knowing Bull, he'd order an enormous fish tank constructed somewhere in the Commons and stock it with several thousand fish, then sell tickets to the feeding shows and lectures. Kit grinned. Sounded like a good subject for a quiet bet or two.

He finished his lunch and headed downstairs to the weapons ranges. Margo was just getting started with Ann when she glanced up. She flushed when she saw him.

"Hi," he smiled, trying to sound friendly.

"Hi." Her closed expression said "I resent you checking up on me."

Well, that was exactly what he was doing and he had no intention of backing down.

"Hi, Kit," Ann said with a friendly nod. "Have a seat."

"Thanks." He settled on one of the benches at the back of the range and slipped in foam hearing protectors.

Ann started Margo off with a relatively "modern" top-break revolver, double-action, very similar to the one Malcolm said she'd been unable to use in London. Margo donned eye- and hearing-protection equipment. Ann did the same and ran out a target, then said, "Whenever you're ready."

Margo took her time and placed five of the six on the paper—but nowhere near the center.

"Front sight," Ann said patiently. "Concentrate on the front sight."

Margo opened the action and dumped out the spent brass. "I thought the whole sight picture was important."

"It is, but the front sight is critical. As long as the front sight is placed properly, your rear sight can be slightly off and you'll still hit near what you're shooting at. But let that front sight drift off, and it won't matter how perfectly your rear sight is aligned, either with the target or with the front sight. You'll miss, clean."

Margo tried again. She was still flinching, but the shots were a little closer together.

"All right, unload the brass and hand me the pistol."

"Why?" Margo asked curiously.

Ann took the pistol—offered, Kit noticed approvingly, in the proper manner, action open, muzzle down. "You've developed a whopping flinch. So we'll do a ball-and-dummy drill. I'll load the pistol for you."

Ann turned away, blocking the gun from Margo's immediate view, then handed it back. "All right. Let's see how bad that flinch is."

Margo fired the first round with a solid bang. The second time, the pistol only went click—and the barrel jerked about an inch anyway.

"Oh!" Margo gasped. "I did that, didn't I?"

"Yes. You're anticipating the noise and the recoil. This drill will help you learn to pull through smoothly without flinching, because you'll never know which chamber might be loaded or empty."

Ann put her through a solid twenty minutes of ball-and-dummy drills. By the end, Margo had developed a much smoother trigger pull and her group size shrank considerably.

"Very good." Ann pulled in the target and ran out a new one. "Now, concentrate on that front sight."

Another fifteen minutes, and the spread of Margo's shots was down to six inches at six yards. Not exactly impressive, but an improvement. Ann drilled her on front sight for another ten minutes, then let her take a short break. Margo pulled off the protective eyeglasses and earmuffs and ruffled her hair. Kit regretted the necessity to dye it. She looked like an abandoned waif with pale skin and dark hair, but it was far safer for her.

The discouragement in her eyes needed dispelling, though.

"You're doing well," Kit said when she glanced his way.

Margo flushed again, but from pleasure this time. "I'm working hard on it."

Kit nodded. "You keep practicing, you'll get much better. Maybe Malcolm will even win that bet."

Margo's whole face went scarlet. "You heard about that."

Kit laughed. "Margo, everyone in La-La Land heard about it."

"That'll teach me to make bets," she said ruefully.

"All right," Ann said, coming back with another case, "back to work. Now we take a step backwards in time. Muzzle-loading black-powder firearms were more common far longer than metallic-cartridge, breech-loading guns. Metallic cartridges didn't become common until the 1870's. The little, low-powered rimfire and pin-fire cartridges date from the decade before the American Civil War, but they were nowhere nearly as common as percussion-fired, muzzle-loading black-powder guns. Flintlock and matchlock guns in particular had a longer period of use than cartridge guns. You'll need to know how to handle these firearms and they're a bit more complicated to use."

Margo gave Ann a brave smile. "All right. Show me."

"We'll start with a little demonstration."

Ann shook out a thin line of various types of powders: smokeless rifle powders, smokeless pistol powders, then black powder. "Modern, smokeless powders are not explosive. They burn. They don't explode. The priming compound in the base of the cartridge case *is* a chemical explosive, but it's a tiny, tiny amount of it. All the primer does is create the spark of flame needed to start the powder burning. This is modern pistol powder and this is modern rifle powder. Now this," Ann pointed, "is *black* powder. Unlike modern powders, it *is* explosive. It burns far, far faster and is much more dangerous, particularly under compression. Watch."

She lit a long match and touched it to the end of the line of powders. The modern rifle powder flared and burned slowly, the pistol powder burned a good bit faster—then the black powder flashed wildly, gone in a split second.

"Good God!"

"Yes. That's to teach you to respect black powder. Be careful when handling it, especially when you're reloading black-powder weapons. A mistake can injure, potentially even kill you."

"Great."

Ann smiled. "Just keep your wits about you and practice. Now, let's start with the components of ammunition for black-powder weapons. In most historical arms, there was no cartridge case, just loose powder, a projectile called a 'ball' and a bit of cloth called a patch, which is greased to help you push the ball down the barrel and to help prevent fouling. During the American Civil War era, a bullet called the minie ball did away with the need for a patch, but it never caught on well with hunters and sportsmen."

Margo said, "Okay, ball and powder and patch. Show me."

Ann demonstrated the whole loading process. "There

are two important things to remember about black-powder firearms. One, be sure the ball is seated all the way to the bottom. Check the length of the ramrod," she showed Margo how, "to be sure you haven't left a gap at the bottom between the back of the barrel and the ball."

"Okay. But why's that important?"

"Remember what I said about thousands of pounds per square inch of pressure inside the cartridge cases of modern guns when smokeless powder begins to burn? Well, black powder doesn't burn, it explodes. If you leave a gap here," she pointed to the bottom end of the barrel, "what you've done, essentially, is build a miniature bomb."

Margo's eyes widened. "Oh."

"Yes. The gun barrel can blow up in your face. The other thing to remember is that sparks can still be smoldering inside the barrel. There isn't any way to get into this end of it. It's all closed up and solid, no breech to open, so you can't just check it. If you try to dump more powder into a hot barrel without swabbing it out first with a wet swab, you could ignite the powder you're pouring in—which could, in turn, set off the powder from the container you're pouring from. That's why you should always load from a measurer that holds just enough powder for one shot. Of course, under battle conditions, you may not have time to swab out the barrel," Ann said with a grin.

Margo gulped and looked massively uncertain.

Ann smiled. "Not to worry. If you hope to use firearms through most of their historical existence, you'll need to master these next lessons, but black-powder firearms aren't dangerous so long as you learn what you're doing and pay attention while you're doing it. Power tools in untrained hands are just as dangerous, if not more so. Any questions before we get started?"

Margo glanced back toward Kit, chewed her lower

lip, then shook her head. "No. Just show me what I'm supposed to do."

Ann started her on a simple replica Colt 1860 Army black-powder revolver, showing her how to load, prime with percussion caps, and fire six shots. Reloading took another entire two minutes. After Margo mastered the concepts involved, she asked cheerfully, "What's next? I know about flintlocks."

"Very good. And here is a beautiful Kentucky rifle to practice with."

"Ooh! Daniel Boone and settlers on the Cumberland Gap trail and . . ."

Kit grinned. His granddaughter's romantic notions had finally landed her with a gun she loved. She even did well with it. Malcolm just might win that bet, after all. After the flintlock, Ann took her on to more esoteric types like wheel-locks and even matchlocks.

"How in the world did people keep these things burning?" Margo demanded with a half-hearted laugh the second time her slow-smoldering match went out. "Am I doing something wrong? Or is it really that hard?"

Ann chuckled. "During battles, they'd keep the matches swinging in circles between shots just to be sure. Looked weird as hell during night fighting."

Margo grinned. "I'll bet. Rain must've been a bummer."

"Yes, it did wreak a bit of havoc on a few plans. But then, rain wasn't kind to bow strings, either, or to paper cartridges. Modern guns are nicely weatherproof compared to most projectile weapons. And speaking of other projectile weapons, we need to train you in crossbows and stickbows, recurves . . ."

Margo's eyes widened. Then she grinned wickedly. "What, no blowguns? Or atl-atls?"

"Oh, goodie! One of my students finally wants to learn flint-knapping and spear throwing!"

Kit couldn't help it. He started to chuckle.

Margo turned on him with a hot glare. "What's so funny?"

"I'm sorry, Margo," he said, still laughing. "But you're so transparent. Learning flint-knapping wouldn't exactly be a waste of time. You literally *could* end up someplace where stone weapons are the only ones available. Remember that scout who just came back from the Wurm glaciation, did the work on Cro-Magnon lifestyles?"

"Yeah, I remember reading that. In the *Shangri-la Gazette*."

"Right. And you did see what fell through the ceiling the other day, didn't you?"

Margo rubbed the back of her neck. "Yeah, well, I *was* thinking about that. What *do* you do if you come face to face with a wooly rhinoceros or something?"

"Look for the nearest tree," Kit advised. "They're mean-tempered brutes. It took a cooperative effort from multiple hunters to bring them down. As for the 'or something,' it depends on what it is. I have a feeling we should add biology and big-game hunting to your curriculum."

She went a little green around the edges.

"Well, there's nothing intrinsically horrible about it," Kit pointed out. "It's useful to know how to kill various species if you're either starving to death or in danger of immediate dismemberment. And I've seen you eat meat, so I know you're not a vegetarian. What *do* they teach in high school these days?"

"Uh, respect for other living creatures?"

Ann just rolled her eyes.

"Well," Margo thrust her hands into her pockets, "I'm not a vegan or anything, and I like steaks and chicken and stuff and a neighbor gave us some venison once. I've just never had to hunt anything to get a meal. I know I grew up in Minnesota and all, but I've never even been fishing," she admitted with a slow flush that made Kit wonder again what her upbringing had really been.

Kit nodded, pleased that she was finally able to admit she lacked knowledge or skills she needed. "That's all right. Lots of city kids don't. As for respecting animals, there isn't a hunter alive that doesn't respect hell out of major predators. And most hunters respect game animals, too. It's a different mindset, maybe, from what you're used to, but the respect is genuine. Now . . . if you plan on stepping through unexplored gates, you'd better know how to forage off the land. Not to mention knowing how to keep local four-footed critters from having you as a light snack between meals. So we'll start you on hunting techniques to get you ready for your first attempt at catching your own food."

"Okay."

"Just remember one thing: try to avoid putting four-footed creatures on some moral pedestal that bears no resemblance whatsoever to reality. Misjudging animal behavior and motives does the animal no favors and can be fatal to you. I think," he stood up, "I'll head back upstairs now. You're making good progress," he allowed, "but you still have a lot of work ahead of you. Ann, thanks. I'll see you at dinner, Margo. Meet me at the Delight."

"Really?" Margo's face lit up.

"Yes, really," he grinned. "See you this evening."

As he left the range, he heard Ann saying, "Now, this is a very early type of firearm called a pole gun. . . ."

CHAPTER TWELVE

Margo was on her way to the Delight when the bones behind her ears began to ache. She frowned and peered toward the nearest chronometer for the scheduled gate postings. "London . . . Primary . . . Rome . . . Denver . . ." She ran down the whole list, but nothing was due to open. The sensation worsened.

"Oh, no, not again . . ."

'Eighty-sixers began to converge. Margo decided she'd better skedaddle, post-haste. She put on a burst of speed—

—and propelled herself straight through a black rent in the air that appeared smack in front of her. She screamed and plunged through the gate before she could halt her forward momentum. She had a brief, tunnel-vision view of a broad, silver river in flood stage, long low banks that sloped gently up to what appeared to be a vast flat plain, and a walled city. A two-part fortified bridge with a tower spanned the river. Standing at the crest of a low, open hill, the city clearly commanded a strategic position overlooking the river. Twin spires of a white stone cathedral were visible above the city walls. *Between* Margo and the walls . . .

It looked like a *battle*.

Then she was through the gate. Margo stumbled right into the thick of it. Men in medieval-looking armor hacked at one another with swords. Horsemen on heavy chargers rode down men on foot. Volleys of arrows fell like black rain, pinioning anything unfortunate enough to be under them. A man right in front of her screamed and clutched at a steel crossbow shaft that appeared from nowhere and embedded itself in his chest armor. He went down with a terrible cry and was trampled by a screaming warhorse. Blood and mud and screams of dying men and wounded horses spattered her from all sides.

Her gaze focused abruptly on a man who'd skidded to a halt right in front of her. Wide, shocked eyes took her measure. *He's younger than I am. . . .* He carried several sheaves of arrows like firewood under his left arm, a bow slung across his back, and a wicked knife in his other hand. He said something and lunged, knife held loosely in an overconfident grip. She whipped around, right side to him, then seized his wrist and yanked forward on it while turning into him. His elbow straightened across her hip. He yelled in pain. Margo kept the elbow forcibly straight and kicked his near ankle with a sweeping blow. She jerked him forward at the same instant. His face slammed into the ground. The knife popped loose.

Thank God. Margo whirled, looking for the gate.

And found an older, far stronger man charging right at her, wild-eyed. He swung a massive wooden maul at least four feet long straight over his head, ready to crush her skull. Margo screamed and ran. The gate pulsed unevenly ahead of her. Two men crashed into her path, slashing at one another with long swords. Margo dodged past and hurtled toward the gate. Then risked a glance over her shoulder. The madman with the maul was still back there.

He snarled something that sounded like *Shawn Dark! Shawn Dark!* A heavily armored horsemen nearby jerked around at his shout—and charged *him*. The rider's shouts made no sense at all. Margo put on a burst of speed. She could just see the Commons as the gate shivered inward and outward again, a quivering hole in the light. *Don't close—oh, God, don't close yet—*

Margo dove through to safety.

And found herself running down a corridor of shocked spectators, straight for a concrete wall. The wild-eyed soldier was right behind her, chased by a suddenly panic-stricken horse. She heard the animal's scream of terror as she turned and flattened against cold concrete.

The soldier charged, wooden maul right over his head, ready to strike. Trapped on either side by milling, confused tourists, Margo saw only one way out. She ran *at* him. Margo lunged with both hands at the butt of the maul handle. Her double-handed blow connected, jarring her to the elbows. The heavy wooden mallet popped loose and clattered on the concrete. The badly startled soldier crashed full-tilt into the concrete wall. He staggered back, dizzy and confused, just as the armored rider came loose from his terrified horse. The animal bucked and shrilled a trumpeting cry. The rider landed with a heavy clang on the concrete floor.

He rolled and came awkwardly to his feet, surprising hell out of Margo. *Good grief, they* could *move around in that armor.* . . . He took one look at Commons through a slitted visor then broke and ran back through the gate without his horse.

The charger reared again, caught sight of the open gate and shied away. A ten-year-old girl in a Frontier Town long skirt tripped directly in its path. Margo reacted without thinking. She grabbed the charger's trailing reins. Margo dug in and hauled its head around just before it could trample the child. The horse screamed savagely and reared to full height. Margo swore and dodged murderous hooves. Someone else grabbed for the bridle and missed. Margo lunged and grabbed the bridle by the cheek strap—and learned why war horses were so valuable.

The bit was a wicked affair, with long, pointed steel

shafts on either side. The horse reared with her, hauling her off the floor. Then it gave a nasty toss of its head. Margo lost her grip on the bridle. She came loose, falling backwards and flailing for balance. The horse—eyes gleaming wickedly—raked that damned bit straight down her arm, catching her thigh for good measure on the way down.

She impacted the concrete floor with a muffled cry of pain.

Someone else snatched the trailing reins, forcing it around before it could strike with murderous hooves.

"Head it into the gate!" someone yelled.

"My God, do you know what that horse would be worth to a guide? Let me try to control him!" In a blur, Margo watched a man leap into the saddle. The horse sunfished, screaming savagely. The rider came adrift with a yell. The warhorse ended facing the pulsing gate. Someone much smarter gave the animal a mighty smack on the hind quarters. It bolted straight through and vanished into the melee beyond. The gate shrank rapidly closed within seconds.

A disturbance somewhere behind them caught Margo's attention. She turned her head to look—

Oh, shit . . .

That wild-eyed soldier hadn't gone back through. Clad in woolen hose, pointed leather shoes, and a quilted leather tunic to which metal plates had been sewn, he was facing down the crowd with that heavy wooden maul of his. Blood snaked downward from his nose and a cut on his brow. An empty quiver for arrows and a bow at least five-and-a-half feet tall lay on the floor.

"Shawn Dark!"

He launched straight toward her. Margo, bleeding and whimpering, rolled awkwardly on the floor. Someone tried to tackle him, but was too late. The soldier brought the maul down in a smashing blow. Margo barely rolled out from under it. An iron band around the end of the hammer sparked on concrete a hair's breadth from her ear. He staggered past, off balance—and ran straight into the arms of station security. Four men put him in a headlock, finally immobilizing him.

Another disturbance in the crowd caught the periphery of her attention, then Kit bent over her. He was utterly ashen.

"Margo! Margo, you're hurt . . ."

She waved an unsteady hand toward the soldier. "He . . . came through the gate . . ."

Kit was examining her arm, her thigh. "Not deep, thank God," he said with a heartfelt grin that actually wobbled.

He really cares. . . .

Margo hadn't realized how much. Kit tore his own shirt for compresses and tied them down. The soldier, still struggling against restraint, snarled something at him. Kit glanced up, looking astonished, then spoke gently in some language Margo had never heard. The man glowered, then slowly stopped struggling. Another few words from Kit and fear began to shine in his eyes. He whispered something to which Kit replied. Whatever Kit said, it terrified the soldier.

"Let him go," Kit said quietly.

The men who'd grabbed him looked uncertain, then released him. The soldier stood uncertainly in the midst of the crowd, looking suddenly terrified and utterly alone.

"He'll need to see Buddy for orientation," Kit said. "Has anyone called him yet?"

Someone near the edge of the crowd said, "He's on his way down."

"Anybody tell Bull what happened?"

One of the Pest Control officers, standing sheepishly by with an empty net, said, "Al's already gone for him. Kit, that grandkid of yours saved a little girl's life before you got here. She acted real quick, caught a French charger by the bridle before any of us were in position to act. It raked her with its spiked bit, but she saved the kid's life. Would've trampled her for sure."

Kit glanced sharply at her, then said, "Can you stand on that leg?"

Margo tried. A nauseating wave of pain swept through her. Kit simply picked her up and strode hastily through the crowd, which gave way with astonishing rapidity.

Margo bit her lips, not wanting Kit to know how badly she hurt. "What did that soldier say, when you talked to him?"

He glanced down just long enough to meet her gaze. "He was at the siege of Orléans. In medieval France. He was fighting for his life. When you appeared out of nowhere, he thought Jeanne d'Arc had opened the gates of hell. Now he thinks you've sent him through *into* hell."

"Jeanne d'Arc, that's what he called me."

Kit tightened his lips. "Yes. He thought you *were* Joan of Arc. Said something about you thrashing another archer?"

"He tried to stab me. I disarmed him, that's all. . . ."

She didn't want to talk. Margo's stomach was so uneasy it was all she could do to swallow down the nausea that accompanied every throb in her arm and leg.

Kit just nodded. "Well, the English army lost the battle at Orléans, rather badly. This fellow's a Welsh archer, a longbowman. Like the English, he thought Joan was a witch. The Burgundians caught her a couple of years after Orléans and turned her over to the English. They burned her."

Margo shut her eyes. "I . . . I fell through the gate when it opened. I didn't have any equipment, I don't know when it was . . ." She started to cry.

"Hang in there, Margo. I'm taking you to Rachel Eisenstein. They're not serious cuts, I promise."

"Good," she whispered.

Kit tightened his arms around her and shoved open the infirmary door with the point of his shoulder.

"Rachel! Emergency!"

The station doctor appeared at a run. "What happened?"

"Medieval warhorse raked Margo with a spiked bit. Slashes to arm and thigh. Unexpected gate into a fifteenth-century battle."

They eased her onto an examining table and Rachel Eisenstein stripped off Margo's ruined clothes. "It isn't as bad as it feels," Rachel told her gently, swabbing out the long slices. She gave Margo a local anesthetic and cleaned the wounds, then stitched them up. She finished off with bandages.

"Your medical records indicate no allergies to penicillin," Rachel said, consulting a computer screen. "That's correct?"

"Yes," Margo said in a small voice. "That's right. I'm not."

The doctor injected antibiotics and anti-tetanus and gave her a prescription for oral capsules as well. "When you're wounded with a down-time weapon that's been only God knows where and in God knows what, we take no chances."

Margo felt sick again, clear through.

"Not to worry," Rachel said with a smile. "We'll take good care of you. Put her to bed, Kit, and feed her when she feels like eating."

Margo felt like a complete fool when they settled her in a wheelchair. Kit wheeled her back out onto the Commons.

"What happened, exactly?" Kit asked quietly.

Margo told him.

"You were lucky," he told her when she'd finished. "Medieval war horses were trained to kill foot soldiers. If the charger hadn't been so spooked by the gate, he'd have crushed you. I'll question the Welshman more closely to see if we can pinpoint more or less when you emerged through that gate."

Don't I even rate a well-done for saving that kid? she wondered miserably.

Evidently not, as Kit didn't say another word on the subject. He took her back to his quarters and tucked her in, the only concession being that he put her in his own bed and carried his pillow and blanket to the couch.

"Hungry?" he asked, settling down beside her.

She turned away. "No."

He hesitated, then touched her shoulder. "You did okay, kid. But you have so much to learn. . . ."

"I know," Margo said bitterly. "Everyone keeps telling me."

Kit dropped his hand. "I'll check on you again later. Call me if you need anything."

Margo didn't want anything more from Kit. She was tired and sick and her injuries throbbed and the best he could manage to say to her was "You did okay."

She muffled her face in the pillow and drowned out all sound of a misery she could hardly bear.

Kit sat in the darkness, nursing a shot glass of bourbon. So close . . . dear God, she'd come so close, and didn't even realize it. His hand was still a little unsteady as he drained the glass and poured again. A knock at the door interrupted an endless stream of graphic images his mind insisted on presenting had the confrontation gone even a little differently.

Kit climbed wearily to his feet and found the door. "Yeah?"

"It's Bull."

Kit unlocked it. "Come on in."

"Drinking in the dark?" Bull asked with a frown.

"Margo's asleep. I didn't want to disturb her." He flicked on a table lamp.

"I won't stay long then. I've spoken with our newest down timer. He's suspicious and unhappy and protested rather violently when I confiscated his weapons, but I didn't order confinement. He seemed genuinely apologetic that he'd attacked the wrong person. Ordinarily, you know, I'd order strict confinement for a fight with lethal weapons, but under the circumstances . . ."

"Yeah," Kit said heavily.

"I'll confine him if you'd prefer."

Kit glanced up. "No. No, don't do that. He was shaken and scared. Battle does strange things to a man's mind, as it is, never mind falling through a gate into La-La Land. What's his name, anyway?"

"Kynan Rhys Gower."

"Poor bastard."

"Yeah. It's rough on the down timers. Buddy's already had a long session with him. He says it's the usual reaction: he's confused, scared, convinced he's in hell. I wish to God the government would come up with some sane policy regarding them, but chances are it'd be worse for 'em than leaving 'em here."

Kit snorted. "When the government gets involved, things *always* get worse."

Bull smiled wryly. "Ain't it the truth? How's Margo?"

"Rachel set fifteen stitches in her arm, nearly fifty in her leg."

Bull winced. "That serious?"

"No, the slashes were shallow, thank God, just long. She should be fine, so long as massive infection doesn't set in. Rachel's put her on antibiotics."

"Good. I hear she saved a little girl's life."

Kit managed a wan smile. "Yes. She's a hero. She was damn near a *dead* hero."

"If you're going to let her scout, Kit, you'd better get used to the idea."

Kit stared at the wall. "Yeah. I know. Doesn't make it any easier."

"Nope. Never does. Get some sleep, Kit. And put away the booze."

Kit grimaced. "Sure, boss." Then he glanced up. "Thanks."

"Don't mention it." Bull smiled, squat and square and for the moment, human instead of demi-legend. Human enough to show how much he cared, anyway, which meant a great deal to Kit in that moment. Bull Morgan thumped Kit on the arm. "See you around, Kit. Tell Margo I asked about her."

Kit nodded and let him out, then locked the door and put away the bourbon. But it was a long time before sleep came. He steeled himself to make the decision and finally settled on Rome as the best place for Margo's next down-time testing ground. Stubborn, brash, untrained . . .

And once again, Kit would not be able to go with her.

The silver lining in all this darkness, Kit grumbled to himself as he sought a more comfortable position on the couch, was that Malcolm Moore wouldn't have to worry about rent and meals for months to come. If he'd thought it practical, Kit would have asked Malcolm to consider scouting again, just to be sure Margo had an experienced partner.

Yeah, right. She'd take to that idea with all the enthusiasm of a wet cat.

He sighed and wondered how she'd receive the news that another down-time trip was scheduled? She'd probably see it as her just reward for playing hero. Kit was rapidly discovering that being a grandfather wasn't half the fun it was cracked up to be. When, if ever, did he get to stop being the "mean one" in Margo's life? Every time things seemed to be straightening out between them, something always seemed to happen to muck it up again.

He blinked a few times, remembering how life with

Sarah had gone much the same way—and how *that* had ended.

He lay quietly in the darkness listening to Margo's steady, even breaths in the next room and tried to keep fear at bay by planning out the next phase of her training.

He wasn't terribly successful at either.

CHAPTER THIRTEEN

Kynan Rhys Gower was trapped in hell.

Everyone here who could actually talk to him said otherwise, of course, but Kynan knew it was hell nonetheless, even if it didn't resemble anything the priests had ever described. The closest thing to a priest here, a man called "Buddy," had told him he could never escape—not to his home or even back to the accursed battle against the witch woman fighting on the side of the upstart French.

It hurt him, gnawed at him, that he was cut off forever from everything and everyone he knew and loved. A king whose laws forbade it, Kynan might have understood. But he could not understand why, if this infernal land's diabolical passageways that opened out of thin air could be made to open with the regularity of the rising and setting sun, *why* could the wizard or demon or hell-spawned sprite who controlled them not reopen the one passageway that would lead him home? Yet Buddy had told Kynan he would never again see the dark hills of Wales or the laughter in his son's eyes. . . .

At least a hundred times every day, as he struggled to understand devilish things beyond his comprehension, Kynan was tempted to do violence to *something*. But they'd taken away his weapons. Without them, he was less than a man. Less, even, than the commonest Welsh farm girl, who at least carried a small knife for chores.

Kynan swallowed his pain, his confusion, swallowed

the demeaning status in which he found himself—a virtual slave in Satan's dominions—and worked hard to earn the scant coins he needed to pay for his tiny sleeping room and the meals of rice and strange vegetables which kept him alive. He missed meat desperately but was unable to afford it on what he earned.

Several times a day, his hatred of the strange, demon birds which lived here—birds with teeth in their bills—deepened as he watched them eat colorful fish *he* was forbidden to take for his own meals. If he hadn't been terrified of incurring the king's wrath for killing one of the protected birds, he'd have killed and eaten one of *them*.

So he carried baggage for rich people whose behavior he could scarcely comprehend and whose language he could comprehend not at all, found a second job sweeping floors in the bewildering place in which he was trapped, and quietly hugged his misery and terror and bitterness to himself. Every time he saw the grinning jackanapes who'd first told him what had happened to him, who had *laughed* at him while four strong men held him down . . .

Every time he saw the man called Kit Carson, Kynan wished to do more than violence. He wished to do murder.

But he'd watched that man practice mock fighting in the huge, lighted hall called "gym." He was a cunning, strong warrior as well as a knave. If Kynan wished to purge the stain of disgrace from his honor, it would have to come through sudden, unexpected attack. Kynan once would have sneered at any man who planned such a treacherous approach to an affair of honor, would have rightly called him blackguard. But Kynan was no longer in a land which made sense. He was in hell.

In hell, a man could be forgiven much.

So he pushed his hated broom down the hated floor,

sweeping up the hated trash while trying to avoid running into hated, arrogant "tourists" and gradually filled his wheeled trash bin with little bits of refuse. Later he would have to open stationary trash bins along the "Commons" and empty them as well, carrying the "plastic" sacks inside down to the "incinerator" and "recycling center." Even the alien, English words that somehow weren't really English made his head ache. Kynan had never spoken much English—his commander had translated battlefield commands—but the so-called English spoken here . . .

Even words he thought he knew made little or no sense.

He pushed his broom and wheeled cart into the area of "Commons" called "Victoria Station"—named, someone said, for a *Queen* of England, who had brazenly ruled in her own name despite a perfectly eligible husband who could have sat the throne in her stead— and filled another tray with dust and trash, emptying it into his bin. A spate of laughter made him grit his teeth. They weren't laughing at him, but Kynan was so lost in despair, he could scarcely endure the sound of another person's joy. It only reminded him how cruelly alone he was.

He glanced up, drawn against his will to look. A group of men in strange, long-coated suits and pretty, sweet-faced women in even stranger dresses were playing an odd game, setting out little wire hoops with weighted feet, standing up two wooden sticks painted with bright bands of color, arguing which of them would claim wooden balls banded with a matching stripe of color.

A pang ran through him. He wondered what his wife and son might be doing now. Wondered if the village men would teach the boy to use longbow and maul—or if the French would even leave enough men alive to return to the village. What would become of his family? A sickness wrought of empty, helpless longing threatened him again, as it did many, many times each day.

Kynan straightened his back against it. He was a Welshman, a veteran soldier. He might be lost, abandoned by God and saints alike, but he would not give Satan the satisfaction of watching him buckle under the weight of fear and loss which hourly were heaped on him. Kynan watched the game players dully, wondering what these particular demons were doing.

Then he noticed the mallets.

Made of wood and banded like the balls, they were smaller than the battle mauls he was accustomed to carrying, but they were hefty wooden mallets, nonetheless. Kynan watched with mounting interest as the players began a baffling game which involved hitting the wooden balls through the wire hoops. None of them knew the first thing about using a mallet, but clearly, despite a smallish size, they would prove formidable weapons in the hands of a trained soldier. Now if he only had a proper mallet like that . . .

He counted the number of players: five. Then he spotted a wooden cart on which a sixth ball and mallet rested, forgotten. None of the players paid it the slightest attention. Perhaps God had not entirely abandoned him after all? *If I cannot escape hell,* he thought, staring intently at that mallet, *perhaps I will at least be permitted a way to restore my honor.* He maneuvered his trash cart around the players, sweeping up dust and bits of paper as he went, pausing to clean up the occasional splatter of bird shit, and worked his way around to the abandoned mallet. None of the players or spectators—many of whom carried odd sticks with tautly stretched shades to protect their heads from non-existent sunshine—paid him the slightest attention.

Good.

It took half a heartbeat to lift the mallet from its resting place and slip it into his wheeled bin. Only after he had made good his escape did Kynan allow himself a long, shuddering breath. Satan's minions had not noticed the theft. If the Evil One had noticed, either he didn't care or thought it amusing to allow his latest victim a chance at vengeance. Kynan touched the hidden mallet handle with trembling fingertips. *At last,* he breathed silently, eyes closed, *I am a man again.* Soon, the knave who had laughed at him would rue the day his betters had failed to teach him manners.

If a man must die in hell, it were best to die with a weapon in hand, striking down an enemy.

Fortunately for Kit's peace of mind, Margo's injuries healed quickly and cleanly. He made certain the leg would hold the strain of a lethal encounter by sparring with her in the gym while Sven evaluated her performance.

"You're favoring it," Sven pointed out. "Does it hurt?"

"No," she admitted. "Not really. I've just grown used to babying it."

The admission brought a scowl to Sven's lips. Kit wisely stepped aside while Sven Bailey *really* put her through her paces. By the time he'd finished with her, she was a limp mass of sweat and aching muscles.

"You're out of shape," Sven told her brusquely. "More practice."

Margo just nodded, too tired to protest.

"How about that dinner at the Delight?" Kit asked. "We, uh, were interrupted last time we tried."

A wan smile came and went. "Sure. No disgruntled soldiers this time?"

"We'll do our best to avoid them," Kit smiled.

The Welsh bowman had certainly avoided Kit. From what he'd heard, Kynan was busy trying to master the modern technology involved in living on a time terminal while taking on odd jobs to keep body and soul together.

"Just let me shower first," Margo said with a grimace. "I stink."

Kit laughed and headed for the showers himself.

Shortly they were back on the Commons, heading for the Delight. Urbs Romae was nearly deserted, as the major gates opening this week were in other parts of the station. A line had formed, of course, in front of the Epicurean Delight, but when Arley saw Kit and Margo standing outside, he waved them in.

"Hello, don't stand out there, your table's ready. Rachel tells me you're healing well, young lady."

Margo smiled ruefully. "Sven Bailey just proved that."

Arley laughed. "You look tired and hungry. Would you like a menu or the House Specialty?"

"A menu!" Margo said hastily.

Kit grinned. "Still upset about those eels?"

Margo managed to affect a wounded dignity despite her youth and state of fatigue.

Arley winked. "I think you'll enjoy the Specialty tonight. Trust me."

"Why do I have a bad feeling about this?" Margo asked as she settled into the chair Arley held for her. "All right, I'll try it, whatever it is."

"Kit?"

"Same for me."

The Delight's owner rubbed his hands. "Good. I'll send out a bottle of something appropriate."

The wine, when it arrived, was a clear red. "Well, at least it won't be eels," Kit remarked as the waiter poured.

"Thank God."

"I thought you *liked* that dinner." He put on his best lecture expression and said, "*Ab uno disce omnes,* Margo."

Margo just looked at him.

Kit frowned. "Margo, didn't you understand that?"

"Uh, no?"

His frown deepened. "Just how well are you doing with your Latin?"

Her face took on a familiar, panic-stricken look. *Oh-oh.*

"I *am* studying!" she said desperately. As though to prove it, she rattled off, "*Abeunt studia in mores!*"

"Quoting Ovid now, eh?" Kit said sourly. "Take that advice to heart. Study harder. Studies *do* turn into habits, but only if you keep up with them."

He made a mental note to check how often she'd actually been to the language lab. She should've been able to translate something as simple as "From one, learn to judge all" by now.

She tightened her lips. "I will. I am. I'm *trying*. Isn't there any easier way to learn all those words and those awful endings that keep changing?"

"Unfortunately, no. Brian's already installed the best language-learning programs available. But learning languages takes work. Constant, hard work."

She sighed, then tried a winning smile that didn't fool him in the slightest. "I learned an interesting thing from Sven today. There was this guy named Musashi, a Japanese guy from the same time period as the Edo gate. He was so good at duelling, he stopped fighting with real knives. Just used a wooden practice sword whenever he was challenged. Isn't that amazing? I wonder if Sven's good enough to do that?"

"Probably," Kit said drily. "I thought you were studying American history, not Japanese?"

"I am," she said hastily, "but Sven was telling me, you know, during our lesson today. I used to be scared of him, but he's really interesting if you can get him to talk."

Clever little minx. Why does she keep changing the subject?

"Hmm, yes, I rather imagine Francis Marion was much the same."

Again, Margo drew an utter blank.

Kit unfolded his napkin with a little snap. "Just what period of American history did you say you were reading? It *was* the Revolution, wasn't it?"

Margo's whole face colored. "Well, yes, I did. I was. I am. I mean—"

"Spill it, Margo. You're not studying. Are you?"

"I study until I'm sick of studying! I learned more in one week in London than I've learned the whole time I've been stuck in that library!"

"Margo—"

"No! Don't say it! All I hear from you is 'Margo, study this, Margo, do that, Margo, pay attention, Margo, that was barely adequate'!"

He thought she might well burst into tears. "I'm only worried about you, Margo," he said quietly. "You have years of studying ahead of you before you can hope to—"

"*Years?*" Her lips quivered. "But I don't have—" She halted. Her chin came up defiantly. "I don't need years. I'm learning a lot and what I don't know, I can fake."

Kit rocked back. *Fake it?* "You can't be serious."

Her eyes flashed. "Why not? I got along just fine in London, except for not knowing that pistol, and I've fixed that problem. Just ask Ann if I haven't. I can shoot anything she hands me. Even that laser-guided blowgun she made me learn to use! Sven said my job is to avoid being seen, anyway, and I'm good at sneaking around in the dark!"

Kit held onto his temper. "Margo, you can't fake languages."

"No . . . but I can fake being a deaf mute, which is just as good! I've worked so hard, dammit! I deserve a chance to prove myself."

Kit didn't know whether to be angry or scared out of his mind. "You'll get that chance. When I think you're ready."

For a moment she just sat there, breathing hard. Tears welled up and spilled down her cheeks. Then, in a low, hurt voice, she said, "I'm not hungry any more. I'll think I'll go *study!*"

She fled past a whole line of waiting tourists who gaped after her. Kit cursed under his breath and shoved back his chair. Arley met him halfway to the door.

"Trouble?"

Kit nodded tightly. "Cancel our orders, would you? Put it on my bill."

"She's young, Kit."

"That's no excuse. The universe doesn't give a damn when it squashes you."

Arley let him go without further attempts at sympathy. Kit headed for the library. He *had* to make her understand. After London—and St. Giles—he'd hoped . . . But all she saw was the need to study fighting techniques, not the history and languages to help avoid the fight in the first place. She clearly understood the tactical advantage of invisibility but wasn't thinking of *knowledge* as one way to achieve it.

Scouting was a career men spent years—sometimes decades—preparing for, only to run into trouble anyway because they slipped up on some tiny, seemingly insignificant detail. He *had* to make her understand that, make her understand she simply *must* take the necessary time to prepare for it.

Otherwise, he'd lose her just as surely as he'd lost Sarah.

Kit was barrelling around the corner past Li's Antiquities when a sixth sense lifted the hairs on the back of his neck. He jerked his gaze up—

—and tracked the lethal swing of a heavy wooden croquet mallet straight toward his skull.

Kit swept his right arm upward by instinct, deflecting the blow at the expense of pain like an electric shock straight to the bone. He leaned away even as he swept the mallet aside. The thick wooden head narrowly missed his temple, lifting hair with the wind of its passage. Kit stepped forward with his left foot, turning with the sweep. He shoved the croquet mallet down and shoved his attacker's face straight into the wall. Both the mallet and someone's skull went *CRACK* against concrete.

A howl of pain reached him. Kit jumped clear. His arm ached, the ache becoming a relentless throb within seconds. He cradled it to his chest and felt for fractures he hoped he wouldn't find. Then his attacker staggered back from the wall.

Aw, nuts. . . .

The Welshman.

"Coward!" Kynan Rhys Gower spat at him. "Filthy dog!"

The Welshman came at him again, mallet raised over his head in a classic attack position. Kit, one arm all but useless, saw no other choice. He threw a sidekick straight into the onrushing Welshman's hips. The blow caught him just above the pubic bone. Kynan Rhys Gower folded up with an ugly sound. The mallet whistled just above Kit's back.

Kit recovered his balance while the Welshman struggled to regain his feet.

"Can't we talk about this?" Kit gasped, using Kynan's native language. *Where in hell did he get a croquet mallet?*

For answer, Kynan swept that damned mallet up and sideways. Kit couldn't get out of the way in time, although he twisted into a pretzel trying. He *felt* ribs crunch. The whole Commons greyed out for a moment while his voice did some creative sound effects.

Fortunately, Kynan Rhys Gower was still off balance and staggering from that blow to the hips. That allowed Kit to recover while the Welshman was still drawing the mallet back for the next try.

Okay, that's it. . . .

Time for a quick *coup de grace* to end this nonsense. Kit attacked first. In one swift motion, he swept the mallet back with one arm then threw a shoulder blow into the Welshman's ribcage. His whole weight hit just below Kynan's raised arm. He felt ribs crack again—but this time they weren't his. A shock of pain jolted through his own broken ribs anyway. Kynan howled and tried to fend him off with the mallet.

Kit grabbed the heavy wooden head and pulled sharply—then slammed Kynan's straightened elbow and shoved back on the mallet. Kynan gasped in pain. Then, with a circular sweep, push, and snatch, Kit simply jerked the makeshift weapon away.

Kynan was left blinking in pain and surprise, disarmed before he quite knew what had happened.

"Now look," Kit wheezed, "I don't know what your problem is . . . and I'm not a vindictive guy . . ."

Kynan started to spring at him, fingers curved into claws ready to gouge whatever they found.

". . . but this has *got* to stop . . ."

Kit swept the croquet mallet around and hit Kynan's ankle on the "funny spot"—just hard enough for the desired effect, but without the force to break it. Kynan gave out a strangled gasp and grabbed for his ankle. Kit shoved gently on his chest. He went down with a sound like a hurt child.

"Oww. . . ."

Kit held the mallet in an easy grip, standing near enough to strike a lethal blow if he wanted. Kynan sat on the concrete floor, holding his ankle, trying to hold his ribcage, and met his gaze. Clearly, he knew he was at Kit's mercy.

Equally clearly, he expected to die.

Pity swept away Kit's rage. He drew several deep, calming breaths. "Do you yield?" he asked quietly.

Surprise flickered through Kynan's eyes. He blinked uncertainly. But he didn't answer.

"I'd like to know why you tried to murder me."

That prompted an answer. "No man laughs at Kynan Rhys Gower and lives! You've taken my honor, my soul. . . . Curse you! Take my life and let this hell end!"

Try as he could, Kit couldn't recall *anything* the Welshman might have construed as being laughed at. "What are you talking about? When did I rob you of your honor? When did I laugh at you?"

Kynan's glance might have sent another man back a step. Kit held his ground, prompting Kynan to drop his gaze.

"You permitted the *woman* to humiliate me," he muttered. "Then you grinned like the gibbering blackguard you are when I was helpless against four!"

Kit was utterly baffled. He'd come in on the very tail end of that fight—how could he have allowed anyone to humiliate this man, when he hadn't even *been* there? In fact, he could identify only one instant Kynan could possibly be referring to. When realization sank home, Kit very nearly swung the mallet at his thick, medieval skull. If his ribs hadn't ached so fiercely, he might have.

"That *woman*," he hissed, "is my *grandchild*. You tried to kill her—after she was wounded trying to save a child from that damned French warhorse! I was not laughing at you! I wasn't even *thinking* about you! I was smiling in sheer relief because she would not lose the use of her leg."

Kynan Rhys Gower looked suddenly doubtful, which was small consolation considering how close he'd come to killing Kit.

Kit tapped Kynan's chest with the mallet. "Is it not bad enough you attacked a lady? Now you take offense where none was given and try to murder a man who has been wronged in his own kin by you!"

"I—"

"Shut up and listen! I didn't 'permit' anyone to humiliate you, much less Margo. I wasn't even *there* when you attacked her. You had better get used to a few new ideas, Kynan Rhys Gower. And the first one is this: women here are perfectly capable of protecting themselves when knaves rush at them with war hammers."

Kynan compressed his lips. "Knave, is it?"

Kit swore under his breath. "What would you call a man who attacked a girl barely eighteen, a girl already cut so badly her leg had to be sewn together—then tried to break a man's skull rather than call him out fairly to ask satisfaction—or at least an explanation?"

Kynan didn't answer. Not that Kit actually expected him to, but Kit always tried reasoning with people whenever circumstances permitted. Unfortunately, some people simply wouldn't be reasoned with. Kit was abruptly disgusted with the whole situation, including his own anger. If he'd dared trust the Welshman, he'd have left Kynan sitting on his backside in the middle of the Commons.

Fortunately, station security arrived on the scene. Mike Benson took one look and hauled Kynan to his feet. Benson cuffed the Welshman's hands behind him, then, in a quick maneuver that was anything but gentle, put him face-down on the floor and hobbled his legs. A strangled sound of pain escaped him.

"Better have someone look at him," Kit sighed. "I think I broke some of his ribs."

Mike Benson grimaced. "Serves him right, I'd say. Where'd this bastard get a weapon?"

"Hell if I know." Kit handed over the croquet mallet. "I'd check the outfitters' stores, see if any of 'em are missing part of a set."

Robert Li spoke up from the doorway of his antiquities shop. "I think he stole it from a group of grad students practicing for the spring garden parties in London. I heard a couple of them talking about a mallet missing out of their set the other day." He glanced at Kit. "I'm sorry, Kit. I had no idea the theft would turn out so serious. I just thought it was part of a practical joke or something. You all right?"

Kit nodded curtly. "I'm fine." Hell would freeze before

he admitted to broken ribs. He'd bribe Rachel Eisenstein, if necessary, to keep it quiet.

Benson ordered his men to take Kynan to a holding cell. The Welshman looked as though he'd considered struggling, then glanced at Kit and settled down to trudge away in his hobbles.

"You're standing mighty funny, Kit." In his late fifties, Mike Benson was solidly built, with thinning grey hair and cold blue eyes that had seen everything, sometimes twice. "How're *your* ribs?"

Aw, hell. . . .

Without asking, Benson peeled back his shirt. "Hmm . . . Better have these x-rayed. I think he broke a few."

"I'll take care of it," Kit grated.

"What was that guff he was giving you when I came up?"

Kit explained.

Mike Benson ran a hand across his short hair and gazed into empty space as though considering the wisdom of speaking. He glanced at Kit's ribs and spoke anyway. "Kit, that girl's been nothing but trouble since she got here. No offense, but she's a magnet for disaster."

"Great. What else has she done I don't know about?"

"Nothing illegal, if that's worrying you. Just . . . well, watch out when she's around. Skeeter Jackson and the occasional drunken billionaire aren't the only hotheads panting over her."

Great. Just wonderful.

A strained smile appeared around the security chief's eyes. "At least it's been more interesting around here since she arrived. Sometimes herding tourists from gate to gate is like dealing with squabbling schoolkids. If I'd wanted that, I'd have stayed on the force in Chicago when they tried retiring me to crossing guard."

Kit forced a laugh. "You'd have lasted six weeks. You thrive on La-La Land's unique brand of lunacy."

Benson sniffed. "Maybe I do. Maybe I do, at that. Of course, I could say the same. You might've retired up-time a couple of years ago. What keeps you hanging around this asylum?"

Kit let his shoulders relax, which was something of a mistake. He hissed softly and adjusted his stance. "Search me. Sheer meanness, I guess. What'll you do with Kynan?"

A wicked grin came and went. "Bull told me to watch out for that one. Almost confined him when he attacked Margo. I think about a month of restricted environment"—Kit mentally translated *jail*—"and community service for assault with a deadly weapon ought to change his attitude. The garbage pits are short of help just now."

Kit winced. "Poor bastard. Sometimes I think it'd be easier on the down timers if we just drugged them until their gates reopened."

Benson shrugged. "Yeah, but some never do. As you damned well know. Be sure Rachel looks at you."

"Huh. I've gone to ground in hog lots with worse than this and survived. Man'd think I'd turned into a mewling baby since I retired, the way people act . . ."

Benson grinned. "Hog lot, eh? You must tell me that story sometime."

Kit laughed. "Sure. You buy the beer and I'll tell all."

"Deal. Stay out of trouble."

Kit watched him stroll away, then winced. His ribs smarted. "Well," he quoted a very ancient comedy team, "this is another fine mess you've gotten us into, isn't it?"

He didn't feel up to tackling Margo's attitude toward education just now. *Better go crawling to Rachel and deal with my injuries.* With any luck, the promise of another down-time excursion would help repair this latest breach in his relationship with Margo. And the trip itself ought to go a long way toward convincing her she couldn't "fake it" down time.

"What're you coming to, Kit," he muttered on the way across the Commons, "bribing your own grandkid with expensive down-time presents?"

Kit knew—from first-hand experience—that once you gave in and paid Dane-geld, the Dane *never* went away.

Well, it was a little late for that now. And she did need a lesson in coping with down-time languages and customs completely alien from her own. Of La-La Land's major gates which fit that bill, Porta Romae was by far the safest.

Margo loose in Rome was an image of sufficient horror to sober even the most reckless of time guides. And Kit had never, in his entire professional career, been considered reckless. *When*, he wondered a little despairingly, *does the worrying end and the enjoyment begin?* Given the way his luck had been running of late, probably never.

"Must be Malcolm's fault," he decided. "His luck's rubbing off."

And that was the very best Kit could find to say about the whole mess.

CHAPTER FOURTEEN

Porta Romae, the Roman Gate, opened into the storage room of a busy wine shop on the Via Appia. Ancient Rome's "Main Street" ran from the Appian Gate to the great Circus Maximus where it turned north past the foot of monumental Palatine Hill, home of gods and emperors.

The hulking Circus rose like a battleship from the valley floor, its bulk silhouetted against a brilliant white sky. In deepest antiquity the Circus had been merely an open sweep of valley where even the Etruscans had run sacred funerary races. Over the intervening centuries the Circus, with its towering monuments and soaring wood-and-stone bleachers, had come to dominate the valley between the Palatine and Aventine Hills, one of the most sacred spots in the city of Rome.

The air of electric excitement which permeated the whole district when a games day approached was apparent the moment one stepped through the Roman gate and heard the screams of caged beasts, the shrill calls of high-strung racing horses, and the roar of Roman voices betting, arguing, laughing, and ordering food.

For Malcolm Moore, the chance to step through Porta Romae, the first of the great time gates to be explored (and subsequently the first owned lock, stock, and barrel by Time Tours) was worth every moment of the heartache, the uncertainty and misery which accompanied the life of a freelance guide. Whenever he stepped through onto the packed-earth floor in a crowd of excited tourists, something in his soul came back to life again.

Stepping through into the midst of the festival of the Magna Mater of Rome was simply icing on the cake.

Malcolm had guided tourists through the Porta Romae many times. But he'd managed to attend the Hilaria and the Ludi Megalenses only twice—and this was the first year Imperial decree would permit the Procession of Attis in its entirety through the streets of Rome. He could scarcely contain an idiotic grin.

Margo, of course, approached the trip in much the same light she'd approached London. Young Margo had no concept what the next two weeks would entail. Given the glimpses he'd seen in London of a bright and thoughtful young mind struggling to overcome something terrible in her past and make something good and decent of her future, Malcolm found himself looking forward to watching her process of self-discovery in Rome. He hoped she would surprise him.

Before new arrivals had finished clearing the gate, Malcolm reminded Margo to take a reading with her ATLS. He pulled her off to one side and put her through the drill of ATLS readings and log updates, then checked her work. He glanced carefully through her notations, double-checked her ATLS readings, and nodded. "Very good. You're getting the hang of it."

She beamed.

He finished his own notations then put away his equipment in the carefully disguised bag he would carry. Malcolm then adjusted his slave's collar and scrutinized the drape of Margo's provincial garb.

"I want her to look like a trader from somewhere really remote," Kit had said in the back room of Connie Logan's Clothes and Stuff. "Ideas?"

"Roman Syria," Malcolm had suggested at once. "Palmyra's perfect."

"Why Palmyra?" Margo asked curiously.

"Palmyrenes were almost unknown in Rome of A.D. 47. No one should question your complete lack of ancient languages—which also means they won't be able to question you about 'home.' And since they can't talk directly with you, I'll be able to 'translate'—and I *do* know the answers. Palmyra was only incorporated as an autonomous part of Roman Syria thirty-seven years before A.D. 47, with very tenuous trading ties to Rome, at best."

The costume Connie had come up with was delightful: draped folds of a Parthian-style tunic with voluminous trousers and leggings embroidered in wine-red designs. Metal "suspenders" supported the leggings, fastening them to the tunic's gold-embroidered hem. The trousers and even the long, narrow sleeves fell in a series of soft, U-shaped drapes down arms and legs. Overhanging the draped tunic came a cloak that fell in loose folds down the back. The shoes were elaborately embroidered "Persian" slippers. Capping off the costume came a cloth belt from which hung a scabbard for a long dagger.

When Margo heard the size of the estimated bill, she actually paled. "My God! Why so much?"

Connie grinned. "Any guesses?"

Margo glanced at the half-finished garments strewn everywhere in Connie's design studio. Computer-controlled sewing machines dominated two whole walls. "I have no idea."

"The chain-stitch sewing machine was invented in 1830. The lock-stitch machine came even later. Before that, all clothing was assembled by hand."

"But not all your costumes are this expensive. Not even close. What are you going to do? Hand spin the thread for this thing?"

Connie laughed. "No, although I've done that, too, on occasion, and spent hours at a loom hand weaving. Most costumes can be assembled by machine from the threads up. Even for pre-sewing-machine time periods, we can sometimes fudge. Take this."

She snagged an extraordinary gown from a peg. In three parts, it consisted of a coat-like overdress, a wide, skirt-like affair, and a triangular piece that was evidently meant to go across the front of the bosom, tapering to a point at the waist.

"This is an eighteenth-century English gown. One of our smaller gates opens into colonial Virginia every five years or so. It's due to open in about a month and a couple of researchers are going through for an extended sabbatical in Williamsburg." She chuckled. "Goldie Morran always makes a killing, exporting China metal to Williamsburg through whoever's going down time. The researchers carry the stuff through to help pay for their research trips."

"China metal?" Margo asked. "What on earth is that?"

"Ordinary nickel-silver," Malcolm grinned. "Not any silver in it, even. It's a base-metal alloy similar to German silver. It's used in cheap costume jewelry, junk trays and candlesticks, that sort of thing."

"Yes," Kit chuckled, "but in colonial Williamsburg it was worth as much as gold." His eyes twinkled. "Much like Connie's gowns."

Connie grinned. "Speaking of which . . . This gown has seven-hundred eleven inches of seams alone, never mind hems for both skirts and the sleeves or the decorative stitching visible from the surface. I can do an average of ten inches of seam an hour by hand, against a few seconds by machine. If I fudge and set the computers to simulate the slight variations in hand stitching, I can assemble a whole gown in a few hours—except for decorative stitching, any quilting the customer wants, and so on. I can't do that by machine. Someone down time would notice. Fashion has always been closely studied, both by practitioners and by poorer folk who want to ape the newest styles in cheaper versions. So some of it can't be fudged.

"Now, with your Palmyrene costume, I can't fudge *anything*. It'll take hours and hours of work to complete. I won't have to hand spin or weave, but the embroidery alone will be murder. I'll have to pull a couple of assistants off other jobs to finish it in time."

"Which is expensive," Margo sighed. "I guess," she said, giving Kit and Malcolm a hang-dog look, "I'd better not get it dirty, huh?"

Malcolm, like Kit and Connie, had laughed.

But now, the overly cautious way Margo moved told Malcolm she was terrified of ruining Connie Logan's exquisite creation.

"Margo," he said, "one piece of advice."

She glanced up, trying to avoid a dusty stack of wine jars. "What's that?"

"That costume is meant to be lived in. It may have been expensive, but it isn't a museum piece. Keep walking around like that and some Roman snob is going to think you're a *puer delicatus* for sale."

Margo's face registered absolute bafflement.

"Pretty boys brought twice as much at the slave markets as pretty girls, whether they were destined for a brothel or a private bed."

Lips and eyes went round with shock.

"This isn't Minnesota. It isn't London, either. Morals here aren't at *all* what they are up time. Not even remotely close. Neither are the laws. So don't go mincing around as if you're afraid to smudge your clothes. You're a wealthy young foreigner, son of a merchant prince in one of the richest caravan states the desert ever produced. Act like it."

She closed her mouth. "Okay, Malcolm."

"Study wealthy Romans on the street for body language. That isn't the same here, either. Neither are common gestures like nodding and shaking your head.

To indicate yes, tip your head back. To indicate no, tuck your chin." He demonstrated. "Shake your head side to side and a Roman will wonder what's wrong with your ears."

"What if I screw up?"

"Intelligent question. Romans were notoriously rude about their cultural superiority. If you make any minor errors, they'll put it down to a rank provincialism without the saving graces of intelligence, manners, or culture."

"Worse than the Victorians?"

"Lots worse," Malcolm said drily.

"Too bad. It's a horrid thing to say about people who invented . . . well, lots of things."

Malcolm sighed. "Margo, you really have to study."

"I know! I *am* studying. I'll study more when we get back! At least I can now tell you everything Francis Marion ever did, said, or thought!"

Still a sore subject. He was sorry, indeed, that she and Kit had fought about it. All La-La Land had buzzed with the gossip when Margo had walked out of the Delight and headed for the library in tears—leaving Kit so rattled a *down timer*, for God's sake, had nearly gotten the better of him in a hand-to-hand with a croquet mallet. That was the primary reason Malcolm was here: to convince her how important those studies were. Malcolm took his job seriously.

Then he had to stifle a grin: If the Hilaria and Ludi Megalenses didn't convince Margo she needed to study, nothing would.

A Time Tours guide opened the outside door again to communicate with employees in the wineshop proper. The roar of noise from the Via Appia just beyond caused a wave of excited laughter to ripple its way back through the tourists. The soundproofed door closed and the Time Tours guide stepped onto a crate to command attention.

"As you know, we'll all be staying at the inn we've

purchased in the Aventinus district, west of the Baths of Decius and southwest of the Temples of Minerva and Luna. That's very close to the Circus Maximus, in the heart of the sacred district, so we're not far from it now. We'll go there first. It's vital that everyone know how to find it. If you get lost, find the Circus and you can find the inn again. The most important instruction I have for you is simple: *Don't get separated from your guides!* There are more than a million people living in Rome right now, not to mention the thousands more who've crowded in for the Games of the Magna Mater. You don't know the language or the customs. If you lose your guide, you could find yourself in fatal trouble very fast. Our porters will carry your luggage, since neither free-born men nor free-born women carried their own parcels. You've already been warned not to venture out after dark. Rome is a deadly city by night. Not even the ruling classes walk the streets after dark. Now . . . are there any questions?"

"What do we do after you show us the hotel?" a man near the center of the group asked.

"You've already been assigned to your tour groups. Each group will follow an itinerary based on the selections you made at the time station. Today is the Sacrifice of Attis, with an historic first procession of the sacred pine, plus the regular annual celebrations and the dedications of new priests. Three days from now the Hilaria begins. The Ludi Megalenses games begin on April fourth and will continue through the tenth, with Circus games and races daily. Chariot races, horse races, and bestiaries are scheduled for the mornings, gladiatorial combats for the afternoons.

"As you know, when the Games open, it will be arena seating"—another ripple of laughter went through the crowd at the silly pun—"so we'll need to find seats quickly to be assured of places. Be ready to enter the Circus by sunrise. The gate back to the time terminal reopens shortly after midnight on the eleventh. You'll probably be exhausted—so don't arrive late!"

"What about the lottery?"

The speaker was another man, near the edge of the crowd.

"We've already drawn the winners of the Messalina lottery but we won't announce the results until tomorrow. As you know, there will be only three winners and the liaisons have to be carefully arranged by our employee in the Imperial palace. With Claudius in town, these trysts have to be set up with care. The winners, as you know, are not guaranteed a night with the Empress. Messalina has the right to refuse any lover she wants, but her tastes in men are generally broad enough we don't anticipate any problems. After all, she does sleep with Claudius."

A titter of laughter ran around the room. Malcolm didn't join in. Everyone had been shown photographs in advance to prevent the disaster of someone laughing at the disfigured emperor should they accidentally stumble across an Imperial procession. Margo, not knowing any better, laughed too, then turned a puzzled glance toward him.

"What's wrong, Malcolm?" she asked anxiously. "That was funny. Wasn't it?"

"No. It wasn't."

She studied his face for a moment. "Why not? You've seen him, haven't you?"

"Yes. That's precisely why I don't find it funny."

Margo's brows drew together, but she didn't respond flippantly. Good. She was learning. Up near the front of the room, the Time Tours guide said, "All right, everybody ready? Any last questions? Good. Let's have some fun!"

Malcolm said quietly, "When we get to the street, it's okay to stare at the buildings. You're dressed like a provincial; it'll be expected."

Margo nodded eagerly. The shine had returned to her eyes.

The door to the street opened once more to a bedlam of noise. Margo craned her neck to see outside, but was too short to see over the people between them and the door. The line moved forward slowly. The tour was permitted to leave in small groups of no more than three or four plus porters and guides. It always took a while to assemble a group for departure or to disperse a newly arrived tour without raising suspicion about the number of people entering and leaving the wineshop.

"Defer to *anyone* wearing a toga," Malcolm went on as soon as the door closed and Margo's attention returned to him. "If you encounter a member of the Praetorian Guard, try to look like the humblest, least important worm on the streets. You *don't* want to catch a Guardsman's attention. If I tell you to do something, do it fast and ask why later."

"Okay. What's the Praetorian Guard look like?"

"Roman soldiers. If you see anyone dressed like the soldiers in *Ben Hur*, get out of the way."

"They look like soldiers? Helmets with plumes, metal breastplates, little skirts, all that?"

"They don't just look like soldiers, Margo, they *are* soldiers. Bloody arrogant ones, at that."

Margo smiled. "Your accent's slipping, Malcolm."

He rubbed the end of his nose. "Well, yes. But the Praetorian Guard is something you don't want to tangle with. A lot of them are *Germans*. They're taller—a lot taller—than Romans. Now, about another important matter, have you studied the money?"

Margo groaned. "A little. Mostly I was trying to cram Latin."

The line moved forward again in a blare of noise from the open door.

"You're dressed as a free man, so you'll be expected to know the use of Roman money. As your slave, all I can do is translate. The more you know about the local money, the less likely you'll be completely rooked. I can tell you fair value for items, but remember we're not here to shop. We're here to learn."

Margo nodded impatiently. They were almost to the door.

"One last thing. I'm dressed as your slave. You're dressed as my *dominus*—my master. That's for public appearances. Don't let the master-slave thing go to your head or I'll turn you over my knee the second we're in private."

Margo shot him a startled glance. "You wouldn't!"

Malcolm grinned. "Oh, yes I would. *I'm* the teacher—the *magister*—and you're the pupil. Forget that and I'll remind you."

The door opened in front of them and Margo let out a tiny squeal of excitement. It was their turn to cross the threshold and enter the street. Then Margo got her first good look at genuine imperial Romans.

Her mouth dropped open. "They're . . . they're so *short!*"

The look on her face was so priceless, Malcolm burst out laughing. Margo was a dainty little thing, but very few of the people on the street were even close to her height. Malcolm towered over everyone in sight. Even the wineshop counter and seats were designed for child-sized bodies.

Margo gaped, staring from one Roman to the next. "They're *tiny!*"

"Among scholars," Malcolm told her with a chuckle, "speculation is rife that Julius Caesar's six-foot height had no little impact on his success as a politician. Everybody had to look up to him."

Margo grinned. "That's funny."

Malcolm laughed. "Yes. *That* is. Ready?"

"And then some! Show me!"

"Okay, hang a sharp right-left-right-left past the end

of the Circus Maximus, then follow the Via Ostiensis until it breaks southwest toward the Porta Ostiensa: the Ostian Gate. We'll take side streets around the Aventine Hill to the inn."

Margo cast a worried glance at him. "If I take the wrong turn?"

"I'll be right behind you. Just don't walk too fast. I *am* carrying all the luggage." That was one of the downsides to freelance guiding in Rome.

Margo set out without further delay. Malcolm hoisted the bundles to a more comfortable position on his back and followed. Crowds jostled him as he made his way down the stone sidewalk. He tried, with little success, to avoid being bumped off into the muck in the streets. When Margo reached the first corner, she paused.

"People are staring at me."

"You're dressed like a provincial. They'll probably laugh at your expense. Ignore them."

"Are those stepping stones to the other side?" She pointed at a series of high, squared-off stones set like miniature tank traps in the street.

"Yes."

"The street stinks. Worse than London."

Several people crossed on the stones, with pedestrian traffic flowing first one direction then the other as people took turns. Those who were impatient braved the muck.

"Yuck. This place is filthy!"

"No, actually it's very clean. State-owned slaves periodically clean the streets and the Cloaca Maxima is still in use in Rome even in our time."

"The what?"

"Main sewer of Rome. Just how much reading did you finish?"

"Uh . . ." She took advantage of a switch in traffic flow to cross the paving stones. Malcolm, caught in a crunch of people, had to resort to wading across at street level just to keep up with her.

"Hsst! Slow down!"

She glanced back and slowed down for all of three minutes, then the lure of more delightful sights down the street caused another lapse. She drew ahead again, paying no attention to Malcolm struggling along with their luggage. Malcolm held his temper and followed, wondering how long it would take her to admit she was in trouble.

She negotiated the dogleg around the end of the Circus just fine, despite the inattention she paid to the directions he'd given her. Malcolm didn't begrudge her the awed stare at the immense arena's facade. A single-story building ran around the outside, crammed with shops selling everything from baskets to hot sausages. Shopkeepers lived on the mezzanine above. Entrances near each shop led directly into the arena-level seats behind the podium wall. Stairs led upward to the second and third tiers where the long stone bleachers of the center sections gave way to wooden bleachers rounding the semicircular end. High overhead, three stories up, rose the colonnade and wooden arches which surmounted the end of the arena.

Margo walked with her neck cricked, staring upward and bumping into Romans who grinned and nudged one another.

"Barbarian's new to town."

"Wonder what gods-forsaken corner that rube's from?"

"Bet his eyes are about to pop!"

"Hey, *meretrix!* Take a look at the barbarian. Could be a good prospect!" This latter was shouted to a nearby woman in a short tunic. She ogled the Palmyrene "boy" hopefully. Margo, oblivious, passed the whore without noticing. Malcolm winked at her. "Maybe later?" he said in Latin.

The woman laughed. "Cheap enough for you? Or expensive enough for him?"

Malcolm grinned. "You look good to me, but who knows what a Palmyrene likes? Sheep, maybe?"

She laughed and passed the joke on to another loitering whore nearby. Several Roman men also laughed, overhearing the exchange.

Margo, oblivious, trailed a wake of good-natured laughter at her expense. She found the Via Ostiensis without difficulty. But she was so busy gawking at the sights, she didn't pay attention to the markings on the buildings when the Via Ostiensis apparently veered southwest. Margo committed the classic folly of taking the wrong fork in the road, wandering enthralled from one shop to the next. Malcolm, sweating under the weight of the luggage, let her walk all the way to the end of the Via Ardeatina. When Porta Ardeatina grew visible in the distance, she paused, then stared uncomprehendingly at her surroundings. She ended with a beseeching look at Malcolm.

"Where are we?"

He caught his breath. "You tell me."

Margo widened pretty green eyes. "*What?* Don't tell me we're lost? I thought you *knew* Rome?"

"I do. *I* know exactly where we are. We're about a hundred yards from the Porta Ardeatina on the southern edge of Rome. Hell and gone, I might add, from the inn."

"*Why didn't you say something?*"

"Margo, I was under the impression you'd learned something from your experiences in London. Was I wrong?"

Margo had the good grace to flush bright red.

"*Pay attention to what you're doing.*" He said it quietly but with enough force to make her hang her head. "I refuse to believe Sven Bailey has trained you for several weeks, yet neglected to mention that little gem of survival wisdom."

Margo's flush deepened. "No harm done. We weren't mugged or anything."

He could have pointed out that *she* wasn't carrying

anything heavy and so wasn't in a fit position to judge harm done, but he'd voluntarily assumed the weight of responsibility when he'd decided to teach her this little object lesson.

"Not yet," he pointed out. "But you still need to pay attention, Margo. There are consequences to everything you do—or don't do. As a scout, you won't have me along to bail you out."

She huffed as only Margo could do. The elegant folds of her costume flounced with the movement, leading Malcolm's attention badly astray from the lesson at hand. When Margo pouted, Malcolm was hard pressed to keep his attention on the job at hand—or anything else, for that matter.

All right, eyes front and center, Malcolm! You were hired to play teacher, not Don Juan. But darn it . . . all that spirit and tenacity and the occasional flashes of warmth and brilliance, glimpsed behind the pert facade and the periodic deep-seated hurt in her eyes, had come gift wrapped in *such* a pretty package. . . .

None of which was her fault.

Maybe Kit picked the wrong guide for this job.

"Okay," Margo sighed. "I screwed up again. It's my fault, I admit it. But I *am* here to learn. So *show* me."

He found it increasingly difficult to remain firm with her. "All right. This time, follow my directions."

Malcolm was tempted to make her retrace her steps and follow the route he'd given her. Instead, he deliberately took her through a maze of narrow, cramped side streets that wandered in zigzags up and down Rome's hills and valleys, just to underscore the lesson in paying attention. They finally emerged on the Via Ostiensis near the Ostian Gate. He led her back north again, to the place where he'd meant for her to leave the Ostian Way, where they should have circled the Aventine Hill. By the time they reached the inn, Malcolm's shoulders ached.

"You're late," the Time Tours employee said sourly, glancing at Malcolm for an explanation as he checked off their names against his master list.

"Object lesson," Malcolm said shortly, offering no further excuses. He retreated to their assigned room and dropped their luggage to the tiled floor then sat down on a wooden bed frame, not even bothering to locate the rolled-up bedding first. He could feel the pull of tired muscles from his neck to the middle of his back. When Margo came in, she caught him working his shoulders in circles. Her face flamed again.

"Are you hurt?"

Contrite as a child, now that the damage was done. He studied her silently. She was biting her lower lip. Malcolm had forgotten how very young eighteen was, with its mixture of invincible assuredness, fragile emotions, and the desperate need to be taken seriously— even when caught in complete ignorance.

Malcolm sighed. "Not much."

She glided across the room in a ripple of Parthian folds, then knelt behind him. Before he could protest, she was rubbing his shoulders. Malcolm shut his eyes. *God . . .* She was surprisingly skilled, working hard knots out of aching muscles from his neck to the middle of his back. *Where'd you learn to do that, little girl?* When her touch lightened to the merest whisper across his neck, Malcolm's insides reacted mindlessly. She didn't know what she was doing to him . . .

Did she?

Malcolm shot to his feet. "Gotta see about lunch," he mumbled, bolting for the safety of the crowded dining tables. The *last* thing any of them needed was for him to lose control. If Malcolm ever kissed her the way his body demanded she be kissed . . .

He called to mind Kit's blackest glower and held it

firmly in place. *Grandpa*, Malcolm warned himself solemnly, *would not be amused*.

Not at all.

Margo had never seen anything like the Procession of Attis.

Their inn lay on the southern side of the Aventine Hill near the Tiber. From there, Malcolm led the way around the end of the Circus where the starting gates overlooked a bend in the river and kept going all the way to the Palatine side of the mile-long Circus.

"Hey!" Margo said, pointing to a small, round temple. "I know that one! That's the Temple of Vesta!"

"Mmm . . . Well, it's been misnamed that for years, yes." Margo's spirits fell. "You're in good company." Malcolm grinned. "Hundreds of books still mislabel it that. Actually it was the Temple of Hercules. And that," he pointed to a squarish temple a stone's throw away, "is the Temple of Fortuna Virilis."

"Fortuna Virilis?"

"Temple of Man's Fate. Fate and the Circus games are *very* closely connected."

That made sense. Men *died* in the Circus.

"See up there?" he pointed to the crown of the Palatine Hill. "That's the Imperial residence. And that," he pointed to a magnificent temple which faced the great Circus, "is the Temple of the Magna Mater Deum Idea."

"What's that?" Margo asked breathlessly.

"What does it sound like?"

She considered, dredging up the bits of Latin she'd absorbed. "Magna sounds like magnificent. Mater . . . I'm not sure. Magnificent Material? Matter?"

"No, *mater* means mother. It's one of the words that sound similar in all languages descended from Indo-European: mater, mere, madre, mutter, mother."

"Oh. Magnificent Mother?"

"Close. Great Mother. What about the Deum Idea?"

"Uh . . . Deum is, like, deify?"

"Good guess. Deum translates 'of the gods'," Malcolm explained.

"Great Mother of the Gods of Ideas?" she guessed.

Malcolm grinned. "Not quite, although it's a logical enough guess. Idea in this case, however, refers to a mountain in Phrygia, near Troy. The Magna Mater is the goddess Cybele, the great mother of the gods from Phrygia. She's an import to Rome, but a very old one. About three hundred years ago, in fact. Her cult's been completely Romanized, of course. The Julian *gens*—Julius and Augustus Caesar's family—claims her as a founding deity. She was sacred to Aeneas, who founded their family. Claudius' family also has ties to her through Claudia Quintas."

Margo stared up the Palatine Hill, wondering what Malcolm saw that she didn't because she didn't know what to look for or what she was looking at. *Okay, I have to study and I will. But if I don't start scouting soon, it'll be too late and I'll never prove anything. . . .*

They fought their way through thick crowds until they could see the Via Appia where it turned to round the Palatine Hill. In the distance they could hear the sound of flutes and drums.

"Just in time," Malcolm grinned.

Margo craned to see. She was taller than the waiting crowd, which was a novel experience. She could see movement now in the street. Sunlight glittered against gold. The shrill of trumpets and the sharp sound of tympani drums rose above the noise of the crowd. Then she could see individuals. The person in the lead wore a long gown with folds of cloth pulled up like a hood. Under it Margo could see some kind of crown with three separate disks across the brow.

"Is that a priestess?" she asked excitedly.

"No, that's the *archgalli*—the High Priest of Attis. He just arrived in Rome through the new port Claudius is building. He managed to secure permission for this procession, to carry the sacred tree to Cybele's temple."

Margo blinked. "But he's dressed like a woman. I mean, he isn't dressed like any of the other men I've seen so far. Is it because he's a foreigner?"

"No, you were right the first time. Attis' priests wore women's clothing. For that matter, so did the priests of Hercules."

Hercules? Mr. Macho himself, the guy with all the muscles who'd done all those impossible labors or whatever they were called? Why would Hercules' priests dress like women? It didn't make any sense. With every maddening snippet of information Malcolm shared, she sensed a vast depth of knowledge he *wasn't* sharing. She glanced up, wanting to ask, but he was so visibly excited by the procession wending its way toward them she decided to hold her question for later. He darted his gaze eagerly, noting details, even mumbling to himself.

The high priest—*archgalli*, Malcolm had called him—neared their position. He moved slowly, wailing in a shrill voice and weeping while beating himself with a long flail. He held a scepter made of reeds in his other hand. Behind him came sweating bearers with a heavy litter. On it rode the gilded statue of a gorgeous young man in a soft, peaked cap. His "shirt" was open to the groin, leaving his chest and belly bare to well below the navel. His trousers were carved with diamond-shaped cutouts like a Harlequin's costume. In one hand he held what looked like a walking cane.

In the other, he held a small tympani drum exactly like the ones carried by wailing priests who trailed behind. They beat their drums with flails, then beat themselves, then sounded the tympanies again. Priests behind them, also wailing at the top of their lungs, carried more of the reed scepters. Behind *them* came another litter carried by sweating priests. On it was a statue of a tree. Sunstruck pine cones glittered with gold leaf.

"A pine tree?" Margo asked doubtfully.

"Shh! Later! Look!"

Margo widened her eyes. "My God . . ."

Half a dozen men each held thick leather leashes which chained a pair of *lions*. The huge cats glared at the crowd with hateful amber eyes. Margo clutched Malcolm's arm. *"They're not even caged!"* The lion handlers were sweating profusely, dragging on the leashes to keep their charges in the center of the street. Behind the stalking lions came another great litter. On it rode a gilded statue of a tall, beautiful woman. She rode a chariot drawn by lions.

"Cybele?" Margo whispered.

Malcolm just nodded. He was listening to the chanting priests. What were they saying? The crowd took up the chant, too, as the Magna Mater passed regally by. Some people tossed coins which weeping priests scooped off the paving stones and dropped into little bowls. Behind the gilded image came two priests who led a great black bull with scarlet robes draped across its back. At the rear of the procession came trumpeters, flute players, and a host of young men who stumbled along with glazed eyes, beating themselves with flails and wailing. They carried no reed scepters.

"Who are *they*?" Margo asked.

"Initiates. They'll dedicate themselves to Attis today. But I rather doubt they'll do it in the traditional Phrygian fashion. Claudius hasn't legalized *that*."

"They look stoned."

"They probably are."

She stared. "Why?"

"Purification ritual. Come on, if we scramble, I know a way up the hill."

Margo followed his lead as they dodged up the Palatine through narrow alleys that led past the Imperial palace toward the crowning Temple of Magna Mater. Crowds had gathered there, too. In a courtyard at the front of the temple they found space to jam themselves close enough to watch. The shrill of flutes, trumpets, and wailing voices drew nearer as the procession wound its way up the far side of the Palatine.

"They're passing through the Forum," Malcolm explained, "down the Sacra Via. Look, here they come."

Margo stood on tiptoe, anxious not to miss anything. What exactly was going on? She didn't know anything about Attis or Cybele—and Malcolm was so caught up in the moment she didn't want to interrupt to ask for explanations. The High Priest arrived first and took a position near a long, deep trench which had been dug in the courtyard. Planks capped it, arranged so that gaps showed. The images of Attis, Cybele, and the pine tree were carried up the steps to the entrance of the temple. The leashed lions snarled at the crowd. The roar vibrated against Margo's chest, bringing a prickle of unreasoning terror to the back of her neck.

The courtyard filled up. The black bull was led in and paraded around the periphery. Over in front of the temple, priests had lifted the gilded image of Attis off its litter. They were tying it to the gilt pine tree with stout ropes. Other ropes served as guide wires to keep the pine tree from toppling under the weight.

A line of robed priestesses—Margo was sure, this time, that she was looking at women—appeared from inside Cybele's temple and took up positions in a semi-circle. The High Priest led the black bull onto the platform, where several attendants held it with strong ropes. A swift glance at Malcolm showed Margo a man completely lost in study. He watched the barbaric scene as though memorizing every baffling detail.

This is his specialty, Margo remembered suddenly, *what he took his degrees in, Classics and Antiquities and stuff. He's forgotten me completely.* She'd seen

Malcolm the teacher, Malcolm the guide, Malcolm the sparring partner, even Malcolm the perennially broke friend who made her smile when she felt like curling into a ball and hiding from the world, but she'd never seen Malcolm the scholar enthralled by his life's passion.

The intensity of his gaze made her wish suddenly he'd look at *her* that way.

You want him to do that, you're going to have to meet him on even ground, Margo. And that meant she had to become a scholar. Well, she'd already discovered a burning desire to learn and understand; what better place to start than with something Malcolm, too, found passionately interesting? *So get started already!*

Margo studied the scene before her, trying to look at it as a student of ancient cultures. She wished she hadn't skipped so many Latin lessons or skimped on the cultural reading Kit had assigned her in favor of more time in the gym. Robed initiates stripped naked and descended into the deep trench. The bull lowed piteously. Its eyes rolled white. Someone she couldn't see too well was doing something under the animal's belly. She caught a flash of sunlight on steel as the High Priest shouted something.

The bull screamed and lunged. The men holding it strained at the ropes. The knife flashed again—to the throat, this time. Margo flinched. *God, they're really killing it. . . .* Blood poured through gaps into the trench. The bull fought, screaming and bellowing and bleeding to death at the end of its ropes. Margo covered her ears. She'd never seen an animal die up close like this, hadn't realized they would scream so pitifully. It was terrible, cruel, monstrous. . . .

You're not in Minnesota, Margo.

But the bull's agonizing death shook her, nonetheless. *They don't take so long to die in modern slaughterhouses,* she told herself. But it would be a long time before she wanted to eat beef again. Eventually the bull sank to its knees, dead. The High Priest held up something long and crooked at one end, like the walking cane on Attis' statue.

Then she realized what it was. "My God!"

Her shocked expletive was lost in the cheer from the crowd. Trumpets sounded again, wild and shrill in the April sunlight. The young initiates emerged, reeling and covered with blood. They looked like they'd been *drinking* it. They stumbled past the High Priest, each touching the bull's severed member in turn, then vanished into the temple. The priestesses followed. The High Priest, too, entered the temple. Other priests took up a chant that lasted a long time. Then, at some signal from inside the temple, the crowd began to cheer wildly. The high priest of Attis returned, still holding the bull's severed genitals.

Margo's head swam. None of this made any sense. The crowd had taken up its own chant. Malcolm looked like he was trying to memorize every word. Then she realized he'd loosened the flap on the bag which held his personal log. How long had he been recording? She caught a glint in his palm and recognized a miniature digitizing camera, one that worked like a video recorder but fed directly to the computerized log. Surely he'd attended one of these parades and ceremonies before?

No, she remembered suddenly, *this was supposed to be a historic first for Rome.*

No wonder he'd been desperate to get here and see this, record it in its entirety. She wondered how many other scholars had come on this tour? Given the questions about the Messalina lottery, probably none. Perhaps Malcolm *was* the only scholar present to record the Procession of Attis. She felt like a heel that she hadn't thought to turn on *her* recorder, too.

"Malcolm," Margo hissed, "just what *are* Attis and Cybele?"

He hushed her. He seemed to be waiting for something,

as though unsure what might happen next. The High Priest bowed low before the great gilded statue of Cybele in her lion chariot. He placed the severed bull's phallus before it and backed away, flailing himself and chanting. Initiates stumbled out, assisted by other priests. Then, at something which completely escaped her, he said, "Ahh" and suddenly relaxed.

The High Priest had obtained a basket filled with reed scepters. He presented one to each reeling initiate. While Margo stared, the new priests broke the reed scepters violently in half, then carried them one by one and tied the broken reeds to the gilded pine tree. The crowd was chanting along with the priests.

"What are they saying?" Margo demanded. "What are they *doing?*"

Once again, Malcolm hushed her. She stood in the midst of an insane crowd and tried hard to figure out the lunacy she'd just witnessed, but didn't come up with anything rational as explanation. *Some scholar I am.* To interpret something, one first had to know something on which to base an interpretation.

Why was it there was never enough time to fulfill one's dreams properly? To be a proper scout would take years. If she took years, the one burning goal that had made the past three years tolerable would never amount to anything more than daydreams. Margo sighed as the priests re-entered the Temple, carrying their sacred images inside. Then it was all over and the crowd broke up. People chattered excitedly, sounding for all the world like sports fans comparing the performances of favorite basketball stars. Malcolm fussed briefly with the bag containing his personal log, sliding the digitizing camera back into it and shutting off everything. Then he stood blinking like a sleepy English spaniel just coming awake in the morning.

"Well . . ." Malcolm's glance rested on her. His face

reddened. "Hi. I, uh, think you had a question?" he asked sheepishly.

"Or three, yes." She stood glaring at him, hands on hips, then had to laugh. "You look so funny when you're embarrassed, Malcolm. What the hell was that all about? I tried to make sense of it, but it was pretty weird."

"Today is known as Black Friday, the day of the Sun's death," Malcolm explained as he led the way down from the sacred Palatine Hill. "Attis is a Solar god, castrated and sacrificed to fructify the earth, then reborn again after coupling with his mother/consort Cybele. The Taurobolium—the ritual slaughter of the bull—is a purification ritual."

"Did they really drink its blood?"

"Yes, indeed. Then each initiate mated with a priestess of Cybele in the Temple of the Magna Mater. I'm surprised they didn't couple in the courtyard. I believe in some areas, the sacred marriages are done publicly." He smiled. "Roman morals, however, are generally much stricter, despite what you may see in movies. Of course," his eyes twinkled, "all bets are off during Hilaria."

A shiver ran up Margo's back. Hilaria was only a couple of days away. Just exactly what *would* the festival be like? And her seventeenth birthday was going to fall right in the middle of it. She couldn't have asked for a better birthday present.

"Anyway, after going inside to mate with the Goddess, our young initiates symbolically castrated themselves by breaking those reed scepters. I'd wondered how they would get away with the ritual in Rome, Imperial law being what it is."

"What do you mean? What's so terrible about breaking a bundle of reeds in half?"

Malcolm grimaced expressively. "It used to be a requirement of the priesthood of Attis for the initiate to castrate himself and present the severed organ to the Goddess."

Margo halted in the middle of the street. "Yuck!"

"Margo, you're blocking the way."

She started walking again, but her expression caused Malcolm to chuckle. "It's a very, very common myth in this part of the world, actually," Malcolm said as they turned into another narrow side street. "It's already ancient by these people's reckoning. The Sun God or Grain God mates the Mother Goddess, sometimes in her incarnation as the Moon, sometimes as Earth. The Solar God reigns as sacred king, is ritually killed, then is reborn again to begin the cycle of seasons and crops all over again. Hercules is another ritually murdered sacred king. But he was burned alive rather than being castrated and hung to bleed to death on a pine. In Carthage, ancient sacred kings were burnt alive on pyres as the solar Hercules. Aeneas barely escaped that fate when he ran away from Queen Dido of Carthage. In Egypt, Ra-Osiris was cut into pieces and scattered—"

"Malcolm, that's gross!"

His glance was highly sardonic. "Well, yes, from our perspective it is. But they really believed sacrificial blood was required to fertilize the earth. Crops wouldn't grow without it. And they really believed the god and his severed phallus were regenerated by the blood and by mating with the Goddess. That's why the full-fledged priests in the procession carried reed scepters. They're symbols of the god's phallus reborn as grain. It's the same reason you'll find Herms—phallus symbols—all over Herculaneum, for instance, which has Hercules as its patron deity. They're considered good luck symbols. People put them up by their doorways, touch them for luck."

Margo could understand rubbing a stone penis for luck better than she could a man mutilating himself. "But Malcolm . . . what kind of man would want to do that to himself? Did they do it voluntarily? Or were they prisoners?"

"No, they were volunteers. Look on the bright side: the tradition was modified years ago to kill the bull instead of the castrated priests. And now the tradition's been modified again, substituting broken reed scepters for the real castration. Roman law wouldn't tolerate the cult, otherwise. Of course, the Romans like to pay lip service to civilized notions about human sacrifices, but they have their own darker element to religious practices."

"Like what?"

"The Games."

"Those are *human sacrifices?*" She halted again, blocking the flow of the dispersing crowd behind her. Someone cursed at her in Latin. Hastily she stepped aside. "Malcolm, you're not serious? Nobody in any of my history classes ever said anything about human sacrifices in Rome and I didn't find anything like that in any of the reading I *did* do. I mean . . . the Romans were supposed to be *civilized!*" She stared down the hill toward the hulking facade of the great Circus. "Why would civilized people do something like that? I don't understand. Malcolm, it doesn't make sense and it ought to, if it's true."

Malcolm's eyes glinted. "I seem to have reawakened that curious itch to learn I first glimpsed in London. All right. Let's see if I can shed some light. Centuries ago, probably during Etruscan times, the Circus Maximus began life as a natural amphitheater of ritual sacrifice. The games, mostly races, were part of elaborate funerary rites. When we watch the Ludi Megalenses in a few days, keep that in mind. We are not merely watching spectator sports. The Games are *not* a Roman form of NFL Football. We'll be watching a sacred drama.

"It's *exciting* drama and the spectacles help the emperor keep the unemployed masses quiet by giving them something to do, but it's still sacred at its core and most people in this time recognize the ritual for what it is—if not overtly, then at some level of awareness.

"You asked if the priests of Cybele were volunteers or prisoners. The participants in Roman games *are* largely prisoners: criminals and slaves, prisoners of war. It's always easier on the king to substitute slaves for the real thing when the king must die. And in this particular time and this particular place, that is precisely what must happen."

The dust and noise of the bright April morning faded from Margo's awareness. She had difficulty taking in everything Malcolm had said. She understood much more clearly now why he'd said most guides held advanced degrees. They had to, in order to explain to tourists what they were watching. *But I can't spend years at this before my first scouting trip!* What she needed to become was a *generalist*. She could learn a little about a lot of things and fake it whenever she had to.

Meanwhile, she'd learn everything Malcolm would teach her.

"Huh. So now what?"

"Now," Malcolm grinned, "I think it's time to scout out some lunch."

"Now *there's* a plan I like!"

Malcolm laughed and took her back down the sacred Palatine Hill in search of her first genuine Roman meal.

Grey light had barely touched the sky when Malcolm stepped out of the Time Tours inn. Wagons and carts, caught like vampires by the sunrise, had been unharnessed and abandoned where they stood. Slaves and yeoman farmers carted off the goods by hand.

"The next three days," Malcolm told Margo as she joined him, "are going to be very much a repeat of yesterday."

"More weird parades?"

He shook his head. "No. That's reserved for the day of Attis' sacrifice. But Attis is a popular cult, particularly amongst the poor in the slums and in the port cities. A lot of people will walk around in a festive state of mourning, if that makes any sense, flailing themselves same as the priests yesterday and weeping for the tragic fate of their god."

She wrinkled her nose. Malcolm chuckled. "Get used to weird sights if you want to scout. Now, since the real fun doesn't begin until the Hilaria, and since that doesn't start for three days, I have a different plan of action in mind."

"That being?"

"Ostia."

"What's that? Another sacred ritual where some poor schmuck gets to play king of the hour?"

"No," Malcolm smiled. "Ostia is the port city downriver from Rome."

"Oh. Oh! That means a sightseeing trip outside Rome?"

Malcolm resisted the urge to tousle her hair. "Yes. Claudius has been building new harbor facilities. I want to see them. You should, too, just to get a grasp of Roman engineering." He chuckled. "The engineers told the emperor the harbor would be ruinously expensive, but it *had* to be built because the main harbor is silting in. I can hardly wait to see it, even if it won't be finished in Claudius' lifetime. It's said to be spectacular."

Margo had brightened visibly. "That sounds super! How do we get there?"

"We hire a boat."

She grinned. "Great! Show me!"

Malcolm made arrangements with a local merchant willing to hire out his little *lenunculi* since he was on holiday for the festivals. The boat reeked of fish, but handled beautifully.

"You know how to sail, I guess?" Margo asked.

"Yep. So will you, by the time we get to Ostia."

She groaned, but took to the lessons cheerfully once they were on the water. Malcolm taught her the rudiments of terminology while he navigated the heavy traffic in the Tiber. Once they were downstream from Rome and into quieter water, he started the hands-on lessons. She was clumsy at first and nearly put them into the near bank a couple of times but eventually caught on. He let her steer for a while and relaxed in the warm morning sunshine.

"You like it here," she said after a while.

Malcolm peeled an eyelid and found her watching him pensively. He smiled. "Yes, I do."

"Even though they're barbaric and put people to death in the arena?"

He considered how best to answer. "Every culture's barbaric in some fashion. It's a matter of perspective. The reverse is generally true, as well. Every culture has something fine and useful to offer. It's a matter of how you look at it. The trick in scouting is to figure out what you're looking at, to decide what—if anything—you can gain from that particular culture and time period, then to make off safely with whatever you've found, whether it's scholarly information or something more lucrative. Like, say, a potential new tourist gate or some treasure that's about to be lost through natural or man-made calamity. The more you know about when and where you are when you step through, the likelier you'll be able to identify what's useful."

"You don't care much about the money, do you?"

He chuckled and tucked his hands more comfortably behind his head. "You're beginning to figure me out, young lady. Nope. Not like some scouts and guides, anyway." He winked. "That's not to say I'd be averse to picking up a nice little treasure if I had the chance. But for me, it's the *learning* that's the kick. It's why

Kit's rich and I'm broke. He likes to learn, too. Isn't a scout alive who doesn't. But he cares more about the money than I do and truthfully . . . I think he's a lot luckier than I am."

"People make their own luck," Margo said with surprising vehemence.

He glanced into her eyes, then smiled. "Well, yes. Maybe they do. You're here, after all. And I'd have bet money you'd never get this far."

She flushed. "Thanks. I think."

Malcolm laughed. "Well, considering the first thing you did in La-La Land was get lost in Residential . . . Straighten the rudder, Margo. We're headed for the river bank again."

She put out her tongue and steered for the central current again. It was a glorious day for a sail, perfect weather and perfect company, but as they neared the new port, river traffic grew much thicker. Malcolm took over and steered a course toward the far bank to get the best view possible when they neared what should be the spot for the new harbor facility.

"There are a lot of boats coming up river," Margo commented.

"Ostia's the grain port for Rome. Italian agriculture's in trouble, mostly for economic reasons. Almost all of Rome's food supply, grain in particular, is imported. In fact, Rome imports far more than she exports. Take that, for instance." He pointed to a heavily laded *corbita*, a kind of heavy freighter, passing majestically on its way upriver. "Those amphorae probably contain wine or olive oil, I can't see the markings at this distance to be sure. Those bales are Egyptian cotton and imported luxury goods." A barge towed by *scaphae* followed. Huddled on its decks were miserable, half-naked men and women in chains.

Margo's eyes widened. "Those are slaves!"

"Ostia *is* a trading port," Malcolm pointed out. "And

slaves are big business. Rome has had a slave economy
for centuries."

She followed the barge's progress until it passed out
of sight beyond a bend, then shivered. They rounded
another curve in the river and the new port came into
view. Ostia was just visible in the distance, more than
two miles away across silty salt marsh. The new port
rose from the marshes as though the gods themselves
had set the giant stones in place.

Margo breathed, "Wow!"

For once, Malcolm shared her awe.

Two curving breakwaters had been constructed across
the entrance to an enormous excavation. The main
harbor—some one-hundred-seventy acres of it—had
already been dug and flooded. Between the two
breakwaters, Roman engineers had built an artificial
island. A tall tower rose toward the bright sky, incomplete
as yet. An artificial channel connected the newly dug
harbor with the river.

Malcolm dragged over the bag containing his ATLS
and log and slung it across his chest, bandolier style,
then risked a quick scan with a digitizing camera which
hooked into the log like an ordinary scanning mouse.
He photographed the entire panorama, then steered
for the middle of the Tiber. Now that he'd seen the
whole layout, he was dying to get a closer look. Margo
leaned over the prow like an excited kid.

"What's that?" Margo asked, pointing to the tower.
"A temple of some kind?"

"No. Much more important."

She glanced around, brow furrowed. "Like what?"

He grinned. "A lighthouse."

"A lighthouse?" Margo laughed. "I never thought
about ancient people building practical things like
lighthouses, but I guess they'd need one, wouldn't they?
Especially to navigate around that island in the fog."

"Yes. It's almost finished. Claudius will dedicate the

new harbor this year, although construction will continue through A.D. 54 under Nero, after Claudius' death. Get your log. I want you to start recording your impressions. Just open the flap on your bag a little and press voice record."

She did so, draping the bag around her own neck and shoulder much as he had.

"Wow. That's really something, Malcolm." She began describing everything in sight, then started asking questions. "How long must it have taken to dig all that out? Months? Years? And look at those walls. What is that? Stone? Or concrete? And look at those piers. They're solid stone! How'd they get those blocks into place? Say, what's that?"

Malcolm grinned. Watching Margo's mind come alive was almost as much fun as studying the new port to satisfy his own scholarly itch. They moved on downriver and spent the day in Ostia, prowling the wharves while merchants offloaded cargo for the river voyage up to Rome and manufactured goods arrived for export to the far-flung provinces. Ostia's harbor was so badly silted, the town was already showing the effects of lost business to overland routes. Eventually, even Claudius' fine new harbor would silt in and everything would come overland from Naples—until Trajan would finally build his non-silting, hexagonal-basin harbor. Almost sixty years from now, Ostia would come into her true glory as a port. But even now, Ostia was an impressive little city.

Malcolm took her to the barracks of the *vigiles* and explained the function of the special cohort.

"Firemen?" Margo echoed. "I thought Benjamin Franklin invented fire departments."

"Say, you *have* been doing that American history reading, haven't you? Very good. In a manner of speaking, he did. But the Romans had a special fire-fighting brigade to protect the grain port and there was even a private company in Rome. Of course, *its* main job was to arrive at a fire and convince the owner to sell out cheap before putting out the blaze. . . ."

"That's *awful!*"

"Free enterprise in action," Malcolm grinned. "The owner got filthy rich."

Margo huffed. Malcolm's gut response disturbed him to his core. *C'mon, Malcolm, she's your student.* But he couldn't help the fact that Margo was doing seriously troubling things to his bodily chemistry.

"Come on, I'll show you the Mithraeum and the Temple of Vulcan."

Margo giggled. "The guy with the ears?"

Malcolm gave her his best disapproving scholar's glare, which reduced her to fits of laughter.

"I'm sorry," she laughed, "but it always tickles me. And you look so funny when you're irritated."

He sighed, feeling suddenly old. *Was* a man old at thirty-six? *Old enough for a bubbly eighteen-year-old to consider funny . . .*

It was just as well. He needed complications in his life the way a flock of turkeys needed Thanksgiving. Malcolm adjusted the fit of his slave's collar and gestured to his "master."

"This way, if you please. The buildings you see here are the *collegia* of the boatmen, professional guilds with considerable clout in Ostia. Down that way are the warehouses and if we look off to the southeast, we can just see the roof of Ostia's Temple of Cybele. . . ."

Margo waited until Malcolm had fallen asleep, then quietly dressed in the darkness and slipped out of their rented room. She wanted to get away by herself to think. What with lessons and down-time adventures, she hadn't really found five whole minutes to just *think* about the enormity of what she was doing. She knew she was taking a risk, going out at night, but Ostia wasn't Rome. *Besides, I need to prove I'm ready to solo.*

Margo gained the dark street without raising an alarm. She leaned against the wall and let go her breath, then grinned. *So far so good.* When her eyes adjusted, Margo caught her breath. *The sky* . . . Clearer even than a Minnesota winter night, the sky was so filled with stars Margo lost whole minutes just gazing upward. *Everybody should see a sky like this, just once before they die.* . . . Margo had met folks who'd never seen anything but the murky yellow glow that passed for night in places like New York. *Maybe if they saw a sky like that they wouldn't feel so . . . so self-important.*

Feeling keenly her own insignificance, Margo found her way to the docks. Wooden hulls creaked in the night. Wind flapped in loose sails, sang through slack rigging. Where ships rode quietly at anchor, a few braziers burned on high stern decks, marking the presence of night watchmen. Margo found a stone archway near the entrance to one long pier and settled in the shadows. Far away, drifting on the spring wind, she could hear a magical chorus of frogs and insects from vast salt marshes. Margo sighed. *I'm really sitting on a dock two thousand years before I was born.*

She'd planned this moment all her life. So why wasn't she happy? Malcolm Moore's smile flitted into her awareness, causing her pulse to dance like mating butterflies. Malcolm Moore was more than a good teacher. He was becoming a good friend, maybe the best friend she'd ever found. She was grateful for that, but . . .

But what?

But deep down, you're afraid of him, that's what. And she wasn't sure she wanted to be, which scared her even worse.

Starlight silvered the rolling breakers. In her own time, the sea had wiped out some of the world's greatest cities. Margo didn't understand all the science and stuff that had caused *The Accident.* All she knew was a burning need to grasp the opportunity before her. And she *would* grasp it. Come hell, high water . . . or Malcolm Moore. How much time was left? She counted backwards in her head. *Three months.* Margo bit her lip. Was she being foolish, rushing her training just to prove *him* wrong?

"I *have* to! I just have to . . ."

Her father's voice, angry and slurred, slapped her from out of the past. "You'll turn out same's her! Filthy, stinking whore—"

My mother was not a whore!

All those years ago, Margo had wanted to shout it back at him. *Not* shouting it had probably saved her life. But not saying it—then or now—didn't change facts. Everyone else *had* said it: the cops, the news people, the foster parents who took her out of a hospital bed and gave her a home in another town. Even the judge who'd eventually passed sentence on her father had said it. Margo, trying to rebuild her life, had turned a dry-eyed mask to the world to hide the pain.

Leaning against a cold stone pier, Margo thought she finally understood what had driven her mother to prostitution. Since leaving Minnesota, there'd been a moment or two when Margo's hunger and desperation had made *any* source of money seem attractive. How much worse must it have been for her mother, with a young child to raise, mortgage payments, groceries, medical bills . . .

And a husband who drank whatever money he got his hands on—including any he could beat out of her.

In that moment, it became doubly critical for Margo to succeed. Not only did she have to prove to her father she could do this . . . *I'll make you proud, Mom. And I'll pay him back for what he did to us. I hate him! I'm glad he's dying, he deserves it* . . . But she wanted him to live just long enough. The only way Margo could find to strike back at him, to really *prove* she wasn't everything he'd ever called her, was to do something no other woman had ever been able to do.

And she had only three months left in which to do it. Three months to convince Kit she was ready to scout, to tackle an unknown gate, to come back with proof of her success. Three months. From where she sat, it seemed as impossible as telling Kit the truth about his only child.

Malcolm Moore's smile, flickering at the edges of memory, seemed nearly as great a threat to Margo's plans as the ticking clock. Men were nothing but trouble. They used you if they could, hurt you when they pleased, shattered your dreams if you didn't run faster than they could punch you to the ground . . .

Malcolm Moore isn't like Billy Pandropolous. Or my father. But it didn't matter. She didn't have time for love. At least Malcolm Moore was too much a gentleman to hurt her the way Billy Pandropolous had. That was very little comfort when Margo crawled back to their rented room in the wee hours and huddled under her cold blanket for the remainder of the night.

Margo tried to keep up a brave front when they returned to Rome. Malcolm, suspecting none of the turmoil inside her every time his wide mouth curved into a smile, showed her the Campus Martius, where the secular games were held in the Circus Flaminius. The area also boasted gardens where young men could exercise and play, the *Villa Publica* where Romans assembled for the census and to levy troops for the legions, the *Septa* where people came to vote, splendid shops where the wealthy purchased luxury items imported from around the empire, even a place along the Tiber where Romans could swim and splash in the shallows.

They toured the Forum Romanum, with its Comitium, the Forum's political center; the religious Regia with the *real* Temple of Vesta, the House of the Vestals, and the seat of the Pontifex Maximus; and the Forum proper, a marketplace, center of civic activities, public functions, and ceremonies. The Forum's famous *rostrum* or speaker's platform was where a man could address his fellow citizens while running for office or just pass along juicy tidbits of news. Decorated with the prows of ships taken in battle, it was impressive, with its backdrop of the Temple of the Divine Julius (on the spot where his body had been cremated), marble-faced *basilicas* or law courts and other public buildings. Margo was surprised to find women lawyers arguing cases in the *basilicas*.

"Yes, women lawyers were increasingly common from the late Republic on," Malcolm explained. "Women in Imperial Rome weren't confined to the home as they were in early times and other cultures."

Margo liked that. The water clocks used to time the lawyers' speeches fascinated her. Some dripped water from a tank into a bowl, lifting a float with an attached rod whose cogs turned the hour hand. Another kind used water pressure to blow a tiny trumpet every hour.

"An alarm clock," Margo marvelled. "They use an alarm clock!"

Malcolm only smiled, which left her insides in turmoil.

They followed the course of the aqueducts through the city, while Malcolm explained how the public fountains worked and how the aqueducts fed the great public baths as well as private homes. He even hired a boat and took her into the immense Cloaca Maxima which drained the city's swampy valleys.

He took her down the fullers' street, showing her how "dry cleaning" was done by slaves who stomped soiled garments into damp fuller's earth. The absorptive clay then dried and was beaten out of the cloth, taking with it oils and dirt. Then he let her watch Roman glass production, following that with a trip to a mosaic artist's studio, a visit to the Porticus Aemelia—the river port of Rome—and its warehouses, called the "Emporia," and another to the slave market.

The sights *there* left her with nightmares.

She was determined not to show it, however. If he could stomach it, so could she. Then, just when her spirits had reached an all-time low, the Hilaria—and her seventeenth birthday—began. It wasn't at all what Margo had imagined. "Hilaria" had conjured images of comic actors staging street performances or maybe people dressing up in funny costumes and laughing at one another, dancing and singing like Mardi Gras, maybe.

Minnesota had not prepared her for Roman street orgies.

"It's a celebration!" Malcolm shouted above the roar. Nearly a million singing, laughing people had taken to the streets, dancing and guzzling more wine than Margo had seen outside a Mogen David warehouse. "Their sun god just got reincarnated today! By the old reckoning, it's New Year's!"

Times Square had *never* witnessed a party like this.

Margo laughed. "Tell you a secret!"

"What?"

"It's my birthday, too!"

"Oh, ho!" Malcolm's grin did seriously dangerous things to her insides. "I can't think of a better way to spend your birthday. Can you?"

She shook her head, grinning like a fool. It occurred to her in that moment, she'd never been so happy in her life.

Someone shoved a wineskin at Margo's mouth. It was drink or drown. She drank—and nearly drowned anyway. Malcolm pounded her back and grinned. "Does Rome know how to throw a bash or what?"

Margo caught her breath and wiped her face. "It's *wilder* than Mardi Gras!" Not that she'd ever *been* to New Orleans. . . .

A girl ran past, shrieking and giggling, while a middle-aged man dashed after in drunken pursuit. When Margo tried to back into an alleyway to avoid being trampled, she literally tripped across a much-occupied couple.

"Oh, my God . . ."

The alley was very much taken. By more than one couple. None of them were vertical. Well, that couple down there was, sort of. She beat a hasty retreat, so embarrassed she hardly knew where to look. Malcolm, the wretch, just waggled his brows. "What's wrong? You're not shocked, are you?"

"Aren't you?" Margo demanded. She didn't know whether to be more embarrassed that she'd seen them, or that her whole body had started to tingle in places Malcolm's grin made hot and fluttery by turns. *Oh, no, Margo, get hold of yourself. This road leads to* trouble. *That's why that Presbyterian preacher the Smiths went to on Sundays always . . .* Quite suddenly she giggled.

"What?" Malcolm asked, leaning close enough to hear over the tumult.

"I just wondered what Reverend Williams would have said if he'd seen that alley!"

Malcolm's eyes widened, then he laughed. "Probably something about fire and brimstone. To a Roman, the Hilaria's a sacred celebration. Casual affairs are *expected*. Of course, the rest of the year women are supposed to be nicely chaste, just like home, and no self-respecting patrician lady would be caught dead out here having the time of her life."

Someone in an outrageous animal mask pranced by, waving a wine jar and singing something that Margo suspected was extremely bawdy.

"I'll bet their husbands and brothers are out in force!"

Malcolm laughed, then snagged a couple of wine cups from a street vendor and bought a whole wineskin. "Too right. Roman gentlemen know how to dissipate with the best of 'em." He hoisted the wineskin with a chuckle. "Come on, let's find something to eat."

Quite unexpectedly, Margo realized she was having a good time. She relaxed. Maybe a little dissipation would be fun. She'd certainly worked hard enough to earn a party. *And if you have to say goodbye to this man someday soon, maybe you should enjoy him while you still have the chance.* So Margo ate sausages that had been cooked in deep vats of olive oil, tried fresh-baked bread hot from the oven and wonderful little cakes made with honey and sesame seeds, and washed it all down with sweet red wine that left her giddy.

Greatly daring, she joined a dance, not caring when people laughed and called her *provincialis*, *rusticus*, and other probably less flattering names. Malcolm roared with laughter, then cut in line behind her. His hands came to rest on her hips, leaving her flushed from scalp to toes. They snaked their way through crowded streets in a wild line dance that ended in front of a tall marble temple. When the dance broke up, Margo staggered dizzily, then fell laughing against Malcolm. He caught her and set her back on her feet. His face was flushed.

Her heart gave a traitorous thump.

"Where are we?" she asked breathlessly. Over there was the long side of the Circus and over that way was the river, but she didn't know what this temple was.

"That's the Temple of Ceres, Liber, and Libera." It came out oddly husky. His eyes were fever bright.

"Who?"

"Ceres, Goddess of Grain and Agriculture. Liber Pater and Libera, very ancient Italian god and goddess. She and Liber Pater celebrate a sacred marriage."

Margo found herself swallowing hard. "Really?"

"They join during the Ludi Ceriales. That's about twenty-two days from now."

The whole city beyond Malcolm's bright eyes was spinning in her awareness. "Do Roman gods do anything besides make love?"

"Not in the spring." He was very close to her. His smile—and that answer—did wicked things to Margo's insides. The way the corners of his eyes crinkled, the way his hair fell across his forehead in an unruly curl, the way he took her questions seriously even when laughter made his eyes sparkle—even the sharp masculine scent of him—

Everything about Malcolm Moore set her blood pounding. *I don't care if this is all there is, I don't care about scouting, I don't care about anything, oh God, let him kiss me. . . .* As though he'd heard her silent prayer, Malcolm bent toward her. April sunlight turned the dark sheen of his hair to the gloss of a raven's wing. Then his mouth covered hers, warm and demanding and gentle all at the same time. Her senses reeled. She found herself clutching the front of his tunic. Margo had never been kissed like this, as though her mouth were a precious jewel which must be handled with exquisite care. Then his hand slipped from her face and touched the side of her breast—

The kiss exploded into a mindless clutching at one another in the bright April sunlight. Afterward Margo was hardly cognizant of stumbling through the streets with his hand on her waist. Was hardly aware of the change when he plunged into a rustling grove of trees and sought a remote, unoccupied corner. Peripherally she noticed low-hanging branches that dipped to screen a tiny glen. A natural spring bubbled up from a rocky basin and poured away through the trees.

Then she was in his arms again and his hands were on her bare skin and the only thing in her awareness was the pounding of his heart against hers as they went to the sweet-scented earth in the tangle of their clothing.

❖   ❖   ❖

Only afterward did the full enormity of what she'd done sink in. Margo lay in the crook of Malcolm's arm, his body pressed warmly against hers, his breath shuddering against her ear. The fire of their joining still lingered in deep tremors inside her.

Then, like icewater through her veins:

I slept with him.

Dear God, I slept with him.

Panic smote her so hard Malcolm stirred. "Margo? What's wrong?"

She couldn't answer. Couldn't put into words the myriad terrors ripping her apart. *Dad was right. I'm nothing but a two-bit whore, I'll never be anything, never amount to anything, I can't even say no when I know it's the wrong thing to do, I could be pregnant. . . .*

Oh, God. She *could* be.

She'd destroyed everything she'd worked for, would never be able to face down that bastard who'd murdered her mother, could never tell him he'd been wrong—

And Kit Carson . . .

If she couldn't even be trusted not to fall into bed with the first man who took her down time . . .

She began to cry. When the dam burst, she couldn't control the flood. Malcolm touched her shoulder.

"Margo? Please, what is it?"

She jerked away, so miserable she wanted to die.

Malcolm's tender concern only made the enormity of her folly worse. Clearly, he'd anticipated a jolly romp in the grass with a woman capable of enjoying the moment. A woman he'd *thought* had just turned nineteen. All she'd managed to give him was a ten-minute quickie with a scared kid. Worse, a scared kid with a past. The fact that it had been the most profoundly shattering experience of her young life . . .

She hid her face in the sweet grass and cried until she thought her heart would burst.

❖   ❖   ❖

Malcolm listened for a long time, damning himself for several dozen kinds of fool. He finally dared a question.

"Margo, I have to ask. Who was he?"

She strangled on another hiccough and stopped crying long enough to ask, "Who?"

Malcolm wanted to touch the nape of her neck, but she wasn't ready for that yet. "The bastard who hurt you."

She finally rolled over to face him. Tear streaks blotched reddened cheeks. Faint surprise flickered in her eyes. For several moments, he thought she wasn't going to answer. When she did, it still wasn't really an answer.

"You sound angry."

This time he did touch her, very gently. And this time, she didn't flinch away. "I *am* angry, Margo. More than you can know."

She held his gaze for long seconds. Behind her, spring water poured over a lip of stone and meandered through Diana's sacred grove down to the Tiber and the distant sea.

Then she turned away again. "You're wrong. It wasn't what you're thinking. And I was wrong, too. About a lot of things."

Malcolm bit one lip. *God, who* did *this to her? I'll take him apart.* . . . "Maybe, but so was he. Whoever he was, whatever reason he had for doing it. He was wrong."

"How—how can you be so—so damned *nice?*"

Meaning you only sleep with boys who are rotten to you?

He decided to introduce a little levity. "But I'm not nice. I'm a calculating cad, Miss Margo." She went very still in his arms. "Consider: I dragged you two thousand years into the past, plied you with sweet Roman wine, then danced you through half the streets in the city for the express purpose of scaring *myself* half witless. We perverts are like that, you know. Devious fellows. We'll do anything to indulge our bent for self-inflicted terror."

His smile, calculated to put her at ease, shattered her fragile self-control. Margo's whole face crumpled, then she turned away from him, shutting him out once again. "Where are my clothes? I'm too naked. If you want to talk, let me get dressed."

"Margo . . ."

She paused, holding the Parthian tunic in front of herself like a shield. "What?"

"You've no idea how sad that makes me feel."

Her brows dove together. "How sad what makes you feel?"

"That you can take your clothes off to sleep with a man, but you can't talk to him afterward. That's what love is all *about*. Touching and talking and caring."

She opened her lips several times, but no sound came out. Then, bitterly, "Who made you the world's expert, anyway? You're a penniless bachelor! You . . . you *are* a bachelor, aren't you?" she asked suddenly, hugging the tunic more tightly to her breasts.

He managed a smile. "Yes. I'm a bachelor, Margo. And I never claimed to be anyone's expert on the subject. But I do think you ought to be at least friends with the people you sleep with. Otherwise, it's the saddest thing in the world, groping after something you can't define with a total stranger who probably can't define it, either."

"*I know exactly what sex is!*" She crouched in the sunlight, fingers dug into the earth, the folds of her tunic forgotten. "It's getting drunk and thinking you're having a good time, then waking up trapped and hurt and scared of everyone you thought you liked! It's miserable and lonely and I'm sorry I ever laid eyes on you! *Damn* you, Malcolm Moore! You *ruined* my seventeenth birthday!"

SEVENTEENTH? Malcolm opened his mouth, but nothing came out. Terror and regret and rage at her lie tore through him so savagely he couldn't even move. *Seventeen? My God, Kit will kill me—*

She flung herself into her Parthian tunic and trousers, then fled. Malcolm swore and hurtled himself into his own clothing, but by the time he gained the street, dodging tree trunks and pleasantly occupied couples, she was gone, swallowed up by the teeming celebration beyond the temple precinct. He stood on the stone sidewalk, shaken so deeply he could scarcely breathe.

Idiot, fool, dolt. . . . You knew she'd been hiding from something! Whatever it is, you just drove her right back into the middle of it. In a moment of utter folly, Malcolm had allowed himself to forget that Margo was young and vulnerable, trying to hide something desperately painful behind a pert, sexy exterior. Donning a mask of confidence and challenging the world didn't change the fact that she was a scared little girl hiding in a woman's body. Memory crucified him. The passion, the quivering fire against him and inside him . . .

There wasn't anything he could do now except pick up the pieces and go on, hoping Margo would eventually forgive him.

It was even money Kit Carson never would.

CHAPTER FIFTEEN

The rest of Margo's stay in Rome was a nightmare.

After fleeing Malcolm, she lost her way in the tangle of narrow, crooked streets. Margo wandered for hours, seeing hardly anything, scarcely paying attention to where she put her feet, much less where she was going. When the light began to go, Margo came out of her mental fog with an abrupt jolt. She blinked at unfamiliar surroundings, discovering she had no earthly idea where she was or where the Time Tours inn might be.

"Malcolm . . ." she quavered.

But Malcolm wasn't there to bail her out. She was on her own in the growing darkness. The crowds had thinned out, leaving her virtually alone on a grimy little street of four- and five-story Roman tenements. Haphazard, rickety wooden buildings a block long, the tenement "islands" sported cheap shops at street level and increasing poverty the higher one climbed the stairs.

She had to find shelter. Rome's streets were deadly after dark. Margo glanced both ways down the street, then, swallowing hard, she headed back the way she'd come. She walked several blocks without finding a trace of anything remotely resembling a landmark she recognized. She moved faster, heart in her throat, abruptly aware of men loitering in darkened doorways and zigzag alleys.

When Margo spotted an inn, she didn't care how dirty it was or how drunk its occupants. She bolted inside, feeling marginally safer in the boisterous, lighted room. She drew immediate attention, but managed to stare down several curious types who shrugged and returned to their wine and dice games. The innkeeper communicated through signs and gestures. She handed over coins and he handed over food and a blanket. The food was hot, the blanket threadbare, and the corner she eventually chose to bed down in drafty, but at least she wasn't alone in the dark on dangerous streets.

Tomorrow she would find Malcolm. Find him and offer an apology and try to explain. . . . She had to find him. The prospect of even one night alone was suddenly more daunting than she'd bargained for. She hid her face in the blanket. Then—asserting itself through rising panic—a spark of intelligence or maybe just Sven's training told her to take precautions. Under cover of her threadbare woolen blanket, Margo transferred her money to her ATLS pouch and drew her short knife, gripping it tightly under the covers. That done, she felt marginally safer.

Even so, sleep took a long time coming. And when she did finally nod off, violent dreams woke her every hour.

By the time sunlight streamed into the room, Margo was exhausted. But her ATLS bag and knife remained in her possession. Her belly rumbled audibly. *Later*, she told her stomach. First she had to find Malcolm. Margo set out to locate the Aventinus district and quickly realized she hadn't absorbed nearly enough of Malcolm's lessons on the layout of Rome. She guessed she was somewhere east of Campus Martius, so she began walking west. That took her into a rat's maze of "islands," private houses, and public buildings strewn haphazardly across Rome's hills.

By midday she was light-headed and still hadn't found the Time Tours inn. The high facade of the Circus, so visible from the Aventinus district, was obscured by clusters of temples and great houses of the rich perched on hilltops. She was so hungry she spent some of her precious money on sausage and wine, then set out again. Hilaria was still in full swing, reminding her all too vividly of Malcolm. What must he be thinking? He'd be frantic by now. What could she possibly tell him to explain, to make this right?

Margo was lost in the worry of what she would say when someone plowed into her, running full tilt. Margo had only a split second to notice the slave's collar, the chains at his wrists, the ripped clothing and wild eyes . . . Then she slammed backwards. Margo felt the back of her head connect sickeningly against stone.

An explosion of darkness wiped out everything after that.

When she woke, Margo had no idea where she was. Her head ached—throbbed—so fiercely she was afraid she might be ill. A weight of blankets covered her. Margo managed to open her eyes and found only darkness. For a moment, panic smote her so hard she struggled against the blankets and the pain. Then a glimmering edge of light revealed the position of a door. She was in someone's bed in someone's house—

And somehow, she'd lost several hours.

She hoped it was only hours.

A cautious exploration revealed her own clothing still in place, although the ATLS bag and knife belt were gone. Someone had tied a poultice around her head. That boded well. *If they're taking care of me, I'm probably not in too much danger.* But where was she? And how much time had passed? Margo didn't feel much like getting up to find her unknown "host" in an attempt to find out.

Eventually the door opened. A young woman carrying an oil lamp peered into the room. Worry creased her brow when Margo met her gaze. She said something

that sounded anxious and called to someone beyond
Margo's view. Then she set the oil lamp down on a table
and bent over Margo.

"Ow!"

The young woman murmured soothingly and
readjusted the poultice. A moment later a thin, balding
man entered the room. He wore several tunics and a
worried expression. Within three sentences, it became
apparent to him that Margo didn't have the faintest
idea what he was saying.

He halted, looked even more worried, and said slowly,
"*Esne Parthus?*"

Margo struggled to find her voice. "*M-minime non
Parthus,* uh, *sed* uh *Palmyrenus sum,*" she quavered,
hoping she'd gotten the "I'm Palmyrene, not Parthian"
correct in her shaky Latin.

"Ahh . . . *Paterne tuus Romae es?*"

Something about her father and Rome. Margo tried
to remember how to shake her head no, decided that
would hurt entirely too much, and tried the Latin again.
"*Non Romae est.*"

He looked disappointed and even more worried.
"*Tuique servi?*"

Servants? Oh . . . Where were her slaves?

To avoid a struggling explanation, Margo touched her
head and moaned. Her host's eyes widened in alarm.
He spoke sharply to the young woman, who carefully
removed the poultice. She applied a new one, then
picked up a basin and set Margo's arm in it. Before
Margo knew what they were doing, the woman had
sliced open Margo's arm. She yelled and tried to jerk
away. The Roman and his servant woman held her down,
murmuring anxiously, then forcibly held her arm over
the basin and let her bleed into it. By the time they
were done, Margo felt light-headed and queasy.

If they keep this up, they'll kill me with kindness. . . .

She was required to drink a noxious potion which

she didn't have the strength to refuse. The Roman touched her hand and said something that Margo supposed was meant to comfort; then they left her alone to sleep. She made an effort to sit up. Between the pain in her head, the forcible bleeding, and whatever they'd made her drink, she was too woozy. Margo collapsed again with a faint moan.

Tomorrow, she promised. *I'll get the hell out of here tomorrow.*

Margo was a virtual prisoner for the next four solid days. Too ill and light-headed to leave the room, she at least convinced Quintus Flaminius, her "host," to stop cutting her veins open every few hours. He wasn't happy about it, but her recovery speeded up significantly—particularly when she insisted on replacing the wine at her meals with as much water as she could drink. She'd learned in basic first aid that recovering from blood loss required replacement of liquids. And alcohol, while liquid, tended to dehydrate, not rehydrate. So she drank water until she thought she would burst and *willed* herself to recover.

Her ATLS bag and knife belt proved to be safely stored in a wooden chest near her bed. Whenever she was alone, Margo updated her log and checked the chronometer to be sure how much time remained before Porta Romae cycled again. According to the log, she had four days remaining in Rome. What Malcolm must think by now . . .

But Margo had no way to get a message to him. The only thing she could do was get well and get the hell out of here. By the fifth day, the headaches had disappeared and Margo was able to walk again without dizziness. Her host was evidently a very wealthy man. The villa she discovered beyond the confines of her sick room was breathtaking with frescoes, mosaic floors, and priceless statuary.

Quintus escorted her into a garden courtyard at the center of his house, guiding her to a marble bench, then clapped his hands. A chained figure Margo vaguely recalled was hauled, weeping and ashen, into the courtyard and thrust to his knees at his master's feet.

Margo stared. *Why, it's just a boy!*

Perhaps thirteen or fourteen, he huddled at Quintus Flaminius' feet and waited. Flaminius spoke harshly to him, pointing at Margo for emphasis. The boy kissed Margo's feet, startling her badly, then huddled almost in a fetal ball beside her toes. Flaminius clapped his hands again. Collared slaves carried out a brazier on poles and set it down near Quintus. Heat shimmered in the spring air. A long iron rod had been thrust into glowing coals.

Flaminius snapped out something to his slave. The boy looked up. . . . A wild cry broke from ashen lips. He started back, trying to scramble to his feet, then flung himself at Flaminius' legs, clinging to his calves and pleading, *"Domine, domine . . ."*

Was he acknowledging Flaminius as his master? Or just begging mercy with the only word he had wit to retain?

The slaves who'd carried the brazier into the courtyard seized him, holding him immobile. Flaminius picked up the iron rod with great deliberation, then nodded to his men. They stripped the boy's tunic back from his thighs. He whimpered. . . .

The sickening smell of seared flesh and a high, ragged scream jolted Margo. *Oh, God.* . . .

They branded him with a lurid "F" across the thigh. Margo gagged and feared she might pass out. By all rights the boy *should* have. He didn't. He just lay on the ground moaning and clutching at the dirt with thin fingers. Flaminius reheated the branding iron. Slaves held the boy again. This time Flaminius moved the iron toward the boy's *face.* . . .

"NO!"

Margo was on her feet, the cry torn from her.

Flaminius halted in surprise. Then stared at the tears welling in her eyes. Then, very slowly, replaced the branding iron in the brazier. He gestured to his men. They released the trembling boy, who kissed his master's feet—then wept on Margo's. She swayed. . . .

Flaminius eased her back to a seat on the marble bench and called to a slave. A moment later, the rim of a goblet touched her lips. She swallowed strong red wine and fought to regain control of herself. Flaminius was speaking quietly to his slave. Margo recognized very little of what he said, catching only the version of her name she'd given him: Margo Sumitus. When Flaminius escorted her back to her sick room, she didn't argue. What surprised her, however, was the boy who'd been branded. He limped after them, still chained and struggling, then took a seat next to her bed. He remained behind even when Flaminius left, putting himself between her and the door as though he intended to guard Margo's very life.

She wondered what his name was and why he'd run away in the first place. He met her gaze, clearly curious about his foreign benefactor who'd kept him from being branded a second time, then flushed and jerked his gaze down again.

She sat up in bed. Then touched her chest. "Margo," she said. Then she pointed to him.

The boy whispered, *"Domine, sum Achillei."*

Domine?

Surely she'd misunderstood? But Malcolm had been clear about the meaning of that word. *Dominus* meant master.

Young Achilles glanced up. *"Esne Palmyrenus?"* he asked, sounding awestruck.

She shrugged. That wasn't important. *"Et tu?"*

His *"Graecus sum. . . ."* came out strangled, so

tremulous Margo's heart constricted. How had this boy come to be a slave?

More importantly, how had he come to be *her* slave? And what was she going to do about it?

When her host returned to check up on her, Margo struggled to ask. Her Latin was insufficient for the question, but Flaminius removed all doubt when he put Achilles' chains in her hands and said, *"Achilles tuus est servus."*

Oh, great. What am I supposed to do with a slave?

He handed her an iron key.

Margo stared at it for a moment. Achilles sat on his heels, head bowed. *Maybe he'll run again, but so what? I won't hunt him down if he does.* She unlocked his chains. Achilles caught his breath, then tears welled up in his eyes and he ducked his head. Flaminius grunted softly, a sound of profound surprise, then shrugged as if to say, "Your loss."

At dinner that night, Margo's unexpected new acquisition waited on her hand and foot. He escorted her to bed, made certain she was comfortably covered, and blew out the lamps. Then took up a guard stance again between her bed and the door.

He was still there the next morning, asleep but in the same spot.

Huh.

By her calculations, she had two days left to find the Time Tours inn, explain and apologize to Malcolm, and go back to La-La Land—a wiser and more cautious trainee scout.

When she tried to leave, Flaminius exclaimed in horror and insisted, by gestures and signs, that she was a guest in his home and he wouldn't think of allowing her to leave while she was still recovering. Desperate to get out of the house, she finally resorted to saying, "Circus, Quintus Flaminius. Ludi Megalenses . . ." figuring if she once made it out into the crowded streets, she'd be able to slip away and break free of his smothering hospitality.

Understanding lit his eyes. Whatever he said, she suspected it ran along the lines of, "Of course, you've come all the way from Palmyra to see the games and here one of my slaves has injured you so you've been too ill to go. . . ."

By gestures and signs, he made it clear that tomorrow they would go to the games. Margo bit down on her frustration and acquiesced. Meanwhile, there was the problem of Achilles. She didn't *like* having a slave. He *hovered*. Everywhere she turned, there he was. If she'd given permission, he'd have dressed and undressed her, even bathed her. Fortunately, the villa had its own private bath which Margo was able to use in complete privacy, barring the door when Achilles tried to follow her in.

Let 'em think I'm an eccentric provincial, she groused. Whatever Margo's host and slave thought, the heated bath was extraordinary. She didn't want to leave. *Ooh, a person could get used to this. . . .*

She lazed in the heated pool of water half the day, just soaking away aches and bruises and scrubbing every inch of herself clean. Then she ate an equally lazy lunch in the courtyard garden, listening to the tinkling splash of fountains and wishing Malcolm were here. *Tomorrow,* she told herself. Tomorrow she would find that opportunity to escape her host's clutches.

Unfortunately, her host had other ideas.

Margo didn't *walk* to the Circus.

She was *carried* there, in a sedan chair supported by long poles. Perched on the shoulders of four sweating slaves, the chair carried Margo well above the heads of the surrounding crowd. She felt ridiculous, conspicuous, and foolish. And utterly helpless to climb down and get *away*. Another sedan chair a few paces behind carried Quintus Flaminius.

Achilles, eyes bright despite the limp which he struggled to hide, followed Margo's chair. Outside the Circus Maximus, thick crowds fought toward the entrances. Dozens of stalls marked the locations of shops selling food, wine, even glass bowls and cups with circus-racing scenes molded into them. *Commemorative sports glasses*, Margo marvelled. *Who'd have guessed?* Other stalls housed "bookies" who took bets on the outcomes of upcoming races and the combats scheduled for afterward. Crowds of men thronged the betting stalls, shouting for their turn to place bets before the games began, collecting their markers, handing over their coins.

She'd read somewhere, in one of those endless books in La-La Land's library, that betting on the games had been illegal in Rome. If that were the case, those charged with enforcing the law apparently didn't mind looking the other way most of the time.

Quintus' slaves set the sedan chairs down near an arched entrance to the great arena. Margo thought seriously about bolting through the crowd, but Quintus took her arm, smiling and chatting, and guided her straight toward the entrance. He paid her admission and collected three red handkerchiefs to cheer on the faction favored by the emperor. At least, she was pretty sure red was the color Claudius favored, since she overheard the words *Imperator* and *Princeps* used in connection with the red handkerchiefs. He handed her one handkerchief and handed the other to Achilles, then dismissed his own slaves.

He gave Achilles some copper coins and dispatched him on some errand; the boy returned sooner than Margo had expected with a basket of food and a jar of wine. Then Quintus escorted Margo into the Circus Maximus. She slowed to stare, overawed. Quintus grinned, then led her to seats midway up a wooden section of the stands, in the second tier near the first turning post. Everyone she saw up in the third tier was either collared as a slave or dressed as a foreigner: no togas. She smiled grimly, pleased she'd understood that all on her own. Doubtless the only reason she was seated here, rather than up there, was because she was the guest of a Roman.

The Circus itself was nothing like she'd imagined. The vast course wasn't an oval. One short end—where the starting gates were located—was essentially straight. Two long straightaways created an oblong ending in a semi-circle. Three levels of seats, some wooden and some stone, rose in tiers. Including the seats, the huge arena was by Margo's estimation just short of a full mile from starting gates to the back of the seating.

Sand over packed earth—except for down near the starting gates where the surface was paved—the track caught the sunlight with an unnatural glitter. She noticed slaves carrying baskets down the track, sprinkling something shiny onto the sand. Some kind of glittering mineral, maybe? She'd seen flakes of mica in granite catch the sun like that. *Expensive, but pretty.*

A long barrier wall perhaps six feet high ran down the center of the track, decorated with tall marble columns which held gleaming female statues—some winged, some wingless. Miniature temples held altars to gods Margo couldn't identify. Crossbeams supported stone eggs and dolphins. A gleaming gold statue even she recognized as Cybele riding a lion stood near one end. Next to the Magna Mater rested a cluster of marble trees, but they didn't look like Attis' sacred pine. She wondered what they were.

In the center of the barrier wall rose a towering Egyptian obelisk. *Now who brought that here?* It must have been quite a feat, getting it across the Mediterranean by sailing ship. A golden flame set onto the top caught the morning sunlight like fire. On the long Aventine straightaway rose a magnificent colonnaded temple built right into the stands. Below it rested a platform. *Bet that's the judges' box,* she decided, spotting a white line chalked in the sand just beneath it.

Visible beyond obelisk and statues, another temple gleamed in the morning sunlight. High above it the Imperial palace rose on the Palatine Hill. Whatever it was, this second temple had been built directly into the lower tiers of seats with a series of columns and a beautiful triangular pediment above a broad stone porch. A number of empty couches awaited occupants. *I wonder if that's where Claudius sits.*

Down at the starting gates, grey and red marble columns decorated the arches of the starting stalls. There were twelve, barricaded at the moment with double wooden doors. Metal grills blocked the tops. An elaborate viewing box with a stone balustrade took up the center portion of the marble facade. Low, round pedestals supporting tall, squarish pillars topped with stone heads stood between each gate. White chalk-marked lanes led from the starting gates to another white line that crossed the whole width of the track at the end of the barrier wall.

Wonder what that's for?

Just below Margo's seat, down on the track itself, stood a small square shrine with columns, resting on circular stone steps. A little tree of some sort grew up from the earth of the track itself beside the shrine. Between the track and the podium wall ran an immense, ten-foot-wide moat filled with water. A high metal grillwork rose from the podium wall in front of the first tier of seats all the way around the elongated horseshoe of the arena.

The turning posts weren't actually part of the central spine, Margo realized. Three tall, tapered stone columns rose from half-moon shaped pedestals. Each tapered column, covered with bronze plaques, ended in an egg-shaped tip. They reminded her uncomfortably of a man's . . .

Huh. Given Roman preoccupation with sex, I wouldn't be at all surprised.

The stands filled up quickly. Margo was surprised how fast an enormous crowd could enter the Circus. She tried to estimate the seating capacity, multiplying by the lines scored into the bleachers, and came up with more than a hundred fifty thousand. Surely that was too high? A group of laughing men and women took seats behind her, jabbing her uncomfortably in the back with their knees. Margo had to sit with her own knees tucked almost to her chin to avoid hitting the people in front of her. *Well, maybe I didn't guess too high.* They were cramming people in like sardines. She hoped the wooden bleachers didn't collapse under the weight.

The stands were almost full when a blare of trumpets signalled activity at the far end. Men on foot appeared, bearing tall standards that glittered brightly in the sunlight. Golden eagles surmounted rectangles marked SPQR. A roar rose from a hundred-fifty thousand throats. The whole stadium surged to its collective feet. Margo stood up, too.

What? Where?

Quintus Flaminius was pointing down the track.

A man had appeared behind the eagle standards, limping awkwardly onto the track from an entrance down near the starting gates. Robed in gleaming white, with broad purple stripes along the edges of a white woolen toga, he was the instant focus of attention. The crowd had gone wild. Whoever he was, he moved on unsteady legs. *Drunk?* Margo wondered. Surely not?

Then the women behind her babbled something about the *Princeps.* Margo gasped. *Claudius!* She hadn't expected the emperor to *walk* at the head of the procession. She'd pictured him as riding in a gilt chariot or something. Maybe that was reserved for generals who'd won battles. Claudius moved carefully, doggedly,

lacking anything like stately grace as he led the procession
into the great Circus.

Unexpectedly, Margo's heart constricted. She hadn't
realized the twisting of his face, so painfully visible in
the Time Tours photograph, had extended to other
physical difficulties. No wonder Malcolm had refused
to laugh at him. The courage—and pain—that
procession must be costing him . . .

Margo gulped and felt her cheeks burn. *She* had run
away from her problem rather than face it head-on the
way Claudius faced his illness. Look where that had
led her. She bit her lip. *Tonight*, she promised herself.
*I'll find him tonight after the games, after I get away
from Flaminius.*

Behind Claudius came musicians: drummers and
pipers filled the arena with rolling thunder and skirling
music while brassy horns sang out in voices so wild
Margo's back shivered. Behind the musicians came
carriages and hand-carried litters on which rode the
Roman gods and goddesses. She had no idea who they
all were, but their statues caught the morning sun in
as splendid a pageant as Margo had ever seen.

The procession made its way around the mica-glittered
track in a complete circuit, ending at the marble temple
on the Palatine side. Claudius ascended a staircase slowly,
followed by bearers who carried the images of the deities
up to the platform to "watch" the games. Claudius
himself took a backless stone chair near the front of
the platform. He lifted his hand and the crowd went
insane.

Popular guy.

Margo discovered unexpectedly that she was glad.

A hush fell across the great Circus. In the sudden
quiet she could hear the scream of high-strung horses,
the thud of hooves against wooden doors. The smell
of sweat and adrenaline drifted on the wind along with
the distant snarls of wild beasts. Margo leaned forward.

A well-dressed official of some sort had appeared in the balustraded box above the starting gates. Other figures were visible as well, fussing over some sort of machinery. A white cloth fluttered from the official's hand. She wished irritably for a lowly pair of binoculars. It looked very much like someone was turning a barrel on a spit and drawing something out of it, but she couldn't see what. *We should've found seats closer to the start.*

Other men had climbed onto the barrier wall, some of them dressed well, others clad in simple tunics. Ladders were run up to the crossbeams holding the eggs and dolphins. Several moments passed while the tension mounted. Men who could only be field judges took their positions. Then, before she was ready for it, the white cloth dropped.

A snapping sound cracked through the breathless arena. The crash of wooden doors flung wide reached her even at the far end of the Circus. Then twelve chariots dashed into view, horses flying four abreast as they raced down the chalked-out lanes. Margo was on her feet with the rest of the crowd. The chariots tore across the pavement toward the first white line in the sand. Trumpets sang out as they flashed past. Then twelve racing chariots like doll's teacups on wheels broke position and flung inward toward the barrier wall.

They tore down the track in a thunder of hooves. Drivers whipped their teams to greater speed. Their short capes snapped in the wind. They'd wrapped long reins completely around their waists, crouched over the tiny platforms like jockeys on skateboards. Green tunics, red tunics, blue and white ones . . . The four racing factions of the Circus stampeded for the best position as they swept toward the first turn. Margo held her breath.

The leader, a green driver, swept around the turn. The second chariot sped around in his wake. The third chariot brushed its wheels against a stone curb. The chariot lurched. The pole snapped. Margo screamed. The delicate chariot, little more than a wooden shell with a lattice-work floor, disintegrated into flinders. Galloping horses dragged their driver out of the wreckage. He fought to draw a knife at his belt. Other chariots swung wide to miss the wreckage.

The driver sliced through the reins and rolled heavily across the track. The other chariots left him lying on the sand. Slaves raced out to pull the driver and the wreckage off the track. Others caught the runaway team and led the horses out of the arena. The remaining chariots swept back toward the first turn for their second lap. Men on ladders had taken down one egg and one dolphin from the crossbeams.

Margo drank in details, determined to think like a scout for a change. The horses wore collars around their necks instead of harness like she'd seen in London. *How can they breathe, pulling against their windpipes like that?* The horses' manes had been tied up so they couldn't stream in the wind. Their tails had been bobbed short, like a Manx cat's. Wickerwork on the lightweight racing chariots bore the teams' colors. The drivers wore slaves' collars.

Malcolm had said the men who raced and fought here were either slaves, prisoners, or criminals. She wondered if the driver who'd been dragged down the track would live. She shivered. Already the chariots were pounding down the straightaway for the next lap. They skidded around the turn, bouncing across ruts left from previous laps, and rounded the turn in a cloud of glittering dust.

Three laps. Four. Five. How many laps in all? She checked the lap counters: two eggs and dolphins each remained on the crossbeams. The chariots fought one another for the lead as they swept into the turn for the sixth lap. Margo held her breath, but they all made it through the jolting one-hundred-eighty-degree turn. The sixth markers came down. Brassy trumpets sang out again. *Final lap*.

A driver in blue was battling it out with a red driver for the lead. Margo waved her red handkerchief with one hand and bit knuckles on the other. Red drivers back in the pack swung wide, blocking blue chariots from coming up to assist their team member. Two of the chariots collided. The crowd roared. Margo hid her eyes. When she dared look, she saw one broken chariot cartwheel into the wide moat with a tremendous splash. A driver in blue was being dragged wide in the turn. His body slammed into the little shrine. She screamed and hid her eyes again.

Another roar shook the stadium. She risked a peek. The surviving chariots had rounded the turning post nearest the start and were thundering toward the finish line. The red chariot shot into the lead as the driver lashed his horses. The blue chariot caught up, passed, then faltered again. The blue driver was whipping his horses mercilessly. Then the red driver swept ahead by a nose just as they flashed past the white chalk line.

The emperor's favorite had won!

Margo found herself shouting right along with the rest of the crowd. Quintus Flaminius exchanged a few coins with the man seated next to him, grinning as he deposited them in his money pouch. Margo noticed other private bets being settled, as well. Achilles' eyes glowed as he watched the driver sweep around the turning post in a wide circle and pass the emperor's platform. The driver completed the victory lap back to the finish line while the other chariots drove disconsolately off the track. The victor pulled his team to a halt. A ramp had been lowered across the moat, allowing him to ascend steps to the judging platform. Margo wondered who was handing out the prizes. She'd expected the victor to receive his reward from the emperor, but he'd stopped on the opposite side of the arena from the emperor's box. It was another man who placed a leafy crown on the driver's head, handed him a palm branch, and placed a bulging leather pouch in his hand. The crowd cheered as he descended the steps triumphantly, resumed his chariot, and drove past the emperor's box once again. Claudius saluted him to thunderous approval from the crowd.

Then he left the track. Slaves carrying baskets began climbing through the stands, tossing out handfuls of little wooden markers. Spectators dove for them, cheering if they caught one, groaning if they missed. When a handful was flung toward Margo's seats, she caught one by reflex, then wondered what it was. She couldn't read what it said. Quintus Flaminius grinned and babbled something incomprehensible. At a signal from the Emperor's box, those who had caught markers descended toward the track. Margo gulped. Surely the "winners" wouldn't be sacrificed in the arena?

Those who had caught the wooden disks grinned like sweepstakes winners. Quintus snapped his fingers at Achilles. The boy bowed and took Margo's wooden disc, then hastily followed in the wake of other winners. When he and the other winners returned, Margo discovered there was a reason those who'd caught the disks grinned like sweepstakes winners: they *were*. Each person who had presented a "ticket" had received a prize. Achilles presented hers formally: a small leather pouch.

She opened it and shook out a blood-red gemstone carved with a racing chariot and the obelisk from the Circus' barrier wall. Margo gasped. "Ohh . . ."

Quintus Flaminius whistled softly and examined the stone. Then smiled and returned it to her. Other lucky winners nearby displayed bags of coins to their friends, or parchments that seemed important. She heard the word *terra* and concluded they'd won deeds to land parcels. Margo tucked her prize back into its leather

pouch and secreted that in her money pouch as the
second event began, a race where jockeys rode horses
in something approaching the modern style of horse
racing. They ran from the turning post near Margo's
seat to the far end of the barrier where the starting
stalls were located, racing past the emperor's platform
in a cloud of dust.

Then another chariot race began, followed by a
wrestling exhibition, followed by a third chariot race.
They sat through a total of ten chariot races, alternating
with other events. Most chariot races were run with
four-horse teams, some with two-horse teams. Some
of the ridden races ended with the jockeys sliding off
and pelting toward the finish line on foot.

Achilles broke out wine and cups, pouring for them,
then handed over parcels of what looked astonishingly
like fried peas. Margo tried them. Not bad. . . .

While they ate lunch, yet another chariot race began,
but this time when the lightweight chariots swept down
the track, Margo burst out laughing. There were no
drivers. No human ones, anyway. Trained *monkeys*
steered the horses around the turning posts in a
ridiculous parody of the earlier races. Laughter rippled
through the stands. When the leading monkey's team
swept across the finish line for the final lap, slaves ran
onto the track and caught the horses. Margo dissolved
into helpless laughter when one of the slaves carried
the victorious "charioteer" up the ramp and steps to
collect his reward: a piece of fruit and a monkey-sized
victory crown.

The little victor actually drove a victory lap, grinning
in a simian fashion that brought roars of laughter from
the crowd.

Once the final chariot had been escorted from the
track, a hush fell over the vast stands. Margo wondered
what was up. Slaves appeared from street-level
entrances, carrying potted trees and bushes. They turned

the Circus into a miniature forest, with screens of
shrubbery, groves of potted trees, even tubs of flowers.
When the preparations were complete, the slaves beat
a hasty retreat to the other side of the podium wall.
Margo noticed that all ramps across the moat had been
withdrawn.

Then she heard the unmistakable grunting roar of
lions. A prickle ran straight up her back. Other wild
screams reached her. The crowd leaned forward. The
stink of sweat and anticipation hung on the bright air.
The familiar snapping sound of the opening gates
cracked through the arena. Margo peered toward the
starting stalls.

A dozen frantic zebras broke into a gallop, veering
to avoid the trees, leaping miniature walls of shrubbery,
braying and bucking as they entered the arena. Behind
them came a dozen ostriches, their black and white
plumage bobbing gracefully as they ran down the long
course of the track, weaving between the potted trees
in visible confusion. Tiny beautiful antelopes darted
into the sunlight and milled about in a frightened herd
near the finish line.

Down at the starting gates, slaves had closed the big
doors again, resetting the bars which held them shut.
Once the job was done, they scrambled up ladders which
were hastily pulled up after them. Margo leaned forward,
watching in morbid fascination as the racing official
who'd presided over the morning's races once again
lifted his white cloth as a signal. The cloth fluttered
toward the ground. The gates slammed open. A defiant
roar shook through the arena.

Enormous cats lunged into the sunlight. Maned lions
snarled at one another and drew blood. Sleek, deadly
lionesses shot past the quarrelling males, homing in
on the terrified game animals already released. The
striking pattern of leopard skin flashed past the starting
gates as half-a-dozen more big cats were released into

the Circus. Margo tried to count. Six leopards, twenty lionesses, at least twenty more heavy male lions . . .

A scream of pain rose from the arena floor. A zebra had gone down, kicking and struggling. Lions closed in, ripping and tearing at its belly. Margo screamed and hid her eyes. More frantic cries and screeches rose on the air. Whenever she dared look, she found big cats swarming across helpless antelopes . . . leopards running down ostriches and slamming them into the sand . . . zebras torn apart while still alive . . .

She hid her eyes until it was over.

Trumpets sang out, a sound of madness in the bright April sunlight. Margo looked up. Then went cold. *Men* were entering the arena. Men with nets and trident-pointed spears, men with swords and helmets, men on foot and on horseback. Lions snarled and backed away or stood their ground over reeking kills. The hunters advanced slowly. A few hung back near the moat, clearly terrified. Then a lion roared a challenge and charged.

It wasn't sport.

It was murder.

Of the fifty men who entered the arena, only six left it alive. They were the only living things still walking on the sand when it was over. Even the horses had been killed, pulled down by murderous cats. The crowd thundered approval of their "victory" as they limped off the sand, bleeding and stumbling. Margo sat frozen in place, shocked to her core. She'd understood at one level what a bestiary was. But to actually watch men ripped to pieces by ravenous hunting cats . . .

She wanted desperately to find someplace quiet where she could be sick. Instead she stayed in her seat and watched while slaves removed the carcasses. The sun journeyed across the sky, leaving Margo light-headed. She wished she hadn't eaten lunch. Down on the sand, another parade began. This time, the participants were gladiators. Some rode horses, some carried nets and tridents like the bestiary hunters. Some wore odd helmets with fish on top. A few rode chariots—the drivers, all but naked, were tattooed in blue over most of their bodies.

The procession wound its way between trees and shrubbery walls, circling the entire arena. Margo tried to count the number of combatants and arrived at the figure of a hundred pairs. The number horrified her. The procession ended. Trumpets blared. The gladiators saluted the emperor, who lifted his hand. Then they broke ranks and began a slow-motion exhibition across the sands, without trying to draw blood. Each gladiator demonstrated the techniques of his unique weaponry while the crowd thundered approval. Then most of them retired from the track. Ten pairs remained. Other men appeared, carrying whips and red-hot prods. Trumpets sang out again. Margo held her breath. . . .

The first pair closed. A fighter tossed his net and missed. He drew it back with a string looped around his wrist while holding off his opponent with a wicked trident. Another pair drove at one another in chariots, looping in and out between potted trees while they slashed with long swords, trying to gain advantage. The audience was shouting strange words, repeating them again and again.

Instructions, she realized suddenly. The shouts were timed to the practiced swing and thrust of the swords and tridents. A couple of men hung back, clearly terrified. Men with whips and branding irons moved in. Margo screamed when the gladiators were herded forward with furious lashes and burns across the backs of their legs.

The first gladiator went down, badly injured by a sword cut across the thigh. He lay flat, helpless under his opponent's long trident. The fallen man lifted his left arm in supplication. The crowd turned all eyes to the emperor. Claudius was looking at the fallen man, then lifted his head to the crowd. The audience broke into factions, some gesturing "thumbs up" and others "thumbs down." More of them seemed to be calling "thumbs up."

The emperor turned his attention back to the fallen gladiator, then lifted his thumb in a sharp gesture toward his breast. Margo started to relax—

The gladiator with the trident stabbed the weapon straight through the other man's throat.

NO . . . !

Margo sat transfixed. She didn't understand. Then a whisper of memory came to her in Malcolm's voice. "Study the body language, it's different here . . ."

Somehow over time the thumbs-up/thumbs-down gestures had become reversed.

It was symbolic of the whirling mess her life was in.

Margo found herself stumbling out of the stands, shoving past shocked spectators. She had to get away, had to get out of this madhouse of sudden death and inexplicable cruelty. . . . She finally gained the street. Quintus Flaminius and Achilles had followed. Her host took her arm, asking questions she didn't understand and didn't want to answer. Margo stood panting heavily for several minutes. Her knees shook. She still felt as though she'd be ill any moment. All she wanted to do was find the Time Tours inn and hide until the gate reopened.

She didn't get the chance. Flaminius' slaves, dismissed to wait outside the Circus for their master, reappeared with the sedan chairs. Margo found herself stuffed into a seat, lifted, and carried away from the Circus before she could find the wit to argue. She slumped in the chair. *Great. Now what?*

She found herself back in her room, alone with Achilles, whose eyes were wide with concern as she sank onto her hated bed. He fussed over her until she wanted to scream at him, but that wasn't fair, so she just held silent and let him fuss. Poor kid. . . .

What would become of him once she left? *If* she left . . .

The situation was so maddening it was very nearly comical. Trapped in time because her host was overprotective. Margo hadn't realized how deadly serious the Romans were about rules of hospitality. *Well,* she told herself with a sigh, *looks like you'll have to engineer a jailbreak tonight. Over the garden wall* . . .

And hope the watchdogs didn't sound an alert.

Naturally, she fell asleep.

Quintus Flaminius' idea of dinner was a twelve-course banquet with little desserts in between and bucketsful of wine. When she woke up, the room was pitch dark. Margo blinked. Then, *Ohmigod . . . What time is it?* She groped, found her ATLS bag, dragged out her log. The chronometer's glow revealed a terrifying set of numbers. She had less than ten minutes to make the cycling of Porta Romae.

In the middle of the night on dangerous, unfamiliar streets . . .

Margo shot out of the sick room as though the villa had caught fire. She jumped over the sleeping Achilles and hit the atrium running. The door was barred. The night watchman had dozed off. Margo flung aside the heavy wooden beam which held the door closed and heard the watchman's startled cry. She jerked open the door and pelted into the street. Panic gave her speed she hadn't thought herself capable of. She remembered the way to the Circus. And from the Circus, she could find the Time Tours wine shop where the gate would be cycling any minute. In the darkness she took several wrong turns and backtracked frantically.

A distant cry caused her to glance back. A bobbing light followed several blocks back. Margo swore under her breath and kept running. She took another wrong turn and sped back the way she'd come. The light had drawn closer: Achilles, carrying a lantern. He called out, "*Domine! Domine!*"

She didn't have *time* . . . .

The boy caught up to her, gasping for breath, and followed when she homed in on the hulking silhouette of the Circus. The glances he shot her told Margo he thought his young master had completely flipped, but he was sticking by her. *Damn, damn, damn* . . . She finally found the Via Appia. Margo raced around the end of the Circus and skidded around the corner. There . . .

What time is it?

She didn't have time to check her log. She just ran for the counter and hoped for the best. Too late, she saw a familiar figure detach itself from the counter and move toward her in the darkness.

Malcolm.

Guilt and fear and relief hit her simultaneously.

As she closed the distance between them, Margo found that she had no idea what to say to him. *Hi, I really screwed up, aren't you happy you went to bed with a dolt and by the way, how do I get rid of this poor slave I seem to have acquired?* stuck somehow in her throat. So she screwed her courage to the sticking place and decided to brazen it out.

She would apologize and eat crow once they were through the gate.

Malcolm hadn't slept in days. Time Tours employees had begun steering clear of him whenever he returned to the inn. He functioned on adrenaline and hope—and the hope was waning fast. He'd never lost a customer. Never mind someone as precious as Margo. What Kit would say, what Kit would *do* . . .

He'd already decided to remain behind when the tour left Rome. He had to find her. Or find out how

she'd died. One or the other. Night closed in on their
final few hours. *Nine days* . . . He'd searched from dawn
until well past dark every day, asking strangers if they'd
seen a young man in Palmyrene dress, searching the
slave markets with sinking horror in his gut, losing hope
with every additional hour that passed.

The agony of guilt was very nearly more than he could
endure.

As the chronometer on his personal log ticked past
eleven-thirty and crept toward midnight, Malcolm found
a corner behind the deserted wine shop's front counter
and waited. He had given up hope; but he would wait,
anyway, until the last possible moment. Then he'd tell
the Time Tours guides to return without him. The big
touring company had lost tourists on occasion—it was
an industry secret closely guarded with massive bribes
to grieving families—but the harsh reality of a tourist's
disappearance shook everyone.

The guides and even the other tourists were subdued
as they made their way into the wine shop for the return
trip. Malcolm huddled in his corner, refusing to meet
anyone's gaze. Ten minutes until midnight. Five minutes.
A ghost of white appeared in his peripheral vision. He
jerked around—

And swore under his breath. Just a white carthorse
pulling a load of hay. The familiar ache of a gate
preparing to open thrummed against the bones of his
skull. The cart rumbled past. The placid carthorse tossed
its head and squealed a complaint its driver echoed.
The man held his ears, muttered loudly enough for
Malcolm to hear, "*Absit omen* . . ." and shook out his
whip. The carthorse broke into a shambling run.

Inside the wine shop, the Porta Romae had dilated
open. A Time Tours guide stepped outside.

"Malcolm? Departures are through. Newcomers are
arriving. You don't have any more time."

"I'm—"

A figure in white ran into view down the block. Malcolm's heart leaped into his mouth. Then he noticed the slave following behind with a lamp. Crushing disappointment blasted brief hope. Then Malcolm did a double-take. The running figure *was* wearing a Parthian-style tunic and trousers. Slender, just about the right height, same fragile, heart-shaped face . . .

He came out of his corner like a gunshot and shoved the Time Tours guide aside. *Please* . . . .

When Margo ran up to the wine counter, bedraggled as a street rat and glaring defiance, he wanted to grab her by both arms and shake her until something snapped. A bewildered boy of about thirteen skidded to a halt behind her, gasping for breath.

"Hi! Did I make it in time? Malcolm, I've got this little problem, how do I free this kid? I, uh, sort of acquired a slave . . ."

Malcolm couldn't speak. Terror had transmuted into a rage so deep he was afraid to touch her. He held her gaze for another agonizing moment, then turned on his heel and strode through the rapidly shrinking Porta Romae. He didn't even look back to see if she'd followed. Nine *days* he had burned out his guts worrying—and she'd been running around Rome *buying slaves.* . . .

His sandals slapped against the grid of the platform. Malcolm shoved aside Time Tours employees and left old friends gaping in his wake. When he hit the gym, he accomplished a lifetime first.

Malcolm Moore laid Sven Bailey flat in a sparring match.

Afterward, he took a cold shower that lasted forty solid minutes. The phone was ringing when he emerged. He jerked it out of the wall and hurled it across the room. Then, very quietly, Malcolm got drunker than he'd ever been in his life.

CHAPTER SIXTEEN

Kit Carson was waiting in the crowd when the Porta Romae opened. Neither Malcolm nor Margo put in appearances. He started to grow seriously alarmed when the Time Tours guides who emerged wouldn't look at him. The whole contingent of tourists, guides, and baggage handlers waiting in the Commons climbed the ramp and vanished through the portal and still there was no sign of his granddaughter or the man he'd trusted with her safety. Then, just as the portal began to shrink toward closure, Malcolm shot through. One look at his face sent Kit's viscera into a tailspin.

The normally unflappable time guide burst past Kit like a damned soul pursued by gleeful demons. He didn't even glance in Kit's direction. Kit shut his eyes, convinced of the worst. Then he risked another look just as the gate shrank closed. Margo had come through. He started breathing again. But she hung back on the platform, looking defiant and sullen and scared all at the same time. She, too, watched Malcolm's stormy retreat down the Commons. Then she saw Kit standing in the crowd below.

She lifted her chin and descended the ramp.

"Want to tell me what's going on?" he asked, falling into step.

"No," she said icily. "I don't."

With that, she, too, stormed off. Kit allowed his

footsteps to slow to a halt. Just what had transpired between those two? Given Margo's temper, he was afraid of the answer. But he had to know. Kit high-signed one of the returning Time Tours guides.

"What gives?"

The woman gave him a guarded look. "Uh . . . Hi, Kit. I think maybe Malcolm ought to be the one to explain." She hurried away before he could ask another question.

Kit muttered under his breath and called Malcolm's number. The answering machine picked up. He swore and headed for the Down Time, but Malcolm hadn't put in an appearance. Then Robert Li, the station's antiquarian, skidded into the bar. He announced to the room at large, "You ain't gonna believe it! Malcolm Moore just wiped up the mat with Sven Bailey. I mean put him on the ground *out cold*. What's going on? I've *never* seen an expression like that on Malcolm's face."

Conversation exploded around Robert Li while Kit beat a hasty retreat. He headed straight for the gym and found Sven in his office, holding an ice pack to his head and groaning.

"Whadda *you* want?" Sven muttered.

"I heard Malcolm knocked you out."

"You don't have to rub it in."

"Did he say anything?"

Sven peeled a swollen eyelid. "No. All he said was, 'Let's spar.' Next thing I know, Ann Mulhaney's bending over me and someone's yelling to call Rachel. Only thing I saw after I woke up was his back on the way out the door. What's eating him, anyway?"

"I was hoping you could tell me," Kit said grimly.

"Huh. Two weeks alone with Margo is my guess. She'd drive any man to violence."

"Great. You're some help, you know that, Sven?"

The weapons trainer just grunted and held the ice pack against his skull. Kit headed for home. Margo wasn't at the apartment. Clearly she'd been there: damp towels and dirty clothes littered the bathroom. Wet footprints crossed the carpet into the living room. But she had departed for destinations unknown well before Kit's arrival. He called Malcolm's again. In the middle of the fifth ring, the connection went dead.

Kit stared at the receiver. "What the hell?"

Someone is going to give me some answers. And it had better be soon. But when he pounded on Malcolm's door, a breakable object of unknown origin crashed against the panel and shattered noisily.

"Go 'way!" He sounded *drunk.* The last time Kit had known Malcolm Moore to get drunk was the night the owner of Time Ho! had fired everyone in his employ, then quietly committed suicide rather than face his creditors.

"Malcolm! It's Kit! Let me in!"

"Go the *hell* away!"

He considered breaking down the door. Instead, he leaned on the buzzer until the noise drove the younger man to distraction. Malcolm finally snatched open the door. His hair was dishevelled and his eyes were bloodshot. He looked like he hadn't slept in a week. He gripped a whiskey bottle by the neck like he contemplated breaking it over Kit's head.

"You *are* drunk."

"An' I'm gonna be drunker. I'm in no mood for a visit."

He slammed the door. Kit caught it before it could close all the way.

"Dammit, Malcolm, talk to me. What the hell happened down time?"

Malcolm glared at him, then dropped his gaze. All the fight leached out of him. "Ask Margo. Your granddaughter is a lunatic. An impulsive, dangerous lunatic. Worse than you, damn your eyes. And a goddamned, bloody *liar*—little bitch just turned *seventeen*, goddammit, not nineteen. Now get out and let me get soused."

Seventeen? Margo was only seventeen? Kit saw several shades of red. *I'll kill her, I swear to God, I'll teach that girl if it's the last thing I ever do not to lie to people who trust her.*

Malcolm was in the act of slamming the door when Kit caught it in one hand. "I, uh, owe you some money."

Malcolm's bitter laughter shocked Kit speechless. "Keep it. I sure as hell didn't earn it."

The door slammed shut.

Kit stared at the reverberating panel. *All right . . .* He stalked down to the Commons on a hunt for his errant granddaughter. He found her at Goldie Morran's, exchanging her down-time currency for modern scrip. Goldie glanced up and smiled. The smile froze in place. Margo swung around and lost color.

Kit was out of patience. He backed Margo into a corner so she couldn't bolt and run. *"Just what the hell happened down time, young lady?"*

"Nothing! I did fine! It's not my fault Malcolm's an overbearing, overprotective, chauvinistic . . ."

She ranted on at length.

Kit finally figured it out.

"You left the tour?" he asked quietly, hardly able to believe his ears.

"Yes, I did! And I did fine! I'm in one piece, aren't I? I'm sick of being coddled, roped in, restricted— dammit, I proved I can handle myself this trip! I want a real scouting job!"

Kit couldn't believe it. She'd actually abandoned the tour, run off on her own . . . No wonder Malcolm was downstairs getting drunk. Kit was tempted to put Margo straight over his knee and wallop her backside until she couldn't sit. But the fire in her glare told him it wouldn't do any good.

"That's it," he said coldly. "You are clearly too reckless

for your own good. I'd thought you were capable of learning something. I was wrong. Worse, you lied to me. Eighteen hell." Margo lost color. "Pack your things. You're going home."

"The hell I am! You're just an overprotective, lonely old man too scared to let me try my wings! I'm ready and you're not letting me prove it!"

They locked glares.

Goldie intervened quietly. "If I might suggest it, why don't you two go somewhere separately to cool off and think this over? Kit, clearly no harm was done. She's made it back just fine. Margo, why don't you come back later and we'll finish this transaction. You might think about the scare you've given everyone. Now, may I help you, sir? Yes, I can certainly exchange that for you. . . ."

Kit stalked out, leaving Margo to make her own way back to the apartment. He was so angry he couldn't think straight. Of all the bone-headed, childish, idiotic . . . He didn't care what Goldie said, Margo was clearly not ready to scout. Goldie had never set foot across a single down-time gate. She had no concept of the dangers that could threaten even an ordinary little tour, particularly when one of the pig-headed tourists abandoned her guides and struck out on her own without knowing so much as half-a-dozen words of the language. . . .

He stormed into the Down Time and snapped out an order for a triple. He knocked it back, then ordered another. *Gotta calm down before I face her again.* Goldie'd been right about that much, at least. He couldn't talk to her in this frame of mind. He had to recapture his composure, marshall his arguments, decide how to approach the very serious problem her rebelliousness had raised.

But . . .

Whatever possessed the brainless little fool to do it?

"Worse than you," Malcolm had said.

Kit winced and downed another triple. Great. That was just great. All he needed to make his life complete was a *seventeen*-year-old *female* carbon copy of himself bent on raising hell everywhere she turned her ambitious little gaze.

He was tempted to haul her kicking and screaming to Primary and toss her bodily through it. But that wouldn't do any good. She'd just come back. Or go to another station and try it from there. He had to find a way to reason with her, convince her to keep training, that she wasn't ready despite marginal success in surviving Rome.

The problem was, Kit had no idea how to go about it.

Everything he did or said only made matters worse.

So he delayed the inevitable and ordered another triple. Just one more for fortitude. Then he'd face her. *Lonely old man,* she'd called him. Well, that much was true. He was lonely and he was afraid of losing her. But that wasn't the reason he was holding her back. Surely he could find a way to convince her of that?

Yeah, right, just like I convinced Sarah to stick by me.

Kit tightened his hand around the shot glass.

Why was it, he always managed to find a way to flub the most important relationships in his life?

He didn't have an answer to that, either.

Margo couldn't believe it. She stood trembling in the corner of Goldie Morran's shop and fought desperately not to cry. After everything she'd been through, after everything she'd proven . . . She'd even risked losing the gate to ask a Time Tours guide to watch over Achilles until she could properly free him the next time the gate cycled. She'd handled every adversity and responsibility chance had thrown at her, doing better than she had any right to expect, but nobody was giving her so much as a moment to *explain*. They all just assumed the worst and dismissed her as a brainless, incapable fool. Worse, Malcolm had told Kit about her lie.

She straightened her back against a weight heavier than the whole Himalayan mountain range and forced her chin up. She might have been kicked out of training, but she wasn't quitting. Somehow, Margo would prove herself.

"Margo?"

She glanced around to find Goldie Morran watching her. The customers had all departed, their business transacted for the moment. Goldie smiled, a sympathetic gesture from one woman to another.

"Don't take it so hard," the older woman said. "You've clearly proven your mettle. A week down time alone, you said?"

"Yes. In Rome."

Goldie nodded. "Why don't we finish that transaction Kit interrupted? I'd like to talk to you."

Margo fumbled in her belt pouch for the coins she'd brought back to exchange. She thought about selling the Circus gemstone, but decided to send it through with a Time Tours guide the next time Porta Romae cycled. Achilles could sell it and use the money to support himself. She was proud of that plan and since ATF would only tax her for it if she tried to take it back through Primary, that was exactly what she intended to do. She might run away from her problems, but she didn't run from responsibility.

Goldie examined her coins and nodded. "Very nice. So . . . you're ready to prove yourself." It wasn't a question.

"Damn right I am," Margo muttered. "I got along fine—and I don't even speak Latin!"

Goldie's eyes widened. "That *is* an accomplishment. You should be very proud." Then she glanced at the doorway as though searching for eavesdroppers. "You want to know what I think?" The older woman's eyes were bright, merry.

"What?"

"I think you're a budding young scout in need of a place to go. And if you're interested, I think I know just the place you need."

Margo's pulse quickened. "Really?" Then she cleared her throat and attempted to assume an air of professionalism. "What did you have in mind?"

"I know of a gate that's in need of a good scout. Someone bright and ambitious. Someone who isn't afraid of a challenge. Someone who'll take a few risks to make a lot of money."

Margo's pulse skipped another few beats. "Why are you telling me?"

Goldie Morran grimaced and gestured to herself. "I'm not a scout and besides, I'm too old. And frankly, I think you've got what it takes. After all, Kit Carson did train you. You've been taught by the best and as far as I'm concerned, you've demonstrated you have what it takes. You've got fire inside you, girl. Besides," Goldie winked, "I'd like to see a woman finally crack that men's club wide open. Interested?"

Margo glared at the doorway where Kit Carson had vanished.

"You bet I'm interested. When do we start?"

"Is now soon enough? Good. First, we allay everyone's suspicions about what you're up to. . . ."

By the time Kit was ready to face Margo with something approaching calm, the "night" had advanced fairly far. Two additional gates had cycled: Edo and Primary. He'd listened to the familiar announcements regarding gate departures while brooding over his bourbon and marshalling his arguments. Significantly, none of his friends even approached his table. Kit finally left the Down Time and brushed through a crowd of new arrivals gawking at the Commons. When he arrived at his apartment Kit drew a deep breath, then unlocked the door. He expected to find her sulking on the couch. He didn't.

Margo wasn't there at all. Her things were gone.

All he found was a scrawled note.

Sorry for all the trouble. It hasn't been fun. I won't be troubling you again. Margo.

Kit crumpled the note in his hand.

Then he sank down onto the couch and cried.

CHAPTER SEVENTEEN

Margo felt free, absolutely and utterly free, for the first time in her life. Goldie Morran was a true savior. After a quick week up time learning to fly the latest ultralight craze, she'd returned to TT-86 with a load of very specialized equipment—all paid for by Goldie. The currency expert had trusted her judgement, relied implicitly on her training, her skills. That alone had been worth all the heartache of the miserable, terrifying week alone in Rome.

Margo had put hours of planning into this, deciding what to take, how to tackle the problem of overland journey and return, selecting equipment; then came the marvelous moment when she stepped through the gate into the twilight of early evening. Two hired hands trailed after her, hauling equipment.

I did it! I'm doing it! I'm really scouting!

ATLS readings widened the grin on Margo's face. "Wow!" The first stars twinkling in the darkening sky allowed her to pinpoint their location. At thirty-two degrees east longitude and twenty-six degrees south latitude, Margo was standing on the southeastern coast of Mozambique in the year A.D. 1542.

The descending African night was soft, the breeze stiff from offshore. They were very near the coast. Margo easily identified a broad stretch of water nearby from geographical records: Delagoa Bay. Around the curving bay from their position huddled a tiny settlement of ramshackle board houses and a wooden fortress, all surrounded by a wooden wall. Not a single light burned in the settlement. Margo grinned. *Like thieves in the night . . .*

She signalled her two assistants to follow, moving down the curve of the bay until they were out of sight of the primitive little town of Lourenço Marques. Then they unpacked their load and got busy. Margo took charge of the Floating Wing. It was the largest commercially available, a high-tech balloon of transparent, gas-tight Filmar, shaped like a pennant flag laid flat. Margo hadn't been able to bring enough helium to inflate it, but she'd studied how to crack hydrogen from water and discovered it was dead easy. She set up the portable generator to power the equipment and got busy.

While she worked on the balloon, her two assistants worked on the gondola. She wasn't sure she approved of Goldie's choices for these two. The big Afrikaner was all right, she supposed, although he was pushing fifty-six, but she was worried about that damned Welshman. He'd tried to disembowel Margo a few weeks ago, mistaking her for Joan of Arc. Now he worked quietly under the Afrikaner's directions, which consisted mostly of hand signals punctuated by grunts and the occasional word in English. Kynan Rhys Gower had learned a few words of English, thank God, since his arrival from Orléans, but his temperament hadn't improved all that much from a month working in the garbage pits while the ribs Kit had broken healed up.

When Margo had protested the choice, Goldie explained, "We don't want anyone blabbing our plans. The Welshman's perfect. He needs money and he can't talk."

"And your Afrikaner?" The Afrikaner could, in fact, speak English, but he usually muttered to himself in his own incomprehensible Afrikaans.

Goldie grinned. "He'll look down that Dutch Afrikaner nose of his, sniff, call you English, and do his job. I know Koot van Beek. He's exactly what you'll need."

"Huh. What kind of name is Koot, anyway?" Margo had muttered, drawing laughter from her dignified partner.

Still, Koot was remarkably cooperative for a close-lipped old man who'd insisted on choosing his own rifle for the journey. He'd even insisted *she* bring a rifle.

"But I don't intend to do any hunting," she'd countered, holding up the laser-guided blowgun she'd used in training. After what she'd witnessed in the Circus Maximus, Margo wasn't sure she wanted to hunt anything for her dinner. "The darts for these are dipped in strong anesthetic. I don't want to kill anything down time unless I absolutely have to."

Koot had muttered under his breath and insisted she bring a rifle, anyway. She'd stowed it away with gear she didn't plan to use unless an emergency threatened.

Koot worked quietly in the starlight, assembling the PVC gridwork that would serve as the platform of their gondola. While Kynan finished tightening connections, Koot attached the ducted fans which would provide propulsion and steering capability. The triangular lifting wing began to swell against the restraining cables as it filled with buoyant hydrogen gas.

The hydrogen was one reason Margo had chosen PVC for the platform. She didn't want metal fittings anywhere on her ultralight. Metal fittings might generate sparks. For the duration of their journey, they would be paranoid about fire prevention. She eyed the slowly filling gas bag and wished again they could have transported in enough helium to do the job, but wishing was pointless. They had what they had and Margo was darned proud of her ingenuity.

Their airship was finally ready. Kynan had covered the PVC gridwork with a "floor" of ripstop nylon to

prevent things from falling through. Koot attached cables
to the hydrogen wing, then helped Kynan load on their
supplies. Margo shut down the generator and packed
it in the wheeled crate it had come in, then returned it
to the vicinity of the gate. Next time the gate cycled,
Goldie would send some down timer through to retrieve
it.

Margo ran through her checklist one last time. Food.
Water purifying equipment. Picks and shovels. Her little
M-1 carbine and ammunition for it. Blowgun and
anesthesia darts. Extra batteries for the laser sight. Koot's
.458 Winchester bolt-action rifle. Emergency medical
kit. Lightweight sleeping bags and mosquito netting.
Ballast they could dump later on when the gas bag
inevitably leaked some of its buoyancy. . . . Yes, they
had everything.

Margo had even made certain they were all inoculated
against cholera, hepatitis, typhoid, meningitis and
diphtheria. They'd begun anti-malarials well before
departure. And even with the extremely good water
filters she'd purchased, she wasn't taking any chances
on contracting bilharzia—she planned to boil all local-
source water for a minimum of ten minutes before using
it. The idea of becoming infected with vicious parasitic
worms in her bloodstream left Margo queasy. Malcolm
and Kit had trained her too well to take stupid risks.

"Are we ready?" Margo asked brightly.

Koot van Beek turned from slinging his rifle across
his back. He grunted in the moonlight. "Yes, English.
We're ready."

The transparent airship, a ghostly sight in the
moonlight, strained against its cables. Margo grinned,
then climbed onto the gondola platform and made
sure everything was secure. She gestured the Welshman
to a place near the front of the platform. He eyed
the gas bag straining overhead with an uneasy glance,
then muttered something entirely incomprehensible

and took his seat. One hand strayed to the case which held his heavy longbow and quiver of arrows. Margo shrugged. They were the weapons he was most familiar with, so she hadn't begrudged him the privilege of bringing them along. How Goldie had weaseled them out of Bull Morgan was something Margo would like to have known.

"Okay, everyone, this show is about to hit the road!" Margo signalled Koot, who loosened his tether at the same moment she loosened her own cable. The airship rose silently into the starlit African night. A strong offshore wind pushed them steadily into the interior. Margo waited until they were well out of sight of the little bayside community below, then fired up the ducted fan engines.

Their noise shattered the night. Kynan covered his ears and glanced over the edge of the platform. He lost all color in the silvered moonlight. The airship dipped and plunged in the air currents like a slow-motion roller coaster. Poor Kynan squeezed shut both eyes and swallowed rapidly several times. Margo grinned and handed him a scopolamine patch, showing him how to put it on, then steered a course northward around the edge of Delagoa Bay for the mouth of the legendary Limpopo River.

Margo thrilled as the dawn came up, spreading fingers of light across the heart of Africa. Beneath their floating platform the distant Drakensberg mountains snaked away southward along the rugged Wild Coast. Directly below, the Limpopo glinted in the early light, a treacherous ribbon of water navigable only during flood stage. According to her ATLS readings, they had emerged in early December, the beginning of the summer season in this part of sub-Saharan Africa. Far to the south, clouds boiled up over the mountains. Flickers of lightning split the predawn sky as the

Drakensbergs roared with another of their legendary storms.

Fortunately, Margo's route lay to the north, following the Limpopo valley in its long, arcing curve through the Drakensberg foothills. With any luck, they'd avoid the worst of the summer storms. Margo peered over the side and grinned even while pulling her jacket tighter. The crystalline chill of the high air invigorated her. The river valley below was a vast carpet of green rising steadily into the foothills. Animals moved in the early sunlight. Vast herds rippled like brown rivers. She wondered what they were. She understood being hungry; but how could anyone hunt such beautiful animals for sport?

She glanced at Koot and wrinkled her nose. *He* hunted for sport and scuttlebutt had it he'd guide down-time safaris, too, but he probably knew what those herds were. She could ask, anyway. "Koot?"

The grizzled Afrikaner glanced back without speaking.

"What are those?" She pointed.

"Wildebeest," he said shortly, "and Cape Buffalo. Very nasty. Most dangerous animal in Africa, the Cape Buffalo. Crocs in that river. Hippos too. Good you decided against rubber rafts."

The sarcasm was heavy enough to weight down the airship. Margo trimmed their attitude by adjusting the amount of ordinary air contained in ballonets inside the hydrogen bag. Her argument with Koot on the subject of air versus water transport had been short, violent, and conclusive. He'd won. That was all right. Flying was more exciting, anyway.

Up in the "bow" the Welshman, too, stared at the tremendous herds. Then he glanced at the hydrogen bag and shivered. Margo felt a moment's pang of pity. What must it be like for him, coming into a time and place where everything he saw smacked of "witchcraft" and left him fighting to hide his fear? She wondered if

Goldie had been right to include him. He needed the work, clearly; but he was having such a difficult time adjusting, Margo would have preferred to leave him on the station and hire someone a little more familiar with modern languages, machinery, and philosophical concepts.

Then she thought about their ultimate destination and grinned. Soon she would fulfill a goal she'd set herself the day her mother had died. A few weeks from now, Margo was going to walk into that prison hospital in Minnesota and show her father just how incredibly wrong he'd been about her, her dreams, everything.

Sunlight flooded the landscape and streamed through the triangular lifting wing which carried them forward into adventure, burning away all trace of bitterness. *Today is the most beautiful, perfect day of my life!* Margo consulted her compass, corrected the direction of the propulsion fans, and came about on the right heading. She thrilled at the touch of the controls. This was *her* airship, *her* expedition, *her* success come to life.

At last, something she had planned was going exactly as it should!

Finding the Seta gravel deposits Goldie had identified was so easy Margo spent the next several days gloating over her success. They anchored the balloon, broke out digging equipment, and busied themselves excavating ore from the potholes along the Limpopo River bank.

When she encountered her first inch-wide sapphire, Margo whispered, "Oh, my God . . ." Then at the bottom of the pothole, they hit diamonds. "Oh, my *God* . . ."

Even the Welshman grinned ear-to-ear as he worked.

They removed yard after cubic yard of matrix, piling it carefully onto the gondola platform, and began hauling it upriver to the site Goldie had marked on her map. Margo had trouble finding that spot. She hovered over the Shashe River, studying the lay of the land, trying to correlate what she saw with Goldie's chart and navigational notations. She finally took an aerial snapshot with the digitizing camera that was part of her personal log, scanned in Goldie's map, and made the best correlation she could.

"There," she decided.

She took the airship down and they buried the first load. They made trip after trip, digging out pits on Goldie's future landholding, seeding them with diamondiferous matrix and returning for another load. It was slow work, because the matrix was heavy. They couldn't lift much at one time. A week passed, blurred easily into two, then three. The January rains of summer hit, flooding their little camp and forcing them onto higher ground. The heat was stifling. Using filter straws which blocked out pathogens, they drank boiled water which had cooled enough to swallow, grinned like fools, and went back to work.

Margo was thrilled her digitizing camera did double duty as a video camera. In her spare moments, she filmed vast herds of antelope, wildebeest, and zebra which stretched away across the grassy veldt. Nearer the river, where trees and scrub grew up, they saw graceful giraffes browsing in the treetops. At night the grunting cough of hunting lions sent shivers through her. Hyenas' wild cackles mingled with the cries of water birds and the bass roar of hippos in the river.

They fished to supplement their supplies. Kynan Rhys Gower and Koot van Beek dined on grilled antelope which Koot brought down. Kynan even joined the hunt, grinning as he transfixed a silver and black gemsbok with a cloth-yard shaft. He cut the long black horns for souvenirs. That night he and the Afrikaner gorged on roast gemsbok. Margo wouldn't touch anything but the fish and her own supplies. Watching them butcher their kills only reminded her of the Roman arena—

and that killed her appetite and curiosity at one fell swoop.

"No, thank you," she said primly when offered a morsel.

Koot just rolled his eyes heavenward, muttered, "*English*," and kept eating.

Elephants appeared in glorious great herds, coming down to the river to drink. Monkeys screamed and chattered in the trees and darted in to try thieving their supplies. Margo laughed and chased them away. In the hay-colored grass of the high veldt, she could even see cantankerous rhinos and long-snouted, suspicious baboons. Those she steered clear of, having no desire to tangle with a horned tank locked on permanent bad temper or an intelligent primate that lived in structured tribal groups, ate a diet that included meat, and sported fangs long as her fingers. But everything else was fair game, both for Margo's camera and her unbounded delight.

They'd nearly finished their work when Margo learned her first valuable lesson about scouting. She and Kynan had left the river, Kynan to hunt his dinner and Margo to stretch her legs and sightsee a little, leaving Koot to guard the camp. Margo carried the carbine slung over her shoulder, but only because Koot always pitched a fit if she didn't. Game was so plentiful Kynan never had to go far and Margo was usually thrilled by whatever they found within a few dozen yards of the campsite. Margo was creeping through tall grass with her digital camera, edging toward a herd of springbok, when it happened. She heard a snort and glanced around to see a massive Cape Buffalo. The bull stood solitary against the skyline.

Oh . . . What a gorgeous animal!

He stared at her through dark eyes, not more than seventy-five yards away. His nostrils flared. He thrust one foreleg out, stiff-legged, as though posing. She lifted

the digital camera and snapped a shot. *Ooh, perfect . . .*
The bull snorted and lowered his head. The horns were
enormous, sharp-tipped, beautiful.

Kynan touched her arm. She glanced around. "What?"

He high-signed her, pointing urgently toward camp.
She noticed he'd notched an arrow to his longbow while
backing away. "There's no danger," she told him. "He's
fifty yards away." Margo clicked the camera from
snapshot to video and began filming again, motion
footage this time. The Cape Buffalo bull lowered his
head even more and snorted again, cutting the turf with
a sharp hoof.

Then he charged.

Oh, shit . . .

Margo fumbled for her laser-guided blowgun, then
realized she'd left it at camp. Then she knew she was
in serious danger. *That animal's as big as a car!* And
he was running straight toward her, bellowing like a
runaway freight train. Terror took hold. Margo fumbled
awkwardly for the carbine and brought it around. The
whole barrel shook, describing wild circles with the
muzzle, but she managed to center the bull. She didn't
know where to aim. She squeezed her eyes shut and
fired. The carbine slapped her shoulder. The crack of
the report sounded above the thunder of hooves.

The bull bellowed and kept coming.

WHACK!

A yard-long arrow sprouted from the bull's chest.

The buffalo bellowed furiously—and kept coming.

"Run!" Margo spun and pelted toward camp. Kynan
was right behind her. The thunder of hooves bearing
down told Margo they'd never make it.

"It's too far!" Margo cried. She turned and fired again,
emptying the magazine into the charging buffalo.

Kynan notched another arrow and let fly. It caught
the bull full in the chest. The crazed buffalo faltered
only one stride then picked up speed again. Two more

arrows followed, pincushioning the enraged animal. Margo fumbled for another magazine to reload the carbine. She was still fumbling with the ammunition when—

KA-RUMP!

The bull went down as though pole-axed. It snorted, screamed, and staggered back to its feet. Then charged again.

KA-RUMP! The thunder of Koot's big rifle barked again.

The buffalo crumpled and slid to a stop. Margo stood where she was, shaking like a leaf. Kynan, poised between her and the maddened bull, slowly relaxed his bow. The bull had skidded to a stop less than four feet from his toes.

"You stupid English!" Koot van Beek muttered, rising from the grass behind them. "You cannot stop a Cape Buffalo with children's toys." He raised the Winchester Model 70 African Special he'd brought along. "*This* is why I brought my own rifle, English."

Margo gulped. "I—I see. Yes. I— Thank you."

Koot grunted once then jerked a thumb back toward camp. "I have fish for supper." The scathing way he said it made Margo wish she could crawl into a hole and pull it in after her. Maybe hunting *did* have its place. . . .

The Welshman slowly, carefully, replaced his arrow in the quiver at his side.

"You were very brave," Margo told him, wondering if he knew enough English to understand her.

Kynan turned to face her. Margo gulped. His whole face was pasty white. He glanced at his bow, stared for a moment at the dead Cape Buffalo, then looked past her to Koot. He said in broken English, "Koot? You show gun?"

Koot grinned. "Sure. Come to camp. I will teach you to shoot."

The look in the Welshman's eyes was one of vast relief.

Wordlessly, Margo followed the men back to camp. *Next time,* she promised, *I'll bring a gun powerful enough to stop anything I'm likely to encounter.* She'd made a mistake. A bad one. Fortunately, it hadn't proven fatal. This time, she'd been lucky.

Margo's second mistake was far more serious than not choosing a powerful enough rifle. Watching the falling fuel gauges—and searching the inhospitable terrain below for nonexistent landing sites—did nothing to slow the alarming rate at which they burned fuel. Far sooner than they should have, the ducted engine fans sputtered and went silent. Terror choked Margo into equally profound silence. *We're out of fuel. Dear God, we're out of fuel. . . .*

Try as she might, Margo spotted nothing that looked remotely like a survivable landing sight for miles in any direction. The fuel gauges read empty—and Margo knew the spare fuel canisters were just as empty as the main tanks. They started to drift rapidly off course.

It's not fair! I was so careful! I figured our exact fuel needs. I got it right for the inland flight! For all those maddening trips upriver. My calculations should've been right for the return to the coast, too. Dammit, I put in every variable I could think of to balance weight against lift—even looked up how heavy that diamond-bearing soil would be! It's just not fair!

But—as Kit and Sven had been so fond of saying— the Universe didn't give beans for "fair." It simply *was*. You got it right or paid the price. And Margo, for all her cautious calculations, had forgotten one simple, critical factor: the wind.

Year round, the wind blew off the coast of Madagascar across the Drakensberg ranges, flowed around the foothills of the Limpopo valley and blasted inland, carrying moisture that kept the eastern half of Africa's tip from baking into desert like the Kalahari and Skeleton Coast farther west. That wind never shifted direction. In all her careful planning, Margo had forgotten to calculate the effect of bucking *headwinds* all the way back along five hundred miles of river valley while summer storms drenched them and threatened to blow their little airship off course.

It wasn't fair; it just *was*.

And now the fuel was gone.

"English!" Koot called urgently. "Fill the fuel tanks!"

Oh, God, I have to tell him . . .

"Uh . . . I can't! We're, uh, out of fuel. . . ."

The hydrogen wing bucked in the wind and dropped sickeningly, then spun lazily at the mercy of rising storm winds. From across the PVC gondola, Koot stared at her, then gave the silent ducted fans a single disgusted glare.

"*English.*"

Margo clung to the gondola with her heart in her throat. She had no choice but to take them down. If they could *get* down. The terrain below was absolutely treacherous: broken rocks and a snaking river bordered by tangles of brush and tall trees. But if they waited much longer, the wind would push them even deeper into the interior, stranding them miles from the Limpopo with no way out but to walk.

"We're taking her down, Koot!" Margo called. "Let's go!"

He gave her a cold glare, but didn't argue. Clearly even he could see the need for getting down *now*. With all three of them fighting the steering controls and hanging on for dear life in the gusting winds, Margo managed to open valves on the lifting wing, draining out buoyant gas. The little ship descended treacherously, canting at wild angles, spinning out of control in gusting winds. Kynan tied down gear that slid and threatened to fall off, then had to grab for a cable to keep from sliding off the edge himself.

"Rope in!" Margo yelled, kicking herself for not thinking of it sooner. One of them might have been flung out. Of course, the way the ground rushed at them . . .

Koot tied himself to the gondola. Kynan and Margo did the same. She trimmed the ballonets, trying to slow their rate of descent. Then dumped ballast overboard. Their wild plunge toward the ground slowed. The flying wing sheered around, flinging Margo against the tiller, then righted itself and continued to descend.

She had no control over where they might land. She searched the ground frantically. If they landed there, they'd break up on the rocks. There and they'd crash through trees and die messily another way. The river was in flood stage, but jagged boulders stuck out of the water like teeth and massive debris including whole trees washed down the raging torrent. They couldn't land in the water. By chance, a freak wind blew them toward a bend where floods had washed out trees and brush, leaving a tiny, muddy clearing. She wasn't sure it was big enough. But if she waited, another gust would blow them past it. Margo released hydrogen with a vengeance. The gondola dropped so fast even Koot yelled.

Please . . . just a little farther. . . .

Margo cut loose half their supplies and kicked the bundles overboard—they landed with a splat in the mud. The gondola slowed, settled toward the ground. Wind blew them sideways toward a snarl of broken trees. Margo yelled and yanked on the valve. Hydrogen hissed out of the balloon. The PVC gridwork thunked wetly into the mud with enough force to jolt her whole spine. *Oww . . . everything* ached.

But they were down. Down, alive, and in one piece. Margo just shut her eyes and shook.

When she opened them again, she found Koot and Kynan staring disconsolately at their wild surroundings. Koot, at least, was busy making them fast with cables and pegs while he stared at the tangle of brush and flooded river. Margo flushed. *Some leader I turn out to be. Stranded two hundred fifty miles from the sea . . .* She wanted to cover her face and cry. But this was her expedition and it was her mistake that had put them all in jeopardy.

"Koot? What do you know about the Limpopo?"

He studied the swollen river. "It is navigable at flood stage. That I know. It will be very dangerous if we try to raft it."

Raft it? "With what?"

Koot just looked at her. "Don't you English learn to think? Our gondola will float. It is PVC plastic. All we need to do is cut up the balloon to waterproof the floor and we can raft on it."

Raft a raging river filled with rocks and whole trees and God knew what else? *Beats walking. . . .* "Yes, you're right. That's a good idea."

He snorted. "Of course it is, English. *I* thought of it."

Margo flushed again, but said nothing. He might be arrogant, but he was right, as usual. Through the effort of gestures and halting explanations, they told Kynan what had to be done. They opened every release valve on the gas bag and deflated it slowly then trod on the ballonets to help deflate them as well. Kynan used his knife to carefully slice open the Filmar wing. Then they unloaded the gondola and covered the rip-stop nylon with a layer of tough, transparent Filmar. Once that was done, they lashed it securely down with the cables which had held the gas bag attached to the gondola. The engines they abandoned by sinking them in the river.

Reloading the raft was tricky as they struggled not

to puncture the layer of Filmar. Once the job was done, Kynan and Koot set to work cutting poles and rough paddles from tree branches. "There will be many dangers," Koot said glumly. "Crocodiles. Hippos. Rapids. We are low on food. We may all die."

Great pep talk. "We're not dead yet!" she flashed back. "And I'm not giving up. Let's push her into the water."

Working together, they hauled the raft to the river and shoved off. Margo scrambled aboard and used her pole to help push them into deeper water. They picked up speed as the swollen current caught them and swept them downstream. She crossed her fingers, said a tiny prayer, and clutched her paddle.

Here goes nothing.

At least she wasn't hiding back home in Minnesota, waiting for life to pass her by the way it had passed by nearly everyone else in that godforsaken little town. If she was going to die out here, she'd die trying! That, Margo supposed as she dug her paddle into the racing current, was something worthy of an epitaph.

She hoped that thought didn't turn into prophecy.

The trip back down the Limpopo was an exhausting, nerve-racking blur of incidents which haunted her at night when she didn't sleep:

"Push off!" Koot screamed. "Now! Now!"

Margo thrust her improvised paddle against a jagged rock higher than her head. The shock of wood on stone all but dislocated her shoulder. Margo went to her knees as the raft spun away from the rock. One kneecap punched through the Filmar floor. Margo dropped her paddle to rig a hasty patch across the spurting hole. Then had to grab wildly for the paddle again as another rock towered in their path. The shock of contact spread white-hot fire through her damaged shoulder. But she held onto the paddle and kept lookout for more boulders. On the other side of the gondola, Kynan hung grimly to a long pole while Koot van Beek clung to his own paddle, trying to steer a course through the flood.

Another day, Margo wasn't sure which one, storm rains lashed them. The river rose swiftly, flinging them from one muddy crest to another. Then ahead, just visible through slashing rain, a sight that brought a cry of terror: wildebeest. A whole herd was trying to cross the Limpopo, thousands—tens of thousands—of animals at a time. The river ahead was a solid carpet of swimming, drowning wildebeest.

"KOOT!"

He came to his feet, swearing. "Try to reach the bank!"

They fought the flood, cracking heavily against a submerged rock. PVC burst along one side of the raft. Then they spun off and bounded downstream again, headed slightly outward toward the far bank. Margo dug in her paddle until her back screamed for mercy— and kept paddling. *If we hit that herd, we're dead. . . .* Closer, closer, they were going to make it . . .

The bank was infested with crocodiles.

"Keep going!" Koot lunged to his feet, rifle in hand, and braced with his legs wide apart.

KA-RUMP!

The rifle barked again and again. Crocodiles died— or thrashed, wounded—on the muddy banks. Others flung themselves into the rain-lashed water or tore into wounded animals for a feast. The bank neared, spun out of Margo's view, came back around closer than before. They were going to make it. . . . They would miss. . . .

The raft grounded, flinging Margo to her chest. Koot leaped ashore, straining to hold the raft by one cable. Kynan jumped out beside him and snatched another slippery cable. Margo screamed. "Look out!"

Koot let go, whirling and bringing up his heavy rifle. He fired once at the croc lunging toward Kynan. It slithered into the roaring whitewater and vanished.

Margo scrambled onto the muddy bank, snatching at the cable Koot had dropped. The raft fought for its freedom. She dug in heels and *pulled*. Rain slashed at her face, making breathing difficult. Lightning flared, but the roar of the river drowned out any thunder.

Koot yanked at another cable. The raft lifted an inch at a time. Margo worked backwards and maintained a steady pull, fearing her back would crack. The raft finally came clear of the river's maddened embrace and slid messily onto the mud. Only a dozen yards distant, crocodiles tore into other crocs brought down by Koot's rifle. Rain washed most of the blood away. Koot shot the nearest crocs then levered them into the water, creating a carcass-free perimeter around their position.

Margo panted, turning her shoulders to the driving rain to regain her breath, then found her M-1 carbine. Kynan Rhys Gower tied the raft down and set about repairing visible damage as best he could. Margo shook so hard she could barely keep her grip on the rifle, but at least she was still alive to shake. Thirty yards downstream, wildebeest struggled in the water and screamed like terrified children while they died. She shut her eyes to the carnage. They'd come so close to plowing straight into that. . . .

More animals died during the next few hours than had died during the entire Ludi Megalenses. Possibly more than had died during the whole previous *year* at Rome. The death of the wildebeest herd didn't change the bloody savagery she'd witnessed in the Roman Circus, but it put life and death in much clearer perspective. Nature wasn't any nobler or gentler than human beings. It was just as deadly and just as cruel and just as savagely "unfair" to the weak. . . .

Maybe more so.

They had to wait hours past the end of the storm before the river was clear enough to risk rafting again.

That night they took turns once again standing watch.

They stayed on the river each night if no rapids threatened, trying to gain time, but dragged the raft onto the banks until dawn if the river was too rough to navigate in the dark. Tonight they'd come ashore rather than risk a treacherous stretch of white water visible just ahead in the fading twilight. That night, Margo spent a lot of time whimpering deep in her throat, glad the roar of white water drowned out the sound of her terror.

So call me Katherine Hepburn and marry me off to Humphrey Bogart. . . .

Margo would have settled for Malcolm Moore's strong arms in a flash. She missed him desperately, particularly at night like this when the screams of hunting leopards and dying animals drifted on the wind like clouds of enveloping mosquitoes. Every time she heard another wild scream on the night air she wanted to grab her rifle, but tonight Margo was so tired she could scarcely pick up the M-1 carbine.

I'm sorry, Malcolm, she found herself thinking again and again, *I was rotten and selfish and I didn't mean it. . . .*

Another drenching summer storm broke over them near midnight, jolting Margo from fitful sleep. Kynan stood watch, a ghostly figure in the flash and flare of African lightning. Koot van Beek, bedded down in his sleeping bag, stirred briefly then went back to sleep.

How could anyone sleep through this?

Lightning screamed through the clouds, slashed downward into trees and the river, dancing and splashing insanely across jagged, arc-lit boulders. Margo was too tired to flinch every time it struck, but fear jolted her with every bolt, nonetheless. *Don't let it strike us. . . .*

Then the rain struck, a solid mass of black, stinging water. Margo coughed and rolled onto her tummy, pulling the sleeping bag right over her head. Water roared louder than ever down the swollen Limpopo.

I'll hear that sound in my grave, Margo moaned. *Why'd we have to arrive in the rainy season?* Then, because she was no longer able to hide from her own folly and its cost, *Good thing it is or we'd really be in a jam.* Rafting out two-hundred-fifty miles still beat *walking* it. Which they'd have had to do, lugging gear every step of the way, if this had been the dry season.

Oh, Malcolm, I really screwed up. . . . She had to get back, not just to prove she could scout and survive it, but to apologize to Malcolm for the cruel thing she'd done to him. It was too late to pursue what might have been the most wonderful relationship in her life, but she could at least apologize.

When, at some later, miserable point in the night, water lapped against Margo's cheek, Margo thought groggily the rain must've seeped into her sleeping bag. Then Kynan Rhys Gower appeared in a strobe-flash of lightning, drenched and white-faced. "Margo!" he cried, pointing toward the nearest edge of the raft. "River!"

The raft was bobbing madly against its moorings.

Huh?

She wriggled free of her sodden sleeping bag. The river had risen swiftly—and rose visibly higher over the next few lightning flashes.

"Koot! Koot, wake up!"

He reacted sluggishly, fighting his way toward consciousness while she shook him. One good look at the rising river brought him to his feet, swearing in Afrikaans.

"Drag her higher!" Margo shouted.

"No use! Look!" He pointed inland.

Lightning revealed a tangle of impenetrable forest. At the rate the water was rising, the whole tangle would be multiple feet deep in flood waters at least five-hundred yards inland from where they floated—probably within another hour.

"Can we ride this out where we are?" Margo called above the sound of river, rain, and thunder.

"Don't know. Rapids downstream looked bad!"

A terrifying *crack* nearly on top of them jolted the raft. Margo screamed. One whole end of the raft disappeared underwater. Kynan scrambled across the tilted deck, knife in hand. The raft jerked, thrashed under the tug of something monstrous. Lightning showed them why: one of their anchor trees had come down.

"Cut the cable! Cut it!" Koot van Beek screamed.

Kynan was already sawing at the taut cable where it vanished underwater. It parted strand by strand, then snapped. The raft lurched and spun sideways. Kynan went overboard with a hoarse yell. Margo lunged forward. Lightning revealed him clinging to a broken PVC pipe with one hand.

"Koot!"

The Afrikaner didn't answer. Margo wrapped both hands around Kynan's wrist. He flailed and caught her arm with his other hand. She lost him in the darkness between flashes, aware of him only through the tenuous contact of hand on wrist. Margo pulled, but her upper body strength was a pitiful match for the tug of the river.

"KOOT!"

The raft slammed around into something hard. Kynan yelled and barely hung onto her arm. Margo sobbed for breath and used toes to dig for the severed cable behind her. She found it and scooted one knee forward until the broken end was under her cheek.

"Kynan! Hold on!"

She drew a breath for courage—

—then let go with one hand and snatched the cable. Kynan yelled—

Margo flung the cable around him.

He grabbed for it as his grip on the raft broke loose.

Margo hung onto one end and Kynan clung to the other. *Please* . . . Margo sobbed under her breath. She rolled over and scooted backwards, hauling with the leverage of arms *and* legs this time. Kynan's arms appeared over the edge. Then his head and back appeared. He slithered forward, clutching at the cable, the PVC, anything he could grasp. Margo pulled until Kynan had wriggled completely onto the raft. Then she fell backwards, panting.

Grimly, Margo tied herself to a lifeline and tied one around the gasping Welshman. Koot was fighting to secure the raft to another tree, braced on one foot and one knee while he struggled with coiled cable and vicious wind and current.

"KOOT! TIE A LIFELINE!"

Before he could respond, another tree went CRACK! The raft lurched underfoot. Margo fell flat. She caught a glimpse of Koot in a strobe-flare of lightning. He was sawing frantically at the other cable with his own knife. Then they spun free. The river sucked them downstream. Margo whimpered, but forced herself to crawl forward.

"Get a lifeline on!" she shouted at him.

Koot, looking numb and shaken, fumbled for a rope.

Then lightning flared and Margo caught sight of the rapids.

"Oh, God . . . Oh, *GOD* . . ."

Margo groped blindly for a paddle, a pole, anything she could use to shove off those looming rocks. The river spat them at those rapids like a watermelon seed in a millrace. Margo found breath to scream just once. Then she was fighting for survival in the strobe-lit night. Every time lightning flared, she shoved the paddle at anything that looked dark. Usually the paddle connected sickeningly with solid stone, jarring her whole body with bruising force. The raft spun, lurched, plunged through the darkness. Spray and rain battered them. Margo couldn't hear anything but the roar of water. If anyone yelled for help, she'd never hear them.

Another shock shook them. A rock nobody'd seen. The whole raft shuddered, bounced off, rocked sideways over a lip of water, dropped sickeningly. The impact jarred her breath out, then they plunged on. She had no idea half the time if she faced upriver or down. Another jolt shook the raft. *It can't take much more of this, it'll come apart on us* . . .

The raft lurched—then either it or Margo was abruptly airborne. Margo screamed. She came down in the water. The muddy Limpopo closed over her head. Margo fought to find her lifeline. The current was savage. She couldn't move against it. She swallowed water, strangled, knew that if she hit a submerged rock, she would die—or worse—

Her face broke the surface. She was moving . . .

Kynan Rhys Gower grabbed her hair and pulled. Margo groped for his arm, his waist. She slithered forward into his lap. The raft rocked violently, spun in a new direction . . .

Then quieted.

They still raced through the darkness like a cork over Niagara Falls, but they'd made it alive through the rapids.

Margo quietly threw up in Kynan's lap, disgorging the water she'd swallowed. He pounded her back, helping her cough it out. Then he helped her sit up and made sure she'd suffered no broken bones. Margo winced a few times, but the worst she'd endured was bruises. Koot watched silently.

She finally met Kynan's gaze. "Thank you."

The Welshman pointed to himself then the river, then pointed to her and the river.

"Yes," she shivered. "We're even now. Thank you, anyway."

He spread his hands and shrugged, then busied

himself checking for damage. Koot watched her without speaking.

"Are you all right?" she called over the storm.

"Yes. You?"

"I'll live. Maybe," she qualified it.

He grunted. "You're damn lucky, English. I'm going to sleep."

Without another word, he collapsed, not even bothering to crawl into his sleeping bag. Margo glanced at Kynan. He gestured for her to rest.

"My watch," he said in his careful English.

Margo just nodded, knowing she'd have found the strength to stand watch if she'd had to, but thanking God and every angel in the heavens she *didn't* have to. If another emergency threatened, Kynan would wake them. She fell asleep before her cheek even hit the sodden sleeping bag.

Five days into their wretched journey, they ran out of food—and Koot van Beek fell seriously ill. He woke with a high fever and terrible chills.

"Malaria," he chattered between clenched teeth.

"But we took anti-malarials!"

"Not . . . not a sure-fire prevention. G-get the quinine tablets."

Margo dug out the medical kit with trembling hands. She read the instructions again to be sure, then dosed him with four tablets of chloroquine and covered him with one of their sleeping bags. They had no food left to help him regain his strength. The river banks were barren of anything that could be shot and fetched back as food.

Where are all those stupid animals when we need them? I'm hungry—and Koot may be dying!

She'd have shot anything that remotely *resembled* food in a heartbeat. She'd even have cooked one of those lousy drowned carcasses, if she could've gotten close enough to one to snag it. She bit her lips and tried to cope with an overwhelming sense of failure. When they stopped for the night, pulling the raft onto the flood-ravaged bank, Margo sat in her miserable corner of the raft and held her head in her hands and started admitting the hardest truths she had ever had to face.

I am not smart. Or particularly clever. Or honest, not even with myself. Kit and Malcolm, everyone was right. I was crazy to think I was ready to scout. . . .

Proving herself to her father seemed utterly pointless now. What had she expected him to do? Take her in his arms and weep on her neck? Tell her the three words she'd wanted to hear all her life? Fat chance.

Sitting there in the darkness, Margo had ample time to review every mistake she'd made, every selfish word she'd uttered, every lamebrained, dangerous risk she'd run because she hadn't learned enough. She'd nearly let a Cape Buffalo kill her because she was too busy thinking how *picturesque* it was to realize her danger. Koot had *warned* her and she'd chosen to ignore him. What was it Kit had told her? Don't put wild animals on some moral pedestal bearing no resemblance to reality?

And she'd nearly killed Malcolm in St. Giles. And in Rome, completely on her own . . . Margo had come to realize she'd come close to being killed in Rome, too, without ever realizing it. She could've stumbled into far less scrupulous hands than Quintus Flaminius'— and his care of her could easily have soured. That lancet they'd used to bleed her could've infected her with something awful, or they might literally have bled her to death, or . . .

Margo's whole experience as a time scout was one unmitigated disaster after another, with some impatient guardian angel finally throwing hands in the air in disgust and going back to whatever heaven guardian angels come from.

All of which left her utterly alone with no supplies on a flooded river miles from help, with a dying man and a scared down-timer on her hands. The only thing that kept her going was her sense of responsibility. She hadn't left Achilles completely without resources and she wouldn't give up on Koot and Kynan, either. Somehow, she'd get them out of this mess she'd made.

Six hours later she woke Koot and dosed him with two more tablets. He complained of a raging headache and fell asleep again. Margo dug out her information on malaria and a flashlight. When she read the list of potential symptoms, Margo felt a chill of terror. The *Plasmodium falciparum* strain of malaria, which included among its symptoms severe headaches, could be quickly fatal if not treated properly. They were several hundred years as well as a hundred or so miles from the nearest medical clinic.

Kynan crouched down at her side and gestured to Koot.

"He die?"

Margo shook her head. "I don't know."

The Welshman's dark gaze flicked to the river. "Bad place."

"Yes. Very bad." She drew a ragged breath. "We have to keep going." She pantomimed paddling and pointed down the river.

Kynan nodded. His expression was as grim as Margo's fading hopes. Somewhere deep inside her, Margo found the courage to keep going. At dawn, they shoved off again. The Welshman wordlessly picked up Koot's heavy Winchester rifle and checked it as he'd been taught, then took up a guard stance in the bow. Someone had to watch for hippos while the other one steered. Margo didn't feel like arguing over which job she was best suited for. She took up position in the stern and did her best to keep them on course.

❖   ❖   ❖

Margo was three-quarters asleep under a starry sky when their raft eddied down the last few miles of the Limpopo. Kynan Rhys Gower shook her gently and pointed. Margo blinked and rose awkwardly. She ached everywhere, making movement difficult, and the hunger gnawing at her had left her muzzy-headed. She stared down the moonlit river for several moments before realizing why it looked so wide.

They had come within sight of the sea.

"Oh, thank God!"

Then another frightening thought hit her.

The mouth of the Limpopo was nearly a hundred miles up the coast from Delagoa Bay and the gate. A hundred miles on a raft on the open sea with no real way to steer and no food or water?

"Kynan! We have to get to the bank!"

Kynan puzzled out her meaning, then nodded and began to paddle. Margo dug her paddle into the current until her shoulders and back were on fire. They moved slowly nearer the bank—but not fast enough. The current was sweeping them inexorably out to sea. Maybe they could swim for it. . . .

Koot couldn't swim. And when she looked closely, Margo saw the gleam of crocodile eyes in the water. Terror choked her breath off. *We'll drift into the Indian Ocean. My God, we could end up anywhere* . . . At the last moment, she thought to fill water cans with river water. Then they were wallowing in rolling swells. The current carried them farther from land.

"A sail," Margo muttered, "we need a sail . . ." Malcolm had taught her how to sail. But not how to build a sailboat out of a PVC and Filmar raft. "Doesn't matter. Gotta have a sail."

Margo dug for the remains of their flying wing. Not much was left. It would have to do. Margo loosened one of the broken PVC pipes and rigged a mast, using cables to tie it in place, then tied the remaining Filmar in place as a rude sail. Wind bellied it out. The raft still wallowed—but in a new direction. For a time, they made little headway. Then they left behind the influence of the Limpopo's strong current and eddied slowly down the coastline, blown slightly shoreward by the wind hitting their sail.

Kynan poured river water through their filtration equipment and used the coleman stove to boil it. Margo was so thirsty she would cheerfully have drunk the ocean dry. He poured a cup and handed it to her. Margo sipped the hot water—

And spat involuntarily.

Salty . . .

She stared in rising horror at the cup. She'd scooped up river water. . . . But she'd waited until they were almost in the mouth of the river to do it. The water she'd retrieved was brackish. And that water was all they had aboard.

She shut her eyes, wishing she could blot out the terrors closing in on her as easily as she did sight of the accusatory cup in her hand. Koot was dying, they were adrift at sea with no water and no food . . .

"Margo?"

She opened her eyes. Kynan's brow had furrowed in the starlight. "Water not good," she said shakily. "Salt."

He frowned and tasted it, then spat. The furrows in his brow deepened. Between them, Koot moaned. Margo checked him and bit her lips. He was extremely weak. When she tried to move him, he vomited over the side, then soiled himself with uncontrollable diarrhea. His skin burned under her hand. Margo poured sea water over him in an effort to bring down his temperature. He moaned and shivered, then subsided into delirium.

Gotta get him back to the gate. HOW?

The raft wallowed in the swells, ungainly as a beached whale. Kynan vomited over the side, too, then wiped his lips and looked embarrassed. Margo dug out another scopolamine patch and stuck it behind his ear, then dosed herself against seasickness for good measure. She wasn't sure she ought to risk dosing Koot, then decided he was so close to death she might as well chance it. If she could keep him from vomiting, maybe he'd survive?

The coastline was a great deal more rugged from the ocean than it had looked from the air. Margo and Kynan took turns at the sail, steering their craft as best they could. They hardly moved in relation to the coast. At Margo's best guess, it would take them *days* to make the gate. Then, icing on a ruined cake, a line of thunderclouds rolled in from the Madagascar Straits, blotting out moon and stars. Lightning flared wildly from clouds to sea and back again.

"Oh, God, no, not now . . ."

The storm swept down on them.

The only silver lining visible in the clouds was their increased speed as the storm drove the little raft southward. Then it began to rain.

"Kynan! Fresh water!"

He'd tilted his head back, letting rain enter his mouth.

"KYNAN!"

He glanced around. Margo tried to explain what she wanted, mimicking the shape of a funnel, then simply tore up part of the flooring and used the plastic to rig a funnel over one of the cans. Kynan did the same, with a bigger sheet of plastic. They filled three cans before the sea grew so rough they had to hang onto the raft to keep from being thrown off the platform. They wallowed and spun around in the swells. Rain pelted down, a wall of solid water that left them blind and drenched. Margo clung to the raft, unable to let go long enough to steer.

Please, let us get out of this alive and I swear I'll do whatever Kit says, study anything Kit tells me. . . .

They ran before the storm, helpless in its grip for

hours. Margo couldn't get to her chronometer, nestled safely in the ATLS bag looped around her torso, but given the changes in the light she guessed the storm drove them down the curving coast for more than twenty hours. She tried to remember what the curve of the coast looked like, wondered if the storm would slam them into the beach or just sweep them on southward past the Cape of Good Hope several hundred miles farther south.

Cape of Good Hope. Hah! Cape of Disasters is more like it. . . .

She and Kynan drank water sparingly, giving Koot a little when he roused, but there was still no food. *Maybe I could rig something to use for a fishing line and hook? When the storm breaks. . . .*

They ran aground without warning in pitch blackness.

Margo was thrown violently clear of the raft. She screamed and landed in stinging salt water. Breakers slammed her into the beach. The force of her landing knocked her breath away and left her floundering in a savage backwash. She crawled forward like a crab scuttling away from the sea, blinded by rain and deafened by the crash of thunder and maddened surf. She finally collapsed above the high water line, drenched to the skin by pounding rain.

Koot . . . Kynan . . .

Malcolm . . .

The last thing to impinge on her awareness was the knowledge that she was an utter failure.

She woke slowly, in pain. Margo heard male voices she didn't recognize, speaking loudly and angrily somewhere above her. She stirred and moaned. *Everything* hurt. Someone slapped her, shocking her more fully awake. Margo gasped and focused on dark-haired men with light, olive-toned skin. They were dressed outlandishly in dirty clothes that reminded her of paintings of Christopher Columbus. Many of them wore slashed velvet breeches and leather armor. One wore metal chest and backplates and carried a fancy wheel-lock handgun. Margo's heart began to pound. She'd been found by sixteenth-century Portuguese from that little settlement on Delagoa Bay.

What about Kynan? And Koot? Had they survived the break-up of the raft? Or had Margo alone failed to drown in the stormy surf? One of the Portuguese, the man in the metal armor, spoke roughly to her. Margo had no idea what he'd said. The man stooped over her, spoke again, then backhanded her. She tried to get away and felt a tremendous blow connect. She didn't feel anything at all for a long time after that. When Margo regained her senses, someone had stripped her naked. The traders had clustered around her, leering. They'd started to unfasten their clothes.

Margo whimpered.

When the first one shoved her knees apart, Margo squeezed shut her eyes.

Malcolm . . .

It took the bastards a long time to finish.

CHAPTER EIGHTEEN

The withered-sea landscape garden of sand and stones
in the corner of Kit's office had lost its ability to soothe.
He slumped in his chair and shoved aside the mountain
of government forms to be filled out, then stared at
the raked sand and dry boulders. *Eight weeks.* It had
felt more like eight years. Kit hadn't believed it possible
to miss someone so keenly after such a short time—
much of it spent arguing, at that. His apartment felt
empty. The Down Time had lost its appeal. The
Commons would have been utterly dead-flat *boring* if
not for the occasional excitement of a crow-sized
pterodactyl raiding lunch from shocked hands or
momentarily unguarded plates.

After a while, even the giggle of watching tourists
dive under lunch tables had worn off. All that was left
was the intolerable weight of government paperwork
and the long hours wondering where she'd gone. He'd
gone up-time long enough to hire an investigative agency
to locate her birthplace in Minnesota and discover her
real name, as well as search other time terminals to
see if she might have gone scouting at one of them. So
far, the agency had drawn an absolute blank. As far as
anyone could tell, Margo had dropped off the face of
the earth.

Which she might have, for all practical purposes, if
she'd gone scouting from another terminal.

Whatever the solution to the mystery of Margo's

whereabouts, TT-86 no longer felt quite so much like home.

Kit ran a hand through his hair and sighed. "Maybe I ought to retire up time." To do that, he'd have to close his accounts, find a buyer for the Neo Edo, locate a place to live in the real world, which had changed a lot—and not for the better, so far as he could tell— during the years he'd been down time.

Kit grunted. "I'm too tired to leave and too bored to stay."

So he picked up a stack of bills and started scanning them for errors, just to avoid government forms. He was halfway through an itemized bill from the library when an entry caught his attention. He hadn't done any research on fuel-consumption and lift-capacity for Floating Wedge ultralight airships.

"What the . . ."

He checked the access code assigned to the bill. It was Margo's. He grunted. So she had been using the library, after all. Then he noticed the date. Kit swivelled in his chair, punching up gate departures for the past two months. There was the day Porta Romae had cycled, the day his granddaughter had walked back out of his life. The library entry on the bill was dated seven days *afterward*.

"Oh, hell, she couldn't even keep her goddamned password a secret. How many other charges did this thief run up against my account?" He found several additional entries, neatly itemized by subject matter and data source as well as computer time logged onto the mainframe. Each one post-dated Margo's precipitous departure through Primary.

Kit slid the bill angrily to one side of his desk. Unless he could locate the access-code pirate, he'd be stuck for one helluva research bill. He switched computer screens, typing out a simple monitoring program to set off an alarm the next time Margo's access code was entered into the system, then e-mailed messages to Brian Hendrickson and Mike Benson, alerting them to the fact that data piracy was occurring.

Then he called Bull Morgan.

"What's up, Kit?"

"We've got a data pirate loose on the station. Someone's used Margo's access code to bill research to my account."

"I'll make a note of it. You're sure it's an account pirate?"

"Margo left a week before the first incident. Went up Primary to God alone knows where. Or when."

Bull sympathized. "I'll do some checking, put Mike Benson on it."

"I've already e-mailed him about it and Brian Hendrickson, too. Thanks, Bull."

He hung up and glared at everything in sight. Then sighed, resigned himself to a long day, and settled resolutely to work again. When the phone rang less than a quarter of an hour later, he cradled the receiver between shoulder and ear.

"Yeah, Kit here."

"Kit, it's Bull."

He sat back in his chair, faintly surprised. "Damn, I knew you were efficient, but I didn't expect you to catch the rat this fast."

Bull chuckled. "We haven't. But I did turn up something odd. I thought you'd want to know."

"Yeah?"

"Margo passed through Primary, all right. Then she came back about a week later."

He sat straight up. "*What?*"

"She came back, but hasn't logged out again. Medical hasn't out-processed her records, the ATF has no trace of her leaving a second time through Customs . . ."

"But—" He closed his mouth again. "What about other gates?"

"Mike's working on it. Hang on a sec."

Kit waited in a swivet. Then Bull came back on. "No, she didn't log out through any of the other gates, either. Not the tourist ones, anyway, and nobody's filed paperwork to scout the unknown gates off Commons."

"Bull, she has to be somewhere. La-La Land's a closed environment."

A brief silence greeted him. "Kit, there *are* unstable gates."

He shut his eyes. "No. Not even Margo's that stupid. She was scared spitless of the Nexus Gate and after Orléans . . ."

"Well, she's still here somewhere, then, avoiding you."

"For seven *weeks?* La-La Land isn't that big. Besides, Margo couldn't stay out of trouble for seven minutes, never mind seven weeks. If she were here, somebody would've seen her. She's not on the station." He thought hard. "Do me a favor, would you? See if anyone else is missing? I'll start asking around on my own, see what I can scare up. Maybe a small gate opened up somewhere we don't know about. Or maybe somebody went through one of the unexplored gates without permission." *It'd be just like that little idiot to pull a stunt like that.*

"Sure thing, Kit. I'll run some checks and let you know."

"Thanks."

Kit hung up and said several biting things to the withered-sea landscape garden, then started placing phone calls.

Kit didn't have much luck. Nobody he talked to had heard a whisper about an unknown gate. A couple of down timers who worked as Time Tours baggage handlers recalled seeing Margo return through Primary, but they had no idea where she'd gone afterward. Kit's granddaughter had managed to vanish without a trace from the heart of one of the most gossip-riddled communities in the world.

Then, when he least expected it, Malcolm Moore showed up.

The younger man had avoided Kit's company for eight full weeks. If Kit arrived someplace and Malcolm was already there, he made excuses to leave within moments. He turned down casual invitations to the Down Time for dinner and had become in general a hard-working recluse. Kit felt sorry for him. Clearly, Malcolm had taken Margo's rebellion and defection deeply to heart, blaming himself entirely. Kit had tried to apologize, to tell him it wasn't his fault, but Malcolm wasn't returning Kit's e-mail or phone calls, either.

When the buzzer on his desk lit up and Jimmy told him Malcolm was headed up, Kit actually sagged in his chair.

"Thank God . . ."

He hated to lose friends.

A hesitant knock at the door signalled Malcolm's arrival.

"Come in, it's open."

The door slid back, Japanese style. Malcolm Moore glanced into the spacious office. He looked massively uncomfortable. "Uh . . . . you busy, Kit?"

Something in Malcolm's eyes told Kit he hoped the answer would be "yes."

"No. Come on in."

Malcolm sighed, then slipped off his shoes and entered. His posture told Kit he'd rather have faced the hangman.

"I, uh . . ." He faltered to a halt, staring at the floor, the walls, anywhere but at Kit.

"Malcolm, it wasn't your fault. She's a headstrong little hellion. It wasn't your fault."

A deep flush darkened the guide's cheeks. "You don't have to be nice about it, Kit. You weren't there." He shoved hands into his pockets, then paced uneasily toward the withered-sea landscape garden, leaving his back to Kit. There were holes in the toes of his socks and both heels were threadbare.

"I, uh, heard she came back. Then vanished."

"Yes," Kit said quietly. "Do you have any ideas at all?"

Malcolm halted. For just an instant his shoulders drooped. "No." Then he straightened his back again. "But I heard something odd this morning. I thought you ought to know. You know, just in case . . ."

"Park 'em. Talk."

Malcolm hesitated, then took the chair. But he still wouldn't meet Kit's eyes. "I was down in the gym working out. Ripley Sneed came in."

"Ripley? Where the hell has he been keeping himself? I haven't seen him in months."

Malcolm grimaced. "Went down an unknown gate and damn near didn't come back. Had some pretty wild stories to tell. Anyway, I mentioned you'd been asking about unknown gates anybody had explored recently. He said he'd gone through one a couple of months back, but it was completely worthless."

Kit frowned. "What gate? Where?"

Malcolm rubbed the fingers of one hand. "He said it opened in the back of Phil Jones' store."

"Phil Jones? Isn't he the nut who goes down time and rescues totem poles?"

"Yeah, that's the one. His shop gives me the creeps. Phil gives me the creeps. Anyway, Ripley said a small gate opened up in his storeroom. He went through, logged it, came back, told Phil the gate was useless."

"Why was it worthless? Where and when did it go?"

Malcolm glanced at his hands, pretending to inspect his fingernails. "He wouldn't say."

Kit tightened his hands down around the edge of his desk. "Ripley Sneed always was a goddamned bastard. How much did he want?"

Malcolm sighed unhappily and finally met Kit's gaze. "A thousand."

"*A thousand dollars?* To tell me where a worthless gate leads?" Kit swore savagely. "Where is that miserly little prick now?"

"The Down Time. He's telling everyone about his adventures in the sultan's harem."

Kit rolled his eyes. "Good God. What an idiot. Okay, Malcolm. Thanks. Maybe this'll be worth it. God knows I haven't had any other clues worth following. I'm afraid she's wandered through one of the question gates without filing proper paperwork with Bull and if she's done that . . ."

Malcolm nodded. "You may be right." He hesitated. "Margo . . . Well, she wasn't in any mood to wait any longer. Something awful happened to that kid before she came here. I'm not sure who she's trying to prove herself to, but it's riding her harder than we ever did."

Kit didn't answer. He'd spent a lot of sleepless hours doing exactly what Malcolm had been doing: blaming himself.

"That doesn't matter, does it, if she's wandered down a gate without telling anyone. She shouldn't have shadowed herself already," he said raggedly, drawing a flinch from Malcolm, "but if she's actually gone down a question gate secretly, she might as well have."

The legal consequences of stepping through an unexplored gate without filing proper forms were minuscule, a mere fine if you actually made it back alive, but the practical consequences . . .

If no one knew which gate you'd gone through, no one could even mount a rescue attempt.

Kit tracked down Ripley Sneed at the Down Time Bar & Grill. Malcolm, to his surprise, followed doggedly. Kit ordered a Kirin, offered to buy one for Malcolm, then shrugged and settled into an empty chair at Ripley's table.

"Mind if we join you?"

"Sure," the scout said with a smile. "What have you been up to, Kit?"

"Oh, this and that. I hear you've been exploring unknown gates."

"Sure have," Ripley grinned. His dark hair needed washing. He smelled bad, like month-old gym socks left to soak in mare's sweat. The regulars at the Down Time had taken tables upwind of him.

Doesn't this jerk ever bathe?

"So, I hear you checked out a gate in Phil Jones' place."

Ripley took a long pull of his own beer. "Yep."

"Odd place for a gate to open up. Of course, they've opened in stranger places." Kit smiled politely.

"You're telling me. How come you're interested in gates again? Thought you'd retired?"

"Oh, just curious. I like to keep up with the business."

Ripley laughed. "You're not fooling anybody, Kit. You want to know about that gate worse than I want to get rich. It'll cost you." His eyes glinted.

"Really?" Kit leaned back and folded his hands across his belly. "You'd charge a man for information on a worthless gate? Hell, I'll just wait until it cycles again and take a look, myself."

Ripley chuckled. "Nope. You're too cautious. You've been through too damned many gates, Kit Carson. You want to step through that bad, it'll really cost you to find out whether or not you'll go 'poof!' before you hit the other side."

Kit restrained the urge to throttle him.

Malcolm leaned forward on his elbows. "You're an unpleasant louse for someone who just spent a week in some poor schmuck's harem, getting his wives pregnant while he was off fighting the Christians."

Ripley laughed, unoffended. "I can afford to be

unpleasant. You can't." He belched. "Okay, Kit, I'll tell you about the gate if I see a thousand up front."

"A hundred, tops."

They fell to serious haggling. Kit finally agreed to pay Ripley five hundred. The scout dug out his log and downloaded a file, then passed the disk over. "There it is. Enjoy."

"Thanks," Kit said drily, passing back a check for five hundred.

"Better not bounce," Ripley said, tacking on a grin at the last moment.

"Watch your mouth," Malcolm growled.

"It's all right, Malcolm. Ripley can't help being abrasive any more than a monkey can help having fleas. Come on, let's see if I got my money's worth."

They left Ripley chuckling as he folded up Kit's check and stuffed it into his wallet.

The file contained very little information. Ripley had gone through the gate and logged in location and time: thirty-two degrees east longitude by twenty-six degrees south latitude, late September of 1542. "There's a small Portuguese trading settlement about two miles north of the gate on Delagoa Bay, Mozambique. A number of native tribal groups in the region are split between Swazi and Shona dialects.

"I see some Moslem influence from contact with Islamic traders, but not much. Relations between the indigenous peoples and the Portuguese is hostile at best. There is absolutely nothing of value to be found in this settlement. Delagoa Bay is merely a stopover to take on fresh water and food supplies for Portuguese ships headed to India. From what I've been able to gather, the Jesuits didn't even leave a mission here when Francis Xavier stopped in 1541. My conclusion is that this is an utterly worthless string not warranting further exploration."

The file ended.

"Well," Kit said heavily. "What do you make of that?"

"Five hundred is a lot of money to demand for that information. Something's going on here."

Kit called up a map of Mozambique and replaced the video scenes on his office wall with the chart of southern Africa. "Mozambique . . ." he mused. "That's hell and gone from anything useful. And in 1542 there wouldn't have been *any* European exploration of the interior. Nothing out there but Shona and Bantu on the high veldt and San nomads in the Kalahari."

"And the Venda-Lemba Semitic groups of the eastern Transvaal," Malcolm added. "*They* were isolated until 1898 for God's sake."

"So why would Ripley demand so much money for this information?" Kit glanced up. "I wonder what Phil Jones has been up to lately?"

"I think we ought to find out."

"Agreed. You want to tackle him or shall I?"

Malcolm managed the first smile Kit had seen out of him in weeks. "You're too conspicuous, Kit. Everybody knows you're looking for traces of Margo. I'll follow that little weasel, see what he's up to, who he's hanging out with these days."

Kit nodded. "Sounds good. I'll give Bull a call. He's trying to find out who else might be missing."

Malcolm left while Kit dialed the phone.

The station manager apologized when he came on the line. "I've been meaning to call you this morning, except that *Pteranodon sternbergi* of Sue's got sick, then we had an emergency with the water filters and . . . Oh, hell, you're not interested in my problems. Only a couple of people I can't account for, but they're interesting."

"Oh?"

"One of 'em's that Welshman you tangled with."

"Kynan? The guy from Orléans?"

"The same. He and his longbow have gone missing."

A chill chased down Kit's back. "Go on."

"Frankly, I was afraid of foul play until I noticed who else is missing. Remember that big Afrikaner who came in a few years back when South Africa went to hell?"

"Yeah, I remember him." South Africa had suffered desperate damage from earthquakes, tidal waves, even volcanic eruptions in the aftermath of *The Accident*. The government had collapsed and thousands of people had fled the ensuing riots, massacres, starvation, and rampant plagues. "Koot van something," Kit said. "Big guy about my age, if I remember right, maybe a little younger."

"Koot van Beek. Took up time guiding. Drifts from station to station, wherever there's work."

"So he's back?"

"Back and missing."

Kit gazed at the map on his video screens and tried to figure out why a freelance drifter like Koot van Beek, a displaced Welsh bowman, and Margo would have hooked up in connection with a gate that led to sixteenth-century Mozambique.

"Thanks, Bull. That's very interesting news. I'll let you know if I come up with anything solid."

Kit pulled out the itemized library bill and studied Margo's recent research. Lift capacity and fuel consumption for a helium-filled ultralight—but with variable equations for hydrogen as an alternative lifting source. Endemic diseases of southern Africa and recommended inoculations or medical treatments where no inoculations were available. Geographical charts of Mozambique, South Africa, Zimbabwe, Botswana. Even—he grimaced—recommended medications to suppress menstrual flow.

"What the hell is that little idiot up to?"

Unless Kit were wide of the mark, Margo planned a lengthy air expedition into the heart of southern Africa, where Zimbabwe, Botswana, and South Africa met along the Limpopo River.

"But *why?*" There wasn't anything out there except crocodiles, wildebeest, and fatal diseases.

The phone rang. "Yeah?"

"Kit," Malcolm said in his ear, "this is really interesting. Phil just left Goldie Morran's. I asked around and people said he's been spending a lot of time with her. A *lot* of time."

Kit narrowed his eyes. "Goldie? Why would Phil Jones be spending time with an expert on currency, precious metals, and . . ."

It hit him. Kit widened his eyes and stared at the map. "My God . . ."

"What?" Malcolm asked sharply.

"Hang on. Hell, get back here. I have to pull a couple of files off the mainframe."

He hung up and swung around, accessing the library's mainframe in a fever of impatience. He sped through several files, correlating data against a search of known mineral sites—and hit paydirt. Kit whistled softly and sat back in his chair.

His office door crashed back. Malcolm was panting. "*What?*"

Kit swung his chair around. "Diamonds. That stupid little featherbrain has gone after a diamond source deBeers doesn't control."

"*Diamonds?*" Malcolm stared at the chart. "But Kit . . . the nearest diamond fields must be, what, five or six hundred miles from Delagoa Bay?"

"Five hundred miles along the Limpopo River valley," Kit said grimly, punching up the chart from the file he'd accessed, "would put you right there."

A geologic map flashed up.

"What's up there? I thought the South African diamond sites were farther south in the Kimberley region or much farther west in the Kalahari?"

Kit strode around his desk and stabbed a finger toward a spot on the Limpopo just east of the confluence with the Shashe River coming down from the Botswana-Zimbabwe border. "That, my friend, is the site of the Seta Mine. Alluvial deposits in potholes along the Limpopo, gravel matrix rich in all kinds of goodies. Garnets, jade, corundum, gold, diamonds . . . That idiot grandkid of mine has vanished into the heart of Africa on a harebrained scheme to bring back diamonds. Bet you the Neo Edo on it. And I can tell you exactly who put her up to it."

Malcolm groaned and said something profoundly ugly.

Kit ran a hand through his hair. "We were in Goldie's shop when I told Margo she was through as a trainee scout. And that avaricious, conniving, greedy old . . ." He couldn't even finish the tirade. "When I get through with Goldie Morran, she's going to wish she'd never laid eyes on Margo."

Kit stormed out of his office. Malcolm Moore trailed hastily behind.

Goldie Morran's smile disintegrated the moment Kit slammed open her door.

"Why, Kit. Hello. What can I do for you?"

"You can tell me why the hell you sent my granddaughter into the high veldt after your goddamned diamonds!"

Goldie Morran actually lost color. "Kit, I don't know what you're—"

"Cut the crap!" Kit stalked over to the counter and slammed both fists down. "You're not talking to a goddamned tourist!"

Goldie adjusted the high-necked collar of her old-fashioned dress. "No, I'm aware of that, Kit. Calm down. I'm not really hiding anything."

"The hell you're not."

"Kit Carson, either control your temper or get out of my shop!"

Kit swallowed the retort on his tongue. Then forcibly

relaxed his fists. "Okay, Goldie. I'll be a good boy and refrain from taking your shop apart. Start talking."

She drew over a high stool and settled on it as though taking a throne. "You're aware, then, of Phil Jones' gate?"

"Yes. And where and when it leads."

"Fortunately for me, Ripley Sneed is an idiot. He didn't even think about the diamonds just lying around the interior waiting for someone to pick them up. Phil and I knew exactly where the most accessible deposits were, but we couldn't get there ourselves. Neither of us is a scout."

"You mean neither of you is crazy enough to risk your own hide. So you conned Margo into doing it for you."

Goldie's eyes flashed angrily. "Margo is an adult, Kit Carson, perfectly capable of making her own decisions. And, I might add, you've treated her very shabbily. She was only too happy to accept my offer."

"Margo is a half-trained child—a *seventeen*-year-old child." Goldie lost a little more color. "She thinks she knows enough to succeed. All she knows is enough to get herself killed. When's she due back?"

Goldie fidgeted and glanced away.

"Goldie . . ."

The severe-faced woman who always reminded Kit of a duchess he'd once known cleared her throat delicately. "Well, as to that, now . . ."

"She's overdue," Malcolm said quietly. "Isn't she?"

Goldie glanced up. "Well, yes. She is."

Kit tightened his hands on the edge of Goldie's shop counter. "*How* overdue?"

"A couple of weeks."

"A couple of *weeks?*" Kit exploded. "My God! Why the hell didn't you *tell* me?"

"Because I knew you'd blow up just like this!" Goldie snapped. "They took plenty of protective gear with them. They'll be fine! They're just a little overdue."

Kit studied her, controlling an ice-cold rage that

demanded physical action. She wasn't telling them everything. For someone waiting on a shipment of first-quality South African diamonds, Goldie was remarkably untroubled about Margo's fate.

"What's your scam, Goldie?"

She widened her eyes at him. "Scam? Why, Margo was just going to dig out some of the Seta deposits and come back, that's all."

Kit leaned over the counter. "You are full of it, Goldie Morran. If Margo was supposed to bring back a shipment of diamonds, you'd have been crawling all over this station looking for someone to go after her when she was two weeks overdue. What kind of scam are you running?"

Goldie pursed her lips like someone who's tasted poison. "You are a royal pain, Kit Carson. She isn't bringing them back. Koot van Beek and I jointly invested in a little piece of property up north of Francistown, in Botswana. No one has ever found the motherlode source of the Seta alluvial deposits. So Margo's going to dig up a couple of potholes' worth of matrix and fly the ore up to our property on the Shashe River. I have a rube up time who's biting at the bait. All I have to do is confirm that Margo's seeded the land and Koot and I will 'discover' samples that match the Seta deposits. This fool will buy the land at a huge profit and we'll make a fortune. We don't even have to smuggle the diamonds past ATF this way. It's all nice and legal."

It was a nice scam. A very nice one. Neat, slick, possibly even legal, leaving out the minor problem of minerals fraud. And given the current state of government in the southern African republics, any fool crazy enough to buy the land would probably end up eating his losses.

Kit said quietly, "You had better pray real hard that nothing has happened to my grandchild, Goldie. Show me this gate."

✧   ✧   ✧

Kit and Malcolm both scanned the gate in Phil Jones' shop during its next scheduled opening. Malcolm double-checked his readings in rising dismay. His heart sprang straight into his throat. "Uh, Kit, are you getting the same readings I am?"

Kit nodded grimly. "It's disintegrating. Rapidly. How often does it open and how long has it existed?"

Phil Jones, a nervous little weasel of a man, cleared his throat. Totem poles loomed on every side, grotesque shapes beyond the shimmering edges of the gate. "Opens every five days, stays open about ten minutes. First saw it about ten weeks ago."

"Have you kept an exact log of its openings?"

Phil exchanged glances with Goldie. "Uh . . . should I have done that?"

Malcolm was afraid Kit might strangle the shop keeper. "Yes, you blithering idiot! You should have!"

The gate shrank, expanded briefly, then vanished.

"Five days," Kit muttered, noting the exact times of its appearance and departure. "I have five days to get ready."

"You're not going through?" Phil gasped. "But I thought—wouldn't it be dangerous for you to—"

One look from Kit was all it took. He gulped and shut up.

Malcolm followed Kit out of Phil's odd little shop. "Have you checked your personal log yet?"

"I have."

"And?"

"It's risky. Damned risky. There's a twenty percent chance I'll shadow myself on stepping through. And if I stay longer than a week, if I have to wait through *two* cycles, a ninety percent chance I'll shadow myself before getting back through. *If* the gate doesn't collapse permanently before then."

"But you're going?"

Kit's eyes were haunted. "Hell yes, I'm going. Goldie admitted Margo should've been back to the gate two weeks ago. What would you do?"

"Go with you," Malcolm said quietly.

Kit swung around. He blinked; then tightened his jaw muscles. "Malcolm, I can't ask you to risk this. You said yourself you weren't cut out for scouting."

"You're not asking and neither am I. I'm going. It's my fault Margo pulled this stunt, say what you will. I'm going."

They locked gazes for a long moment. Then a suspicious film moistened Kit's eyes.

"All right. You're going. The Portuguese aren't real cheerful about strangers in their African outposts."

"No."

"Those traders are likely to kill any European they find sneaking around their settlement."

"Yeah." Malcolm wasn't thinking about himself. He was picturing Margo in their hands.

"Jesuits," Kit said finally. "You speak Portuguese?"

"Some. I studied it for Edo, back when I was with Time Ho! My Basque is better, though."

"Good. I speak Portuguese very well. You'll be a Basque Jesuit, I'll play your superior in the Society. Let's find Connie. This is going to be one helluva rush order."

Five days.

Malcolm just prayed the gate hadn't already disintegrated so badly that it never opened again.

CHAPTER NINETEEN

They emerged onto a rain-lashed beach. When Kit didn't vanish like a shimmer of heat over Kalahari sands, Malcolm started breathing again. The pallor in Kit's cheeks told its own story. *Now all we have to do is try to find Margo—and beat ninety-percent odds if we don't do it in a week.*

With the entire southern tip of Africa to search, Malcolm wasn't terribly sanguine about their chances.

He finished his ATLS readings and log update a hair sooner than Kit. The retired time scout was out of practice. They hid their equipment deep in camouflaged bags beneath vestments, censers and other priestly paraphernalia. Among their personal "effects" were handbound copies of not only the Bible in Latin but also of the Jesuit *Spiritual Exercises* written by Ignatius Loyola, the Basque founder of the Society of Jesus. Connie Logan had outdone herself on this one.

Malcolm closed his bag and turned his attention to their surroundings. In the short minutes they'd stood on the storm-lashed shore of Delagoa Bay, their long, heavy habits were already soaked. Wind whipped sodden wool around their ankles. They had decided to approach the Portuguese first, to find out if Margo had, in fact, made it back this far or if they would have to mount an expedition into the heart of the interior to search for her.

"This storm will work in our favor!" Kit shouted above

the crash of thunder. "I've been worrying about how to explain our sudden appearance. Claiming we've been shipwrecked is more credible in the middle of a storm!"

Malcolm nodded. "The Wild Coast is notorious for shipwrecks, particularly when summer storms hit the Drakensbergs. And as Jesuits, we ought to be welcomed."

They both carried bladed weapons just in case they weren't.

Lightning flares cut through the gloom of early evening, revealing the miserable little fort and ramshackle houses of Lourenço Marques huddled on the bay. A stout *kraal* wall enclosed the whole community. Kit marked the spot where the time gate had closed by piling stones into a small cairn, then he and Malcolm slogged down the rainswept beach toward the trading settlement and prayed for the best. They passed grain fields where straggling wheat lay flat under the onslaught of the storm.

Vegetable gardens sprawled in patchwork confusion beyond an unguarded *kraal* gate. Wet chickens hid under the houses. Pens for hogs stank and leaked filth into the mud streets. Thin, forlorn cows huddled against the rain and a few sheep and goats milled uncertainly in a high-walled pen. A horse neighed once, answered by others in the distance.

"Where is everyone?" Malcolm wondered aloud. "There should be a watch set, even in this storm."

Kit cupped hands over his eyes to blink them clear of streaming rain. "Probably at the fort," he decided. "The wall's higher, stouter in case of emergencies. We'll try there."

When they stumbled between the houses into "town square" they halted in unison. The residents of Lourenço Marques had set up a crude pillory along one side of the square. Hanging from the stocks was a familiar, grizzled figure. Malcolm and Kit glanced swiftly around but saw no sign that anyone was watching. The whole town was shut up tight against the storm. Malcolm got to him first. Koot van Beek was dead. Had been dead for several hours, maybe as long as a day. Kit was ashen in the wild flares of lighting.

Margo . . .

They searched the body for signs of violence, but found no trace of systematic torture. Malcolm swallowed once, then followed Kit through ankle-deep mud past an idle blacksmith's forge, what was clearly a cooper's workshop, and a small gristmill. In the distance, the fort's rough wooden gates were shut.

"Lean against me," Kit muttered from cover of the gristmill.

"You're older, more likely to succumb to exhaustion. You lean against me. I know enough Portuguese to get by until you 'come around.' "

Kit didn't argue. He just draped one arm across Malcolm's shoulder and let his weight sag. Malcolm hastily slid an arm around Kit's back. *All right, we're shipwrecked Jesuits who've struggled up the coast in a terrible storm. . . .*

He half carried Kit across the open, muddy ground toward the gates. "Help! Hello inside, help us!" Malcolm shouted in rough Portuguese, heavily accented with Basque pronunciation. "In the name of Christ, help us!"

A suspicious sentry appeared at the top of the wall. "Who are you? Where have you come from?"

"We are Jesuits! Father Francis Xavier sent us to you from Goa. Our ship went down in this storm, south of here! This *is* Lourenço Marques, is it not? Please God let it be . . ."

The sentry's eyes had gone wide. A hasty shout relayed Malcolm's message. A moment later the gates creaked open. Then Portuguese traders swarmed outside, lifting Kit's stumbling figure to carry him while others supported Malcolm. He staggered like a man in the final stages of exhaustion and allowed his escort to take most of his weight.

The residents of Lourenço Marques stank of onions, sweat, and dirt. Their voluminous, slashed breeches needed washing. Food and wine stained leather jerkins and slashed velvet doublets. Malcolm saw at least six professional soldiers in leather armor, half of them carrying matchlock arquebus carbines rendered useless by the storm. They'd drawn wicked swords which they now resheathed, but the other half of the military detachment, carrying steel crossbows, remained alert until the gates had been closed and barred once again.

Other men had come running, dressed as rough tradesmen and humble farmers. Many carried long pikes and daggers. One burly bear of a man carried what looked like an honest-to-God wheel lock rifle. Another man carried an enormous, full-length matchlock arquebus. None of these men wore helmets; only a few possessed leather jerkins. *Six professional soldiers and a surprisingly well armed auxiliary of tradesmen and farmers. And those fellows over there look like sailors.* Malcolm counted five men who had probably been left behind by the last ship, to recover from illness or be buried.

Shortly, Malcolm and Kit found themselves in a grimy, smoke-filled room which was clearly the best accommodation in the fort. Real chairs stood around a scarred wooden table covered with the remains of the evening meal. A real bed stood in the corner. A man in plate armor—at least a chest and back plate—blinked when they came in, then lowered a "high-tech" wheel lock handgun and carefully pulled back its "dog," making it somewhat safer, although still loaded and ready for use.

"Sergeant Braz, who are these men, where have they come from?"

The sergeant said importantly, "They were sent by Father Francis Xavier to us, Governor, but their ship was wrecked in this storm. I don't know any more than that."

Kit coughed violently and moaned. The soldiers carrying him asked anxiously, "May we put the Father in your bed, Governor?"

"Of course, of course. Hurry, the good Father is exhausted and ill." The governor tucked his pistol into his belt and helped lower Kit into his own bed.

Kit gasped and clutched at his benefactor's hand. "Bless you, my son," he whispered faintly. "God has preserved us in an un-Christian land." Then his eyelids fluttered closed.

Malcolm hastened to his side. He knelt and clutched Kit's hand, giving every evidence of terror. "Father Almada . . ." Malcolm turned to the anxious Portuguese. "Have you any hot broth? He is exhausted from fighting the sea and then we had to walk miles and miles up your treacherous coast. I feared God would call him away before we saw your walls."

"You sound like a Basque," one of the men dressed as an artisan said excitedly. Another had gone in search of something to feed their unexpected visitors.

"Yes, I am Father Edrigu Xabat. I had the grace to be ordained in Rome by the General of our Order, Father Loyola. Father Almada is . . ."

Kit "roused" with a faint moan. "Where . . . where are we, Edrigu?"

"God has delivered us safely to these Christian men, Inigo, praised be His name." One of the farmers handed Malcolm a cup. "Oh, bless you, my son . . ."

Malcolm held it to Kit's lips and helped him drink hot soup, then consented to eat some himself. It was terrible, no salt, no pepper, watery and thin—but it was hot. Kit struggled to sit up, then begged to know who their rescuers were.

"I am Vilibaldo de Oliveira Salazar, the military governor of Lourenço Marques," the governor introduced himself proudly, sweeping a courtly bow. He was a small man with sharp eyes and a thin face. He wore expensive velvet garments under his armor despite the grime. "This is Joao Braz, the Sergeant of my command, and these are my soldiers, Francisco, Amaro, Lorenco, Mauricio, Ricardo."

The soldiers saluted sharply.

The big man with the wheel lock rifle shuffled forward. "Please, Father, I am Rolando Goulart, a humble blacksmith. I speak for the artisans of Lourenço Marques when I bid you welcome. This is Bastien, my assistant."

Bastien was the man who'd been so excited by Malcolm's Basque name and accent.

"And this is Vincente, our butcher and tanner, Huberto the miller, Nicolau the cooper, Xanti our baker, and Mikel his assistant . . ." *More Basques*, Malcolm realized. The farmers and husbands who tended the community's herds also proved to be Basques: Narikis, Mikolas, Peli, Kepa, Posper, and Satordi.

The other five men were stranded sailors, as Malcolm had suspected. Three were Portuguese, introducing themselves shyly as Rodrigo, Adao, and Pedro. Erroman and Zadornin were both Basques. There were no women in evidence.

"Please," Vilibaldo de Oliveira Salazar begged, "if you are strong enough, Father Almada, tell us of yourselves and your misfortunes."

Kit rose to the occasion with wonderfully fluent Portuguese, embroidering on Malcolm's original tale. He described the conditions in Goa and Father Francis Xavier's concern that the men here at this desolate outpost had no priests to confess or shrive them. He elaborated on their harrowing journey back to Africa from India, described the terrifying shipwreck which had drowned all the ship's company sparing only the two of them, spoke with tears in his eyes and a choked voice of reading last rites to the crashing waves, then of their struggle up the coast, praying that they stumbled in the direction of the outpost, not deeper into trackless wilderness . . .

Even Malcolm was impressed.

Several of the men cleared their throats and stamped their feet to hide their own emotions. Vilibaldo insisted they change out of their sodden cassocks into something warm and dry, producing good quality, simple tunics and cloaks in which they wrapped themselves. The farmers hung their wet things to dry in one corner of the room. Vilibaldo then broke out wine and shared it around, making certain his new priests were warm and comfortable. The governor spoke of the hardships they had endured in the outpost, the troubles they had with the natives who stole Portuguese cattle or ran their own cattle through the grain fields, destroying the crops utterly, and the illnesses which had befallen them, the men they'd lost.

Finally, insisting that the soup and good company had revived him, Kit suggested that he and Malcolm hear confessions without delay. "Clearly, my son, you have been without the comforts of a priest for too long. It would be best to relieve your souls of the burden of sin you carry now, before another moment passes. I am only glad that God has sent us to minister to your needs."

The traders mumbled and looked embarrassed, then hastily rigged blankets to form two crude confessionals. Kit insisted they put on their wet cassocks again, then Malcolm took one side, Kit the other, and they began hearing confessions. They were not even through the first one when Kit emitted a roar of outrage and snatched back the curtain.

"Witches!" he cried, wild-eyed. "What say you, *witches!*"

The artisans crossed themselves. The soldiers paled.

Vilibaldo stared at the floor for a moment, then cleared
his throat. "It is true, we have a prisoner who is a witch,
Father. The other witch has died of some evil disease
he brought upon himself."

Sergeant Joao Braz ventured, "We have closely
questioned the other and—"

"*You* questioned this person? Are you a man of God?
Do you presume to know witchcraft?"

The sergeant paled and stumbled to a halt.

"But—but Father—" one of the sailors, Rodrigo,
protested. "They *were* witches! Seven weeks ago it was,
I saw with my own eyes a terrifying sight, a great glowing
raft of white sticks that sailed through the heavens far
away to the north. Then last night terrible storms raged
all night and well into the morning. You see how the
witch-brewed storm has nearly destroyed even you, who
are men of God? What do you think we should find
on the beach, Father, but that same great white raft,
broken it is true, into pieces, but there were devilish
items on the sand and the man and woman wore Satan's
garments and—"

Kit groped for the nearest chair and sank into it. "And
the other witch? What have you learned?"

The men of Lourenço Marques glanced at one another
again, clearly uneasy.

"Father, the dead witch," governor de Oliveira Salazar
said quietly, "he babbled in a possessed madness. He
spoke *Dutch!*"

Malcolm and Kit exchanged glances.

"I speak a little Dutch, Father," Sergeant Braz put
in. "The witch was raving about another of their
company, who is not with them. We have search parties
out looking for him and have told the black heathens
hereabouts there is a reward for capturing this other
witch and bringing him to us."

The Welshman, Malcolm realized. *Poor terrified
bastard . . .*

"You must take me to the witch you have captured," Kit said severely. "I must examine the woman and see if Satan's hand is truly upon her. Has she spoken at all?"

One of the Basque farmers spat onto the floor. "No, only to scream."

Kit lost all color. Malcolm hastened to his side. "Father Almada, you are still unwell. You should be in bed."

"How can I sleep when God's work is waiting? Come, show me this witch."

What are you going to do, Kit? We can't escape through the gate for another five days. She'll tip our hand for sure.

But the desire to know what condition these men had left her in worried at him like a rat gnawing at his foot. How much worse must it be for Kit? The governor and soldiers led them through the downpour to a tiny stockade on the far side of the fort. The rest of the community trailed behind. Sergeant Braz produced an iron key. It grated rustily in the lock. The room beyond was so dim Malcolm couldn't see a thing. Kit gestured impatiently for a lantern. The smith, Rolando Goulart, gave Kit his.

"Leave us," Kit said harshly. "Father Xabat will examine the witch with me."

"But Father Almada, she might do you an injury—"

"God is the sword of the Jesuit, my son. Do not fear for our safety. Go. We will lock her in again when we have examined her."

The soldiers shuffled uneasily, then retreated to the far end of the overhang, refusing to go farther. Kit lifted the lantern, drew a hasty breath, and stepped into the foul little room beyond.

Margo shivered in a corner of her prison, hating with a greater passion than she had ever felt in her young life. She hurt so desperately, tears formed. They tracked

down her cheeks in the darkness. These brutal *animals*—
no, they were *worse* than animals, that was an *insult*
to animals—had raped her, beaten her, demanded things
in as many languages as they spoke and hit her every
time she couldn't answer. They'd finally stumbled on
broken English in their efforts to find out who she was.

They had ordered her to reveal who the other man
was, the one who had escaped, ordered her to explain
why she and the other witches had come, demanded
to know what terrible evil they planned to do
Portugal. . . .

The insanity had gone on and on until Margo had
been capable of nothing but screaming at them.
Whereupon their pig of a leader had raped her again,
then tossed her naked into this earth-packed cell and
locked her in without food, water, or a blanket. They
had come back only to inform her that Koot van Beek
had died and that she would die next.

Margo had never known such black despair in all
her life. She cried until there were simply no more tears
left in her. She'd stupidly set out to prove a childish
point—but the only thing Margo had succeeded in doing
was getting Koot van Beek killed and the Welshman
even more lost in time than ever. Not to mention getting
herself raped and imprisoned.

Tremors shook through her at the memory. She would
have killed for soap and water or a gun to shoot the
bastards. *If they could even be killed.* Their sweat still
stank on her skin. Every time she closed her eyes, she
saw their faces, leering down at her while they held
her down and hurt her. . . .

Oh, Malcolm, why did I run from you? That memory
was torture, too, the sweetness and gentleness contrasted
with abuse beyond anything she'd been capable of
imagining. *I'm sorry, Malcolm, I'm sorry, I failed you,
failed Kit, failed men who counted on me to get them
out alive, I even failed Mom—*

At least Margo's mother had died doing something to keep her child alive. All Margo had done was behave like a reckless, ungrateful brat. Locked naked in a Portuguese prison awaiting execution was a helluva time to learn one's lesson.

"I'm sorry," she whispered over and over, "I'm so sorry. . . ." She wiped her nose and sniffed, surprised she was able to conjure more tears. Life had handed her a precious friend and she'd fled, too much a baby to face what a wonderful relationship he'd offered. Now she was going to die and she would never have a chance to tell him what a thoroughgoing, cowardly *fool* she had been.

And Kit. He'd never know what had become of her. What she'd done to him was inexcusable. If she ever, ever had the chance . . .

But life wasn't like that. The cavalry came over the hill only in fairy-tale Westerns. And the prince on the shining charger had vanished right along with blunderbusses and sailing ships and gentlemen who tipped their top hats and smiled when a lady walked past. She'd never get to tell him how sorry she was or to beg forgiveness and the chance to go to college for several years before trying it again.

What must he have thought when he'd found her hateful little note?

"I'm sorry," she whispered again.

She didn't know what else to do.

Then, with a terrifying, rusty grate of iron turning in the lock, the door swung open. Dim light silhouetted the whole pack of slavering murderers who'd captured her. Margo bit back a terrified cry and came to a low crouch.

They would doubtless kill her. She was too weak and too badly hurt to stop them. But she could at least put up a fight. Maybe, if she were really lucky, she'd manage to send one of them to hell a few minutes ahead of her.

◆   ◆   ◆

Kit stepped through first, lantern held aloft. Malcolm followed and hastily closed the door, then turned and found a shocking tableau. Kit had frozen in place, lantern still uplifted. Margo huddled in the corner, squinting against the lantern light. She'd come to a defensive crouch . . .

She was naked, covered with bruises. Dried blood showed dark on her thighs . . .

"Oh, my God," Kit whispered.

Malcolm whipped off his cassock to wrap around her. Her eyes widened. Then she burst into tears and hurled herself forward. Malcolm expected her to go for Kit. She flew into his arms instead, staggering him off balance. She hugged him so tightly he had to fight for breath.

"Malcolm," she was whispering raggedly, "oh, God, Malcolm . . ."

He wrapped the cassock gently around her shoulders. She dragged his head down and kissed him so desperately all he could do was close his eyes and hold her. At length sanity returned.

"Your grandfather's here, too," he said quietly.

She turned and saw Kit. "Oh, God . . ."

Kit was staring at them, pale and silent in the lantern light. Malcolm swallowed hard and met Kit's gaze. Their position was painfully clear. Margo clung to him, not to Kit, had kissed him as only men and women who have become lovers kiss.

Margo forestalled the explosion by throwing herself into Kit's arms. "I'm sorry, I'm so sorry . . ."

"Shh . . ." He held her as though she might break, but his look over her shoulder boded ill things to come in Malcolm's immediate future.

Malcolm met that cold gaze steadily. He was ashamed of the fact he hadn't told Kit sooner and he was ashamed of the fact he'd been drunk when he'd gone to bed with her. But he wasn't ashamed of the way he felt about Margo, and it wasn't his fault he hadn't known she was only seventeen at the time. At least, that's what he'd been telling himself for weeks. So he held Kit's gaze and said quietly, "We aren't out of danger yet."

He halfway expected Margo to wail, "What do you mean?" but she didn't. She let go of Kit and carefully pulled Malcolm's cassock more tightly around herself. Then she straightened against obvious pain and said quietly, "What do we have to do?"

Her voice shook a little, but childish petulance and every trace of impatience were gone. Terrified and battered and clearly only beginning to dare hope she might live through this, Margo met his gaze and faced the possibility she could yet die. Moreover, she did it with a quiet dignity he'd first glimpsed in London, standing on a street of kosher shops and rebuilt dreams.

Malcolm swallowed hard. When Margo looked at him now, an adult met his gaze. A *real* adult. Regardless of the number that represented her birthdate. In that moment, he fell in love all over again.

"Malcolm?"

He cleared his throat. "I'd say that's up to Kit. This is his rescue, I just sort of invited myself along."

She swung her gaze around. Kit continued staring at Malcolm for another long moment, then bit out, "Yes. And now I see why." Then he met Margo's gaze. "The gate doesn't reopen for five days. If it reopens. The string's disintegrating fairly rapidly. I'd be very surprised if it opens more than once or twice more before failing completely.

"Kynan Rhys Gower is still at large. The indigenous people in this region are being encouraged to capture and turn him in. Portuguese search parties are out hunting him. The traders are convinced you're a witch. One of them saw that damned balloon of yours seven weeks ago and now they have your 'devilish' equipment as further damning proof.

"They'll expect us," he nodded to Malcolm, "to examine you for witchcraft. Given the circumstances, there's only one verdict possible. They'll expect us to proceed quickly with the execution. We're outnumbered twenty-five to two and they're heavily armed. More so than I'd feared."

"And there's a ninety percent chance," Malcolm added heavily, "that if we miss the next cycle of the gate, Kit will shadow himself before it reopens the next time. It's possible he'll shadow himself as it is."

Margo just covered her face with her hands. "You shouldn't have come," she whispered brokenly. "You shouldn't have risked it. I'm sorry. I'm not worth it, not even close to worth it—"

Kit lifted a hand, hesitated, then touched her hair. She glanced up, eyes brimming in the lamp light. He managed a pained smile. "Did you actually transfer those damned diamonds to Goldie's worthless piece of property?"

The ghost of a smile flickered into being. "I sure did." Then her smile crumpled. "But Koot's dead and everything's gone to ruin. It's my fault! I screwed up the amount of fuel we needed. We ran out bucking the headwinds. We had to raft out and Koot contracted *malaria* of all things trying to get downriver, and we ran out of food, then that storm broke up our raft . . ." She drew a deep breath. "I'm not making excuses. I'm to blame for all of this. You were right. I'm not cut out to be a scout."

Kit traced an ugly bruise on her cheek. "Don't tell me you're giving up so soon?"

Her chin quivered. "I—I wanted to ask for a second chance, but I—I screwed up so bad, I—"

"Promise me you'll go back up time and study. Provided we get out of this mess alive," he added with a wry smile. "You get those college degrees, okay? We'll talk about it then."

She started crying again, silently, desperately. Malcolm wanted to hold her, but left that to Kit, who pulled her close and rocked her in his arms. Malcolm's throat thickened. He'd never seen such an expression on Kit's face. Eventually she sniffed and pulled back a step. "Okay. We'll talk about that when we get there," she said, sounding exactly like her grandfather. "But first, we have to get out of here. Any suggestions?"

"None whatsoever," Kit said cheerfully. "I generally make things up as I go along. Although for the sake of verisimilitude, I would suggest you scream, very loudly and most convincingly, right about now."

Margo didn't even hesitate. She screamed, a piercing sound of agony that raised fine hairs on the back of Malcolm's neck. Then she whimpered loudly enough to be heard through the closed door. They waited for a moment, then Kit signalled to her again. She let out another gawdawful cry and started sobbing.

Kit said quietly, "I'm sorry, but Malcolm has to keep this." He took Malcolm's cassock and handed it back. Then he stepped to the door and opened it.

"Governor Salazar, whether this girl is witch or not, I have still not decided in my heart," Kit said. "But the girl has been badly brutalized." Reproach darkened his voice. "God does not approve of such violence against the weaker sex. Worse, you have left her naked and starving. We may chastise the body for the sake of the soul, but we are still Christian men. Bring the poor child a blanket, clothing, something hot to eat. Let her pray and sleep. Tomorrow we will examine her further."

He lifted his hand in a Latin benediction, then motioned to Malcolm. Margo bit her lips as he turned to leave. He said with his eyes, *Hold on, kid. Just hold on.* Then the traders brought a coarse shirt, a blanket, and a mug of soup. Kit saw to it that she was clothed and wrapped in the blanket, watched her finish the soup, then consented to lock her in again for the night.

Then—and only then—did he and Malcolm finish the "confessions" they had begun. Neither of them was in any mood for it, but the charade had to be maintained at all costs. The confessions proved astonishingly petty, yet gave great insight into the factions which split the isolated men of Lourenço Marques.

"The tradesmen," Sergeant Joao Braz complained bitterly, "act like they are in Lisbon, not this forsaken wilderness! The miller demands his twentieth part for grinding flour. What will he spend it on? And the husbands are lazy! All they do is stand around and watch their chickens scratch in the dirt while we guard their miserable lives. . . ."

The Basque baker, Xanti, ranted against the soldiers, who treated everyone in the community like peasants, putting on arrogant airs and shirking their duty. "Do they stand night watch? Ha! They *sleep* through night watch, unless a rat runs over their feet. Then they scream like women and swear that Satan himself is loose in the town. Why, that idiot Mauricio even shot at a shadow at *three o'clock in the morning!* Woke up the whole town. . . ."

The governor complained bitterly that the men were slovenly, undisciplined, and lazy. Nicolau the cooper's confession was one endless tirade against everyone and everything in Lourenço Marques. "The town would not even *exist* but for me! My barrels hold the water this fort was built to supply for the ships bound for India! Without me, Lourenço Marques would still be a stretch of mud held by devil-worshipping heathens!"

The blacksmith, too, had his complaints. "Three times in the past month, that idiot of a cooper has broken the handles of his drawing knives. What does he do with them, to break the handles? And the governor demands more guns, then complains at the price when

I tell him what it will cost and how long it will take my assistant and myself to make even the simplest . . ."

The farmers hated the sailors with a Basque passion. "We work hard," Mikolas cried, "feeding those lazy louts. What do they do all day? They sit by the water, eat ten times what any other man would consume in a day, and sing bawdy songs while they make *rope!* Why do ships need more rope? Every time a ship comes, there are miles of rope coiled on deck, and God preserve you if you so much as step on one little pile . . ."

You know, Malcolm thought quietly while the Basque ranted, *it wouldn't take much to set these men at one another's throats.* Malcolm filed the thought away and finished hearing their bitter complaints, then doled out suitable penance for their sins, expressing shock and dismay when he learned that half the men in town didn't possess so much as a simple rosary. Malcolm might have felt guilty about deceiving these men, but for one fact. Cold rage filled him every time memory revealed Margo crouched naked in that filthy corner, ready to fight off her attackers.

As for Kit . . .

Malcolm glanced at the blanket separating his "confessional" from Kit's. He would deal with Kit when they came to that quarrel. No sense setting himself up for more worry than he already had. They would either get out alive or they wouldn't. Only then could he and Kit settle the matter between them.

Kit's stony silence the rest of the evening didn't bode well at all.

Kit had to plausibly stretch their "examination" of the so-called witch over five full days. He lay awake far into the night, trying to put out of his mind what these men had done to Margo. If he let himself dwell on it, he'd never be able to think straight. He knew he ought to consult Malcolm, but was too deeply angry to speak to him. *'It's my fault she's pulled this stunt,'* Malcolm had said.

What did you do to her in Rome, my friend? You seduced her, hurt her, drove her away . . .

I trusted you, Malcolm.

That hurt almost as much as what Margo had suffered.

Malcolm's breathing told him the younger man hadn't fallen asleep, either. *Good.* He hoped Malcolm Moore spent a night in hell. Kit turned over with a creak of bed ropes and presented his back to the guide.

"Get some sleep," he said roughly. "You'll need it."

Malcolm didn't answer.

At two o'clock in the morning, Kit rose and lit a lamp, then kicked Malcolm into wakefulness. The guide stirred under dirty blankets and groaned, then struggled to his feet. His eyes showed the strain of sleeplessness. Malcolm faced him squarely, however, neither flinching nor apologizing. Kit grunted. "Time to wake these sinners up for night office. I want them half asleep and off balance for the next five days."

Malcolm only nodded. He vanished outside to search for the fort's alarm bell. Kit heard Malcolm speak with the night watch, then the bell sang out a dirge which brought men stumbling out of the houses to the fort. They clutched weapons a little wildly as they searched for danger.

"What is it?" one of them cried, darting frightened glances into the darkness. "What danger threatens, Father?"

"The danger of damnation and hell everlasting," Kit said sternly. "The Evil One has been at work among you, by your own admission. God has sent us to save your souls. All of you, put away your guns and crossbows. Kneel for Matins."

The men of Lourenço Marques exchanged dismayed glances in the dim light from Kit's lamp. Then, with a low muttering and a shuffling of feet, they knelt in the

darkness. Kit began Matins in high Latin, speaking out
the service in a slow, rolling way that spun out the
observance as long as he could stretch it. Then, just
for good measure, Malcolm repeated the whole thing.
The traders yawned and dozed until Kit switched them
awake with a small stick and an admonishing glare.

They finally allowed the bewildered Portuguese to
get off their knees and stretch. But when the traders
headed for the gate to return to their warm beds, Kit
called them back. "My sons, think you that you return
to bed now? Lauds must now be read before you may
sleep safely in the knowledge that you are saving your
souls."

When the military governor complained bitterly that
his men needed to sleep, Kit held up a hand. "Until
the matter of these witches is settled and I know that
the souls of my new flock are safe from harm, I must
ask that you abide by my decree. Kneel, then."

In the flickering lamplight, dismay showed plainly
in swarthy faces. "My sons," Kit said gently, "too long
have you been living ungodly lives. Have you considered
that your own wickedness has brought the witches and
the devil himself among you?"

Several of the men crossed themselves fearfully. No
one else complained as they knelt to hear Lauds. By
the time this second service had ended, dawn had
begun to creep across the sky. Kit let them go, enjoining
them to sleep with prayers upon their lips, then
stumbled back to his own wretched bed. Malcolm
glanced once at Margo's prison, then followed. They
slept for exactly three hours, then roused the traders
at six o'clock and conducted the Prime service. Only
then did they allow the traders to eat breakfast. Kit
ordered that the poor girl be fed, as well, then faced
his uneasy new "flock."

"I would know what manner of devilish things these
witches brought among you. Father Xabat and I will

examine the evidence for what we may find of the Evil One's presence."

He and Malcolm made a great show of examining the wreckage of the raft with its PVC gridwork, the transparent Filmar and ripstop nylon, the medical kit with its shiny foil packets and brightly colored pills, and the water purifying equipment which had washed ashore in the wreckage.

"And was this all?" Kit asked worriedly.

"No, Father," Sergeant Braz answered. "There were strange, devil-made guns which we cannot make sense of and even more frightening things."

They brought out an M-1 carbine, a beautiful .458 Winchester that must have belonged to Koot van Beek, and a stained leather bag containing Margo's ATLS and personal log. Kit and Malcolm exclaimed to one another in Latin, made worried sounds, conferred at length, took apart the "devil" guns to see what might be inside, and admitted bafflement over the strange equipment.

Kit finally announced Tierce service, which ate up a good bit of time, then returned to examining the "evidence" until time for Sext. After that, he questioned each of the traders closely about everything he had seen and done and felt and thought during the past six weeks. That took them to None service, which he and Malcolm dragged out nicely.

They had just finished None when a disturbance outside the fort brought a shout from one of the traders.

"The search parties are returning! Open the gate!"

Kit and Malcolm exchanged glances, then hurried after the soldiers who ran to open the fort's high wooden gates.

Kynan Rhys Gower was a strong swimmer. But when the raft broke up, throwing him into the water, something heavy caught him a grazing blow across the temple, stunning him. He floundered in the breakers, swept away from the wreckage by a powerful southerly current. Kynan managed to keep his face above water and let the sea carry him, too dazed to struggle and wise enough to marshall his strength before trying for shore.

Lightning flares showed him the curve of Delagoa Bay and the wretched little settlement he'd first seen seven weeks previously. The current swept him past it, inexorably southward. By the time he'd recovered enough to move his arms and legs against the current, Kynan estimated he'd been swept several miles south of the settlement on the wide bay—which meant Margo and Koot were trapped north of it, on the wrong side of the bay to reach the gate.

Kynan struck out for shore, wincing slightly at pulled muscles in his shoulder, and finally groped his way onto a rocky beach. He pulled himself on hands and knees above the line of crashing breakers, then collapsed to catch his breath. Rain pelted his back. He hadn't eaten a proper meal in days, felt dizzy and weak from hunger and his struggle with the sea.

Am I going to die here? And where am I, really? he wondered bleakly. *Africa,* Margo had said, but Kynan had only the haziest idea where Africa was—somewhere far south of Wales—and he hadn't known how to interpret the glowing chart she'd shown him on her "computer." He knew the men in the bay settlement were Portuguese. Kynan shivered. No love was lost between Welshmen and Portuguese.

The other men who lived here . . . The pictures Margo had shown him were difficult to credit. *Black* men in strange garments, carrying long, wicked spears he wouldn't have wanted to face one-on-one, not even on his best day. Which this clearly wasn't. Slowly Kynan sat up, squinting into the rain and dark wind. Lightning flares revealed the sea, lashing furiously at the coast.

As alone as he'd felt in the time station, the isolation he felt now paled that into insignificance. He was lost

a century after his own time and five centuries before
"TT-86" would exist, in a land where he looked nothing
like the native people and where the only men born in
Europe were his enemies. He had no food, no water,
no weapons, and no way of reliably obtaining more.
Without so much as a knife, he couldn't even make a
bow to hunt game. Of course, he could probably find
the gate again, if he stumbled around long enough
looking for it.

Kynan grimaced. *Never thought I would long to crawl
back into hell. . . .*

Of course, he'd begun to doubt that TT-86 *was* hell
over the past few weeks. He'd begun to change his mind
about the girl, Margo, too. She was a young fool
sometimes, but she had courage to match a warrior's.
He didn't understand why she had left her grandfather's
protection to hunt diamonds, any more than he
understood the reasons *any* "'eighty-sixer" did anything,
but he thought her grandsire would have been proud
to see her on their journey down the river to the sea.

The last he'd seen of her, she'd been struggling in
the sea, same as him. Kynan spat sand out of his mouth
and stumbled to his feet. He'd accepted her leadership
of his own free will. Kynan Rhys Gower did not abandon
his leaders when they were in trouble. Margo was
somewhere to the north. It was up to Kynan to find
her again and help her bring Koot van Beek back with
them through the gate.

He started walking and kept doggedly on, pausing
to rest only when his legs threatened to buckle. Each
time he rested, weariness urged him to just lie where
he'd fallen and sleep, but each time, he forced himself
back up. He kept going through the night and the long,
steaming day which followed, moving steadily northward
along the wild strand. Kynan caught the scent of the
Portuguese settlement before he came within sight of
the ramshackle little town: wood smoke, hogs, refuse.

He skirted inland past the broad bay where the Portuguese fort was, fighting exhaustion and thirst and trying to edge his way northward without raising an alarm. Kynan closed his hands, longing for some sort of weapon to defend himself, but he had none. He had only a sense of duty to drive him forward, step by aching step. Which did him no good at all when he staggered, unwitting, into an ambush.

One moment he was alone beneath a steaming forest canopy. The next, he was on the ground with Portuguese shouts in his ears and hard hands on his arms and legs. Kynan heaved and broke loose. He rolled and came to a crouch with his back against a tree trunk. Then swallowed hard. He faced half a dozen snarling Portuguese, all of them armed with guns or crossbows.

Honor demanded he fight. Duty demanded he try to escape and rescue his lost comrade and commander. A strong sense of practicality told him he could do neither, given his exhaustion and the unwavering weapons trained on him. One of the men grinned slowly and said something Kynan didn't understand. Then, in bad English: "Witch . . ."

Kynan's blood ran cold.

They'd found Margo or Koot van Beek or the raft—they would torture and burn him alive—

He groped behind the tree trunk, closed his hand around a chunk of stout deadwood. He'd rather be shot with gun and crossbow than burn. Then another, worse thought came to him. They would burn Margo, too, and the sick Afrikaaner who had taught Kynan to shoot the semi-magical rifle. If Kynan let these men kill him now, the others would have no chance of escape at all. If he let them take him alive . . .

They had to get free only long enough to gain the gate.

Kynan caught a ragged breath.

Then quietly surrendered.

✦   ✦   ✦

Kit and Malcolm gained the gates in time to see the search party return with a bloodied, bruised prisoner. Vines secured his wrists behind his back. The Welsh soldier was ash-pale but he stood erect, facing his doom with all the bravery in him.

One of the soldiers still inside the fort called out, "Looks like he put up a fight!"

Kynan's captors grinned. "Naw. Looked like he might for a minute, but he surrendered quiet as a lamb."

Kit narrowed his eyes. They'd beaten him afterward, then, badly, from the look of it. Why had he surrendered? That didn't fit the image of the Kynan Rhys Gower who'd attacked both Kit and Margo with single-minded, near-unstoppable fury. Kynan kept his gaze stonily on the ground, clearly aware that he faced his doom.

The Portuguese were gloating.

"Put him in the stocks," the governor crowed.

"No," Kit countered, allowing weariness to color his voice. "Put him in the cell with the woman. Father Xabat and I must examine him for Satan's mark."

Kynan flinched visibly at the word "Satan." He didn't quite struggle when the Portuguese shoved him toward the stockade, but he cursed them under his breath in Welsh. One of the soldiers struck him across the mouth, splitting a barely scabbed-over lip. Kynan stumbled and glared at his captors, but made no further sound. Kit and Malcolm exchanged glances.

"Brave man," Malcolm's look said.

Kit just nodded, then followed. Malcolm fell into step behind him. Their heavy cassocks dragged in the mud. Sergeant Braz unlocked the cell and shoved Kynan inside, then stepped aside for Kit and Malcolm. Once again, Malcolm shut the door. Margo sat in the corner, alert and silent. She took one look at Kynan and swallowed hard, but her eyes had begun to shine with hope. Kynan swayed, clearly at the end of his strength, but he said in broken English to Margo, "I . . . I look you. Portuguese," he snarled, spitting blood onto the dirt floor, "find me. I—I come, no fight. We run gate. I help, yes?"

Margo's eyes widened. She looked past Kynan to Kit, who had difficulty finding his voice. Kynan had surrendered, knowing what the Portuguese would do to them. . . . What had happened during the past seven weeks, to change Kynan's opinion of her so thoroughly?

Kit cleared his throat. "Kynan Rhys Gower."

The Welshman jerked around. His eyes widened. His mouth worked several times before any sound came out. "*You*—"

Then faint hope began to burn in his eyes. "Have you come to help us?" he asked quietly in his native tongue.

Kit didn't answer the obvious. Instead he asked, "Did you really surrender to the Portuguese to help my grandchild escape?"

Kynan flushed and dropped his gaze. "I accepted her leadership."

Ahh . . .

"Yes, but it was still uncommonly brave, duty or not. I will not forget this. Malcolm, free his hands. Do you have any idea where and when you are?"

The Welshman paused while Malcolm untied him. "I know we are in Africa and that Africa is south of Wales," he said, rubbing his wrists. "I know those whoresons are Portuguese, a pox on them all. I think it is a hundred years after . . . after I left my home."

"Yes, the year is 1542. The Portuguese think you and Margo are witches."

Kynan lost color again. "I know. They said so when they began to kick and beat me." He winced and shrugged. "I feared for a time they would kill me without benefit of a trial."

His smile was bitter and short-lived.

Kit said quietly, "We are still in very serious danger. There is a chance I will die before the gate opens again. It's complicated and you haven't learned enough about the gates yet, but the simple truth is, a man can't exist in two times at once. I am going to come very, very close to doing that. If I stay here too long, past the time when I exist someplace else this year, I will die."

The Welshman's face went through a whole series of unguarded expressions. Then, to Kit's astonishment, he went down on one knee. "I offer fealty, then, liege lord. Command me, that I may finish your task should you perish in this rescue."

Now was neither the time nor the place to try and explain that no oath of fealty was necessary. He simply accepted the pledge of vassalage. If they lived, he'd sort it out later. Margo looked on, wide-eyed.

"Now," Kit said quietly, "what we must do is hold a mock trial for witchcraft. . . ."

Malcolm ordered that the Welshman be given food and water, then treated his injuries. Kit ordained that he should be given a night's rest before the holy examination began. When they left, Malcolm felt marginally better about abandoning Margo. At least now she wasn't alone in that wretched little room.

They "examined" the Welshman in that same little room the next day, making a whole day affair of it— and really spent the time quietly discussing their plans, coming up with alternative courses of action should something go wrong. They planned the fake trial like a Broadway production. Only this play's outcome was far more critical than any theatrical spectacular ever to hit the streets of New York. And when they finished their plans, silent looks which passed between them said everyone was aware just how easily something could still go wrong.

The African sun was low in the summer sky when

Malcolm finally stepped out of the filthy little cell and held the door for Kit. The lean time scout wouldn't look at him. Margo had clung to Malcolm before their departure, revealing her feelings so transparently a blind man would have seen how she felt. Her farewell to Kit had been far more restrained. Her demonstration had shaken Malcolm, but it hadn't done anything to heal the breach between Kit and himself. As they shut the door, Kynan moved protectively between her and the Portuguese who locked them in, bringing Malcolm's opinion of the Welshman another notch higher.

Malcolm and Kit took the traders through Vespers before consenting to sit down to the evening meal. Dark looks and angry words between several of the men convinced Malcolm to put a plan of his own into action. If Kit wanted these men off-balance, he saw a golden opportunity to set them at one another. So at dinnertime, which the entire community had begun taking together at Kit's insistence, he lifted his hands and launched into a sermon on the evils of witchcraft in his Basque-accented Portuguese.

"Know you that the Evil One has demons to sniff out all your grievous sins and tempt you to even greater evil. You must be on your guard against anything that entices you to stray from God's path. If you see your neighbor shirking his duty, be assured Satan is working within that man, leading him down the path of damnation. Be harsh with your neighbor. Correct his behavior that you might guard his soul. You must help one another to find the narrow path again. If your neighbor indulges that cardinal sin of greed, you must help him to resist the error of his ways. If you stand guard at night and see the Evil One and his minions prowling about the town, looking for ways of creating mischief, you must charge him to be gone!"

Several of the soldiers lost color. Clearly, they'd seen *something* prowling the night. Monkeys, Malcolm was willing to bet, intent on raiding the garbage middens, possibly even leopards after the livestock. Tonight's watch ought to prove interesting.

"Does your fellow man swell with insufferable pride? Teach him humility, that he might rescue his soul from damnation. Avarice, pride, *gluttony*. Watch for these deadly sins. You *must root them out!*"

He delivered a final benediction. The whole cadre of soldiers, artisans, farmers, and landlocked sailors sat speechless, eying one another with growing suspicion and fear. The governor crossed himself and began to eat—but slowly, to avoid the impression that he had fallen prey to the sin of gluttony. The other men followed his example, eying one another uneasily while they ate. *Which of you*, Malcolm could practically read their thoughts, *summoned the Evil One with his wickedness?*

Later, alone, Kit eyed him coldly. "Hope to hell you know what you're doing."

"You wanted them off balance. Next couple of days ought to be interesting."

Kit just grunted and stomped off to bed. Kit's plan to keep the men unsettled and tired was certainly working on *Malcolm*. He was numb with exhaustion.

"Good night," Malcolm said quietly.

Kit's only reply was a brusque, "Hope you sleep like hell, buddy."

Malcolm held his tongue. He'd take Kit's anger and swallow it raw. *Consider it penance, Father Xabat.* Malcolm did manage to fall asleep eventually; but his dreams were violent, waking him well before midnight. He rolled over in the darkness and stared at the invisible wooden ceiling.

How could he ever patch his friendship with Kit? Malcolm owed the retired scout more favors than he could ever repay, not the least of which was the trust Kit had placed in him to guard Margo. The knowledge that she huddled in the darkness, locked into a filthy cell with nothing more than a coarse shirt and a flea-ridden blanket to cover her, when she needed medical treatment . . . He closed his fists in his own coarse blanket. Those wretched traders could have given her venereal diseases, could've gotten her pregnant—

Malcolm turned onto his side and clenched his teeth. *He* could have gotten her pregnant. He couldn't blame Kit one jot for the cold, murderous looks. Malcolm couldn't help the way he felt about Margo, but he could've restrained that wild, drunken impulse on a street in Rome. *That*, he could have prevented.

I'll make it up somehow, he promised. *Somehow.* He hadn't yet figured out how when a wild scream and gunshots shattered the silence. Another man screamed in mortal agony.

Then the alarm bell clanged wildly.

Kit rolled out of bed, one hand going for the push daggers in his ATLS bag. Then he blinked and said, "What the hell?"

"My plans coming to fruition, I think," Malcolm said drily.

Thudding footsteps ran toward their door. Then a frantic knock shook it on its hinges. Malcolm struggled to his feet and threw the door wide. "What is it?" he asked worriedly. "We heard the shots and the bell—"

"Oh, Father, come quickly, please . . ." It was Francisco, one of the soldiers. His voice shook.

Malcolm followed, with Kit hurrying in his wake. They found Zadornin, the Basque sailor, lying in the mud near the fort wall. He'd been shot through the chest. Clearly, the man was dying.

"I did see a demon, Father," the sailor gasped, "atop the wall. I screamed and the watch fired. . . ."

"It was a misshapen beast," Peli, one of the soldiers quavered. "It had the likeness of a man and it cried out with Zadornin's voice. We fired and it vanished with a screech, leaving poor Zadornin to die in its place."

The sailor was fainting from shock and blood loss. The hole in his chest was at least eighty caliber. Malcolm took his hand and spoke last rites while he died. The sailor's death shook him badly, but Malcolm steeled himself with the thought that these men had permitted Koot van Beek to die and planned to kill Margo and Kynan using the hideous methods reserved for witches. He crossed himself in time to hear a fight break out among the soldiers of the watch.

"If you hadn't been asleep, God curse you—"

"If you could shoot an arquebus as well as you shirk your duty—"

The fist fight was brutal and short. Malcolm and Kit watched wordlessly. Malcolm, at any rate, had no intention of soothing the shaken soldiers. When it was over, Amaro sported a broken nose and Lorenco spat out a couple of teeth.

"I suggest," Kit said coldly, "that you bury the man you have murdered. Do so at once. When you have finished, we will begin Matins."

The soldiers grumbled into the stubble of their beards and went in search of shovels to dig the grave.

Margo sat in her prison until nearly mid-morning, overhearing the sound of violent quarrels between her captors. Whatever Kit and Malcolm were doing, it was creating havoc. *Good!* The gunshots the previous night had jolted her out of nightmares. She had no idea what had happened, but hoped neither Malcolm nor Kit had been directly involved. Her greatest terror was that Kit would die before they could make good their escape, leaving Malcolm alone in a hostile camp of abruptly suspicious Portuguese.

The soldiers came for her shortly before mid-morning. She was clad only in a rough shirt that covered her to her thighs. Margo snatched the blanket and wrapped it around her waist as a skirt. When that hideous Sergeant

Braz seized her wrists, Margo spat in his face. He backhanded her into the wall. She slid to the floor, weeping and holding her face. Dimly, she heard Kit's voice, speaking angrily in Portuguese.

Then Malcolm appeared out of the blur. She retained just enough sense not to throw her arms around him. He helped her to her feet, then escorted her outside. A table and chairs had been set up in the fort's open courtyard. The military governor—Margo shuddered at the memory—sat in the front row of seats. His soldiers stood guard, looking like they'd been in a fist fight half the night. Other men squatted on the ground or stood in uneasy clusters, watching the proceedings.

Kit seated himself behind the table and dipped a quill pen into an inkwell, writing something meticulous on thick sheets of parchment. He glanced up and gestured Malcolm to the front of the table. Malcolm led Margo to the open space between table and audience. Kit sat back and looked up at her. Margo felt a chill. If she hadn't known he was playing a part, she would have despaired.

He spoke in Portuguese. Malcolm said in English, "You are on trial for witchcraft, girl. What is your name?"

There was at least one man in that audience who understood a little English. Margo lifted her head. "Margo Smith."

"And you are English?"

"I am."

Malcolm spoke briefly to Kit in Portuguese. Kit scribbled something onto his parchment. Then he began to speak. Malcolm translated a list of charges, which began with "You are accused of consorting with the devil to make yourself and others fly through the air by means of foul magic" and ended nearly half an hour later with "and lastly, you are accused of summoning storms by the combing of your hair, which did cause the wreckage of a Portuguese ship and the loss of all hands but two." They even threw in summoning demons to make the sheep bleat at the wrong hour of the night.

"How do you plead to these serious charges of witchcraft?"

Margo turned her head just far enough to stare directly into the military governor's eyes. She curled her lip. "Even if I were a witch, I would not waste such powerful magic on these men. They are not worthy of it. I am innocent and they are liars, murderers, and rapists."

Malcolm translated her reply. The governor came to his feet with a roar and threatened Margo with the back of his hand. Malcolm snapped something that caused him to resume his seat.

The "trial" was the most amazing thing Margo had ever witnessed. She was required to repeat phrases in Latin. Every syllable she stumbled over was duly noted on Kit's parchment and commented on by the sullen audience. She was stripped naked and searched. Birthmarks and a tiny mole were pointed out and recorded. She glared at Kit, who returned her gaze coldly.

Malcolm said, "Put on your clothes, English. You offend God."

"Not as much as you do!" she snapped.

Kit glanced up reproachfully.

Then they escorted her down to the bay. Two soldiers picked her up bodily and heaved her into the water. Margo squealed in shock and landed with a heavy splash. The water was *deep*. She swam for the surface, gasped, and glared at the soldiers. The men were muttering worriedly. When Malcolm fished her out, she snapped, "What are you trying to do? Drown me?"

"Witches," Malcolm said coldly, "float. The innocent sink."

"Huh!" *Great way to get rid of a problem. Drown 'em or burn 'em.*

By the time they dragged her back to the fort, it was

nearing noon. Kit asked her questions which made absolutely no sense at all. Most of them she couldn't begin to answer. Kit shook his head mournfully and wrote in his parchment. It was nearly dark when they finally escorted her back to her cell and gave her bread, soup, and wine.

If Kit hadn't made clear yesterday that he intended to find her "guilty" she would have been terrified. Margo shivered as it was. What if something went wrong? What if they began the execution and Kit simply vanished, having shadowed himself? Not only would Kit die, so would she, and most likely Kynan and Malcolm, too. The idea of burning to death left her sweating into her coarse, filthy shirt. She clenched her hands and tried to pray, then paced the little cell. Surely they would pull it off. Kit knew what he was doing.

But as Kit had admonished her time and again, even trained scouts ran into fatal trouble sometimes.

The next morning, they took Kynan away. He was gone all day, put through the same ordeals she'd been through. When the lock finally grated open and Kynan was thrust bodily inside, he was pale. In his bad English, he said, "Is not good. Portuguese scared. Mad. Not good."

"No. It isn't good. I'm . . ." She hesitated, then said it anyway. "I'm scared."

He took her hand, holding it gently. "Yes. Margo is brave. Brave have fear. Is true."

She swallowed hard. "Yes. Very true."

He managed a rueful smile. "In Orléans, Kynan fear. Fear French. Fear Margo. True."

She started to laugh and ended up crying on his shoulder. If he thought less of her for it, he didn't let it show.

During the night, more screams and gunshots rang out. Margo started awake, then muttered, "Good!" and heard an answering grunt from Kynan. No one shouted for Kit or Malcolm, though, so no one must have died this time. The next day—the day the gate was supposed to reopen—the Portuguese brought them both out to hear the "testimony" of their accusers. Not that it did Margo or Kynan any good. The testimony was all in Portuguese. But the angry, fearful looks sent their way and the sleepless hollows under most eyes told Margo that Kit and Malcolm's plans were bearing fruit.

Given the shouting match and fist fight that ensued during the afternoon, the Portuguese had begun to accuse one another of witchcraft charges. Kit ordered Margo and Kynan locked up while the soldiers broke up the vicious little fight with blows from the butts of their arquebuses. Margo wondered when Kit would make his move. They were running short on time. The gate would be opening in just a few hours—if it opened at all.

The longer they waited, the more terror stretched her nerves taut. Something had gone wrong. They'd slipped up, somehow, their ruse had been discovered, or Kit had vanished, leaving Malcolm to face the whole superstitious, murderous bunch. . . .

The sun was sinking into the heart of the distant Drakensbergs when the door opened a last time. Margo's heart pounded unsteadily beneath her rib cage as she came slowly to her feet. Kynan, too, scrambled up to face the Portuguese sergeant who'd unlocked their cell. The sergeant wouldn't meet their gaze. He crossed himself and moved hastily aside. Malcolm stood behind him. He gazed coldly into the cell without speaking, then said roughly, "You have been found guilty of witchcraft, Margo Smith. You will be taken far from Lourenço Marques where you will be put to death by burning. May God pity your soul."

Margo stared at him, hardly recognizing the gentle man who had loved her in Rome. Then, recalling the part she had to play, Margo gave out a shriek and sank toward the ground. Her theatrical faint was so convincing, Kynan caught her with a cry. He held her protectively. Kit appeared behind Malcolm and said something in Welsh. Kynan didn't speak a word. He just snarled like a trapped wolf.

Oh, God, Margo thought while her heart triphammered, *let this work!*

Soldiers herded them out of the cell. They were taken across the open courtyard while the rest of the men crossed themselves and avoided their gaze. Kynan marched stolidly between the soldiers, placing one hand protectively on Margo's waist. The gesture brought tears to her eyes.

Kit and Malcolm followed, intoning something in Latin. Both of them had slung their ATLS bags over their shoulders. It was the only hopeful sign she saw. They passed a wagon and a thin horse in harness. The remains of Margo's PVC raft and Filmar balloon and everything which had survived the wreck had been piled into it. An ominously large stack of wood and two long, thick stakes also weighed it down. Several of the Portuguese stood near it, holding pikes and lit torches. Margo let her steps falter. Then she sank to her knees, weeping. Given the fear jolting through her that something would yet go wrong, tears were remarkably easy to conjure. Kynan lifted her back to her feet and glared at their executioners.

Farther along, waiting for them to pass, were that pig of a military governor and the rest of his disgusting, unwashed swine. All of them carried weapons: black powder firearms, cocked crossbows, swords, or murderous long pikes and daggers. Margo tried to keep her spirits from sinking, but she couldn't see how Kit planned to escape with an armed contingent that size acting as guard.

They marched completely out of the walled village and moved down the beach, heading south around the

wide curve of the bay. Margo remembered the layout
of the land. Kit was herding them closer to the gate.
The whole parade marched down the wave-scoured
beach, moving grimly, silently. Only the creak of the
wagon and the crackle of the torches rose above the
sound of sea and wind. Kit moved into the lead as though
searching for something. Whatever it was, he clearly
wasn't finding it. Margo knew the gate would open
somewhere close to here, but she couldn't remember
precisely where, either.

Kit finally lifted his arms and spoke in Portuguese.
The wagon rolled to a halt near him. Roughly dressed
men began unloading it. An enormous bear of a man
hammered the terrifying stakes into the ground. Sailors
piled wood high around them. Kit spoke earnestly in
Latin to the skies as though she and Kynan didn't even
exist. The wreckage of Margo's raft was added to the
pile, along with everything else which had survived.
She checked the slant of the sun. *Any time now,
surely . . .*

If the gate opened again.

Or if Kit didn't die any moment, shadowing himself.
If, if, if . . .

She noticed sweat on his face and began to tremble.
Malcolm's skin had taken on a ghastly hue. He produced
a coil of rope and bound one of Margo's wrists securely.

"Pretend I've tied your other wrist behind you once
you're at the stake," he hissed in her ear. Then he dragged
her toward the pile of wood.

Margo screamed and struggled. He caught her wrists
and lifted her off the ground, doggedly climbing the
stacked wood and shoving her against the stake. Margo
begged for mercy, sliding to her knees and clutching
his robes. He sobbed out something in Portuguese
and snatched her back to her feet, then dragged her
hands behind her. He jerked her wrists behind the
stake. Margo screamed again. The audience hung on

their every movement like hypnotized sports fans. Margo felt sick. Malcolm wound the rope around her hand without looping it around her wrist. All she had to do was let go and she'd be free. Margo slumped against the stake as though tightly bound and gave in to wretched sobs.

Kit dragged Kynan Rhys Gower to the stake. From her vantage point, she could see that Kit repeated the same procedure with the Welshman's wrists. Kynan was white to the lips. He held his head high and intoned something in a loud voice, speaking in his own native tongue. He might have been heaping curses on the Portuguese or praying to God to let this mad scheme work.

Kit stumbled back down the piled wood and turned to face them. He lifted both hands, a crucifix clenched in one fist. He began to chant in Latin. Whatever it was, it went on and on. Sweat beaded up on his lips and dripped down his chin. Malcolm kept darting nervous glances in the direction Margo thought the gate ought to lie.

Nothing was happening.

The sun sank lower, vanishing behind the distant peaks of the Drakensbergs. The crash of waves was loud in her ears. Seabirds screamed overhead. *It's not opening, oh God, it isn't going to open . . .* On the ground below the pyre, Kit sank to his knees and bowed his head. Malcolm followed suit. The rest of the company went to their knees as well. Torches crackled in the growing twilight. Still no gate opened. Kit couldn't delay this much longer. The military governor was staring at him, darting uneasy glances toward the as-yet unlit pyre. A few glimmering stars appeared in the darkening sky.

Then the bones behind Margo's ear began to vibrate.

She caught her breath on a sob—

Then let out an ear-piercing shriek.

❖   ❖   ❖

At the first buzz of the gate, Malcolm went giddy with relief. Then Margo screamed. He started and whirled to stare at her. Even Kit jumped.

"HEAR ME!" Margo shouted. "I CALL UPON THE POWERS OF HELL!"

Malcolm staggered to his feet, holding up his crucifix. The soldier who spoke a little English began to shout that she was calling upon the Evil One himself.

Kit ran toward the pyre, snatching a torch from a dumbfounded farmer. "Minion of hell!" he cried. "Cease thy conjuring! I command thee in the name of Christ!"

Margo shouted at him to stuff it. Then she started ranting. "You will all die hideous deaths if you lay that torch to this pyre! I call on Beelzebub! I call on Satan, Lucifer, St. Nick—"

St. Nick?

From Malcolm's vantage point, Kit nearly lost it. With masterful skill, he converted sudden laughter into a cough and a cry of pain. He sank to his knees, gasping and clutching his chest as though her curses were having real effect. Semi-hysterical images flitted briefly through Malcolm's head, threatening to loose his own laughter—

But Margo was still shouting.

And the soldiers nearest her were swearing in terror, pointing their crossbows right at her. *Oh shit . . .*

Malcolm flung himself between the crossbows and the still-unlit pyre. "No! Do not interfere in God's work!"

"But Father—" one of them cried, ashen and sweating in the descending gloom.

The vibration of the gate had grown so painful several farmers and sailors had dropped their weapons. They clutched their ears, staring wildly around for the appearance of the most profoundly expected demons. Malcolm lifted his own crucifix and advanced toward the piled wood. Kit outdid himself. He twisted on the ground, then crawled to his knees, coughing and holding up his own crucifix.

In a voice faint with terror, Kit cried, "I command thee, in the name of Christ, begone Satan! God will protect us!"

"Satan will eat your entrails for lunch!" Margo screamed right back.

One of the shaking farmers let out a wail of terror—and hurled his torch straight onto the pyre. Wood shavings crackled and roared into flame. Margo screamed, then shrieked at the poor farmer, "St. Nick will have your guts for sausages!"

Kit, not to be outdone, rose tottering to his feet and lifted both arms, trembling so violently even Malcolm was halfway convinced he was about to fall down again. "Jesu Christo! Open the gates of hell itself! Send these minions of damnation to their deaths!"

Then Kit hurled his own torch like a thrown javelin—
—straight at the source of the sound that wasn't a sound.

Twenty-five yards down the beach, a crack appeared in the fabric of reality. The torch sailed straight through it. Someone behind Malcolm screamed. Someone else began chanting hail Marys. Another man began to sob. Half the Portuguese broke and ran for town, wailing in terror. The gate dilated open, pulsing savagely in the mad rhythm of an unstable string.

"NOW!" Kit yelled.

Margo flung herself down the pile of burning wood, jumping right through the flames. Kynan Rhys Gower followed with a wild yell. Malcolm caught a blur of motion—

The huge blacksmith had aimed his weapon at Margo's back.

Malcolm lunged forward. He knocked the barrel of the smith's rifled wheel lock upward just as the piece discharged. The smith roared. Malcolm dodged away.
—Then delivered a snap kick that flattened an arquebusier trying to fire on Margo.

Then he ran through the confused, shaken crowd. "Kit! Run!"

The time scout dove at the fire instead, snatching something out of it, then whirled, knocking aside a white-faced soldier just before his arquebus went off with a roar. A lead ball slammed into the beach less than a foot short of Margo's flying feet. The soldier snarled and charged. Kit brushed him to the ground. The man screamed. Malcolm caught the glint of push daggers in the firelight. *Nothing like Aikido and a push-dagger blade to ruin your whole day.*

Someone else levelled a crossbow at Kit's back.

Malcolm delivered a flying kick that knocked the man to the sand, then he was past and running for the gate.

"Kit!" he yelled. "It's disintegrating!"

Margo reached the gate first. It shrank savagely to a pinpoint. She sobbed out something Malcolm couldn't quite hear. Kynan skidded to a halt beside her. The gate roared open again. Kynan glanced back and shouted. Malcolm looked wildly over one shoulder. Behind them, Amaro had taken a careful bead on Margo with his crossbow. Malcolm couldn't do anything to stop him and Kit was out of position—

Kynan yelled and flung himself between Margo and the arbalestier. The Welshman knocked her to the ground with a sweeping blow, shoving her out of harm's way. The slap of the steel spring was a hideous sound. Kynan screamed and collapsed like a punctured balloon. A steel shaft thick as Malcolm's thumb slammed through Kynan's body instead of Margo's chest.

Margo sobbed once and crawled to him, trying to stanch the bleeding with her hands. Malcolm lunged the final yard to the gate. "Go!" He shoved her bodily through. She sprawled into Phil Jones' shop with a hoarse yell. Malcolm scooped up the injured Welshman in a fireman's carry. Kynan groaned and fainted. Malcolm lunged through, tripping over Margo and dropping

Kynan to the concrete floor. Margo howled in pain and crawled out from under him. Malcolm came to his feet and whirled. "Kit!"

He was running for the gate.

The time scout gasped with effort and dove forward. He crashed into Malcolm just as the gate shrank with a roar like a freight train. Malcolm landed on hard concrete. Kit swore hideously and cradled one arm. A crackle of fire and thick, acrid smoke roared into Malcolm's awareness. One of the totem poles in Phil Jones' store room had caught fire from Kit's thrown torch. A crossbow bolt, covered with blood and bits of Kynan's flesh, stuck obscenely out of another.

Above them, the gate vanished as though it had never been.

CHAPTER TWENTY

An instant later, the fire-control system cut in, spraying clouds of halon into the room.

"Out!" Kit cried.

Malcolm helped carry Kynan into Phil Jones' office. Margo ran for the phone to call in a medical emergency, then ran interference, as well, driving Phil Jones bodily out of their way when he started shouting that they'd ruined his inventory, his business, and his life. When he didn't shut up, she tossed him through the doorway into his showroom. The last glimpse Malcolm had of her, she was *standing* on him.

Kit stripped off Kynan's shirt and stanched bleeding as best he could with direct pressure. Malcolm stripped off his woolen cassock and cut thick compresses. "Here . . ."

They applied the compresses and more pressure. Kynan moaned. His eyelids fluttered, then he sought Kit's gaze. His eyes were glazed.

"My lord . . . I'm . . . dying . . ." He groped weakly for Kit's arm.

"No," Kit said roughly, "you won't die, Kynan Rhys Gower. I won't allow it."

"Aye," Kynan breathed, allowing his eyes to close again. "My life is . . . yours. . . ."

Kit had said just the right thing. Maybe—just maybe—the man's superstitious faith that his liege lord could work magic would keep him alive. Long enough for station medical to arrive, anyway. . . . The bleet of the medi-van's siren was the most welcome sound Malcolm had heard since the buzz of the gate in the African twilight. Rachel Eisenstein and another duty doctor raced into the office.

"Cross-bow bolt," Kit said tersely.

Rachel took over, rigging pressure bandages, stabilizing Kynan's vitals with IVs, treating for shock. "Prepare for thoracic surgery," Rachel said into her radio link with the station's hospital. "Stat! We're bringing in a bad one."

"Roger."

They lifted Kynan carefully onto a gurney and ran for the medi-van. Silence, sudden and brutal, descended on the smoky office. Kit scrubbed his brow with the heel of a bloody hand. Malcolm leaned against Phil's desk and rubbed aching ribs where Kit's lunge for safety had caught him. For a moment, neither of them spoke.

Then Kit glanced his way. "Malcolm . . ."

He looked up. A rarely seen look which everyone dreaded having pointed at *them* was levelled straight at him. Malcolm winced. *Well, you've been waiting for this.*

"All right," Kit said quietly. "Let's hear it."

"What do you want me to say, Kit? I'm sorrier than you'll ever know. Breaking a friend's trust . . . Well, I *am* British. For whatever that's worth. I've no excuses, Kit. So I won't even try to make any. But lame as it sounds, I thought she'd just turned nineteen, Kit, not *seventeen*, and . . . and dammit, that headstrong little idiot does something to me. . . ."

Kit snorted.

Malcolm adjusted himself against the hard desk, wincing slightly. "She's been hurt, Kit. Desperately. If I ever find out who did it, I think I might actually kill him. There's something fine inside her fighting to get out. I see glimpses of it all the time. First in London,

again in Brighton. Then in Rome . . ." He swore softly.
"We were both a little drunk. Hilaria was in full swing.
She was doing so well and I was so proud of her and
the next thing I knew . . ."

"Stop." Kit held up one hand. "Please."

Malcolm halted. Then, very quietly, "It isn't much,
but I never meant any of this. I'm bloody sorry, Kit. I
won't say I'd undo the way I feel about her, but I'm
bloody *damned* sorry for how I've handled this, the mess
I've caused. If it's any consolation, I went through nine
days of absolute hell, thinking I'd killed her." He groped
for something else to say and ended lamely with the
only thing he *could* say. "I'm sorry, Kit."

"So am I," his one-time friend sighed.

"I'll . . . I'll go to another station, I guess, get out of
your way . . ."

"Malcolm."

He shut up, ready to take whatever bitter anger his
friend vented.

"I ought to break your neck, you know. I'm tempted
to saddle you with the Neo Edo. The punishment ought
to fit the crime, after all. You *deserve* that paperwork
and the government auditors and the inspections
and . . ."

Malcolm winced.

"But . . ." Kit's faint smile shocked him. "At least she
had enough sense to pick someone like you."

Malcolm didn't know what to say.

"It *might* have been Skeeter Jackson, after all."

Malcolm found his voice after all, surprising both of
them. Kit just stared. "Where *do* you pick up language
like that?"

Malcolm managed a wan smile. "Believe it or not, I
overheard that one from a Praetorian guardsman the
day Caligula was murdered."

"Really? Some day you *must* tell me the whole story
about that day."

Malcolm let his gaze focus on something far beyond Phil Jones' sordid little office. "Maybe. I'm not sure I'll ever tell anyone the *whole* story."

Kit cleared his throat. "Know the feeling," he muttered. He scrubbed bloody hands on his ruined Jesuit cassock, then cleared his throat again and held out one hand. "I don't have enough friends to lose one. Not even for something like this."

Malcolm paused only a moment, then shook it. "I'll make it up, Kit."

The lean time scout grinned. "You sure as hell will. And if she's pregnant . . ." He let the threat dangle.

Malcolm just groaned.

The office door opened. Kit and Malcolm looked up to find Margo staring down at them. Clad in a ragged Portuguese shirt, face and hands smeared with soot and blood, eyes hardened by what she'd been through, Malcolm hardly recognized her.

"No broken bones, I see," she said quietly. "Good. Because Rome was my fault, too. In fact, Rome was *mostly* my fault." Malcolm didn't know what to say. Clearly, Kit didn't either. "I would just like to say for the record that I don't deserve either one of you. But I think I've learned my lesson—oh, hell, I've learned more lessons in the past seven weeks than I have in the last seventeen years. I screwed up *everything*. Everyone was right and I was wrong and I'm so damned sorry I nearly got us all killed, I . . . I could almost go back to Minnesota and hide. . . ."

Her voice cracked.

Oh-oh. Better try and lighten the mood a bit . . .

"You know," Malcolm said off-handedly, "there's something you really ought to know before your next scouting trip."

She blinked tears, sounding absolutely miserable. "What?"

"Mmm . . ." He glanced at Kit and winked. "There's

rather a large difference between *Old* Nick and *Saint* Nick."

She stared at him, so nonplussed she forgot to keep crying. "Old Nick? Saint Nick? What are you talking about?"

Malcolm glanced at Kit. The scout's lips quirked. Then his eyes crinkled and he couldn't contain it any longer. He started to laugh. Malcolm grinned. Margo, clad in nothing but an Irish alley-cat glare and a too-loose sixteenth-century shirt, glared from one to the other as though they'd misplaced their collective wits.

"What's so funny?" she demanded.

Kit lay back and roared.

Malcolm wiped his eyes. "You called down the wrath of *Santa Claus* . . ."

Margo opened her lips over air. Then she started to chuckle. "I did?"

"Oh, Margo," Kit gasped, "you sure as hell did, honey."

Malcolm was still wiping tears. "It was priceless. I had visions of the heavens splitting open and a vengeful team of reindeer screaming down at Mach eight while the jolly old elf threw Christmas boxes like grenades. . . ."

That set Kit off again. Margo just grinned, taking the ribbing with surprisingly good humor. Then her laughter vanished.

Kit sat up hastily. "What's wrong? Oh, hell. . . . You're hurt and here we are laughing like idiots—"

"No . . . no, it's Kynan." She sank to her knees beside him. "Why did he do that? Throw himself in front of me that way?"

Kit touched a bruised cheek. "He pledged me as his liege lord. You instantly became the object of his sworn protection, his liege lady if you will. He considered it a sacred duty to die in my service, protecting you."

Margo swallowed hard. "I see. I . . ." Her face crumpled. "I'm sorry. I don't mean to snivel. Will he live?"

Kit smiled. "I'd say you earned a sniffle or two. And Rachel doesn't like losing patients. He has a very good chance, anyway." Kit dragged a scorched leather bag out of the corner. "I rescued your ATLS and log from the fire, by the way."

She opened the bag slowly, removing the ATLS, the personal log, even a folded chart.

"What's that?" Malcolm asked curiously.

"The map Goldie gave me." She thrust it at Kit. "I don't want it."

Kit took it wordlessly and tucked it into his own ATLS bag. "Speaking of Goldie . . . I think we need to hold a little chat with that avaricious old shark."

"You're telling me! She almost got us killed!"

Kit turned a reproachful glance on her.

"Well, all right, I almost got us killed. But she *knew* I was hopelessly unqualified!"

"Comes with the territory," Malcolm told her unsympathetically. "It's too bad her scam will work. She deserves to lose her shirt."

Margo sniffed. "As much trouble as I had finding that stupid spot on the river, those damned diamonds had *better* be there. I'd hate to think I put everyone through all this and got poor Mr. van Beek killed, only to find I'd screwed up and stuck them in the wrong place."

"You had trouble finding the right spot?"

Malcolm knew that tone. Kit was suddenly and profoundly interested. "What trouble, exactly?"

Margo wiped her nose. "The maps didn't match, not exactly. Here." She dug out her log and pulled up a file, then turned the screen to face him. "That's the digital snapshot I made of the river valley where we buried the stuff. I had to scan in Goldie's chart and superimpose the two. They still didn't quite match up, but I'm sure I got the right plot of ground."

Kit studied the screen intently, then started to grin.

"What?"

"Margo, I think I just might be able to pay back every scam Goldie has ever run on me. Malcolm, take a look."

Malcolm peered over Kit's shoulder. Then he, too, began to grin.

"What?"

"The river changed course."

"So?"

Malcolm said patiently, "Look. Here and here and here. See? It's at least a hundred yards off right here and more than fifty here . . ."

Margo frowned. Then she got it. Her eyes widened. "You mean—" She started to laugh.

Kit grinned. "Yep. Hell, it's *better* than beating her at pool." He tottered to his feet and gave Margo a hand up. "You, young lady, march straight to the infirmary. Leave Goldie to me."

Malcolm rubbed metaphoric hands in anticipation. He could hardly wait to see this one.

EPILOGUE

Goldie Morran wandered into the Down Time and sank into a chair. Kit and Malcolm left their table and sat down at hers.

"What's wrong, Goldie?" Kit asked.

The gems and currency expert sniffed autocratically. "It's that stupid granddaughter of yours. She put the diamonds in the wrong place."

"Oh?" Malcolm asked innocently.

"We dug up a square fifty yards on a side around the spot on that map. Nothing. Not a trace. My up-time rube has withdrawn his offer to buy the whole parcel. I can't believe we went through all that and she didn't get the right place. God *knows* where she put them."

Kit had received his own confirmation from up-time sources that Goldie was, for once, telling God's own truth.

Malcolm put in, "Well, Margo buried them—what? Four hundred fifty years ago? Anything could have happened. A flash flood might have washed the whole mess out. Or someone could have dug the stuff up years ago and quietly sold it off. Who could tell? It was a great idea, Goldie. Too bad it didn't work."

"Yeah," she said glumly. "Too bad. *Damn* that girl. . . ."

Kit consoled her by ordering Goldie's favorite. She sipped disconsolately.

"How much money did you lose?" Kit asked quietly.

"Ten thousand dollars! I paid for that whole benighted expedition, not to mention that worthless piece of farmland! It's so riddled with tse-tse flies you can't even run cattle on it!"

"I feel really terrible," Kit said earnestly. "After all, I did train Margo. Her mistake is my mistake."

Goldie sniffed again. "You always were too nice for your own good, Kit. Thanks anyway. I'm still out ten thousand."

"Tell you what. I'm determined to drive home the lessons Margo's learning from this fiasco. How about I make her pay you back?"

"Pay me back?" Goldie echoed. "Why?"

"To teach her the value of getting her geography right."

Goldie sniffed once more, but her eyes had begun to gleam. "What did you have in mind?"

Gotcha! "Margo will be spending the next eight years or so in college. She's agreed to pay back every penny of her education out of what she earns as a scout. I'd like to tack an extra ten thousand onto the price tag. How's this? I'll buy the land. Then, every vacation Margo has, I'll go up time and make her fly, walk, and *crawl* every inch of that river valley until she learns how to do aerial mapping *right.*"

Goldie hesitated, a veteran angler playing her "fish" with seasoned skill. "I don't know, Kit. That's an awfully expensive lesson."

Kit grunted. "Not half as expensive as losing your granddaughter. Which, I might add, I damn near did."

"Not to mention my life and Kit's," Malcolm added. "And that Welshman almost died on the operating table. Koot van Beek *did* die."

Goldie hurried to change the subject. "About this proposition of yours . . . are you serious?"

"Dead serious," Kit muttered darkly. "Margo isn't setting foot across another gate until she's learned every lesson I insist she master. Getting geography right is critical. If she'd done a better job of it, Koot van Beek might still be alive."

Goldie tossed back the rest of her drink. "All right. I'm willing to help teach her a lesson. Come on, I have the paperwork down at my office."

Malcolm, God bless him, maintained an absolute poker face.

Goldie couldn't sign over the deed to the Shashe River property fast enough. Kit duly transferred ten thousand from his account into hers while Malcolm witnessed the signatures. "Goldie," Kit said, kissing her hand gallantly, "you have a grandfather's undying gratitude."

"My pleasure. Young people must learn, after all." Goldie's cheeks were faintly flushed. No one loved a scam quite as much as Goldie Morran.

Unless, of course, it was Kit Carson.

Two weeks later, Malcolm Moore's computer-mail queue beeped, letting him know he had a package from up time waiting at Customs. He signed for the box, which had been sealed by up-time ATF customs authorities. The return address was scrawled in Margo's hand. Malcolm spotted a second package like it for Kit.

He grinned, then made tracks for the Neo Edo.

"Kit around?"

"Yeah," Jimmy told him. "It's paperwork day again. You want me to buzz him?"

"Nah. I'll surprise him."

Jimmy grinned. "That man will do *anything* to avoid paperwork."

Malcolm laughed. "Can you blame him?"

"Hell, no."

Malcolm rapped on the office door. Kit's "Yeah, it's open" sounded vastly relieved.

Malcolm slid back the door and kicked off his shoes. He held up his mail. "Package from Margo. There's one for you, too, waiting at Customs."

Kit came around the desk like a thrown baseball. "Well, open it!"

Malcolm tore the seals and ripped open the cardboard. Inside was a metal box which he tilted carefully out. The lid slipped back to reveal a single item: a glittering diamond in the rough, nearly as big as Malcolm's thumbnail.

Kit whooped. "*She did it!*"

Malcolm held it up to the light, then whistled. She sure had. "That," Malcolm sighed, "is truly beautiful." And if she still felt the same way in a few months, maybe he'd even have it made into a ring . . .

Well, stranger things had happened to him lately. Their parting had been enough to shake both of them to the core. Who knew? Maybe she'd even broken his notorious string of bad luck?

Now *that* would be a switch.

"I think," Malcolm grinned, "this calls for a celebration."

Kit broke out champagne from his private stock and poured bubbly, then handed over a glass. "How about a toast?"

Malcolm waited expectantly.

Kit lifted his glass. "To the best damn time scouts in La-La Land. Partner." He slid over a signed document giving Malcolm and Margo each a third-share interest in the land Kit had bought from Goldie Morran. Malcolm just gaped.

"You earned it. We all did. Hope you don't mind paying Kynan Rhys Gower out of our joint profits?"

Malcolm's eyes misted. "Hear, hear. I'd say that's a bargain any day of the week." They touched glasses with a musical *clink*.

"Now, partner," Kit grinned, "about that story you were going to tell me . . . the one about Caligula's murder and Claudius' ascension to the Principate of Rome."

"Oh, no," Malcolm laughed. "First you have to spill the beans about what really happened when you spent the night hiding under Queen Victoria's bed."

Kit grinned. "I *never* compromise a lady. You first."

No one, Malcolm chuckled, could bamboozle and flummox his way out of the truth like a time scout. At last, La-La Land was back to normal. Thank God. Malcolm settled back in one of Kit's chairs and started spinning the tallest tale he could concoct about that day in Rome five years previously—and two thousand years in the past—and made himself a silent promise.

If Margo could risk it, so could he. *Malcolm Moore and Margo Smith, Time Scouts . . .*

It had a nice ring to it.

continued ☞

DAVID WEBER

The Honor Harrington series: *(cont.)*

Field of Dishonor

Honor goes home to Manticore—and fights for her life on a battlefield she never trained for, in a private war that offers just two choices: death—or a "victory" that can end only in dishonor and the loss of all she loves....

Flag in Exile

Hounded into retirement and disgrace by political enemies, Honor Harrington has retreated to planet Grayson, where powerful men plot to reverse the changes she has brought to their world. And for their plans to suceed, Honor Harrington must die!

Honor Among Enemies

Offered a chance to end her exile and again command a ship, Honor Harrington must use a crew drawn from the dregs of the service to stop pirates who are plundering commerce. Her enemies have chosen the mission carefully, thinking that either she will stop the raiders or they will kill her . . . and either way, her enemies will win....

In Enemy Hands

After being ambushed, Honor finds herself aboard an enemy cruiser, bound for her scheduled execution. But one lesson Honor has never learned is how to give up! One way or another, she and her crew are going home—even if they have to conquer Hell to get there!

continued ☞

PRAISE FOR
LOIS MCMASTER BUJOLD

What the critics say:

The Warrior's Apprentice: "Now here's a fun romp through the spaceways—not so much a space opera as space ballet.... it has all the 'right stuff.' A lot of thought and thoughtfulness stand behind the all-too-human characters. Enjoy this one, and look forward to the next." —Dean Lambe, *SF Reviews*

"The pace is breathless, the characterization thoughtful and emotionally powerful, and the author's narrative technique and command of language compelling. Highly recommended." —*Booklist*

Brothers in Arms: "... she gives it a geniune depth of character, while reveling in the wild turnings of her tale.... Bujold is as audacious as her favorite hero, and as brilliantly (if sneakily) successful." —*Locus*

"Miles Vorkosigan is such a great character that I'll read anything Lois wants to write about him.... a book to re-read on cold rainy days." —Robert Coulson, *Comics Buyer's Guide*

Borders of Infinity: "Bujold's series hero Miles Vorkosigan may be a lord by birth and an admiral by rank, but a bone disease that has left him hobbled and in frequent pain has sensitized him to the suffering of outcasts in his very hierarchical era.... Playing off Miles's reserve and cleverness, Bujold draws outrageous and outlandish foils to color her high-minded adventures." —*Publishers Weekly*

Falling Free: "In *Falling Free* Lois McMaster Bujold has written her fourth straight superb novel. ... How to break down a talent like Bujold's into analyzable components? Best not to try. Best to say 'Read, or you will be missing something extraordinary.'" —Roland Green, *Chicago Sun-Times*

The Vor Game: "The chronicles of Miles Vorkosigan are far too witty to be literary junk food, but they rouse the kind of craving that makes popcorn magically vanish during a double feature." —Faren Miller, *Locus*

PRAISE FOR
LOIS MCMASTER BUJOLD

MORE PRAISE FOR
LOIS MCMASTER BUJOLD

What the readers say:

"My copy of *Shards of Honor* is falling apart I've reread it
so often.... I'll read whatever you write. You've certainly proved yourself a grand storyteller."
—Liesl Kolbe, Colorado Springs, CO

"I experience the stories of Miles Vorkosigan as almost
viscerally uplifting.... But certainly, even the weightiest
theme would have less impact than a cinder on snow
were it not for a rousing good story, and good story-
telling with it. This is the second thing I want to
thank you for.... I suppose if you boiled down all I've
said to its simplest expression, it would be that I immensely enjoy and admire your work. I submit that, as
literature, your work raises the overall level of the
science fiction genre, and spiritually, your work cannot
avoid positively influencing all who read it."
—Glen Stonebraker, Gaithersburg, MD

" 'The Mountains of Mourning' [in *Borders of Infinity*]
was one of the best-crafted, and simply best, works I'd
ever read. When I finished it, I immediately turned back
to the beginning and read it again, and I can't remember
the last time I did that."   —Betsy Bizot, Lisle, IL

"I can only hope that you will continue to write, so
that I can continue to read (and of course buy) your
books, for they make me laugh and cry and think ...
rare indeed."   —Steven Knott, Major, USAF

What Do You Say?

Send me these books!

Shards of Honor	72087-2 ◆ $5.99	☐
Barrayar	72083-X ◆ $5.99	☐
Cordelia's Honor (trade)	87749-6 ◆ $15.00	☐
The Warrior's Apprentice	72066-X ◆ $5.99	☐
The Vor Game	72014-7 ◆ $5.99	☐
Young Miles (trade)	87782-8 ◆ $15.00	☐
Cetaganda (hardcover)	87701-1 ◆ $21.00	☐
Cetaganda (paperback)	87744-5 ◆ $5.99	☐
Ethan of Athos	65604-X ◆ $5.99	☐
Borders of Infinity	72093-7 ◆ $5.99	☐
Brothers in Arms	69799-4 ◆ $5.99	☐
Mirror Dance (paperback)	87646-5 ◆ $6.99	☐
Memory (paperback)	87845-X ◆ $6.99	☐
The Spirit Ring (paperback)	72188-7 ◆ $5.99	☐

LOIS MCMASTER BUJOLD
Only from Baen Books

If not available at your local bookstore, fill out this coupon and send a check or money order for the cover price(s) plus $1.50 s/h to Baen Books, Dept. BA, P.O. Box 1403, Riverdale, NY 10471. Delivery can take up to ten weeks.

NAME:

ADDRESS:

I have enclosed a check or money order in the amount of $